S0-BEG-119

SHOWDOWN!

"Howdy, spy!" Ash called.

"Glad to meet you, beef rustler," returned Rock.

Ash's muscles seemed to ripple. Rock could catch gleams of blue fire under the wide black brim of Ash's hat.

When Ash jerked to his fatal move, Rock was the quicker. His shot cracked a fraction of a second before his adversary's.

Rock felt a shock, but no pain. He did not know where he was hit until his right leg gave way under him, letting him down.

Books by Zane Grey

The Arizona Clan
Black Mesa
The Border Legion
Boulder Dam
The Call of the Canyon
Drift Fence
The Dude Ranger
Fighting Caravans
Forlorn River
The Fugitive Trail
Lone Star Ranger
Lost Pueblo
The Lost Wagon Train
Majesty's Rancho
The Maverick Queen

Raiders of the Spanish Peaks
The Rainbow Trail
Riders of the Purple Sage
Rogue River Feud
Stairs of Sand
30,000 on the Hoof
Thunder Mountain
Under the Tonto Rim
The U.P. Trail
The Vanishing American
Western Union
Wilderness Trek
Wildfire
Wyoming

Published by POCKET BOOKS

Most Pocket Books are available at special quantity discounts for bulk purchases for sales promotions, premiums or fund raising. Special books or book excerpts can also be created to fit specific needs.

For details write or telephone the office of the Vice President of Special Markets, Pocket Books, 1230 Avenue of the Americas, New York, New York 10020. (212) 245-6400, ext. 1760.

ZANE GREY

SUNSET PASS

PUBLISHED BY POCKET BOOKS NEW YORK

POCKET BOOKS, a Simon & Schuster division of
GULF & WESTERN CORPORATION
1230 Avenue of the Americas, New York, N.Y. 10020

Copyright 1931 by Zane Grey; copyright renewed 1955 by Lina Elise Grey

Published by arrangement with Harper & Row, Publishers, Inc.

All rights reserved, including the right to reproduce
this book or portions thereof in any form whatsoever.
For information address Harper & Row, Publishers, Inc.,
10 East 53rd Street, New York, N.Y. 10022

ISBN: 0-671-45642-3

First Pocket Books printing May, 1975

10   9   8   7   6   5

POCKET and colophon are trademarks of Simon & Schuster.

Printed in the U.S.A.

SUNSET
PASS

Chapter One

The dusty overland train pulled into Wagontongue about noon of a sultry June day. The dead station appeared slow in coming to life. Mexicans lounging in the shade of the platform did not move.

Trueman Rock slowly stepped down from the coach, grip in hand, with an eager and curious expression upon his lean dark face. He wore a plain check suit, rather wrinkled, and a big gray sombrero that had seen service. His step, his lithe shape, proclaimed him to be a rider. A sharp eye might have detected the bulge of a gun worn under his coat, high over his left hip and far back.

He had the look of a man who expected to see some one he knew. There was an easy, careless, yet guarded air about him. He walked down the platform, passing stationmen and others now moving about, without meeting anyone who took more than a casual glance at him. Then two young women came out of the waiting-room, and they shyly gazed after him. He returned the compliment.

At the end of the flagstone walk Rock hesitated and halted, as if surprised, even startled. Across the wide street stood a block of frame and brick buildings, with high weatherbeaten signs. It was a lazy scene. A group of cowboys occupied the corner; saddled horses were hitched to a rail; buckboards and wagons showed farther down the street; Mexicans in colorful garb sat in front of a saloon with painted windows.

"Reckon the old burg's not changed any," soliloquized Rock, with satisfaction. "Funny, I expected to find her all built up. . . . Let me see. It's five—six years since I left. Well, I never ought to have come back, but I just couldn't help it. Somethin' roped me in, that's sure."

Memory stirred to the sight of the familiar corner. He had been in several bad gun fights in this town, and the scene of one of them lay before him. The warmth and intimacy of old pleasant associations suffered a chill. Rock wheeled away and hunted up the baggage-room to inquire about his saddle and bag, which he had checked at Deming. They had arrived with him. Reflecting that he did not know yet where to have them sent, Rock slipped the checks back into his pocket, and went out.

A subtle change had begun to affect his pleasure in returning to Wagontongue. He left the station, giving a wide berth to the street corner that had clouded his happy reflections. But he had not walked half a block before he came to another saloon, the familiar look of which and the barely decipherable name—Happy Days—acted like a blow in his face. He quickened his step, then reacting to his characteristic spirit, he deliberately turned back to enter the saloon. The same place, the same bar, stained mirror, and faded paintings, the same pool tables. Except for a barkeeper, the room was deserted. Rock asked for a drink.

"Stranger hereabouts, eh?" inquired the bartender, pleasantly, as he served him.

"Yes, but I used to know Wagontongue," replied Rock. "You been here long?"

"Goin' on two years."

"How's the cattle business?"

"Good, off an' on. Of course it's slack now, but there's some trade in beef."

"Beef? You mean on the hoof?"

"No. Butcherin'. Gage Preston's outfit do a big business."

"Well, that's new," replied Rock, thoughtfully. "Gage Preston? . . . Heard his name somewhere."

"Are you a puncher or a cattleman, stranger?"

"Well, I was both," replied Rock, with a laugh. "Reckon that means I always will be."

Several booted men stamped in and lined up before the bar. Rock moved away and casually walked around, looking at the bold pictures on the wall. He remembered some of them. Also he found what he was unostentatiously seeking—some bullet holes in the wall. Then he went out.

"Reckon I oughtn't have looked at that red liquor," he decided.

2

There were times when it was bad for Trueman Rock to yield to the bottle. This was one of them. The sudden cold in his very marrow, the blank gray shade stealing over his mind, the presagement of a spell of morbid sinking of spirit—these usually preceded his rather rare drinking bouts. He had not succumbed in a long time now, and he hoped something would happen to prevent it in this instance. For if he fell here in Wagontongue, it would be very bad. It would be folly and the poorest kind of business. He had been industrious and fortunate for some years in a Texas cattle deal, and had sold out for ten thousand dollars, which amount of money he carried in cash upon his person.

Rock went to the Range House, a hotel on another corner. It had been redecorated, he noticed. He registered, gave the clerk his baggage checks, and went to the room assigned him, where he further resisted the mood encroaching upon him by shaving and making himself look presentable to his exacting eyes.

"Sure would like to run into Amy Wund," he said, falling into another reminiscence. "Or Polly Ackers. Or Kit Rand. . . . All married long ago, I'll bet."

He went downstairs to the lobby, where he encountered a heavy-set, ruddy-faced man, no other than Clark, the proprietor, whom he well remembered.

"Howdy, Rock! Glad to see you," greeted that worthy, cordially, if not heartily, extending a hand. "I seen your name on the book. Couldn't be sure till I'd had a peep at you."

"Howdy, Bill!" returned Rock, as they gripped hands.

"Wal, you haven't changed any, if I remember. Fact is you look fit, an' prosperous, I may say. Let's have a drink for old times' sake."

They went from the lobby into a saloon that was new and garish to Rock's eye.

"Fine place, Bill. Reckon you've been some prosperous yourself. Do you still run the little game upstairs that used to keep us punchers broke?"

"It's a big game now, Rock," replied the hotel man as they tipped their glasses. "How long since you left Wagontongue?"

"Six years."

"Wal, so long as that? Time shore flies. We've growed

3

some, Rock. A good many cattlemen have come in. All the range pretty well stocked now. Then the sheep business is growin', in spite of opposition. We have two lumber mills, some big stores, a school, an' a town hall."

"Well, you sure are comin' on. I'm right glad, Bill. Always liked Wagontongue."

"Did you jest drop in to say hello to old friends, or do you aim to stay?" inquired Clark, his speculative eyes lighting.

Rock mused over that query, while Clark studied him. After a moment he flipped aside Rock's coat.

"Ahuh! Excuse *me*, Rock, for bein' familiar," he went on, with a slight change of manner. "I see you're packin' hardware, as usual. But I hope you ain't lookin' for some one."

"Reckon not, Bill. But there might be some one lookin' for me. . . . How's my old friend, Cass Seward?"

"Ha!—Wal, you needn't be curious aboot Cass lookin' for you. He's been daid these two years. He was a real sheriff, Rock, an' a good friend of yours."

"Well, I'm not so sure of that last, but Cass was a good fellow all right. Dead! I'm sure sorry. What ailed him, Bill?"

"Nothin'. He cashed with his boots on."

"Who killed him?"

"Wal, that was never cleared up for shore. It happened out here at Sandro. Tough place then. But for that matter it still is. Cass got in a row an' was shot. There was a greaser an' a cowpuncher shot up the same night, but they didn't croak. The talk has always been that Ash Preston killed Seward. But nobody, least of all our new sheriff, ever tried to prove it."

"Who's Ash Preston?"

"He's the oldest son of Gage Preston, a new cattleman to these parts since you rode here. An' Ash is as bad a hombre as ever forked a hoss."

"Bad? What you mean, Bill?"

"Wal, I leave it to you. I ain't sayin' any more, an' please regard that as confidence."

"Certainly, Bill," replied Rock, hastily. After another drink and some casual conversation about the range they parted in the hotel lobby. Rock took an instinctive step

4

back toward the saloon door, hesitated, and turned away. He was still stubborn about giving in to the desire for liquor. He declared to himself that he did not really need or want whisky. It was just a need to drive away a mood. He had not calculated that it would hurt to come back to Wagontongue. He told himself that there was no reason why it should. Suppose he had been in love with Amy Wund, and later with Polly and Kit? That had never hurt him, or even prevented him from falling in love with Texas girls. He had never been proof against a pretty girl. He sensed a moral lapse that would land him good and drunk if something did not counteract it. He had always been rather disgusted with this weakness, though he believed it was less pronounced in him than in most cowboys. Sitting there in a chair, he recalled friends and enemies of the old Wagontongue days. It developed that there were many friends and but few enemies. One of his best friends had been Sol Winter, a kindly storekeeper who always overrated a service Rock had once rendered. Whenever Rock got into a scrape, provided it was not a shooting one, Sol was the one who helped him out of it. And as for money, Sol had always been his bank. Rock, remembering many things now clear, one of which was that he had left Wagontongue hastily and penniless, thought he recalled a debt still unpaid. With that he sallied out to find Winter's store.

It should have been a couple of blocks down the street. Some of the buildings were new, however, and Rock could not be sure. Finally he located the corner where Sol's place of business had been. A large and pretentious store now occupied this site. Rock experienced keen pleasure at the evidence of his old friend's prosperity, and he stalked gayly in, sure of a warm welcome. But he was only to learn that Sol Winter did not occupy this store.

"Ah!—Is Winter still in business?" inquired Rock, conscious of disappointment.

"After a fashion. He has been sort of run out of the best part of town."

"Run out? How?" sharply returned Rock.

"Better store and stock took his trade. If you want anything you'd—"

"Thanks. I don't want anythin'," interrupted Rock, and departed.

Through inquiry, he located Sol Winter's store at the end of the street. It was by no means a small or cheap place, but it was not what it had once been. Rock entered. Sol was waiting upon a woman. He looked older, thinner, grayer, and there were deep lines in his face that seemed strange to Rock. Six years was a long time. Rock gazed round him. It was a large store room crowded with merchandise—hardware, groceries, saddles and harness and farm implements.

"Well, sir, what can I do for you?" inquired a voice at Rock's elbow. He turned to find Winter beside him.

"Howdy, Sol, old-timer!" said Rock, with a warm leap of his pulse. "Don't you know me?"

Winter leaned and crouched a little, his eyes piercing. Suddenly the tightness of his face loosened into a convulsive smile.

"True Rock!" he shouted incredulously.

"Sure as you're born. How are you, Sol?"

Winter seized him with glad hard hands. "If it ain't really you! . . . Why, you ole ridin', drinkin', shootin', love-makin' son of a gun!"

"Glad to see me, Sol?" returned Rock, tingling under Winter's grip.

"Glad?—Lordy, there ain't words to tell you. Why, True, you were always like my own boy. An' since I lost him—"

"Lost him!—Who? You never had any boy but Nick. What you mean?"

"Didn't you ever hear aboot Nick?" queried Winter, with jaw quivering.

"No. I've never heard any news from Wagontongue since I left," returned Rock, bracing himself.

"Nick was shot off his hoss out near Sunset Pass."

"Aw—no! Sol?—Nick shot! Aw, say he wasn't killed?"

"Yes, he was, True," replied Winter, sadly.

"That fine sweet lad! . . . My God! I'm sorry," exclaimed Rock, huskily, as he wrung Winter's hands. "But it was an accident?"

"So they say, but I never believed it. There's still bad

6

blood on the range, True. You must remember. In fact there's some new bad blood come in since you left."

Here a customer entered, and Rock was left to himself for the moment. He seated himself on the counter and put aside his sombrero, to find his brow clammy and cold. Nick Winter dead! Shot by rustlers, probably, or some enemy of Winter's, or perhaps by this new bad element hinted at by Clark and Winter. The last thing Rock would have expected was that anyone could do violence to gentle, kindly, crippled Nick Winter. Here was something to keep Rock around Wagontongue, if nothing else offered. Rock pictured in mind the wild range south of Wagontongue and particularly the broken Sunset Pass country with its sage flats and cedar ridges and piñoned gorges and the purple timber uplands. There had never been a more beautiful wilderness known to Rock or one harder on riders, horses, and cattle.

"True, it's good to see you sittin' there," said Winter, returning to place a hand on Rock's shoulder. "I never saw you look so well, so clean an' fine. I don't need to be told you've worked hard."

"Yes, Sol. I've been five years on a cattle job in Texas. Cleaned up ten thousand, all honest and square. I've got a roll that would choke a cow."

"No! Ten thousand? Why, True, that's a small fortune! It'll make you. If only you don't get drunk an' begin to gamble."

"Well, Sol, maybe I won't. But I've gone straight so long I'm worried. . . . How much do I owe you?"

"Owe me? Nothin'," replied Sol, smiling.

"Look over your books before I hand you one," ordered Rock, fiercely. Whereupon he helped Winter find the old account, which was not small, and forced him to accept payment with interest.

"Say, Rock, to be honest, this little windfall will help a lot," declared Winter, brightly. "I got in a cattle deal some time past an' lost out pretty much in debt. Then the new store—Dabb's—ate into my trade. I had to move. Lately, though, my business has picked up. Old customers have come back. I think I can pull out."

"That's good. Who'd you go in cattle deals with?" rejoined Rock, gruffly.

7

"Dabb."

"Dabb? Not John Dabb who ran things here years ago?"

"Yes, John Dabb."

"Well, Sol, you ought to have known better."

"Sure. But it seemed such a promisin' deal, an' it was for Nick's sake. . . . But I'm out of cattle deals for good."

"Go on. Tell me some more bad news," said Rock, gloomily.

"I guess that's aboot all, True."

"What's become of my old girl, Kit Rand?" inquired Rock.

"Kit. Let me see. I know she married Chess Watkins—"

"What! That drunken loafer?" interrupted Rock, indignantly.

"Yes, an' she couldn't change him, either. Kitty had to go to work in a restaurant here, an' finally they left Wagontongue. Never heard of them since."

"Kitty Rand? That dainty, clever little girl a waitress! Good Lord! . . . How about Polly Ackers? There was a girl who was sure to be a success."

"Polly went to the bad," returned Sol, gravely. "Some flash gambler got around her. She's been gone for years."

Rock groaned. "I'm sorry I ever came back to this darned Wagontongue. . . . I'll risk one more question. How about my best girl, Amy Wund?"

"Worse an' more of it, True," rejoined Winter. "After you left, Amy played fast an' loose with many a puncher. There are some who say yet she never got over your runnin' away."

"Thunder! They're crazy!" burst out Rock. "She played fast an' loose with *me*. She never cared two snaps for me."

"Yes, she did, if there's anythin' in gossip. Mebbe she never found it out till you were gone. Amy was a highstrung lass. An' you know, Rock, you were sweet on Polly at the same time."

"Lord forgive me, I was," replied Rock, miserably.

"Boys will be boys. I reckon you didn't know your

mind any better'n Amy knew hers. An' now brace yourself for a shock, True."

"Fire away, you old Calamity Jane."

"Amy broke the hearts of all the cowboys on the range—an' then up an' married John Dabb."

Rock glared speechlessly at his friend.

"Dabb was a widower with a daughter 'most as old as Amy. They were married a year or so ago. It was a poor match, they say about town. Amy is not happy an' she flirts as much as ever."

Trueman Rock dropped his head.

"Son, it's the way of life," went on Winter. "You've been gone a long time. An' things happen to people, most of it sad, I'm sorry to say."

"Sol, will you keep my money till I come askin' for it?" queried Rock, with his hands inside his waistcoat.

"Now, True, what're you up to?"

"I'm goin' out and get awful, terrible drunk," declared Rock, tragically.

Winter laughed, though he looked serious enough.

"Don't do it, True."

"I am, by gosh!"

"Please don't, son. It'll only fetch back the old bad habit. You look so fine now, I'd hate to see you do it."

"I'm goin' to drown my grief, Sol," declared Rock, solemnly.

"Well, wait till I come back," returned Winter. "I've got to go to the station. My clerk is off today. Keep store for me. There's not much chance of any customer comin' in at this noon hour, but if one does come, you wait on him—like you used to."

"All right. I'll keep store. But you rustle back here pronto. I tell you I want to get terrible drunk."

Winter hurried out, bareheaded and in his shirt sleeves, leaving Rock sitting on the counter, a prey to symptoms he well knew. This time the still small voice of conscience was lacking. He felt the wild, unreasonable, sickening yearnings to do himself wrong—a black shade encroaching upon the wholesomeness of his mind. If Sol did not hurry back—

A light quick step arrested the current of Trueman's thoughts. He looked up. A girl had entered the store. His first swift sight of her caused him to slip off the counter.

She looked around expectantly, and seeing Rock she hesitated, then came forward. Rock suddenly realized that to get terribly drunk was the very remotest thing that he wanted or intended to do.

"Is Mr. Winter in?" asked the girl, pausing before the counter.

"No. He had to go to the station. Reckon he'll be there quite some time."

"Oh—I'm sorry. I—I can't wait, and I wanted him particularly," she said, a little embarrassed and impatient.

"Can I do anythin' for you?" inquired Rock. He was cool, easy, respectful.

"Are you the new clerk Mr. Winter was expecting?" she queried.

"Yes, miss, at your service."

"I've quite a list of things to get," she said, opening a handbag to pry into it.

"I'll do my best, miss. But I'm a little new to the business."

"That's all right. I'll help you," she returned, graciously. "Now where is that paper?"

The delay gave Trueman opportunity to look at her covertly. She was thoroughbred Western, about twenty-one or two, blond, with fair hair more silver than gold. She was not robust of build, yet scarcely slender. She wore a faded little blue bonnet not of the latest style, and her plain white dress, though clean and neat, had seen long service.

"Here it is," she said, producing a slip of paper and looking up somewhat flushed. Her eyes were large, wide apart, gray in color. Rock looked into them. Something happened to him then that had never happened before and which could never happen again. "Now, shall I read the list off one at a time or altogether?"

"Well, miss, it really doesn't—make any difference," replied Trueman, vaguely, gazing at her lips. They were sweet and full and red, and just now curved into a little questioning smile. But, as he watched, it fled and then they seemed sad. Indeed her whole face seemed sad, particularly the deep gray eyes that had begun to regard him somewhat doubtfully.

10

"Very well—the groceries first," she said, consulting her list. "Five of sugar, five of rice, five—"

"Five what?" interrupted Trueman, with alacrity, moving toward the grocery department. Everything was in plain sight. It ought to be easy, if he could keep his eyes off her.

"Five what!" she echoed, in surprise, raising her head. "Did you think I meant barrels? Five *pounds*."

"Sure. That's what I thought," replied Trueman hastily. "But some people buy this stuff in bulk. I used to."

"Oh, you were not always a clerk, then?" she inquired, following him.

"Oh no! I've been a—a lot of things."

She looked as if she believed him. Rock began to grasp that he was bungling the greatest opportunity of his life. He found the sugar and had almost filled a large sack when she checked him: "Not brown sugar. White, please."

There was something in her tone that made Rock wonder if she were laughing at him. It stirred him to dexterity rather than clumsiness. He filled a large paper bag with white sugar, then turned to her, essaying a smile.

"But you didn't weigh it," she said.

"I never weigh out small amounts," he returned, blandly. "I can guess very accurately."

"There's more than five pounds of sugar in that bag," she protested.

"Probably, a little. Sure I never guess underweight." He laid the bag on the counter. "What next? Oh, the rice." And he dove for the bin containing that staple.

"Can you guess the weight of rice, too?" she inquired, as if consumed with curiosity.

"Sure can. Even better. It's not near so heavy as sugar." And he filled a larger bag. In attempting to pass this to her he accidentally touched her bare hand with his. The soft contact shot a thrilling current through him. He dropped the bag. It burst, and the rice poured all over her, and like a white stream to the floor.

"There—you've done it," she said, aghast.

"Excuse me, miss. I'm sure awkward this day. But rice is lucky. That might be a good omen. I'm

11

superstitious," went on Trueman, waxing toward the confidential.

"Well, young man—" she interposed, almost severely. But his gaze evidently disconcerted her.

"You never can tell," he said. "Spillin' rice might mean a weddin'?"

She blushed, but spoke up with spirit. "It couldn't, so far as I'm concerned," she said. "Of course I don't know your affairs. . . . But you are wasting my time. I must hurry. They'll be waiting."

Rock humbly apologized and proceeded to fill another bag with rice. Then he went on with the order, and for several moments, in which he kept his eyes averted, he performed very well as a clerk. He certainly prayed that Sol Winter would not come back soon. Who was she? He had never in his life met such a girl. She could not be married. Too young and—he did not know what! But the thought that she might be made his heart sink like cold lead. He stole a glance at her left hand. Ringless! What a strong, shapely hand, neither too large nor too small, nor red and rough like that of most ranchers' daughters. It was, however, a hand that had seen work. Naturally Rock wondered if she rode a horse. The goddess of every cowboy's dreams was a horsewoman. Did he dare to ask her if she loved a horse? Rock divined that his usual audacity and adroitness with the feminine sex were wanting here.

"That's all the groceries," she said. "Now I want buttons, thread, calico, dress goods, linen and—"

"Is that all?" queried Rock, as she paused.

"It's all *you* can get for me," she answered, enigmatically.

At the dry-goods counter Rock was in a quandary. He could not find anything. The young lady calmly walked behind the counter.

"Can't you read?" she inquired, pointing at some boxes.

"Read!" exclaimed Trueman, in an injured tone. "Sure I can read. I went to school for eight years. That's about four more than any cowpuncher I ever met."

"Indeed! No one would suspect it," she returned, demurely. "If you're a cowboy—what're you doing in here?"

"I just lately went to clerking," he hastened to reply.

"Show me the buttons. There—in the white boxes. . . . Thank you."

While she bent over them, looking and assorting, Trueman regained something near composure, and he feasted his eyes on the little stray locks of fair hair that peeped from under her bonnet, on the small well-shaped ear, on the nape of her neck, beautiful and white, and upon the contour of cheek.

"It isn't pearl?" she inquired, holding a button in her palm.

"Sure is," he replied, dreamily, meaning her cheek, suddenly, terribly aware of its nearness and sweetness.

"That pearl!" she exclaimed in amazement, looking up. "Don't you know bone when you see it?"

"Oh—the button! I wasn't looking at it. . . . Sure that's bone. If you want pearl buttons, maybe I can help." And he bent over the box. It was not necessary to bend with his head so close to hers, but he did so, until he felt one of those stray silky locks of hair brush his cheek. She felt it, too, for there seemed to come a sudden still check to everything in connection with the business at hand. Then she drew away.

"Thank you. I can help myself. You find the thread."

It turned out that she had to find the thread, too, and she did it so readily that Trueman inquired if she had ever been a clerk in this store. She laughed merrily and informed him that once, during fair week, she had helped Mr. Winter out for several days.

"That explains. So you're a good friend of Sol Winter's?" went on Rock.

"Oh yes indeed, ever since we came here."

"Well, I'm a good friend of Sol's, too."

"You must be—seeing he keeps you in his store," she said, slyly.

"You think I'm a poor clerk?"

"Not from a customer's point of view."

"But I'm a poor clerk for Mr. Winter?"

She caught herself again being drawn into conversation and asked to see some calico. Rock espied the only bolt of this commodity on the shelves and drew it down.

"Calico! Sure this reminds me," he said with such enthusiasm that she had to attend. "Once in Colorado

I rode into a town. Gunnison. It was a Saturday. Big day. All the outfits were in. Everybody for miles around. Horses, wagons, buckboards on the streets. I bought a bolt of red calico, tied one end to the pommel of my saddle and left the bolt lyin' on the ground. Then I rode up and down. In about ten minutes that street was a roarin' millin' *mêlée*."

"Please cut me ten yards of this," she said, with steady eyes of disfavor upon him.

Trueman made a mess of the job, to his secret chagrin and her evident despair. Then she asked for a certain kind of dress goods, utterly foreign to him, and which she had to locate herself.

"How much of this?" asked Rock, stripping off yards of the soft material.

"Five. And I want it cut on the bias," she returned.

"On the bias," he echoed. "Oh, sure." And he went at the task desperately, realizing full well that he could not stand this deception much longer. But he had not progressed very far when she interrupted: "You're measuring too much. I said yards—not miles."

Trueman vowed he would finish as he had begun. He went on.

"You can't guess on dress goods like that," she protested.

"Me! I could guess on anythin' once," he retorted, wildly.

"Indeed you look it. I never saw such a—But I can't afford—I *want* only five yards."

"Miss, this *is* five yards, roughly," he rejoined, beginning to cut.

"Stop! You'll ruin it. That's not the way I want it cut!" she cried.

"You said on somethin' or other."

"Excuse me, Mr. Clerk," she returned, manifestly at the end of her patience. She brushed him aside, and taking up the shears began carefully to cut the material to suit herself.

"I'm sorry, Miss—Clerk," spoke up Rock contritely. "I'm not usually so dumb. But you see I never before waited on such a—a girl as you."

She shot him a gray glance not wholly doubtful or

14

unforgiving. And meeting his eyes caused her to look down again with a tinge of color staining her cheeks.

"I'm not a clerk. Good Heavens! If the gangs I've ridden with would drop in here to see me—doin' this. Whew! . . . my name is Trueman Rock. I'm an old friend of Sol Winter's."

"Trueman Rock?" she repeated almost with a start, as she swiftly lifted big, questioning surprised eyes. That name was not unfamiliar to her, but Rock could not tell whether she attached good or bad to it.

"Yes. I used to ride this range years ago. I've been gone six years—five of which I've spent in Texas, workin' hard and—well, I'd like you to know, because maybe you've heard talk here. Workin' hard and goin' straight. I sold out. Somethin' drew me back to Wagontongue. Got here today, and when I ran in to see Sol he left me here in charge of the store. Said no one would come in, but if some one did to wait on him . . . Well, as you see, *some one* did come in. I'm sorry I've annoyed you—kept you waitin'. But it was Sol's fault. Only, I should have told you first off."

"You needn't apologize, Mr. Rock," she replied, shyly. "There's no harm done, except to the rice."

"I'm not so sure of that," he returned, coolly. Now that the deception was past, he had begun to feel more like himself.

"Please wrap these for me," she said, pushing the cut goods along the counter, but she did not look up.

Elaborately Trueman wrapped those parcels.

"Charge to Thiry Preston," she said.

He found a pencil near at hand, and bending over a piece of wrapping paper, very business-like, he inquired:

"*Miss* Thiry Preston?"

"Yes, *Miss,*" she replied.

"Thiry. Pretty name. How do you spell it?"

"T-h-i-r-y," she replied.

Trueman wrote down the name, in a clear bold hand, obviously to impress her.

"What place?" he went on. Then as she stared, he continued, "Where do you live?"

"Sunset Pass."

"Way out there?" He glanced up in surprise. "Sixty

15

miles. I know that country—every waterhole, stone, bunch of cactus, and jackrabbit."

She smiled fully for the first time, and that smile further fascinated Rock.

"You were well acquainted, weren't you?"

"I expect to renew old acquaintances out there. And I may be lucky enough to make new ones."

Miss Preston did not meet his glance and there was other evidence of discouragement.

"What instructions about these parcels?"

"None. I'll carry them."

"Carry them! All this heavy load? Thirty pounds or more!"

"Surely. I'm quite strong. I've carried far more."

"Where to?'

"Out to the corral. Our buckboard is there. They'll be waiting and I'm late. I must hurry."

In rather nervous haste she took up the several light packages and moved toward the other counter. Rock got there first and intercepted her.

"I'll carry these."

"Oh, thank you, but you needn't trouble. I can carry them easily."

"Sure, I'm sorry, but I really can't think of it," returned Trueman, gathering together the bags of groceries. They made a bulky, if not heavy load.

"But you shouldn't leave the store," she protested.

Fortunately, at this juncture Sol Winter hurriedly entered.

"Well, now, what's this?" he queried, with broad smile. "Thiry, to think you'd happen in just the wrong minute."

"Oh, Mr. Winter, I didn't miss you at all," returned Thiry, gayly. "Your new clerk was most obliging and—and capable—after I found the things I needed."

"Haw! Haw!—He's shore a fine clerk. . . . Thiry, meet True Rock, old rider an' pard of mine."

"Ah—I remember now," she flashed. "Is Mr. Rock the rider who once saved your son Nick?"

"Yes, Thiry," he replied, and turning to Rock he added, "Son, this lass is Miss Thiry Preston, who's helped to make some hard times easier for me."

16

"Happy to meet you, Miss Preston," beamed Rock, over his load of bundles.

"How do you do, Mr. Rock," returned Thiry, with just a hint of mischief in her gray eyes.

"Sol, I was clerk and now I'm delivery boy," said Trueman. "I'll be back pronto."

"You've forgotten your hat," announced Thiry as he started off.

"So I have. Sol, it's there behind the counter."

The storekeeper picked up the sombrero and grinned as he placed it on Rock's head.

"True, I'll be gibbered if I don't believe you hid it."

"Sure did."

Thiry laughed with them. "Well," she said, "if you'd worn *that,* I'd never have taken you for a clerk."

They went out together and Trueman felt that he was soaring to the blue sky. The heavy bundles were as light as feathers. Outside in the sunshine he could see her better and it was as if some magic had transformed her. Really he had not seen her at all. He felt more deceitful than ever, for he kept turning to her to say ordinary things, about the heat, the dust, and what not, when he only wanted to look at her. They soon reached the end of the street and started across an open flat toward the corrals. How well Rock remembered them! A strange pang tore his breast. Was it regret and shame for the past—of something of which this girl might have heard?

"You're in an awful hurry," finally complained Trueman.

"Yes, I am. I'm late, and you don't know—"

She did not complete the sentence, but nevertheless it told Rock much.

"This load is heavy. You'd never have packed it," declared Trueman, slowing up. Any excuse was better than none. He was going to lose this wonderful girl in another moment. He wanted to prolong it. Slyly he pinched a hole in the bag of rice and it began to spill out in a thin stream.

"There! We've rushed so we've broken the sack," he went on. "And it's the rice, too! . . . Miss Thiry, it's an omen."

"Bad or good?" she asked, archly.

"Why, good, of course—wonderful."

17

"Mr. Rock, I fear you are many things besides a clerk," she said, shaking her head sadly. "Here, let me take the bag. I'll turn it upside down. If I had far to go with you I'd have no groceries left."

"But wouldn't it be great *if* we had farther to go?" he asked.

"I can't see that it would," she replied, dubiously. "Especially if my dad was at the end of the walk."

"Your dad. Is he Gage Preston?"

"Yes."

"Is he a terror?"

"Indeed he is—to boys who come gallivanting after me."

"Pooh!" exclaimed Trueman, coolly.

By this time they had reached the first corral. The big gate swung ajar. The fence was planked and too high to see over. Loud voices and thud of hoofs came from somewhere, probably the second corral. Thiry led the way in. Rock espied some saddle-horses, a wagon, and then a double-seated buckboard hitched to a fine-looking team of roans.

"Here we are," said the girl, with evident relief. "No one come yet! I'm glad. . . . Put the bundles under the back seat, Mr. Rock."

He did this as directed, and then faced her, not knowing what to say, fearing the mingled feelings that swept over him and bewildered by them.

"After all, you've been very kind—even if—"

"Don't say if," he broke in, entreatingly. "Don't spoil it by a single if. It's been the greatest adventure of my life."

"Of many like adventures, no doubt," she replied, her clear gray eyes on him.

"I've met many girls in many ways, but there has never been anything like this," he returned, tensely.

"Mr. Rock!" she protested, lifting a hand to her cheek, where a wave of scarlet burned.

Then a clink of spurs, slow steps, and thuds of hoofs sounded behind Rock. They meant nothing particular to him until he saw the girl's color fade and her face turn white. A swift shadow darkened the great gray eyes. That broke Rock's emotion—changed the direction of his thought.

"Hyah she ish, Range," called out a coarse voice, somehow vibrant, despite a thick hint of liquor. "With 'nother galoot, b' gosh! Schecond one terday."

Slowly Rock turned on his heel, and in the turning went back to the original self that had been in abeyance for a while. When it came to dealing with men he was not a clerk.

Two riders had entered the corral, and the foremost was in the act of dismounting. He was partly drunk, but that was not the striking thing about him. He looked and breathed the very spirit of the range at its wildest. He was tall, lean, lithe, with a handsome red face, like a devil's, eyes hot as blue flame, and yellow hair that curled scraggily from under a dusty black sombrero. He had just been clean-shaved. Drops of blood and sweat stood out like beads on his lean jowls and his curved lips. A gun swung below his hip.

The other rider, called Range, was a cowboy, young in years, with still gray eyes like Miss Preston's, and an intent, expressionless face, dark from sun and wind. Rock gathered, from the resemblance, that this boy was Thiry's brother. But who was the other? Rock had not met many of this type, but a few was enough.

"Thiry, who's thish?" queried the rider, dropping his bridle and striding forward.

"I can introduce myself," struck in Rock, coolly. "I'm Trueman Rock, late of Texas."

"Hell you shay!" returned the other, ponderingly, as if trying to fit the name to something in memory. "Whash you doin' hyar?"

"Well, if it's any of your business, I was in Winter's store and packed over Miss Preston's bundles," replied Rock, in slow, dry speech.

"Haw! Haw!" guffawed the rider, derisively. He did not appear to be angry or jealous. He was just mean. Rock had formed his idea of what this man's wrath might be. That, and mostly a consideration for Miss Preston, made Rock wary. Who was he? Surely not a lover! The thought seemed to cut fiercely into Rock's inner flesh.

"Wal," went on the tall rider presently, swaggering closer to Rock, "run along, Big Hat, 'fore I reach you with a boot."

19

"Ash! You're drunk!" burst out the girl, as if suddenly freeing her voice.

The disgust and scorn and fear, and something else in her outbreak, caused Rock to turn. Miss Preston's face most wildly expressed these things. They instantly gave Rock tight rein on his own feelings. This rider, then, was Ash Preston, of whom Rock had heard significantly that day. Her brother! The relief Rock experienced outstressed anything else for the moment.

"Whosh drunk?" queried Preston, placatingly, of his sister. "Your mistake, Thiry."

"Yes, you are drunk," she returned, with heat. "You've insulted Mr. Rock, who was kind enough to help me carry things from the store."

"Wal, I'll help Mishter Rock on his way," replied Preston, leering.

Range, the other rider, like a flash leaped out of his saddle and jerked Preston's gun from its sheath.

"Ash, you look out," he called, sharply. "You don't know this fellar."

Chapter Two

Whash I need gun fer?" demanded Preston, half resentful of his brother's precaution.

"Sure you don't, but you might if you had one," replied Range, with a grin. "Anyway, Ash, you're shootin' off your chin enough. I tell you this fellar's a stranger to us."

The younger rider had been bending his intent, clear gaze upon Rock and had formed conclusions.

"Whash the hell we care? He's Big Hat, an' I'm a-goin' to chase him pronto."

Thiry Preston stepped out as if impelled, yet she was evidently clamped with fear. Rock was learning a good deal, but could not determine if her fear was on his account or on her brother's. Rock, swift in his impressions, conceived instant cold suspicion of this Ash

20

Preston. He thought, for Thiry's sake, he had better make as graceful an exit as possible.

"Please, Ash, be decent if you can't be a gentleman," begged Thiry.

For answer Preston lurched by Thiry and swept out a long slow arm, with open hand, aimed at Rock's face. But Rock dodged, and at the same time stuck out his foot dexterously. The rider, his momentum unchecked, tripped and lost his balance. He fell slowly, helplessly, and striking on his shoulder he rolled over in the dirt. He sat up, ludicrously, and wiping the dust off his cheek he extended a long arm, with shaking hand, up at Rock.

"Shay, you hit me, fellar."

"Preston, you're quite wrong. I didn't," replied Rock.

"Whash you hit me with?" he went on, sure that indignity had been committed upon him. Plain it was that his presence there on the ground was sufficient proof.

"I didn't hit you with anythin'."

"Range, is thish hyar Big Hat lyin' to me?"

"Nope. You jest fell over him," returned the younger rider, laconically.

"Ash, you're so drunk you can't stand up," interposed Thiry.

"Wal, stranger, I'm 'ceptin' your apology."

"Thanks. You're sure considerate," returned Rock, with sarcasm. He was not used to total restraint and he could not remember when any man had jarred him so. Turning to the girl, he said: "I'll go. Good-by, Miss Preston."

With his back to the brothers Trueman made his eyes speak a great deal more than his words. The dullest of girls would have grasped that he did not mean good-by forever. Thiry's response to his gaze was a silent one of regret, of confusion, of something more of which she was unconscious.

Rock did not pass the riders. He stepped up on the corral fence, reached the top rail, and vaulted over. Outside he saw men and horses coming, and was glad that they were not in line with him. Thoughts and emotions almost overwhelmed Rock.

"Ash Preston! Bad medicine! And he's her brother!"

21

muttered Rock, aloud. "Sure as fate we're goin' to clash."

At first he wanted to go off alone somewhere to think, to try and figure out what had happened and what to do about it. He halted on a street corner long enough to see the buckboard, the wagon, and several mounted riders move away briskly toward the south. Rock's sharp eye picked out Thiry's white dress and blue bonnet. Amazing and stirring was it to Rock that she turned to look back. She could see him standing there. Quickly the little cavalcade passed out of sight behind trees. Far to the southward rose a dim outline of rugged country, hazed in purple. Rock divined now that always he had been destined to return to this wild range. He broke away from the corner and the spell which had gripped him. What he must have now was information.

He strode back to Sol Winter's store. The day was hot, and what with brisk exercise and the emotion under which he labored, he was wet with perspiration when he confronted his friend.

"Now, son, what's happened?" queried Sol, with concern.

"Lord knows. I—don't," panted Rock, spilling off his sombrero and wiping his face. "But it's—a lot."

"True, you took a shine to Thiry Preston. I seen that. No wonder. She's the sweetest lass who ever struck these parts."

"Sol, we'll investigate my—my state of mind last," replied Rock, ruefully. "Listen. I ran into the Preston outfit."

"Humph! You don't look happy over it," said Winter, bluntly.

"I should smile I'm not. But I only bumped into two of them. Thiry's brothers, Range and Ash."

"Ahuh. Hard luck," replied Winter, pertinently. His tone implied a good deal.

"Think I saw the rest of them as I came away. Sol, I had to jump the fence."

"No!" exclaimed the storekeeper, unbelievingly.

"I sure did," said Rock, with a laugh. "Listen." And he related to his friend all that had occurred at the corral.

"Aw! Too bad for Thiry. She's always being' hu-

22

miliated. No wonder she comes to town so seldom. Why, Rock, she's liked by everybody in this town."

"Liked! Sol, you old geezer, this here town ought to do better than that. . . . But I sure agree with you. Too bad for Miss Thiry. Oh, she felt hurt. I saw tears run down her cheeks."

"An' you took water from that Ash Preston?" mused Winter.

"I sure did. Gee! it felt queer. But I'd taken a beatin' for that girl."

"Rock, you have changed. You're bigger, stronger. You've grown—"

"Hold on, Sol. Don't make me out so much that you'll have to crawl later. But if I have improved a little I'm thankin' the Lord. . . . Sol, I meant to get terrible drunk till that girl stepped in this store."

"An' *now* you don't?" queried Winter, gladly.

"Hell! I wouldn't take a drink for a million dollars," replied Rock, with a ring in his voice. "You should have seen Thiry's face—have heard her when she said, 'Ash—you're *drunk.*'"

"Yes, I know. Thiry hates drink. She has cause. Most of the Prestons are a drinkin' lot. . . . But, son, are you serious?"

"I'm serious? I think so," rejoined Rock, grimly. "What about?"

"Has bein' with Thiry Preston for a little while changed your idea about red liquor?"

"Sol, it sure has. I don't know just what's happened to me, but *that* you can gamble on."

"Son, it sounds good. If it isn't just excitement. Why, most every young fellar—an' some older ones—in this country have been struck by lightnin' when they first seen Thiry. But I can't see that it did them good. For they drank only the harder. Thiry isn't to be courted, they say."

"Struck by lightnin'. Sure that might be it. But never you mind about me. I'm solid on my feet even if my head's in the clouds. . . . Tell me things. I want to know all about this Preston outfit."

"Rock, you're hot-headed. You fly off the handle,"

returned Winter, gravely. "You might give me more trouble with the Prestons. I've had considerable."

"Sol, you can trust me," said Rock, earnestly. "We're old friends. I'm back here for good. I'll absolutely not give you any more trouble. I'm goin' to help you. So come out with everythin'."

"Same old Rock," mused Winter. "No, not the same, either. There's a difference I can't name yet. Mebbe it's a few years. . . . Wal, this Preston outfit is sure prominent in these parts. They call them 'The Thirteen Prestons of Sunset Pass.' It's a big family. Nobody seems to know where they come from. Anyway, they drove a herd of cattle in here some time after you left. An' 'ceptin' Ash Preston, they're just about the most likable outfit you ever seen. Fact is, they're like Thiry. So you don't need to be told more about that. They located in Sunset Pass, right on the Divide. You know the place. An' it wasn't long until they were known all over the range. Wonderful outfit with horses and ropes. Fact is, I never saw the beat of Gage Preston for a real Westerner."

"Go on, Sol. It's sure like a story to me. What was the trouble you had?"

"They ran up a big bill in my store. The old store, you remember. I taxed the boys about it. Didn't see Gage along there. Well, it was Ash Preston who raised the hell. He wasn't drunk then. An', son, you need to be told that Ash is wild when he's drunk. When sober he's—well, he's different. . . . Nick was alone in the store. Nick was a spunky lad, you know, an' he razzed Ash somethin' fierce. Result was Ash piled the lad in a corner an' always hated him afterward. Fact is the range talk says Ash Preston hates everybody except Thiry. She's the only one who can do anythin' with him."

"She didn't do a whole lot today. The drunken—! . . . And Nick was shot off his horse out there in Sunset Pass?"

"Yes. An' I've never breathed to anyone my natural suspicion. I think Ash Preston must have killed Nick. They must have met an' fought it out. Sure it wasn't murder. Ash would not shoot any man in the back. There were four empty shells, fresh shot, in Nick's gun."

24

"The boy had nerve and he was no slouch with a six-shooter. I wonder—"

"Well, Gage paid the bill first time he came to town. Then for a while he didn't buy from me. But one day Thiry came in, an' ever since I've sold goods to the Prestons. But none of them save Thiry have ever been in my store since. She does the orderin' an' she pays pronto."

"Ahuh. . . . Any range talk among the punchers about these Prestons?"

"You mean—"

"Sol, you know what I mean?"

"Well, son, there used to be no more than concerned the Culvers, or Tolls, or Smiths, an' not so much as used to be about the little outfits down in the woods. You know the range. All the outfits eat one another's cattle. It was a kind of unwritten code. But, lately, the last two years, conditions have gone on the same, in that way, an' some different in another. I hear a good deal of complaint about the rustlin' of cattle. An' a few dark hints about the Prestons have seeped in to me off the range. Darn few, mind you, son, an' sure vague an' un-trailable. It might be owin' to the slow gettin' rich of Gage Preston. It's a fact. He's growin' rich. Not so you could see it much in cattle, but in land an' money in bank. I happen to know he has a bank account in Los Vegas. That's pretty far off, you know, an' it looks queer to me. Found it out by accident. I buy from a wholesale grocer in Los Vegas. He happened here, an' in a talk dropped that bit of information. It's sure not known here in Wagontongue, an' I'm askin' you to keep it under your hat."

"Is Gage Preston one of these lone cattlemen?" queried Rock, thoughtfully.

"Not now, but he sure was once."

"Who's he in with now?"

"John Dabb. They own the Bar X outfit. It's not so much. Dabb has the big end of it. Then Dabb runs a butcher shop. Fact is he undersold me an' put me out of that kind of business. He buys mostly from Preston. An' he ships a good many beeves."

"Ships? Out of town?" asked Rock, in surprise.

25

"I should smile. They have worked into a considerable business, with prospects. I saw this opportunity years ago, but didn't have the capital."

Rock pondered over his friend's disclosures, trying to reduce them down to something significant. They might be and very probably were perfectly regular transactions. He could never split hairs over deals pertaining to the cattle range. Thiry Preston's sad face returned to haunt him. Surely she was too young, too healthy and good for marked sadness of expression, such as had struck him forcibly. He felt more than he could explain. This girl had dawned upon him like a glorious sunrise. His perceptions and emotions had been superlatively augmented by he knew not what. He could not be sure of anything except that he vowed to find out why Thiry's eyes hid a shadow in their gray depths.

"Sol, what do you think about Ash Preston?" asked Rock, coming out of his reverie.

"Well, son, I'm sure curious to ask you that same question," replied Winter, with humor. "You used to be as wild as they come. You know the range. How did this fellow strike you?"

"Like a hard fist, right in the eye," acknowledged Rock.

"Ahuh. I'm glad your sojourn in Texas hasn't dulled your edge," said Winter, with satisfaction. "Rock, the Prestons are all out of the ordinary. Take Thiry, for instance. How did *she* strike you?"

Trueman placed a slow heavy hand on the region of his heart, and gazed at his friend as if words were useless.

"Well, I wouldn't give two bits for you if she hadn't. Son, I've a hunch your comin' back means a lot. . . . Wal, to go on—these Prestons are a mighty strikin' outfit. An' Ash Preston stands out even among them. He's a great rider of the range in all pertainin' to that hard game. He can drink more, fight harder, shoot quicker than any man in these parts. You used to throw a gun yourself, Rock. I'm wonderin' did you get out of practice in Texas? But Texas, now—"

"Go on," interrupted Rock, curtly. He was shy on talk about gun-play.

"Excuse me, son. Well, to resoom, Ash Preston is sure the meanest, coldest, nerviest, deadliest proposition you're likely to stack up against in your life. I just want to give you a hunch, seein' you went sweet on Thiry."

"Thanks, old friend. Forewarned is forearmed, you know. The man was drunk when I met him, but I think I grasped a little of what you say."

Winter evidently found more in this reply to worry him.

"Well, then, you know what the risk is."

"Sol, what do I care for risks?" burst out Rock, contemptuously.

"True, you always were a sudden cuss, but even so, you could hardly get serious—real serious over Thiry Preston so quick."

"What you mean—serious?" snapped Rock.

"Sweet on her, I mean," answered Winter, hesitatingly.

"Sweet on *that* girl! No! I've been sweet on a hundred girls. This is different. I don't know what. I'll have to dig into myself and see. But it's somethin' terrible. Ten thousand times sweet!"

"Son, you needn't bite my head off," protested Winter. "If you want to know, I'm tickled stiff—an' scared to death. I love that girl. An' if you haven't forgot, I was once some fond of you."

"Sol, I haven't forgotten," replied Rock, with warmth. "But don't you dare ever mention my—my old girl friends. And if you'd dare to tell Thiry I'd murder you."

"Somebody will tell her, son. For instance, Mrs. John Dabb. She likes Thiry. She'll tell her. I see them together occasionally."

"Mrs. John Dabb. She couldn't know much."

"I told you she was Amy Wund."

"Oww!" wailed Rock, bending double.

"Trueman, your trail will sure be rough," returned Winter, wagging his grizzled head.

"Listen, old friend. There's only one thing that could stump me. I don't know what I'm goin' to do. But I mean there's only one thing that could queer this—this beautiful dream almost before it starts."

"An' what's that?"

"Tell me. Do you know Thiry real well?"

"Yes, son, an' I can answer that question so plain in your eyes. Thiry is not in love with anybody. I know, because she told me herself, not so long ago. She loves her family, especially Ash. But there's no one else."

"That'll—help," replied Rock, swallowing hard. "Now, Sol, I'll sneak off alone somewhere and try to find out what's the matter with me—and what to do about it."

Trueman sallied forth into the sunlight like a man possessed. He did not know whether he was trying to escape from himself or find himself. It had been all very well to talk loftily to Sol Winter, but now that he was out in the open many feelings began to edge into his incomprehensible buoyancy.

He did not notice the heat while he was striding out of town, but when he got to the cedars and mounted a slope to a lonely spot he was grateful for the cool shade. He threw aside coat and sombrero, and lay down on the fragrant mat of cedar needles. How good to be there! He became aware of his labored breathing, of moist, restless hands, of hot face. Excitement was strong upon him.

It would not do to dream—at least not until he had settled things with himself. Rock always went to the loneliness and silence of desert or forest when in any kind of trouble. He had not been in this shady spot for five minutes before the insidious spell of nature prevailed. He could think here. He heard the hum of bees, melodious on the mellow summer air; and the shrill call of a yellowhammer. A jack-rabbit went bobbing by, and there was a rustling of the dry leaves of brush near at hand.

Only one thing had stood in the way of a happy return to Wagontongue, and that had been the possibility of a clash with Cass Seward, the sheriff. This now no longer perturbed him. It had been reckless, perhaps foolish, for him to come back, when he had known that the probabilities were that Cass would try to make him show yellow and clap him in jail, because of a shooting affray which Rock had not started. But it had been Rock's way to come, not knowing; and there certainly had been only a remote chance of his surrender to Cass. That hazard was past. Rock paid tribute to the dead sheriff, and gladly welcomed the fact that he had a clean slate before him.

That gray-eyed girl Thiry Preston! Here he did surrender. He had been struck through the heart. And all
the fight there was seemed directed against himself—a
wavering, lessening doubt that he could be as marvelously
transformed as he thought. And then, one by one, in
solemn procession, there passed before his memory's eye
the other girls he had known, trifled with, liked, or loved.
A few stood out brightly. He watched them pass by, out
of the shade, it seemed, into the past forever. He had
imagined he had cared; he had thought he had suffered.
All that had been nothing. Thiry Preston had made them
vanish, as if by magic. Trueman did not sentimentalize
or argue about it. She was the girl. All his life he had
been dreaming of her. To realize she actually lived! Nor
did he ask himself any questions about love. Whatever
it was, it had been sudden, inevitable, and fearsome only
in its premonition of tremendous might.

This was not decision, but a realization and acceptance.
Decision had to do with remaining at or near Wagontongue, and it was made the instant the question presented.
He would ask Gage Preston for a job riding, and
if one was not available he would ask some other cattleman. Not likely was it that any rancher thereabouts
would not find a place for Trueman Rock. In such event,
however, he could go into the cattle business himself.
He had enough money for a good start, and the idea had
always appealed to him. Still, he did not want to hurry
into that. Range conditions had changed, and no doubt
competition was greater. Also sheep-raising had begun
to eat its way out over the pastures. Rock had a cattleman's healthy dislike for sheep. It would be better
to start again as he had started there years ago—a poor
cowboy. What to do with his money? It had somehow
become precious. Always it had been his habit, when
he had any money, to carry it on him until he spent it.
And that had not been long. This, however, would never
do now. He would ask Winter about a safe investment.
And as for minor considerations, there seemed to be some
reason or other for Trueman to have a couple of
thoroughbred horses to go with his showy saddle and
the other fine accouterments he had brought with him.

The thought of Ash Preston was disturbing. When
Rock, having burned his bridges behind him, tried to

give up to the trance-like memory of Thiry, this wild brother obtruded his evil fame and person to spoil it. Rock had a premonition that he would have trouble with Preston, but he deliberately refused to harbor it. He absolutely must not fight with Thiry's brother. There might be ways to propitiate Ash, and Rock promised himself that he would go far. But if he could not get along with Ash he could keep out of his way. Fortunately, it was not likely that the range would ever believe True Rock shied from meeting any man. Rather it had been that he had gone out of his way to meet men. Had he not come back to Wagontongue ignorant of Seward's death? He had always intended to return.

At length Rock left the cedar nook and started to retrace his steps. He had come quite high up the slope, and he could see the town below, and beyond it, to the south. Wagontongue had grown considerably, and from this vantage-point it looked promising. Some day it would grow into an important center.

Far to the south, across a belt of gray desert, rose the range country. It looked its reputation. It rolled away to east and west, far as the eye could see, an empire for cattlemen, needing only water to make it a paradise. Capital and labor would some day bring that vast land to its limit of production.

Folding down over the range at its southern line lay the purple broken highlands of rock and gorge and forest, and above these rose the black mountains, not peaked, but wave on wave of great flat domes limned against the blue. The scene caused Trueman to draw a deep breath. He could not discern Sunset Pass from that point, but he saw the bulge of mountains into which it opened to the west.

Rock returned to town and Winter's store. His friend was busy with customers, so Rock betook himself towards the hotel. A young woman, coming out of Dabb's large establishment, almost ran into Rock. It might have been his fault, because he was lost in thought. He tried to avoid her, but she did not make a like effort.

"Excuse me," he said, touching his hat.

"True Rock—aren't you going to speak to me?" she burst out.

He knew the voice, the face, too, the dark, sparkling,

astonished eyes. But who was this holding out both gloved hands?

"True—don't you know *me*?" she asked, with mingled reproach and gayety. "It's Amy."

Indeed it was. Amy Wund, older, fuller of figure, with dark flushed face and roguish eyes. She was richly and fashionably dressed, and that fact, somehow, put surprise and confusion far from Rock.

"Why, Mrs. Dabb, this is a surprise!" he said, doffing his sombrero, and bowing over her hand. "I'm sure glad to see you."

"Mrs. Dabb? Not Amy?" she rejoined, with captivating smile and look Rock found strangely familiar.

"Some one told me you were married to my old boss, John Dabb," said Rock, easily.

"Yes, it's true, but you can call me Amy, as you used to."

Rock smiled, but did not avail himself of the gracious privilege. "You sure look well and fine. And prosperous, too?"

She did not like his penetrating gaze and his slow, cool speech.

"True, I can return the compliment. You are handsomer than ever."

"Thanks."

"You don't look your years, cowboy."

"Am I so ancient? I plumb forget."

"True, you're not glad to see me," she rejoined, almost petulantly.

"Why, sure I am! Glad you're settled and happy and—"

"Happy! Do I look that?" she interrupted, bitterly.

"If my memory's any good you look as gay and happy as ever."

"Your memory is bad—about that—and other things. . . . Trueman, have you come back on a visit?"

"No; I aim to stay. I always was comin' back."

"If you only had come!" she sighed and looked eloquently up at him. "I'm glad—terribly glad you're going to stay. We must be good friends again, True. You'll come to see me—ride with me—like you used to. Won't you?"

"I'm afraid Mr. Dabb wouldn't like that. He never had any use for me."

"It doesn't matter what he likes," returned the young woman, impatiently. "Say you will, Trueman. I'm horribly lonesome."

Rock remembered that Amy had always been a flirt, but he had imagined she would change after marriage. Evidently she had not changed. It was rather a melancholy moment for him, realizing that he could no more dangle after her than fly, and he was sorry for her and wished to spare her discomfiture.

"I'll call on you and John sometime," he replied, with all friendliness.

"Me and—John! . . . Well, your long absence in Texas hasn't made you any brighter. I dare say it hasn't changed you any—about girls, either."

"No?" he drawled.

"I saw you with Thiry Preston," she went on, spitefully. "At your old tricks, cowboy!"

"Did you? I don't call it old tricks to carry a few bundles for a girl," replied Rock, stiffly. It annoyed him to feel the blood heat his face.

"Bundles, rot!" she retorted. "I saw you through a window and anybody could have read your mind."

"Indeed! Could you read it?"

"I sure did."

"Well, if you're such a mind-reader, what am I thinkin' about now?"

"It's not flattering to me—I have that hunch," she snapped. "Oh, I know you, True Rock, inside and out. You've lost your head pronto over Thiry Preston."

"I'm not denyin' it, am I?"

"You're flaunting it like a red flag right in my face. Well, I'm telling you, cowboy, that this once you've lost your head for nothing. Thiry Preston will have none of you. I know her. She is not your kind. She's cold as ice to every cowboy on this range. Heaven knows, they've run after her."

"Thanks for that last news, anyhow," he responded, dryly.

She was searching the very depths of him, her eyes keen with jealous intuition.

"More. Thiry Preston has no use for lovesick cowboys,

32

much less one like you, who've been at the beck and call of every girl in the land. And she worships that handsome devil of a brother, Ash."

"I'll hold it a virtue for a girl to love her brother—whether he was bad or good."

"Bah! Thiry Preston is queer. Some folks say her love is unnatural."

"Folks around Wagontongue talk a lot," returned Rock, significantly. "Sure used to say some unkind things about you. . . . Good day, Mrs. Dabb," he concluded, rather coldly, and replacing his sombrero he turned away, not, however, without catching a last angry blaze of her eyes. Could he ever have been in love with that catty woman? But he tried to feel kindly, in spite of vague pain she had aroused. Sober thought acquitted him of any blame for her evident disappointment with life. She had trifled with love; she had never known her own mind; and now she was reaping the tares. She would be his enemy, of that he was full sure, unless he allowed himself once more to be attached to her train. The idea was preposterous. In a few short hours—no, they were hours incalculably long in their power—he had grown past flirting with any woman. Life had suddenly become sweet, strange, full of fears and hopes, something real and poignant, such as he had never experienced before.

Rock, instead of entering the hotel, returned to Winter, whom he found unoccupied, and proceeded to unburden himself. He told the last thing first.

"So you run into Amy," meditated Sol, with a thoughtful twinkle. "Reckon you might have expected that. An' she knocked the wind out of you?"

"She sure did. You see, I'd really forgotten Amy."

"Wal, son, take my advice and keep shy of Amy. She's got old Dabb so jealous he can't attend to his business. She always has some buckaroo runnin' after her. That won't do for you. Dabb had reason to hate you long ago."

"Huh. I reckon I haven't forgotten. But no fear, old pard. I wouldn't run after Amy even if Dabb wanted me to."

"It'd be like her to hate you, same as he did. An' that'd not be so good. The Dabbs about own Wagontongue, not to say a lot of the range outfits. Sure John's

33

brothers are ruled by him. I told you he bought beef from Gage Preston. Then I always see Thiry with Amy, when she comes to town. If you aim to snub your old girl for this new one—wal, son, you'll have a rough row to hoe."

"Sol, I'll not snub Amy, but I can't go playin' round with her."

"Wal, that's what she'll expect."

"Sol, what did Amy mean by sayin' Thiry had an unnatural love for her brother."

"I don't know. Sure I never seen anythin' unnatural about Thiry. An', Rock, I've heard that very same remark before. It's just low-down talk by nasty people. All the same, it bothered me."

"It sort of jarred me. Funny how gossip can sting you, even when you know where it comes from."

"Son, I seen you'd been jarred some, when you first come in. You went out ridin' the air. Anythin' else happen beside buttin' into Mrs. Dabb?"

"Yes, a lot. But it all happened *in*-side me. . . . Sol, how much money do you owe?"

"Couple of thousand, an' when that's paid off I'll be on the road to prosperity again."

"Old-timer, you're on it right now. I'll take that much stock in your business," went on Rock, crisp and business-like, as he took out his pocketbook.

"Son, I don't want you to do that," protested Winter.

"But I want to. I think it's a good investment. Now here's your two thousand. And here's five more, which I want you to put in your bank, on interest, but fixed so you can draw it out quick."

"You want it to your name, of course?"

"No. Put it in yours. Reckon we'd better add another thousand to that five. I only need enough money to buy a spankin' outfit."

"Son, suppose somethin' happened to you," said Winter, gravely, as he fingered the money. "It might. You know this is a sudden country. An', Rock, you've got fire in your eye."

"Sol, my parents are livin', an' though old, they're in good health. They live in Illinois. I was brought up in western Illinois, town of Carthage. Went to school there till I was fourteen. Then we moved to Nebraska.

34

Dad went in for ranchin' and lost all he invested. Then my folks went back home, but I stayed on, and drifted all over till I landed here."

"Son, I always was curious about you—where you come from, if you had any folks. I'm sure glad they're livin'. How old are you, Trueman, if I may ask?"

"Reckon I'll never see thirty-two again," returned Rock, ruefully.

"Wal, you don't say, really. Thirty-two! Cowboy, you sure hide your age. Fact is, you always was a mysterious cuss."

"To go on about the money. If anythin' should happen to me—which I'm gamblin' it won't—you send this six thousand to my folks. I'll leave the address with you. Also some papers and things for safe-keepin'."

"An' how about the two thousand you're investin' with me?" queried Sol, with a smile.

"You can just forget about that, pardner."

Winter shook his lean old head sagaciously, almost sadly. "Son, you were always open-handed. How did you ever save all this money?"

"Never did save it, Sol," returned Rock, with a laugh. "Went in with a pretty big rancher in Texas. He had enemies—one of them a sure-enough crooked hombre. I just naturally gravitated toward removin' that hombre from disfigurin' the general landscape down there. My pardner did well after that. Then a railroad came our way. We sold out, and I found myself with ten thousand."

"Ahuh!" exclaimed Winter, his eyes narrowing to slits. "An' you found yourself needin' to get out of Texas?"

"Well, Sol, there sure wasn't any need of my gettin' out at all," replied Rock, dryly. "I hung round for weeks to give my pardner's enemies the chance they circulated round they were lookin' for. But they didn't seem to be lookin' very bad for it. So I got homesick and hit out for Wagontongue."

"I'm sure glad, yet I know you'll keep me scared stiff all the time. . . . Wal, son, out with it. What's under that big hat?"

"I'm goin' to be a plain cowpuncher and start in where I left off here six years ago."

"What's the idea of pretendin' to be poor, when you've got a big stake for a cowboy?"

"Sort of suits me, Sol."

"You'll need an outfit."

"Sure. I want a jim-dandy outfit, you bet. Two saddle-horses—the best on the range, if money can buy them."

"We can find one of them pronto," replied Winter, with satisfaction. "Come out to my house for supper. Wife will be happy to see you. She was fond of you, son. . . . After supper we'll walk out to Leslie's. He's sellin' out an' he has some good stock. One horse in particular. I never saw his beat. Dabb has been hagglin' with Leslie over the price. It's high, but the horse is worth it."

"How much?"

"Three hundred."

"Whew!—When I used to buy the best of horses for fifty."

"Reckon you never laid eyes on one as good as Leslie's. Wait till you see it."

"All right, Sol. We'll buy. But reckon one saddle-horse will do. Then I'll need a pack-horse and outfit. In the mornin' we'll pick out a tarp and blankets, grub and campin' outfit. I've got saddle, bridle, spurs, riata—all Mexican, Sol, and if they don't knock the punchers on this range, I'll eat them. My Texas pardner gave them to me. And last, I reckon I'll require some more hardware."

This last came reluctantly with a smile not quite grim from Rock.

"Ahuh! . . . An' with all this outfit you're headin' for Sunset Pass," asserted Winter, wholly grim.

"Yeah. I'm goin' to ride down slow and easy-like, renewin' old acquaintances and makin' new ones. Then I'll end up at Gage Preston's and strike him for a job."

"What at? Ridin'?"

"Milkin' the cows, if nothin' else offers."

"Son, it's a bold move, if it's all on account of Thiry," returned Winter.

"Sol, I don't mind tellin' you it's all on account of Thiry," replied Rock, imitating his friend's solemnity.

"Gage Preston can't hardly refuse you a job," went on Winter. "He needs riders. He has hired about every cowpuncher on the range. But they don't last."

"Why not?"

"Ash gets rid of them, sooner or later. Reckon about as soon as they shine up to Thiry."

"How does he do that?" queried Rock, curiously.

"Wal, he scares most of them. Some he has bunged up with his fists. An' several punchers he's driven to throw guns."

"Kill them?"

"Nope. They say he just crippled them. Ash shoots quick an' where he wants."

"Most interestin' cuss—Ash Preston," said Rock, lightly.

"Son, this is what worries me," went on Winter, with gravity. "It'll be some different when Ash Preston butts into you."

"How you mean, pardner?"

"Wal, no matter how easy an' cool you start—no matter how clever you are—it's bound to wind up a deadly business."

"Thanks, old-timer. I get your hunch. I'm takin' it serious and strong. Don't worry unreasonable about me. I've *got* to go."

Chapter Three

Trueman Rock was not one of the cowboy breed who cared only for pitching, biting, kicking horses. He could ride them, when exigency demanded, but he never loved a horse for other than thoroughbred qualities. And sitting on the corral fence watching Leslie's white favorite, he was bound to confess that he felt emotions of his earliest days on the range.

"Wal, True, did you ever see the beat of that hoss?" asked Sol Winter, for the twentieth time.

Rock shook his head, silently.

Leslie, a tall rancher in overalls and boots, stood inside the corral. "Reckon I haven't had time to take care of him lately. He's had the run of the range. There hasn't been a leg thrown over him for a year."

"I'll take him, Leslie, and consider the deal a lastin' favor," replied Rock.

"Reckon I'm glad. Dabb said yesterday he'd buy him an' send out today. But you beat Dabb to it. Somehow I didn't want Dabb to have him."

"What have you against Dabb?" inquired Rock.

Leslie laughed shortly. "Me? Aw, nothin'."

"Mrs. Dabb has been wantin' this hoss, didn't you tell me, Jim?" asked Winter.

"Wal, I reckon so. She has been out here often. But I don't think Mrs. Dabb really cared about the horse so much. She just wanted to show off with him. But today there was a girl here who loved him, an' I'd shore have liked to let her have him."

"Who was she, Jim?" asked Winter, with a knowing wink up at Rock.

"Thiry Preston. She passed here today with her dad an' some of the boys. Gage stopped to have a talk with me. All the Prestons are keen on hosses, but they won't pay much. Hossflesh is plenty cheap out Sunset Pass way."

"What did Miss Preston do?" queried Rock, causally.

"She just petted the hoss while the other Prestons walked around, talkin' a lot. Miss Thiry never said a word. But I seen her heart in her eyes."

"Speaks well for her," replied Rock, with constraint, as he slid off the fence and approached the animal. If this beautiful white horse had appeared desirable in his eyes upon first sight, what was he now? Rock smoothed the silky mane, thrilling at the thought that Thiry's gentle hand had rested there. "Leslie, I'll come out in the mornin'. I want a pack-horse or a mule. . . . Here's your money. Shake on it. What's one man's loss is another's gain."

"I'll throw the pack-horse in to boot," replied Leslie.

"Sol," said Rock, thoughtfully, as they retraced their steps toward town, "I'll hardly have time to look up folks I used to know. Reckon it doesn't matter. I can leave that till I hit town again. . . . Do the Prestons come in often?"

"Some of them every Saturday, shore as it rolls round. Thiry comes in about twice a month."

38

"Pretty long ride in from Sunset. Sixty miles by trail."

"There's a new road, part way. Longer but better travelin'. Goes by Tanner's Well."

"Reckon the Prestons make a one-night stop at some ranch?"

"No. They're not much on that sort of travel. They camp it, makin' Cedar Creek, where they turn off into a flat. Good grass an' water. There's an old cabin. It belonged to a homesteader. Preston owns it now. Thiry was tellin' me they'd fixed it up. When they're comin' to town, she an' the other womenfolks sleep there, an' the men throw beds outside."

"Queer how all about these Prestons interests me so," said Rock, half to himself.

"Not so queer. Leavin' Thiry aside, they're a mighty interestin' outfit," returned Winter. "You'll find that so pronto."

"Reckon I'll find out a lot pronto," said Trueman. "Never could keep things from comin' my way, particularly trouble. But, Sol, in all my life no adventure I ever rode down on could touch this one. I'm soberin' a little and realize how crazy it seems to you."

"Not crazy, son," replied Winter, earnestly. "It's wild, perhaps, to let yourself go over this girl all in a minute. But then, wild or no it might turn out good for Thiry Preston.

"Sol, why is her face so sad?" queried Rock, stirred by his friend's implication.

"I don't know. I've asked her why she looked sad—which you can see when she's not speakin', but she always makes herself smile an' laugh then. Says she can't help her face an' she's sorry I don't like it. Rock, it hurts Thiry, sort of startles her, to mention that. It makes me think of somethin' unhappy."

"It's for me to find out," said Rock.

"You bet. I've always been puzzled an' troubled over Thiry. My wife, too. An' True, it'll please you that she took kindly to your sudden case over Thiry. She says, 'If Trueman Rock stops his drinkin' an' gun-throwin' an' settles down to real ranchin' he could give that girl what she needs.' . . . She didn't say *what* Thiry needs. So we can only guess."

"Sol, I'll sure have to get away from you. Else you'll have me locoed."

"True, I may be wrong thinkin' you've growed to be a man. . . . But one last word. This here has been stickin' in my craw. These Prestons have heard all about you, naturally, an' when you ride out on the range it'll all come fresh again. No cowboy ever had a finer reputation than you—for bein' keen an' honest an' clean, an' a wonder at your work. You never drank much, compared to most cowboys. . . . But your gun record was bad—forgive me, son, I don't want to offend. Remember I'm your friend. Every old-timer here knows you never went around lookin' for trouble. It's not that kind of a bad reputation. It's this kind. You've spilled blood on this range, often, an' more'n once fatal. That made you loved by a few, feared an' misunderstood by many, an' a mark for every fame-huntin' sheriff, gambler, an' cowpuncher in the country. Now you're back again, after some years, an' all you ever done here will come up. An' your Texas doin's, whatever they were, will follow you. . . . Now the point I want to make is this: Preston knows most of this or will know it soon, an' if he keeps you in his outfit it will be pretty strong proof that these queer dark hints from the range are without justification."

"Sol, it would seem so," replied Rock, meditatively.

"Wal, it'll be good if you find it that way. For Thiry's sake first, an' then for everybody concerned. Then these hints against Preston will be little different from those concernin' other ranchers. Most outfits have cowboys who brand calves an' kill beeves they oughtn't to. That's common, an' it don't count, because they about all do it."

Rock regarded his anxious friend a thoughtful moment. "Winter, you've made a point you weren't calculatin' on. You're *hopin'* I'll find Preston one of the common run of ranchers. But you're *afraid* I won't."

It was nearly noon the following day when Rock had his pack outfit ready for travel. Leslie came up presently with the white horse.

"Black leather an' silver trimmings," said the rancher, admiringly. "Never seen him so dressed up. An' the son-of-a-gun is smart enough to know he looks grand."

"He's smart, all right," agreed Rock, with shining eyes. "Now we'll see if he'll hang me on the fence."

"Reckon you can ride 'most anythin'," observed Leslie, his appreciative glance running over Rock.

The white horse took Rock's mount easily, pranced and champed a little, and tossed his head.

"Good day and good luck, rancher," said Rock, lifting the halter of the pack animal off a post.

"Same to you, cowboy," replied Leslie, heartily. "Reckon you don't need any advice about them hard nuts down in the Pass."

"Need it all right, but can't wait. When you see Sol tell him I'm off fine and dandy," rejoined Rock.

With that he headed down the road which the Prestons had taken the preceding day. Before Rock was far out of town he had ascertained his horse was a fast walker and had an easy trot. For speed and endurance, Leslie had committed himself to the claim that no horse in the country could approach him.

"I've hit the trail," sang out Rock, explosively, though it was a broad, well-trodden road that he was traveling.

As many times as he had ridden out from Wagontongue and other towns, and from the innumerable range camps all over the West, not one of them had ever been like this venture. He laughed at himself. His boyhood had returned. There was nothing but good and joy in the world. The hot June sun pleasantly burned through his shirt sleeves; the dust tasted sweet; the wind, coming in puffs, brought the fragrant odors of the desert, spiced by a hint of sage; the hills slumbered in blue haze.

Out of town a little way he caught up with a young rider who had evidently seen him.

"Howdy, cowboy!" he greeted Rock.

"Howdy, yourself!" returned Rock, genially.

"I seen you was up on Leslie's white hoss, so I waited."

"You know the horse?"

"Shore do. I ride for Spangler out here an' we often had Leslie's stock to pasture. . . . Reckon you own the white now. You kinda have thet look."

"Yes, I went broke buyin' a horse to go with this saddle."

"Wal, you shore got two thet fit. You-all make a flash outfit. . . . Where you ridin', cowboy?"

"I'm aimin' for Sunset Pass."

"Got a job with Preston?"

"Nope, not yet. I hope to land one."

"Easy, if you will stand long hours an' poor wages. Preston pays less than any rancher hereabouts."

"How much?" queried Rock, as if it was important.

"Forty, with promise of more. But no puncher ever sticks long enough to get more."

"What you mean by easy?"

"Preston is always hard up fer riders. Reckon he's only got a couple beside his sons. He asked me yestidday if I wanted a job."

"What's the reason no cowboy ever rides long for Preston?"

"I knowed you was a stranger round Wagontongue," said the other, grinning.

"Sure I am, lately. But I was here years ago."

"Before my time, shore. 'Cause I'd remembered you. What's your handle?"

"Trueman Rock, late of Texas."

" 'Pears to me I've heerd that name, somewheres. Wal, I'm glad to meet you. I'm Hal Roberts. An' if you don't tie up with Preston, come back en' try Spangler."

Rock thanked him and asked questions about the range. Soon afterward the cowboy bade him good-by and turned off. Back from the road Rock espied a new ranch house and corrals that had not been there in his day. Then as he passed on he drew away from the dry-farming levels and the wastes of cut-over land, to get out into the desert proper. It waved away to the southward, gray and yellow, with spots of green cedars and dotted groups of cattle, on and on to a beckoning horizon line. Familiar landmarks stared at him, and grew in number and power to stir him, as he went on. His quick eye made special note of improvements along the road. Stone culverts had been put in at some of the deeper washes.

Rock kept looking for a cabin where he had stopped many a time. He could not recall the name of the homesteader who had located there. Coming to the top of a low rise of ground, he saw a little valley beyond, with a fringe of green. Then he found the cabin. It had been long deserted; the roof had fallen in, and the outside chimney of yellow stone had partly crumbled away. What had become of the homesteader and his hard-working wife and tousle-headed youngsters?

Rock rode on. Further along he saw a dam of red earth that had been built in a depression, where in the rainy season water ran. A red, sun-baked, hoof-marked hollow glared there now. Cattle were few and far between. But this was barren desert. Some miles on, over the summit of this long slope, conditions would improve.

In due time he reached the top and there halted the horses to spend a few moments in reveling in the well-remembered country.

A thirty-mile gulf yawned wide and shallow, a yellow-green sea of desert grass and sage, which sloped into ridge on ridge of cedar and white grass. The length of the valley both east and west extended beyond the limit of vision, and here began the vast cattle range that made the town of Wagontongue possible. Rock's trained eye saw cattle everywhere, though not in large herds. It was a beautiful scene for any rider. Rock feasted his eyes, long used to the barrens of the Texas Panhandle. The rough country commenced some fifteen miles or more farther on. Sunset Pass and its environs were not in view, nor even the mountain ranges that were visible from the town.

The valley smoked with the thick amber light of the warm June day. Lonely land! Rock's heart swelled. He was coming back to the valleys and hills that he now discovered he had loved.

An hour's ride down the slow incline brought Rock into a verdant swale of fifty acres, fresh with its varied shades of green, surrounding a pretty ranch house. Here Adam Pringle had lived. If he were still there, he had verified his oft-repeated claims to Rock that here had been the making of a prosperous farm and cattle ranch.

The barn and corrals were closer to the road than the house. Rock saw a boy leading a horse, then a man at work under an open shed. The big gate leading in was shut. Rock halloed. Whereupon the farmer started out leisurely, then quickened his steps. It was Adam—stalwart, middle-aged, weatherbeaten settler.

"True Rock, or I'm a born sinner!" shouted Pringle, before he was even near Rock.

43

"Howdy, Adam! How's the old-timer?" returned Rock.

"I knowed that hoss. An' I shore knowed you jest from the way you straddled him. How air you? This is plumb a surprise. Get down an' come in."

"Haven't time, Adam. I'm rustlin' along to make camp below. . . . Adam, you're lookin' good. I see you've made this homestead go."

"Never seen you look any better, if I remember. Thet's a hoss an' saddle you're ridin'. You always was hell on them. Whar you been?'

"Texas."

"Reckon you heerd aboot Cass Seward bein' popped off, an' you ride back to the old stampin'-grounds?"

"Adam, I didn't know Cass was dead till I got to Wagontongue. Guess I was homesick."

"Whar you goin'?"

"Sunset Pass."

"Cowboy, if you want work, pile right off heah."

"Thanks, Adam, but I've got a hankerin' for wilder country. I'll try Preston. Think he'll take me on?"

"Shore. But don't ask him."

"Why not?"

"I'm advisin' you—not talkin'," returned the rancher, with a sharp gleam in his eye. "You know me, True."

"Used to, pretty well, Adam. And I'm sort of flustered at your advisin' me that way," replied Rock, keenly searching the other's face.

"Stay away from Sunset Pass."

"Adam, I just never could take advice," drawled Rock. "Much obliged, though."

"Cowboy, you may need a job bad, an' you shore always hankered for wild range. But it ain't that."

"What you aimin' at, Adam?" asked Rock, with a laugh.

"I ain't aimin', True. I'm tellin' you. It's thet tow-headed lass of Preston's."

"Well, considerin' we're old friends, I won't take offense," drawled Rock. "How you doin'?"

"Been on my feet these two years," returned Pringle, with satisfaction. "Been raisin' turnips an' potatoes an' some corn. Got three thousand haid of stock. An' sellin' eight hundred haid this fall."

44

"Bully! I'm sure tickled. Losin' much stock?"

"Some. But not enough to rare aboot. Though I'm agreed with cattlemen who know the range that there's more rustlin' than for some years past."

"Is that so?"

"Queer rustlin', too. You lose a few haid of steers an' then you never hear of anyone seein' hide nor hair of them again."

"Nothin' queer about that, Adam. Rustled cattle are seldom seen again," returned Adam, for the sake of argument. But there was something unusual about it. Pringle, however, did not press the point.

"Many new cattlemen?" went on Rock.

"Not too many. The range is healthy an' improvin'."

"How's Jess Slagle? I used to ride for Jess, and want to see him."

"Humph! Didn't nobody tell you aboot Slagle?"

"Nope. And I forgot to ask. You see, I only got to town yesterday."

"Jess Slagle couldn't make it go in Sunset Pass after the Prestons come."

"Why not? It's sure big enough country for ten outfits."

"Wal, there's only one left, an' thet's Preston's. Ask Slagle?"

"I sure will. Is he still located in the Pass?"

"No. He's ten miles this side. Stone cabin. You'll remember it."

"If I do, that's no ranch for Jess Slagle. Marshland, what there was of it fit to graze cattle, salty water, mostly rocks and cedars."

"Your memory's good, Rock. Drop in to see Slagle. An' don't miss callin' heah when you come out."

"Which you're thinkin' won't be so very long. Huh, Adam?"

"Wal, I'm not thinkin', but if it was anyone else I'd give him three days—aboot," replied Pringle, with a guffaw.

Rock's misgivings grew in proportion to the increasing warmth and pleasure of this ride toward old haunts. The fact that nothing was spoken openly detrimental to the Prestons was a singular feature that he had encountered once or twice before. The real Westerner, such as Leslie or Pringle, was a man of few words. This reticence sprang

45

from a consciousness that he was not wholly free from blame himself, and that to be loose with the tongue entailed considerable risk. Rock could not prevent his growing curiosity and interest, but he succeeded in inhibiting any suspicions. He wanted to believe that Thiry's people, including the redoubtable Ash, were the very salt of the earth.

Toward sundown he reached the south slope of the valley and entered the zone of the cedars. These gray-sheathed trees, fragrant, with their massed green foliage and grotesque dead branches, seemed as much a part of a cowboy's life as grass or rocks or cactus. Rock halted for camp near a rugged little creek, where clear water ran trickling over the stones. He went off the road and threw his pack in a clump of cedars where he could not readily be seen. How long since he had camped in the open, as in his earlier days on the range!

Then he unsaddled the white, and hobbled both horses, and watched them thump out in search of grass. He unrolled his tarp under a low-branching cedar, and opened his pack, conscious of pleasurable sensations. It had been years since he had done this sort of thing. In Texas he had ridden out from a comfortable house, and back again, sooner or later, as he liked. But this was the real life for a rider. When the dead cedar branches burst into a crackling fire he seemed magically to find his old dexterity at camp tasks. And the hour flew by.

After sunset, sky and cloud and valley were illumined by a golden ethereal light. Twilight stole from some invisible source, and night followed, a mellow warm summer night, with hum of insects and croak of frogs, and the melancholy music a cowboy found inseparable from his lonely vigil—the staccato cry of coyotes. Rock lingered beside his dying red cedar fire, listening, feeling, realizing that the years had brought him much until now never divined, and that something as mystical in the future called to his being. Not by chance merely, nor because of a longing to return to this range, nor impelled by the restless wanderlust of a cowboy, had he journeyed hither. Around every thought, almost, seemed to hover the intangible shadow of Thiry Preston. But he would not make of her a deliberate object of conjecture, of reality. That would come later, when he had found her again, and understood himself.

The night darkened, the air cooled, the camp fire flickered out. Rock crawled into his blankets under the widespread cedar. The soft feel of wool, the hard ground, the smell of cedar, the twinkle of a star through the branches, the moan of rising night wind, the lonesome coyote bark, and the silence—how good they were and how they recalled other days!

Rock was awakened at dawn by the thump of hoofs. The white horse had come into camp, which was something horses seldom did.

"You early-risin' son-of-a-gun," called Rock, as he rolled out of bed. "Want your oats, huh? I just figured you'd want a snookful of oats, so I fetched some."

He was on his way before sunrise, and in an hour or so had reached Cedar Creek, with its green banks and clusters of trees, its little flat where stood a cabin new to Rock. It was locked. He could not see in. But in the sand before the door he saw little boot tracks that surely had been made by Thiry Preston. This was the halfway house used by the Prestons, going to and from town.

From there the road circled a ridge to the west, and a well-defined trail led up the slope. Rock knew the trail, and believed that the road would come back to it over the hill. He took the short cut, and almost it seemed that he had ridden the trail only yesterday.

When he achieved the summit, the sky had become overcast with heavy white and black clouds, darkening the day. From here he gazed over into country that deserved its repute. Wide and far away it flung defiance, menace, and call to the long-absent rider. Below him spread a white-and-green checkerboard of grass and cedar, leading with striking boldness up into leagues and leagues of black timber, mesas with crowned walls of gray limestone, cliffs of red rock, fringed by pine, all mere steps up to the mountain kingdom into which the great gap of Sunset Pass yawned, purple and dim and forbidding.

About noon Rock halted before the stone cabin that he knew must belong to his old friend and employer, Jess Slagle. Rock rode into what was a sorry excuse for a yard, where fences were down and dilapidated wagons, long out of use, stood around amid a litter of stones and wood, and all kinds of débris characteristic of a run-down range. The corral in the back was a makeshift, and the log barn would have shamed a poor homesteader. It amazed and shocked Rock, though he had seen many cattlemen start well and never finish.

Dismounting, Rock went to the door and knocked. He heard steps inside. The door opened half a foot to disclose a red-haired, homely woman, in dirty garb, more like a sack than a dress.

"Does Jess Slagle live here?" asked Rock.

"Yes. He's out round the barn somewheres," she replied, with a swift flash of beady eyes that took him in.

As Rock thanked her and turned away he saw that she was barefooted. So Jess Slagle had come to squalor and poverty. Who was the woman? Rock certainly had no remembrance of her. Presently he heard the sound of hammer or ax blows on wood, and he came upon Slagle at work on a pen beside the barn.

"Howdy, Rock! I knew you were in town. Range Preston rode by this mornin' an' passed the news."

This gaunt man was Slagle, changed vastly, no doubt like his fortunes. He showed no surprise or gladness. The grasp of his hand was rough, hard, but lacked warmth or response. Rock remembered him as a heavy, florid Westerner, with clear eyes, breezy manner, smooth of face, and without a gray hair.

"Jess, I'm sure surprised and plumb sorry to find you—your condition so—so different," began Rock, a little uncertain.

"Reckon that's natural. Not much like when you rode for me, years ago," replied Slagle, with the bitterness of the defeated.

"What happened, Jess?"

"About everythin', I reckon."

"Sheeped off the range?" went on Rock, hazarding a query.

"Hell no! There's no sheep on this side, an' never will be, so long as Preston lives."

"How'd you lose out?"

48

"Well, Rock, I had hard luck. Two bad years for water and grass. Then Dabb shut down on me. I held the little end of a deal with him. Next I sold some cattle, put the money in a bank, an' it busted. Then Preston moved into the country—an' here I am."

"How in the devil did you get here?" demanded Rock, bluntly, spreading his hands significantly.

"Right off I made a mistake," returned Slagle, nodding his head. "Preston was keen about my ranch in the Pass. He made me a good offer. I refused. He kept after me. I had some hard words with his son, Ash, an' it all led to a breach. They kept edgin' my stock down out of the Pass an' I didn't have the riders to drive it back. That way, then, an' in others I fell more in debt. No banks woud give me credit. An' as I said before, here I am."

"It's a tough story, Jess. I'm sorry. But it doesn't explain how you lost your ranch in the Pass."

"I forgot to tell you, I had finally to sell for about nothin'."

"To Preston?"

"Sure. No one on the lower range would take it as a gift. It was a poor location, if any other outfit rode the Pass."

"Ahuh! Then as it stands, Preston about ruined you?"

"No, Rock, I couldn't claim that. My deal with Dabb hurt me most—started me downhill. Gage Preston never did me any dirt that I actually know. When I went to him an' told him his outfit was drivin' my stock off grass an' water, he raised the very old Ned with his sons, in particular Ash Preston, who's sure rotten enough to taint the whole other twelve Prestons."

"So this Ash Preston *is* rotten?" queried Rock, deliberately, glad to find one man not afraid to voice his convictions.

"Rock, I don't talk behind any cattleman's back," returned Slagle, forcefully. "I told Gage Preston this, an' I told Ash to his face."

"Then what happened?"

"Well, the old man stalled off a shootin' match, I reckon."

"Have you ever met since?"

"Lots of times. But I've never had the nerve to draw on Ash. I know he'd kill me. He knows it, too."

"What you mean by rotten?"

"Mebbe it's a poor word. But I know what I mean. Did you ever see a slick, cold, shiny rattlesnake, just after sheddin' his skin, come slippin' out, no more afraid of you than hell, sure of himself, an' ready to sting you deep?"

"Reckon I have, Jess."

"Well, that's Ash Preston."

"Ahuh! And that's all you mean?"

"Reckon it is, Rock. I've lost cattle the last five years, some hundreds in all. But so has Preston an' other ranchers, all the way from Red Butte to the sand. There's rustlin', more perhaps than when you helped us clean out the Hartwell outfit. But sure as I am alive I never laid any of it to Ash Preston."

"I see," rejoined Rock, studying the other's masklike face. "Glad to get your angle. I'm goin' to ask Preston for a job."

"I had a hunch you were. I'm wishin' you luck."

"Walk out with me and see my horse, Jess," rejoined Rock, turning. "Do you aim to hang on here?"

"Thank God, I don't," replied Slagle, with a first show of feeling. "My wife—she's my second wife, by the way—has had a little money an' a farm left her, in Missouri. We're leavin' before Winter sets in."

"Glad to hear you've had a windfall, Jess. . . . Now what do you think of that white horse?"

Rock had been two hours leisurely climbing the imperceptible slope up to the mouth of Sunset Pass. It was mid-afternoon. The clouds had broken somewhat and already there were tinges of gold and purple against the blue sky.

At last he entered the wide portal of the Pass, and had clear view of its magnificent reach and bold wild beauty. The winding Sunset Creek came down like a broken ribbon, bright here and dark there, to crawl at last into a gorge on Rock's left. The sentinel pines seemed to greet him. They stood as he remembered, first one, isolated and stately, then another, and next two, and

50

again one, and so on that way until at the height of the Pass they grew in numbers, yet apart, lording it over the few cedars on the level bench, and the log cabins strange to Rock, that he knew must be the home of the Prestons.

Many and many a time had he camped there, realizing and loving the beauty of that lovely aloof spot, yet never had he imagined it as a site for a ranch. But it was indeed the most perfect situation of any he had ever seen. And it was Thiry Preston's home.

Rock was still a mile or more distant. Slowly he approached, holding in the white horse that scented water and grass. The ascent here was gradual, as was the constriction of the Pass. The breath of sage blew strong, sweet, heavy on the breeze that came through from the west. Already the sun hung low, directly in the center of the great V-shaped gap which appeared to split the very heart of the mountain range. And the gold was growing vivid. Preston's ranch, at least the six cabins, occupied the divide, which hid the lower and the larger end of the Pass from Rock's eager gaze. He remembered it so well that he could scarcely wait.

Slowly he rode up and entered the beautiful open park. It was just naturally beautiful, level, with white grass surrounding the patches of brown mats of needles under the pines. The road cut through the center and went down the other side. Rock had a glimpse of gardens, corrals, fields, and then the purple pass threaded with winding white.

There were no rocks, no brush, no fallen logs or dead timber. The few cedars and piñons and pines stood far apart, as if distributed by a mighty landscape artist. Some of the cabins were weathered and gray, with more green on the split shingles. They had wide eaves and sturdy gray chimneys built outside, and glass windows. Other cabins were new, especially a little one, far over under the overhanging green slope and near a thin pile of white water falling from mossy rock. The largest of the pines marked this little cabin, and towered over it protectingly. The only living things in sight were two deer, standing with long ears erect, a horse and a colt, and a jack-rabbit, bounding away across the waving grass.

Just then a hound bayed, deep and hollow, no doubt

announcing the advent of a stranger in the Pass. Rock, having come abreast of the first cabin, halted his horse.

The door of this cabin opened. A tall, lithe, belted and booted man stalked out, leisurely, his eagle-like head bare, his yellow hair waving in the wind—Ash Preston.

Chapter Four

Rock felt that seldom indeed had he been looked over as he now was by this Ash Preston. No hint of recognition in that live blue gaze!

"Howdy, stranger! Are you off the trail?"

The omission of the invariable Western "Get down and come in," was not lost on Rock.

"Howdy to you!" he returned. "Is this Gage Preston's ranch?"

"Yes."

"Then I'm on the right track. I want to see him."

"Who're you, stranger?"

"I'm Trueman Rock, late of Texas."

"Rock. . . . Are you the Rock who used to ride here before we came?"

"Reckon I am."

Ash Preston measured Rock again, a long penetrating look that was neither insolent nor curious, but which added something to his first impression. It was impossible to tell what he thought. He was hard to reach, aloof and cold. Like every meeting Rock ever had with anyone, this one made its own reaction. He could not be other than himself, even though most desirous of being agreeable.

"You can tell me what you want with Preston. I'm his son Ash."

"Glad to meet you," said Rock, pleasantly, and that was true, even if he had to feign the pleasure. "Do you run Preston's business?"

"I'm foreman here."

"Reckon my call's nothin' important," returned Rock,

easily. "But when I do call on a cattleman I want to see him."

"Are you shore it's my father you want to see most?" asked Ash, without the slightest change in tone or expression.

"Well, I'm callin' on Miss Thiry, too, for that matter," rejoined Rock, with a laugh. "But I'd like to see your father first."

According to Western custom it was natural and courteous for a rider to call upon any rancher, if he chose to; and in most cases he would be received hospitably. And it was permissable for him to pay his respects to a young unmarried woman. Rock let it be assumed that there was no reason why the Prestons of Sunset Pass were any different from other Western people.

"Miss Thiry ain't seein' every rider who comes along," said Preston.

"No? Well, that's unlucky for some," rejoined Rock.

"An' dad ain't home."

That would have made the matter conclusive for most men confronting Ash Preston.

"You mean *you* say he isn't home to *me?*" queried Rock, deliberately.

"Wal, I didn't expect you to take it that way, but since you do we'll let it go at that."

Here was the first hitch in the situation. It had to be met. Rock accepted the inevitable. Harmony, let alone even agreeable acquaintance, was utterly impossible between Preston and himself.

"Excuse me, Preston, if I can't let it go at that," he returned, coolly. "Would you mind tellin' me if any of the other ten Prestons are home?"

There the gauntlet went in the face of Ash Preston. Still he did not show surprise. The intense blue of his eyes, steady on Rock, changed only with a flare. Whatever he might be when drunk, when sober as now, he was slow, cold, complex, cunning. He was flint, singularly charged with fire. Rock would have felt easier in mind if Preston had shown less strength and perception. But he gave Rock the same status that Rock gave him. It augured ill for the future.

"Wal, Rock, all the Prestons are home, if you're so

53

set on knowin'," returned Ash. "But there's one of the thirteen who's advisin' you to dust down the road."

"Reckon that must be you, Mister Ash?" inquired Rock, nonchalantly.

"An' that's shore me."

"Well, I'm sorry. I don't know you. And sure you don't know me. I can't ever have offended you. Why are you so uncivil?"

Preston's glance, straying over Rock, and the flashy saddle and beautiful horse, betrayed something akin to disfavor, but he did not commit himself further than to make a slight gesture, indicating the road down the Pass.

"Plain as print," went on Rock, bluntly. "But I'm not takin' your hunch, Ash Preston. I'll stay long enough, anyhow, to see if the rest of your family is as rude to a stranger as you are."

In one sliding step Rock reached the ground. And at that instant heavy boots crunched the gravel.

"Hey, Ash, who're you palaverin' with?" called a deep, hearty voice.

Ash wheeled on his heel, as on an oiled pivot, and without answer strode back into the cabin, to slam the door. Then Rock turned to see who had intervened so timely. He saw a man of massive build, in the plain garb of an everyday cattleman. Rock perceived at once that he was father to Thiry and Range Preston, but there seemed no resemblance to Ash. He might have been fifty years old. Handsome in a bold way, he had a smooth hard face, bulging chin, welk-formed large lips, just now stained by tobacco, and great deep gray eyes.

"Stranger, I reckon Ash wasn't welcomin' you with open arms," he said.

"Not exactly. . . . You're Gage Preston?"

"Shore am, young man. Did you want to see me?"

"Yes, I asked for you. He said you weren't home."

"Doggone Ash, anyhow," replied the rancher, with impatient good-humor. "Whenever a cowpuncher rides in hyar, Ash tells him we've got smallpox or such like. He's not sociable. But you mustn't judge us other Prestons by him."

"I was tryin' to argue with him on that very chance,"

said Rock, smilingly. It required only a glance to define Gage Preston as the type of Westerner Rock liked.

"Hope Ash didn't take you for a hoss thief. Course he knowed Leslie's white hoss. We seen him only yesterday."

"Well, your son didn't say. But I reckon he thought so. I bought this horse from Leslie."

"Grand hoss he is, you lucky rider," replied Preston, with a huge hand on the white flank. "Hyar, Tom," he called, turning toward a lanky youth in the background, "take these hosses. Throw saddle an' pack on the porch of the empty cabin. . . . Wal, stranger, you're down, so come in."

Rock had not noticed that the next cabin, some distance away under the pines, was a double one of the picturesque kind, long, with wide eaves, a porch all around, and ample space between the two log structures. Water ran down from the stream, in a chute hollowed from saplings. This house was one of the older ones, which had become weathered, with roof greened over with moss. The nearer cabin had two doors and a window that Rock could see. Evidently the second cabin was a kitchen. But both had large stone chimneys. Deer and elk antlers, saddles and skins, hung on the walls between the cabins. Table and benches there indicated where the Prestons dined.

"Reckon it'll be pleasanter sittin' outside," said Preston, and invited Rock to a rustic seat under the trees. "What'd you say your name was?"

"I didn't say—yet," laughed Rock. He liked Preston, and could not help but compare the son most disparagingly with the father.

"Thiry didn't tell me either," went on the rancher. "But I know you're the young fellar who was polite to her an' did somethin' or other for her thet made Ash huffy."

"Yes, I am. It wasn't much, certainly nothin' to offend Miss Thiry's brother."

"Aw, Ash was drunk. An' he shore ain't no credit to us then. Range, the other boy who saw you, said you was pretty decent. Thet you only stuck out your foot fer Ash to tumble over. I reckon he didn't need thet to take a dislike to you."

"He didn't recognize me, I'm glad to say."

"Young man, I'll say you didn't lose any time trailin' Thiry up," went on Preston, quizzically, with a twinkle in his big gray eyes. "Shore you must be one of them sudden fellars."

"Mr. Preston, you—I—I—" began Rock, somewhat disconcerted, more from the rancher's genial acceptance of a fact than from being discovered.

"You needn't lie about it. Lord knows this hyar has happened a hundred times."

"I wasn't goin' to lie, Mr. Preston," went on Rock.

"Don't call me mister. Make it plain Preston, an' Gage when you feel acquainted enough. You're not tryin' to tell me you didn't foller Thiry out hyar."

"No—not exactly. Now you make me think—I'm afraid it must be—somethin' like that. But I came to ask you for a job."

"Good. What'll you work fer?"

"Reckon the same as you pay any other rider. I'm an old hand with ropes, horses, cattle—anythin' about the range."

"Wal, you're hired. I'm shore in need of a man who can handle the boys."

"Say, Preston, you don't mean you'll put me to handlin' Ash! He said he was foreman."

"I run two outfits. Ash bosses the older riders. If you fit in with the youngsters it'll shore be a load off my mind."

"That suits me fine. I reckon I can hold up the job."

"Wal, you strike me all right. But I gotta tell you thet no young man I ever hired struck Ash right. An' none of them ever lasted."

"Why not?" inquired Rock.

"Say, you seen Ash an' you ask me thet?" exclaimed Preston, spreading his big hands.

"Preston, if I turn out to be of value to you, will *you* want me to last?" queried Rock, and this was the straight language of one Westerner to another. Preston appeared to be confronted with a most pertinent question.

"Have you any money?" parried Preston.

"Well, I'm not quite broke."

"Jest a poor cowpuncher with your fortune tied up in hoss an' saddle?"

"Reckon that's about the size of it."

"How aboot red eye?"

"Preston, I used to drink a little, now and then. But I've quit."

"Fer good?"

"I believe so. I never quit before. But I'm not a man to go back on my word. And I promise you I'll never drink while ridin' for you."

"Wal, I like your talk an' I like your looks. An' I'll say if you can handle my boys an' stick it out in the face of Ash, I'll be some in your debt."

"I don't know Ash, of course. But I can take a hunch, if you'll give it."

"Wal, Ash sees red whenever any puncher looks at Thiry. He cares fer nothin' on earth but thet girl. An' she's awful fond of him. She's never had a beau. An' Thiry's near twenty-two."

"Good Heavens! Is her brother so jealous he won't let any man look at her?"

"Wal, he wouldn't if he could prevent it—thet's daid shore. An' far as the ranch hyar is concerned he does prevent. But when Thiry goes to town accidents happen, like you meetin' up with her. Thet riles Ash."

"In that case, Preston, I'm afraid Ash will get riled out here. For I reckon the same kind of accident may happen."

"Hum! Hum! You're a cool hand to draw to," exploded the rancher, boisterously. "What'd you say your name was?"

"I haven't told you yet. It's Trueman Rock, late of Texas. But I used to ride here."

The rancher apparently met with instant check to his mood. "What? . . . Trueman Rock!—Are you thet there True Rock who figgered in gun-play hyar years ago?"

"Sorry I can't deny it, Preston," replied Rock, his steady glance on the gray thought-clouding eyes of the rancher.

"You rode fer Slagle—when he had his ranch down hyar below in the Pass?"

"Two years I was with Slagle."

"Also the Cross Bar outfit, the Circle X? An' once you was with John Dabb?"

"Sure you have me pat, Preston."

57

"It was you who run down thet Hartwell rustlin' outfit?"

"I can't take all the credit. But I was there when it happened."

"Say, man, I've heerd aboot you all these years. Damn funny I didn't savvy who you were."

"It's been six years since I left here—and perhaps you heard some things not quite fair to me."

"Never heerd a word thet I'd hold against you."

"Then my job stands, in spite of my bein True Rock?" asked Rock, eagerly. What a vast importance seemed to hang on this!

"Say, why'n hell didn't you yell who you was fust off?" retorted Preston.

"You didn't ask me—and I guess I've always been a little backward about my name, at least."

Preston had undergone further subtle change that to Rock's quick intelligence indicated he was finding favor with the rancher. Something of Preston's pondering speculation might have had to do with the future.

"Rock, shore you couldn't know thet when you killed Pickins—"

"I'd rather you didn't dig up my past," interrupted Rock, sharply.

"Hell, man! You're listenin' to Gage Preston. An' he's tryin' to tell you how you once did him a good turn."

"I'm glad, even if I don't understand."

"Wal, I'll tell you some other time," rejoined Preston, evidently relieved to be checked in his impulsive speech. "Come now, an' meet these hyar eleven other Prestons."

Rock faced the ordeal with mingled emotions, chiefly concerning Thiry, but with nothing of the inhibition he had labored under while encountering Ash. Thiry, however, to his keen disappointment, was not one of the half dozen Prestons who answered the rancher's cheery call.

Mrs. Preston appeared a worthy mate for this virile cattleman. She was buxom and comely, fair like all of them, and some years younger than Preston.

"Ma, this is Trueman Rock, who's come to ride fer me," announced Preston. Then he presented Rock to Alice, a girl of sixteen, not by any means lacking the good looks that appeared to run in the family. She was shy, but curious and friendly. Rock took instantly to the ragged, barefooted, big-eyed children, Lucy and Burr; and signs were not wholly wanting that they were going to like him.

"Where's Thiry?" asked the rancher.

"She's ironin', Dad," replied Alice.

"Wal, didn't she hyar me call?"

"Reckon she did, Pa, for you'd 'most woke the daid," replied his wife, and going to the door of the second cabin she called, "Thiry, we've company, an' Pa wants you."

Rock caught a low protesting voice that came from inside.

"Nonsense, daughter," replied the mother. "You don't look so awful. Anyway, you can't get out of it."

Whereupon Thiry appeared in the door in a long blue apron that scarcely hid her graceful symmetry. Her sleeves were rolled up to the elbow of shapely arms. She came out reluctantly, with troubled eyes and a little frown. She showed no surprise. She had seen him through the window.

"Good afternoon, Miss Preston," greeted Trueman, evincing but little of the pleasure that consumed him.

"Oh, it's Mr. Rock, our new grocery clerk," she responded, with manner and tone that was a little beyond Trueman. "How do you do! And aren't you lost way out here?"

"Reckon I was, but there's hope of me gettin' back in the trail."

"Hey, Rock, what's thet aboot you bein' a grocery clerk? I reckoned I was hirin' a cowboy."

Whereupon Rock had to explain that he had been keeping store for Sol Winter when Thiry happened in. Thiry did not share in the laughter. Rock thought he saw the gray eyes quicken and darken as she glanced swiftly from him to her father.

"Thiry, he's goin' to handle the boys," replied Preston, as if in answer to a mute query.

"You are a—a cowboy, then," she said to Rock, struggling to hide confusion or concern. "You don't know the job you've undertaken. . . . What did my brother Ash say?—I saw you talking with him."

"He was tellin' me your dad would sure give me a

59

job. . . . And that you'd be glad," replied Trueman, with the most smiling and disarming assurance.

"Yes, he was," retorted Thiry, blushing at the general laugh.

"You're right, Miss Preston," returned Rock, ruefully. "Your brother was not—well, quite taken with my visit."

"What did he say?"

"He told me you didn't see every rider who came along. And that your father was not home. And that—"

"We apologize for Ash's rudeness," interposed Thiry, hurriedly. She had not been able to meet Rock's gaze.

"Never mind, Rock. It's nothin' to be hurt aboot," added Preston. "Ash is a queer, unsociable feller. But you're shore welcome to the rest of us. . . . Thiry, if you never heerd of True Rock, I want to tell you he's been one of the greatest riders of this range. An' I need him bad, in more ways than one. An' I can tell you somethin' thet'd make you glad he happened along."

"Oh, Dad, I—I didn't mean—I—of course I'm glad if you are," she returned, hurriedly. "Please excuse me now. I've so much work."

Somehow Trueman divined that she was not glad; or if she were, it was owing to her father's need, and then it was not whole-hearted. The knowledge fell upon him with unaccountable dismay, so much so that he could scarcely conceal it. But the youngsters saved him this time. They sidled over to him and began to ply him with questions about the white horse, which had captivated their eyes.

"What you call him?" asked Burr.

"Well, the fact is I haven't named him yet," replied Rock, surprised at the omission. "Can you think of a good one?"

"Sure. Call him Whiteface or Longmane."

"Not so bad. What do you say, Lucy?"

"I like what Thiry calls him," she said, shyly. "Oh, we've seen him often. I was once on his back."

"Your sister has a name for him? Well, that's nice. Tell me. Maybe I'll like it," said Trueman, with a feeling of duplicity.

"Egypt," announced Lucy, impressively. "Isn't that just grand?"

"Egypt?—Oh, I see. Because he's like one of the white stallions of the Arabians. I think it's pretty good. . . . We'll call him Egypt."

"That'll tickle Thiry. I'll tell her," cried the child, joyously, running into the kitchen.

Rock contrived, while letting Burr drag him round to look at the antlers of deer and elk, to catch a glimpse of Thiry at her work. She was alone in there, for Lucy had come running out. Rock thought she looked very sweet and domestic and capable. On the way back round the porch he stopped a moment to have another glimpse. This time she glanced up and caught him. Rock essayed to smile and pass on, to make his action seem casual. But her gaze held him stock-still, and it was certain he could not find a ready smile. She ceased her ironing and transfixed him with great eyes of wonder and reproach, almost resentment. She accused him, she blamed him for coming. He had brought her more trouble. Rock was so roused that he forgot himself and returned her look with all the amaze and entreaty he felt. Then the paleness of her face seemed suddenly blotted out; hastily she bent again to her work.

"Come, Rock, let me show you the ranch," called Preston. "We're shore some proud of it."

"You ought to be. I've seen a sight of ranches, but this one is the finest," returned Rock, as he left the porch. "Slagle once told me he didn't build here because he thought it'd be cold and windy."

"Ha! I had the same idee. But I found out thet the wind blows only in summer, when you want it. Fall an' winter this high saddle is protected. Prevailin' winds from the north."

"Pa, soon as Thiry's done we'll have supper, so don't go far," spoke up Mrs. Preston.

"All right, Ma. I reckon Rock couldn't be driv very far," replied the rancher, drawing Rock away. "When we first come hyar, aboot five years ago, Slagle, as you know, lived down below. He wouldn't sell, an' he swore this divide was on his land. But it wasn't, because he'd homesteaded a hundred an' sixty acres, an' his land didn't come halfway up. Wal, we threwed up a big cabin, an' we all lived in it fer a while. The kids were pretty small then. Next I tore thet cabin down an' built the double

61

one, an' this one hyar, which Ash has to himself. He won't sleep with nobody. Lately we throwed up four more, an' now we're shore comfortable."

The little cabin over by the creek under the largest of the pines was occupied by Alice and Thiry, and they, according to Preston, had just about put that cabin up themselves. But Rock's quick eye gathered at once that Preston or some one of his sons was something of an architect and a most efficient carpenter. Except the two large cabins, nearest the road, the others were some distance apart. The small empty cabin, where Rock's packs had been left, was off among the trees fully a hundred yards; the next, where Preston's sons, Tom, Albert and Harry, lived, appeared an equal distance farther, and the last, occupied by Range Preston, and some of the other boys, stood close under the north slope of the Pass.

The grassy divide sloped gradually to the west, and down below the level, where cedars grew thicker and the pines thinned out, were the corrals and barns and open sheds, substantial and well built. Another log chute brought running water from the hill. Rock found his white horse in one of the corrals, surrounded by three lanky youths from sixteen to twenty years old. Preston introduced them as the inseparable three, Tom, Albert, and Harry. They had the Preston fairness, and Tom and Harry were twins.

"Rock, if you can tell which is Tom an' which is Harry, you'll do more'n anyone outside the family."

"Son-of-a-gun if I can tell now, lookin' right at them," ejaculated Rock.

"Boys, I've hired Rock to ride with you, an' reckon you'll get along," said Preston.

"Like my horse?" asked Rock.

"By gum! he's the only hoss I ever seen thet gave me the feelin's of a hoss thief," vouchsafed Albert Preston. The twins admired Egypt in silence.

The barns were stuffed full of hay and fodder, some of it freshly cut. A huge bin showed a reserve of last year's corn. Wagons and harnesses were new; a row of saddles hung opposite a dozen stalls, where the Prestons no doubt kept their best horses. But these were empty now. A long fenced lane ran down to pastures. Horses were whistling down there, cows mooing, calves bawling. The whole environment reeked with the heady odor of stock, hay, and manure.

Both money and labor had been lavished on this ranch; and it was something to open the eyes of old-time homesteaders like Slagle. Even prosperity would not have induced Slagle to such extremes of improvement. But then, Rock reflected, Preston must be a hard worker, and he had seven stalwart sons.

"Preston, if I owned this ranch I'd never leave it a single day," was Rock's eloquent encomium.

"Wal, I'd shore hate to leave it myself," returned the other, tersely.

"How many cattle have you?" queried Rock, because he knew this was a natural question.

"Don't have much idee. Ten thousand haid, Ash says. We run three herds, the small one down on the Flats, another hyar in the Pass, an' the third an' big herd up in the Foothills."

"Naturally the third means the big job," said Rock.

"Shore will be for you boys. Thar's a lot of cattle over thar thet ain't mine. Ash said eighty thousand haid all told in the Foothills. But thet's his exaggerated figurin'."

"Gee! So many? In my day half that number would have been a lot. But it's a big country. Who's in on that range beside you?"

"Wal, thar's several heavy owners, like Dabb, Lincoln, Hesbitt, an' then a slew of others, from homesteaders like Slagle an' Pringle to two-bit cowpuncher rustlers. It's sort of a bad mess over thar. An' some of the outfits haven't no use fer mine."

"Ha! That's old cowboy breed. You can't ever change it. . . . I know Lincoln. But Hesbitt is a new one on me."

"Yes, he came in soon after me," replied Preston, shortly. His speech, to Rock's calculating perceptions, had lost heartiness and spontaneity. But Rock doubted that he would have observed this subtle little difference had he not come to Sunset Pass peculiarly stimulated by curiosity.

"Sol Winter told me you'd worked a new wrinkle on the range," went on Rock, matter-of-factly. "Wholesale butcherin'."

"Yes. Always did go in fer thet. Hyar in this country I first set in killin' an' sellin' to local butchers. Then I got to shippin' beef to other towns not far along the railroad. An' all told I've made it pay a little better than sellin' on the hoof."

"Reckon it's a heap harder work."

"We Prestons ain't afraid of work," said the rancher. "But it takes some managin' as well. I made a slaughter-house out of Slagle's place, an' then we do some butcherin' out on the range."

"What stumps me, Preston, is how you get beef to town in any quantity," responded Rock.

"Easy for Missourians on these hard roads. We got big wagons an' four-hoss teams. In hot summer we drive at night."

"So you're from Missouri," went on Rock, with geniality. "I sort of figured you were. I once worked with an outfit of Missourians. They have a lingo of their own, somethin' like Texans. Better educated, though."

"My girl Thiry went to school till she was seventeen," Preston spoke with pride. "But the rest of them had little schoolin' 'cept what Thiry has taught them out hyar. . . . Wal, you'll want to unpack an' wash up fer supper."

It was just sunset when Rock came out of the cabin assigned him. Sitting down on the stone steps of the porch, he found there was an open place between the trees permitting unbroken view of the Pass.

Here, striking him like an invisible force in the air, was the wild scene famous among riders all over the Southwest. For riders wandered from range to range, and round camp fires and while on guard or in the bunkhouses they were wont to tell about the outfits with whom they had ridden and the ranges they had known. Rock had been asked about Sunset Pass more than once while he was in Texas. He recalled how he had used to rave. Small wonder!

From Preston's ranch the Pass spread into a wider stretch of grassy knolls tipped by cedars, and grassy flats dotted by cedars, and grassy ridges sloping like hog-backs down from the walls of gray and green. Ten miles and more of the most beautiful meadow and pasture land in the West! Dots and strings and bunches of cattle gave

64

life to the scene. The mellow murmur of a stream came on the summer wind. Water was falling somewhere, and Rock had to search to find it, close under the right wall, fringed by green that was turning to gold.

Beyond the grassy levels and mounds the Pass changed to a verdant floor, only here and there showing a glint of open parks, like lakes of gold set in a forest. The walls leaned away, less rugged and rocky. From the league-wide forested floor, then, the Pass restricted to one third that width and began its magnificent step by step, up and up, to open into the golden foothill country. The white stream fell and paused and fell and paused again, as if loath to plunge into the purple gorges. Magic lights of gold and lilac and rose, transparent as the rainbow, gathered strength, and spread from rays and streaks to a mantle that slowly dimmed the outlines of the lower reaches.

Beyond and above the foothills yawned the western end of the Pass—the grand gap that split the mountain range and gave the felicitous name to this beautiful rent in the crust of the earth.

The sun was setting in the notch, with broken clouds above, pearl and mauve and opal, with hearts of rose and edges of saffron. How intense the blue far above! How like yellow lightning low down near the sinking orb, that now slipped its blazing under side below the clouds! A colossal reflector of nature—the great stone slopes of the mountain, magnified the brilliance, the color, the glory. And what had been beautiful before now seemed transformed to enchanted realms beyond the earth. What pure gold burned on the winding high walls of rock! The royal purple hue of Pharaoh's raiment slanted down from the peaks, its source invisible, to vanish in the white fire-streaked gorges. Over the western wall, between its end and the foothills, now mystic and dim, poured a medium like transparent lilac water. It moved. It flashed and glinted, as if falling stars shot through it down to the depths of amethyst. And every second there was change, until the blazing sun slid below the notch, and as swiftly the color and beauty and glory faded, to show Sunset Pass only a wild, broken defile, shading to gray and black.

65

A bell called Rock to supper. When he reached the cabin, to find the Preston boys straddling the benches, it was to be accosted by the rancher.

"Say, cowboy, when you hyar the supper bell you come a-r'arin'. Never wait for a second bell."

"Did you have to ring a second bell for me?" queried Trueman, in surprise.

"I did—or you'd have missed your supper," returned Thiry. She was standing near where Preston sat at the head of the table. Her face seemed to catch the afterglow of sunset, and her eyes, too.

"Thanks. . . . I'm sorry to be late. I didn't hear. Guess I was lost in the sunset."

"Wal, it wasn't it's best tonight. Too much sun. You want more cloud, so you can see. . . . Rock, you set hyar on my right. Thet'll put you across from Thiry. Hope it doesn't spoil your appetite!"

"Dad, instead of cracking jokes you should introduce Mr. Rock to the other boys," reproved Thiry, calmly.

"Scuse me. Let's see. Are we all hyar? . . . . Whar's Ash?"

"He rode off somewheres," replied one of the boys.

"Wal, Rock, meet Range Preston, an' thet's his real name . . . an' Scoot, which is short for some handle Ma gave him once . . . an' Boots, whose proper name is Frank. . . . Boys, this is Trueman Rock."

Preston's humorous introduction, and Rock's friendly response, elicited only a "howdy" from each of these older sons.

"Reckon we can eat now." added Preston. "Sit down, Rock, an' pitch in."

The long table was bountifully spread, steaming, savory. Mrs. Preston sat at the foot, with Lucy on one side and Burr on the other. Alice's place was next to Rock, and she most solicitously served him. The twins and Albert, with their silver hair wet and plastered back, sat next to Thiry, faces over their plates. The elder brothers occupied seats on the bench beyond Alice. There was hardly any unnecessary conversation. The male contingent, Rock observed, devoted themselves to the supper, like any other hungry cowboys. Presently Rock stole a glance at Thiry, to catch her eyes on him. That made him so happy he did not dare risk another. But he could see her plate, and that the food on it diminished slowly. She was not hungry. His coming to Sunset Pass had unaccountably troubled her. It puzzled and annoyed Rock. It was far from flattering. He was not such a cad that he would impose himself upon a girl who disliked him on first sight. But Rock could not believe that could be wholly true. What had he done to deserve that? If he had been rude or bold that day of the meeting in Winter's store, he could understand. But he had only been full of fun—he could not remember saying anything to which Thiry could take exception, unless it was that silly remark about the spilled rice being an omen. So his mind ran, and the remainder of the supper was not a satisfaction to him.

When it ended, dusk had just fallen. It was not going to be very dark, at least early in the evening, for a half-moon soared out from under the white fleecy clouds.

Rock sat on the edge of the porch, attended again by the children. The older sons stalked away while the younger lingered, evidently accepting the newcomer. The womenfolk, except Thiry, who had gone into the other cabin with her father, were in the kitchen.

"Can you tell Tom from Harry?" Burr asked, mischievously, of Rock.

"No. Can you?"

"Sure can," he replied, then whispered, "I'll tell you how if you get stuck."

Presently the rancher came out alone. There was a lighted lamp inside.

"Boys, hyar's some work fer you to break Rock in on tomorrow," he said. "Grease the wheels of the green wagon. Then hitch up an' go down to the slaughter-house. Fold tight an' pack all the hides thet are dry. Haul them up to the barn. An' Tom, next mornin' soon as it's light you hitch up again an' drive down an' meet us at the Flats. Then you come back home."

"Walk, I reckon?" asked Tom, laconically.

"Wal, you can run if you like. An' thet day an' till I come back you-all work on the new pasture fence."

"All right, Pa," drawled Tom.

"Rock, thet doesn't sound much like work to you. But your job is to keep these three harum scarums from ridin' off into the woods. You'll have your hands full, fer they're shore Indians."

"Boss, if I can't hold them in I'll do the work myself," replied Rock.

Before the hour passed, Mrs. Preston and Alice came out, and Thiry, too, and they all sat around on the porch and grass enjoying the cool breeze coming up the Pass. The moon shone brighter as the clouds grew more open. There were moments of pale gloom, then a long interval of silver light. The shadow of the pines on the white grass fascinated Rock. And presently he found that being there, except for the silent Thiry so disturbing to him, was no different from being in the company of most any hospitable Western family. The discordant note—Ash Preston—was absent. Rock made himself as agreeable as he knew how, to the youngsters especially, and then to the mother, who responded readily. She was of pioneer extraction, simple, virile, and sincere. She had a hearty laugh; she liked news of the outside world.

Preston retired within his cabin, and soon after the boys slouched away, their spurs jingling, their dark lank forms silhouetted against the moon-blanched grass.

Trueman rose to say good night.

Thiry had been standing some moments, in the shadow of the cabin, apparently listening.

"Mr. Rock, would you like to walk with me to my cabin?" she asked.

"Why—pleased, I'm sure," replied Rock, haltingly, scarce able to conceal his amaze and joy. What old-fashioned courtesy! Good nights were exchanged, and Rock found himself walking away under the great dark pines, in the shadowed moonlight, with Thiry beside him.

Chapter Five

Thiry walked beside him, slender, light-stepping, with her profile showing clear-cut and cold in the moonlight. As she did not speak, Trueman dismissed the idea that her invitation was simply an old fashioned courtesy. Therefore he made no attempt at conversation. When they had covered most of the distance to her cabin, without exchanging a single word, he felt anew and provokingly the growing excitement of this situation.

At last she slowed her step, hesitated, and halted under the magnificent pine tree that made dark shade around her cabin. Outside the circle there were spaces of silver moonlight, and then streaks and bars of black shadow across the light. The night wind breathed in the huge spreading mass of foliage overhead. How supernaturally beautiful the place and moment!

The girl confronted Trueman, and her face had the sheen of the moonlight, her eyes the darkness and mystery of the shade.

"Mr. Rock, I want to talk to you," she said, very quietly.

"Yes?" rejoined Trueman, encouragingly, but he was not in the least encouraged.

"Have you been—wholly honest in coming out here to Sunset Pass?" she asked, gravely.

"Honest!—What do you mean?" flashed Rock, his pride cut and his blissful anticipations fading.

"What did you tell father?"

"I asked for a job," returned Rock, curtly.

"Did you let him believe the job was your sole reason for coming?"

"No. He said I hadn't been long in trailin' you up. He was good-natured and nice. So I didn't deny it. I laughed and agreed with him."

"Oh—you did!" she exclaimed, somehow shaken out of her reserve. "That's different. I apologize."

"Miss Preston, you don't owe me any apology," rejoined Rock, stiffly.

"Yes, I do. I thought you'd deceived Dad—the same as so many riders have done."

Rock had averted his face. He was astounded and hurt, suddenly, coldly checked in his romantic imaginings. What manner of girl was this Thiry Preston? It might be that she was a worthy sister to unsociable Ash Preston. But that resentful thought could not abide with his loyalty.

"Mr. Rock, do you remember the last moment, when you were with me at the corral in Wagontongue?" she asked.

"I'm not likely to forget it," he returned.

"You looked something at me. You didn't say so, but you meant you'd see me again. Now didn't you? Honest?"

"Miss Preston, I—I certainly did," answered Rock, hastily. "But, indeed, I didn't mean to be rude or—or bold."

"I don't think you were either," she said, earnestly. "I—But wait a moment. My sister is coming."

Rock glanced up to see the slim figure of Alice pass by toward the cabin.

"Good night, Mr. Cowboy," she said, naïvely.

"Good night, Miss Preston," replied Rock, trying to be gay.

She went into the cabin and closed the door. Soon a light gleamed pale through a curtained window.

"We might sit down," suggested Thiry, indicating a rustic bench under the pine. "I am tired."

The bench appeared to catch a gleam of shadowed moonlight. Thiry could here be seen more clearly than while she stood in the shade. Rock preferred to stand, and he wished he could not see her so well.

"Mr. Rock, please don't misunderstand," she began, looking up. "I was far from being insulted or even offended that day in the store and at the corral. . . . At the last, there, you meant you'd see me again. And you've done it. Now we're concerned with that."

"Reckon I might have waited a decent little while," responded Rock, as she paused. "But I never met a girl like you. I wanted to see you again—soon. Where's the harm?"

"Indeed there isn't any harm *in* it, Mr. Rock, but harm can come *from* it."

"How?"

"Through my brother Ash."

"Well, that's not hard to believe," rejoined Rock, with sharpness. "The other day he was a drunken, vulgar lout. He ought to have been kicked out of that corral, and I'd have done it but for you. Today, when he was sober, he was a different proposition to meet. He was cold, mean, vicious. He had no hospitality of the West—no idea what was due a tired and hungry stranger. But at that I'd prefer him drunk. In my day on the range I've met some—"

Trueman bit his tongue. The girl had suddenly covered her face with her hands. He could see her strain and almost writhe.

"Aw, Miss Preston, forgive me," he burst out. "I didn't mean to distress you. I just spoke out quick, without thinkin'—"

She drew her hands away and lifted her head. "You're quite right—Mr. Rock," she said, unsteadily. "Ash is—all that you say. To my shame I confess it. All my life I've made excuses for him. It's no use. I—I cannot do it—any more. . . . But that's not the point."

Rock sat down beside her, his anger flown, but there was another kind of heat runing along his veins. How this girl must love her brother!

"I know. The point was the harm that might come through Ash. Please be frank with me. If I've brought this distress upon you, I'm entitled to know why."

"I've always been very—very fond of Ash," she said, tremulously, struggling for a composure that would not return. "Partly because he was always so bad—and I seemed the only one who could influence him for good. Ash cares for nothing but me. Not for father, mother, brothers, or his other sisters. He hates men—he hates horses—he hates cattle. . . . And through these things I—I've stuck to him until now I—I—Mr. Rock, I can't tell you."

"Spare yourself, Miss Preston," returned Rock, im-

71

pulsively. "It's wonderful—beautiful of you. I admire and respect you for it. But I can't understand."

"No one can," she said, sadly. "Alice thinks I'm mad. . . . Oh, how I dread this! But it has to be done—more with you than with any other who ever tried to be friends with me. I've known lots of boys, and liked them, too. But not lately. As I grow older Ash grows more jealous. He fears I might like some cowboy."

"Oh I see! Is such a remarkable thing possible?" returned Rock, unable to resist a slight sarcasm.

"Of course it is," she retorted. Her eyes flashed at him. "What do you think I am, anyway?"

"Under the present circumstances I reckon I dare not tell you."

"Mr. Rock, you are going to disappoint me, presently."

"Good Heavens! What do you think I am, anyway?" retorted Rock, in turn, growing almost desperate.

"I make a good deal of what Mother and Alice and Dad think," she said, gently.

"Well, what's that?" he queried, suddenly mollified. She could do anything with him.

"I would dare tell you, but it would only make this unfortunate situation worse. I only hint of it—because it's not fair to let you think we—or I—dislike you."

"Oh, then you don't?"

"No. I—I think I really like you, though it's such short notice for me. . . . And, Mr. Rock, if I had my way, I'd like to be friends with you."

"Thank you, Miss Thiry," he returned, gratefully, swayed by her unexpected avowal. "Honest, I didn't hope for so much. All I wanted was a *chance* to prove I could deserve you—your friendship."

"I—I dare say you could," she returned, looking away. "Mr. Winter used to tell me about you. How fond you were of Nick—how you saved his life once. Then Dad. He likes all cowboys, but I never saw him taken with anyone as he is with you. . . . But the thing is I *can't* be friends with you."

"Because of Ash?"

"Yes. That's where the harm would come in. He will not let any boy or man be friends with me—at least out here at Sunset."

"Very well. I give up my job and go ride for some ther outfit—*if* you will be my friend."

"That's fine and square of you, Mr. Rock, and I might romise so much."

"Much? That isn't much. I mean only friendship. Do ou think I'm the kind of a man who'd want a girl to ;ive more than friendship until he'd earned it? Well, 'm not. And I wouldn't ask anythin'."

"Mr. Rock, you're making this harder for me," she aid, with pathos.

"I'm sorry. But go ahead."

"Cowboys have called on me here and many have :ome to ride for Dad. Just the regular run of cowboys. Ash soon got rid of them."

"I wonder how he did all that. I know cowboys well, where a pretty girl is concerned. And I'm just curious."

"I'll tell you. Ash has chased them away in every :onceivable manner. He's lied, as he lied to you about my not seeing riders who came to Sunset. He'd coolly invite them to leave. He'd bluff. He'd threaten. He'd cripple and shoot their horses, Oh, that was the vilest thing! He'd get them drunk while on guard—which Dad couldn't forgive. He'd ridicule any sensitive cowboy before the outfit—so terribly that the poor fellow would leave. He'd concoct devilish schemes to make a cowboy seem negligent or crooked. And as a last resource he'd pick fights. Oh, he has beaten several cowboys brutally. Then worst of all—he has thrown his gun on more than one. Archie Black will be a cripple for life. And Jack Worthington nearly died of a gun shot."

"How very interestin'!" exclaimed Rock, and for the life of him he could not keep his voice normal. "And has nothin' ever happened to this bully?"

"Oh, Ash didn't always come out scot-free. But nothing to bother him. I don't believe Ash has nerves or heart or feeling."

"Yet you love him!" ejaculated Rock, bitterly.

"I do—more because I seem the only one. But it's not so much that. I've kept him from going to the bad."

"How could he be any worse?" asked Trueman, incredulously.

"Oh, he could be. You don't know—you can't understand. But I do."

73

"Miss Thiry, have you been so vastly concerned for the good health of all these poor lovesick cowboys as you seem about mine?" asked Rock.

"You are sarcastic again. Oh, you're not—so nice as I thought you'd be. . . . Yes, I was concerned—worried about these boys. But I've never been so—so scared as I am over your coming."

"Scared!—For me?"

"Yes, for you—a little. Oh, I can't lie to you. I'm scared because of the—the harm that may come—if you stay."

"A little! How nice of you! All you think of is poor dear Brother. For my face to be beat to a jelly or my leg shot off or worse—that causes you only a little concern. Thanks, Miss Preston. I'm beginnin' to believe I idealized you rather high."

"You're perfectly horrid!" she cried, passionately.

"Yes, indeed, you must have idealized me beyond my merits."

Rock leaned closer to study the lovely face, the deep eyes that flamed at him yet tried to hide true feelings. He could speak bitter words, but was instantly full of remorse. Yet how sweet to hurt her!

"Look me straight in the eyes," he said, suddenly. "You can't—you can't."

"Why—you—certainly I can," she returned, startled. And she did, gravely, tragically. What a marvelous abyss Trueman Rock gazed into! He lost himself there.

"You said you couldn't lie?" queried Rock, cruelly, overcome by his own catastrophe.

"I never told—a—a—black lie in my life," she faltered, with her head lifting.

"Then—are *you* honest with me? What is the reason you want me to run off like a coward?"

"I've been trying to tell you," she replied, hastily ignoring his first query, which he saw had made her start. "But I don't want you to be a coward. I'd think it brave, generous, to help me. I told you and I tell you again harm, terrible harm, might come of this, if you stay. Ash will not try any of his tricks on you. For you are different. Why, my dad said to me, not an hour ago, 'There, lass, is a cowboy whose face Ash won't rub in the dirt. An' he won't be throwin' guns around so careless. For, Thiry, this fellow, True Rock, is a different kind of a hombre

74

from all those Ash has stacked up against. . . .' Those were Dad's very words. I was thunderstruck. It seemed almost as if Dad was *glad*. I never saw him speak like that. And lightning flashed from his eyes. . . . Oh, this spurred me to speak with you. Can't you see? You are different. You're a man—and one with a—a—please forgive—a bloody record. I don't despise you because of that. Mr. Winter told me of your meeting with that vile Pickins. That same Pickins was once an enemy of father's. Since I've lived West I've learned there are bad gunmen and good gunmen. My brother Ash is one kind—you are the other."

"Thiry Preston, first you are cruel, then you are kind," replied Rock, hoarsely, as she paused to catch her breath, with a hand pressed upon her heart. "If you want to drive me away I advise you to keep on bein' cruel."

She was in the grip of strong emotion now, beautiful and soul-moving to Rock.

"You wouldn't stay here—with us—and—and leave me alone?" she asked, with a simplicity wholly free of vanity.

"Yes, I might—if you cut me cold or slammed the door in my face," he answered.

"That I couldn't do. If you stay on, living here and eating at our table, I could not help but talk to you, be with you some. I think it would be nice—if Ash wasn't around to make me so sick. I—I'm afraid I might like you. There isn't any reason why I shouldn't. . . . Now, if you stayed—you'd—you'd——"

She broke off as if unable to find adequate expression. But her voice, her look, were more than sufficient to make Rock fight temptation. How easy to lie to this innocent girl! He could do that and stay on here, and deceive Ash Preston, too.

"Yes, Miss Thiry, I would," he returned, swiftly, to get by the danger. "I would be a very great deal worse than any cowboy you ever knew."

"So—you see," she said, entreatingly. "Then you and Ash would fight over me. . . . First with fists, probably, like a couple of beasts. Then with guns! . . . Oh, that's the horror of it. . . . There would be blood spilled. He might kill you, which would be terrible. But most likely you would kill *him*."

"Suppose I did?" flashed Rock, torn between pity and jealousy.

She leaped up to stand rigid, with clenched hands and swelling bosom, with such blazing eyes of passion that he was stunned.

"If it was not my death—I'd kill you myself," she cried, intensely.

How wonderful she was! Almost he forgot all in sheer ecstasy. Then remorse laid hold of him again. He was torturing her.

"Miss Thiry, forgive me again," he pleaded. "You've said an awful thing. But I was to blame. Please sit down. . . . That was only my temper. Listen. I hope I'll never get into *any* kind of a fight with Ash."

"Oh, what are good intentions to men—where a woman is concerned? You couldn't keep out of it. You have a fiery temper. . . . And Ash—that devil would make a saint fight."

"I'll just make up my mind I won't fight. I'll keep out of his way. I'll do anythin'."

"Except let me alone. Oh, I can't trust you, Mr. Rock. I daren't trust the situation."

"But, girl, be reasonable. No one yet ever made me do what I didn't want to do. If I say I won't fight with words or fists or guns—I won't."

"Not if he insulted you vilely before my family—and others? Not if he slapped you, spat in your face, kicked you as if you were a dog?"

"Girl, in that case I couldn't be so sure of myself. But I might stand all that for you."

"Then I wouldn't have you do it," she cried. "I wouldn't let you be a coward—be despised by my people—all these range-riders, and your friends."

"Those who know me would understand. Reckon I wouldn't care about others."

"But it'd be dreadful to make such—a—a fool of yourself over me," she protested, hotly. "I—I wouldn't allow it."

"You might not be able to help it. I'd have to be a fool—or else True Rock—one or the other. And I'd certainly rather be a fool than hurt you."

"But you've only seen me once!" she exclaimed, despairingly.

"I'm not committin' myself yet, because I'd hate to embarrass you more without bein' sure. But I'm afraid, if seein' you the other day wasn't enough, this time *is*."

"Oh, please go away tomorrow—before it's too late," she implored.

"You want me to go as bad as that?" asked Rock, weakening.

"I beg you to. I've begun to be afraid of you, and I wasn't at first. You're so sharp—so keen. You'll—"

Suddenly in her agitation, she jerked a hand to her lips, as if to silence them. Her eyes dilated. She stared up at Rock like a child who had almost betrayed herself. And Rock, if he did not read her mind, had intuition enough to grasp that part of Thiry's fear, perhaps the greater, was not due to the inevitable clash between him and Ash. She was afraid he would find out something. Rock hastened to thrust the insidious thought from him.

"Afraid of me!" he ejaculated, hurriedly. "Why, Thiry—Miss Thiry, that's absurd! Right this minute I'm the best friend you have in the world."

"Then prove it," she said, bending closer.

"How?"

"Go away tomorrow."

"And never see you again?" he queried, blankly.

"It would be best," she returned, and looked away. "But I didn't say you'd never see me again. Perhaps I—we might meet in town. I'm going in over the Fourth. Mrs. Dabb is to give a dance. I could see you there."

At that Rock laughed rather wildly. "At Amy Wund's house? Not much. . . ."

"Then at the dance. It won't be at her house. I—I'll go with you—if you ask me."

"Don't bribe me to run off from Sunset Pass," he said, ponderingly. "But thank you for sayin' you'd go with me. I'd like to. But I'm not invited and don't expect to be."

"I'll see you get an invitation, Mr. Rock."

"Don't tempt me. I'd almost give my head to take you to a dance. I'd almost quit my job here and then come back to it again."

"But that would be a lie," she returned, severely.

"Well, I might lie, too. I don't mean *to* you, but *for* you."

77

"Please, Mr. Rock, go away tomorrow before trouble comes. I'll never be able to thank you enough. It's the only chance you have to be my—my friend."

"You're a queer, wonderful girl," he replied, puzzled and sad.

"I will come to town oftener—then," she almost whispered.

"You'd meet me in town and hope to deceive Ash?" queried Rock, bluntly.

"Yes. I—I'll try," she faltered.

"But he'd find it out. You can't fool that hombre. Then he would have a real case against me. He'd hunt me down, force me to meet him."

"Oh!" she cried, poignantly.

"If I give in to you and leave Sunset Pass, I'd never willingly see you again," he went on, with more bitterness.

"Mr. Rock, that wouldn't be such a—a loss to you as you imagine now," she answered.

"I don't know. All I know is that I hate to refuse you anythin'. Reckon I can't, if it's for your sake. But if I do it, I'll go plumb to hell!"

She questioned him with mute lips and beseeching glance.

"Listen. There's two sides to this deal, and here's mine," he began, leaning close so that he could see her better in the pale shadow. "I want you to know about me. I was born in Illinois. My mother and father are livin'. They're quite old now. I was home five years ago. I have a sister. She ought to be nineteen now—a fine, pretty girl. Well, I went to school till we moved out West. Then I went to ridin'. My father lost out in the cattle business and took the family back home. I stayed. That was—fourteen—sixteen years ago. Durin' these sixteen years I've lived the life of a wanderin', ridin', drinkin', fightin' cowboy. I stuck here on this range longest of all. I don't say I was bad, but I wasn't much good. . . . I was always gettin' in trouble for other people. . . . That's how I came to shoot Pickins. It was a good riddance. But the sheriff then—Cass Seward—was a friend of Pickins's. I didn't want to kill Seward, so I left Wagontongue. I stayed away six years. Then had to come back. I got there the day I met you. Found out Seward was gone. Found out a lot of other things. I wanted to know about my old girls. I had always been crazy over pretty girls. Ran after anyone. Liked some—and, reckoned I loved—or imagined I loved others. Sol Winter told me a lot of bad news about the girls—and about his son Nick. So I lost my happy mood. I wanted to go out and get drunk. Sol asked me to keep store for him. And I sat there sinkin' into one of the old black spells that had kept me from makin' some one out of myself. Pretty soon I would go and get awful drunk. I had a hunch that it'd be kind of climax in my life. But I didn't care. . . . Then you, Thiry Preston, walked in that store. And I didn't want to go out and get drunk. Somethin' happened. I don't know yet what it was. But it was wonderful. Sure you remember how funny I was—don't you?"

"Oh, I thought you funny then, but now I see you weren't," she said.

"No, I'm sure not so funny now," he went on, with dark passion. "Somethin' happened to me. It's been such a tearin', changin' somethin' that I don't know myself. I'm findin' out little by little. Seein' you this second time has helped a lot. I'll make a clean breast of all—soon as I know. But right now I know—if you don't turn your back on me—I'll never drink again. Or hunt for a fight! Or waste my time and money!"

"Mr.—Rock!" she exclaimed, rising, low-voiced and trembling. "Are you telling me you—you love me?"

"No, I'm not tellin' you that," he returned, doggedly. "But I'm sure afraid somethin's terrible wrong. . . . It's this here wrong, Miss Thiry—that if you *make* me, by your coldness to me and your pleadin' for that no-good brother, leave Sunset Pass, I'll go plumb to hell. I know that. It'd be too much."

"Coldness? . . . I think I have been anything but cold," she murmured, sinking back on the bench.

"You've frozen me so I'm stiff. I can't talk. But it'll be good for me. I've been spoiled. I've grown conceited. I need just this lesson you're teachin' me. . . . But, Miss Thiry, please—please don't make me go away."

"Could I make you do anything? How silly!—But if you're manly enough to save me misery, you'll go."

"That's hittin' hard," he returned, shrinking. Then

he jerked up his drooping head. "Suppose I get it into my mind that by *stayin'* I can save you *more* misery?"

"Mr. Rock!" she cried, shocked.

His sudden query had been a random shot, but it struck home. Rock's heart leaped. He had to stifle a wild impulse.

"Quien sabe? I might," he returned, almost coldly. "Give me a day to think over whether I'll go or stay. Reckon so far the fight's one-sided and in your favor. . . . I'll meet you tomorrow night and tell you."

"Tomorrow night.—Here at this hour?" she returned, rising from the seat.

"Yes. Good night, Miss Preston."

"I'm very, very sorry— You. . . . Good night."

Rock gave her one long look as she stood now in the moonlight. He would carry that picture in his heart of hearts all his days. Then he strode away, and when he turned, at quite some distance, she was still standing like a white statue.

He made his bed on the porch, so that he could lie there and watch the moon, and think over this maddening situation.

For hours it seemed he never got anywhere, so far as decision was concerned. His mind was chaotic. The moon soared white and grand above the pines and the night wind roared. Coyotes mourned eerily. A deep-voiced hound bayed them in answer. A low soft murmur of running water came to him in the lulls of the wind.

At last he admitted that he loved Thiry Preston. Time was nothing. He had always known her, and though the hours were but few since their actual meeting, he was now measuring their incomprehensible length and fullness. But he hated the idea that he only loved her. That was putting her with the others. His love for Amy, Polly, and Kit had merely been growing pangs toward this real and beautiful thing.

It was great and would suffice Rock for all time. Not one second longer did he hesitate about sacrificing himself for her happiness. He could glory in that and still keep from going to hell, as he had childishly threatened.

This resolve cleared his mind of vacillation and bewilderment and conflicting tides of emotion. The rest was easy and required only intelligence. If he could best serve Thiry Preston by passing out of her life as quickly as he had come into it he would do so. But he had a strange persistent recurrence of a doubt. He recalled her words, her looks, her actions, and relentlessly analyzed them. His love, once acknowledged, incited and stimulated his mind.

Before the moon tipped the pines above the rim of the Pass, which was late in the early morning hours, Rock had solved at least the second of his three problems.

Thiry Preston was honestly afraid her brother Ash would kill him or that he would kill Ash. So she wanted to send Rock away. But only so far was she wholly honest.

She feared Rock would discover something wrong there at Sunset Pass. Ash Preston was crooked. No doubt of this! Perhaps the father was, too, and some of the brothers. But Mrs. Preston was ignorant of it; so were Alice, and the younger brothers. Thiry bore this burden alone. That was the secret of her sad eyes and lips. That was the power Ash Preston had over her—love for him and fear. It did no longer seem unnatural. That was why no cowboys ever got a fair chance to win Thiry Preston's friendship.

What a terrible situation for Rock to fall upon! It was at once the most maddening and thrilling and irresistible thing that had ever happened to him. It was the big event of his life. It called to all the heights of emotion of which he was capable.

To go or stay—that was the question! If he left her, she might love him, surely would always remember him regretfully, tenderly. If he stayed she would hate him. But then he might save her.

Rock knew the West. He had become a part of it. The Prestons were new, comparatively, to this wild range. He knew Western men, their slow evolution, their uncanny power to suspect and search out and find among them the cattleman who transgressed the unwritten laws. All cattle-raisers stole from one another. But there was a distinction with a difference.

Gage Preston was getting rich—a little bit swiftly for a rancher on an ordinary scale. How? Rock answered the query in many ways, but only one way seemed tenable. Preston sold cattle on the hoof, the same as other

81

ranchers. None but rustlers ever sold cattle that did not belong to them. And certainly Preston could not be a rustler. It was inconceivable that Ash Preston could be a rustler, either, at least without his father knowing. But Rock scouted the rustler idea.

The Prestons had become butchers of cattle on a considerable scale. Did any one, outside themselves, know just how many steers they butchered? What a pertinent question here! Rock was certain that he would find out that no outsiders knew how many head of stock they killed. And here was the gist of the matter.

Some of the Prestons, with Ash at the head, and the father either in with them or unable to prevent it, were killing cattle not their own, burning or hiding the skins, and selling the beef at near and distant points.

"Good Lord!" muttered Rock, under his breath. "I've hit it plumb center.—The damn fools, thinkin' they can hide that long! . . . Gage Preston ought to have more sense. He struck me queer, though. But it's that rattlesnake son who's got this outfit buffaloed. No wonder poor Thiry has sad eyes. . . . Well, by Heaven, I'll stay at Sunset Pass!"

Chapter Six

A bell awakened Rock from late slumbers. The sun was up, and as he peeped out over his blanket covering he saw the grass shine gold under the cedars. He had overslept, which was not a remarkable fact, considering how long it had taken him to get to sleep. As he had neglected to undress, except to remove his boots, it did not take him long to get ready for the day.

While performing his ablutions his thoughts whirled, and then steadied to the stern consideration of the task before him. In the sober light of day it seemed tremendous. He had to prove his suspicions, which had lost no strength during sleep, and if they were well founded, then he must somehow stop the illicit proceedings before the Prestons were overwhelmed by catastrophe.

No new thing for Rock was it to appear a lighthearted, careless cowboy when underneath this guise he was hard and cautious, keen as a blade. The Prestons, excepting possibly Ash, would be easy to deceive.

Briskly he strode toward the double cabin, conscious of heart-beating anticipation, and when he thumped upon the porch Alice Preston came out of the kitchen, carrying plates and cup, which she set upon the table. She smiled at him. How pretty she was!

"I'm ashamed, Miss Alice," he said as he stepped over the bench. "Think of a cowboy late on his first mornin' of a new job!"

"It took three rings this morning to fetch you."

"Did it? I must have been dead to the world. Who rung them?"

"I did."

"You're very good to persevere. But I promise it'll not happen again."

Mrs. Preston looked out of the kitchen and greeted Rock with pleasant smile and words.

"Are the boys up, too?" he asked as he fell upon the ham and eggs and hot biscuits.

"Land's sake! they're up an' gone long ago," she replied. "They were sure funny. Tom said: 'Let him sleep, Ma. The longer the better.' . . . An' Al said: 'Don't wake the new boss, Ma. He won't never get no sleep when Ash is here, so let him get some now.' . . . An' Harry said: 'Ain't Thiry up yet, either? Reckon settin' up in the moonlight is bad for some folks.' "

"It sure is, Mrs. Preston," laughed Rock. "I'm sorry, though, if I'm to blame."

"Oh, Thiry was up hours ago," Alice informed them. "Saw Pa and the boys ride away. I know she had a run-in with Ash, because she had been cryin'."

"That's too bad," said Rock, bending over his plate and eating fast. He had seen the mother's face change very slightly, almost imperceptibly. Ash Preston was a thorn in the flesh of this wholesome family.

Rock made short work of his breakfast, and glad somehow that he had not encountered Thiry, he hurried away down toward the corrals. Pre-occupied as he was, he yet saw and felt and smelled afresh the incomparable beauty and spirit and fragrance of this Sunset Pass. Already the wind had begun its roar in the pines.

At the barnyard Rock found Al Preston leading in some horses; and one of his brothers was jacking up a hind wheel of the green wagon.

"Mornin', boss. Hope you're not sick," drawled Al.

"Boys, I was plumb dead. I'll sure let you punish me for bein' lazy."

The other boy nodded at Rock.

"Are you Tom or Harry?" asked Rock, suddenly reminded of the twins.

"Wanta bet on it?" queried the other.

"I'll be darned if I do."

"I'm Harry."

"All right, Harry, I'll know you tomorrow or bust. Where's Tom?"

"He left us to grease the wagon and went off after a horse for you."

"For my white horse, Egypt?" asked Rock.

"No—I'm sorry to say," returned Harry, haltingly, as if he had bad news.

"Did Egypt jump the pasture fence?"

"No. Ash saddled him and rode off on him."

Rock sat down suddenly, stifling the yell that leaped to his lips.

"It was just daylight when I got down here," went on Harry. "Range and Scoot were just ridin' off. Ash had your horse and saddle. Pa was cussin' Ash awful. Reckon they'd been arguin', 'cause Pa never cusses till he's wore out. Well, when he got done Ash says, 'Pa, how'd you like to go to hell?' Then he forks your horse and rides after the boys. Pa 'peared to be chokin' mad. All of a sudden he busted out laughin'. He climbed up on the wagon with Boots, and they left."

Rock for the moment succumbed to a silent fury. But seeing the gray-eyed brothers watching him curiously, keen to catch how he would take this first move of Ash's, he thought he had better explode naturally and wholesomely, as might any cowboy.

"— — — — —!" he yelled, lustily. "He took my new white horse! And my saddle that I wouldn't lend to the King of England! . . . Never had that happen to me. Doggone!—Boys, was it supposed to be a joke?"

"Joke nothin'. Ash was just mean, like he always is when we get a new rider. But reckon you'll have to take it as a joke."

"Huh! I will—like the old lady who keeps tavern out West!" replied Rock, with a short laugh.

"How's that boss?" inquired Al, hugely delighted.

"Like h—," answered Rock. "Boys, I reckon I'm the maddest cowpuncher that ever was. I think I'll get a horse and saddle from you, and go after my own."

"If you take my advice you'll swallow it—leastways till Ash comes back. Chances are he won't do Egypt no harm. If you follow Ash now, mad as you are, there'll only be another fight."

"Take it as a joke. Or better be nice about it," added Harry. "That always stumps Ash. If he can't make you mad he let's up—for a while, anyway."

"Thanks, boys. I'll think it over," rejoined Rock, grateful for their solicitude. "But I reckon the good Lord himself couldn't keep my mouth shut—after that."

"Let's get to work," suggested Harry. "We're late. And Ash ain't the only one Pa can cuss."

While Rock and Al greased the wagon wheels, Harry hitched up, and by the time this task was done Tom rode in, leading a horse. It was a bay that instantly took Rock's eye, and which would have made up for the loss of 'most any horse, except one like Egypt.

"Where's Ash's saddle?" he asked.

"It's hangin' there," replied Al. "But, gee! you won't ride his, will you?"

"I'll be darned if I won't," returned Rock, with grim humor. "You boys rustle along. I'll catch up."

"Come down the road by the pasture, boss," said Al. "Then take the right-hand road. You can't miss the slaughter-house, for the stink will knock you down."

After the boys left, Rock proceeded to put Ash's saddle and bridle on the bay horse, but he was not in any hurry. This first trick of Ash Preston's rankled in Rock. "Wonder what Thiry will say," he soliloquized. "She must have seen Ash on my horse. That's what upset her. . . . Damn him!—He must be one of those people who make the angels weep. And here I am with my hands tied!"

When Rock rode around the barn he espied the wagon far ahead down the gentle slope. He moved on at a trot, his mind busy, his active eye on the gardens and fields where he saw Mexicans at work. He came to the forks of the road, and taking the left one he entered the cedars, climbed the ridge, and descended to a grassy open meadow, only to mount another cedared ridge. He remembered this part of the Pass, though not so well as the general view of it from the divide. Willows and cottonwoods lined the brown brook; jackrabbits were numerous; hawks sailed over the open country and blue jays screeched from the slope. It was not long until the sweet sage-wind suffered a change and became tainted. Rock rode up a sparsely cedared slope to a level bench and soon came upon the site that had once been Slagle's ranch. The boys were halting before the several cabins. As Rock rode up, the stench unmistakably heralded a slaughter-house. Cabins, corral fences, barns and sheds and even the trees bore ghastly evidence of the nature of what this old Slagle ranch had sunk to. Skins of cattle hung everywhere.

The horses were turned loose to graze, and Rock, with the three boys, set to work. It was no easy task for one man, or even two men, to fold a stiff hide and compress it into small space. But that was what they had to do. The Preston boys might have been skillful and diligent at other kinds of ranch work, but at this particular job they were lazy. They made no bones of saying they hated it and particularly the inescapable smell. As the day grew warmer the odor increased. Rock did not drive the boys, but he drove himself. He heard Al say to his brothers in an aside, "Sure he's a hawg for work." Rock felt it good to sweat and toil again, despite the unpleasantness of the task.

Nevertheless, during this labor, and while joking with the brothers, without any ostensible interest in the place or the hides, Rock was bending all his keen faculties toward the end that he had determined upon. Nothing escaped his sharp eye, yet during the half day that it took to complete this job he did not observe anything that struck him significantly. Toward late afternoon, owever, he happened to kick a piece of white substance, ot stone, and of a color markedly contrasting with the ed earth. When he picked it up he thought it was clay. He smelled it—tasted it. Quicklime! Rock put it in his ocket.

In due time Tom mounted the loaded wagon to drive ome, while the other brothers rode off toward the woods, ach now with a rifle over his pommel.

"I'll poke along, Tom," said Rock.

"You been callin' me Tom all day an' I'm Harry," etorted the other.

"I'll be darned if I believe you," replied Rock. "You ellows are havin' fun with me."

Presently Rock was left alone. He was satisfied that e had gotten along well with the boys and that they ked him. They were so guileless that he knew he could ursue his suspicions almost before their backs were urned. They surely were as honest boys as any one ould find.

He took out the piece of quicklime. It did not appear o be very old. He looked around where he had found t to see if there was more. After diligent search he found . smaller piece. Quicklime in any quantity there, might e used to deaden the stench of decaying offal, blood, nd bones. Rock searched all the cabins, sheds, bins, vithout finding any more. None had ever been used upon he horrible pile that had accumulated in the hollow elow the slaughter-house. This heap had been left to he hogs, the coyotes and the weathering process of ature.

"Reckon no little piece of quicklime could get down ere of its own accord," muttered Rock, deliberating. It sure never flew. It must have been fetched here with nore of the same. What for?"

He had no other answer than the first he had con- ectured. Manifestly the Prestons left the entrails and keletons of their cattle there on the ground to rot. No leed to waste valuable time destroying what the ele- nents, the dogs, coyotes, and hogs would soon do away vith. But they might have left something here that they vanted to destroy quickly. Hides! Cow hides they could lot sell because these did not bear their brands!

All of a sudden, into Rock's searching mind there

87

flashed memory of a deep well he had once helped to dig on these premises. It had been a job, he recalled, that every one of the half dozen cowboys had rebelled at, and had scornfully told Slagle was labor wasted. The digging had not been without considerable hazard. They had to go so deep that it was necessary to enlarge the hole. Slagle wanted to get water close at hand, to obviate the necessity of packing it uphill from the brook. But they never struck water, and at eighty feet abandoned the effort.

Since that time brush had grown heavily all around the ranch houses, but after some search Rock located the well. The edges had weathered, widening the mouth. He could not get right to the brink at this point. On the opposite side, however, opened a break in the brush. He was about to crash his way through the bushes, around to this opening, when his caution urged him not to leave a trail. Carefully he retraced his steps, worked around into a narrow path, in which he saw boot tracks.

Reaching the well, Rock peered down. He saw only the gravel sides and the black hole. He dropped a stone into it. No sound! He thought that strange. Selecting a larger one he leaned over and let it fall. The hole certainly was deep. A low soft thud, barely distinguishable, came to his taut ears.

"By gum!" he ejaculated. "That well had a rock bottom. . . . We had to quit diggin' because of rock. Son-of-a-gun if this isn't gettin' hot."

Rock cautiously stretched himself on the ground, and putting his head over the brink of the well he sniffed like a tracking hound. He caught a faint scent of something that was not earth or brush and certainly not rotting hides. And it was rotting cattle hides which he expected to smell.

Resting a moment, he tried again. This time he caught the scent strongly enough to recognize it. Quicklime!

Rock sat up, suddenly sweating, though he felt a cold chill. He felt no doubt that down this well, hundreds, perhaps thousands, of cattle hides had been dropped—not one of which bore the Preston brand.

The knowledge staggered him. Suspicion, after all, was not fact. And logic told him that until he had actually seen hidden hides, with other brands than Preston's, he

88

ad no actual proof. Yet he would have staked his life
that his suspicions were correct. He would bide his time,
and at favorable opportunity he would come down here
with a hook of some kind, and plenty of rope, and he
would fish one of those hides up out of the well.

Rock crawled on hands and knees back along the edge
of the path, making certain not to leave the slightest
mark. He found another piece of quicklime, and several
smaller pieces. No doubt they had spilled out of a sack.
When he got to the boot tracks he scrutinized them with
the photographing eyes of a trailer of long experience. He
cut twigs from the under side of a bush, and with minute
care measured the length and breadth of the most clearly
defined print. These twigs he stored in his pocket.

He retraced his steps back to the open, and saddling
the horse the boys had brought up before they left, he
mounted, and rode quickly away to get out of the stench.

"More than one kind of a stink there, I reckon," he
muttered.

The daily phenomenon that gave this Pass its name
was in full and glorious sweep when Rock reached his
cabin. Weary and worried as he was, he had to sit down
and watch the beautiful end of day.

There were fewer clouds and these hung round the
distant peaks, as if anchored to the steep higher slopes.
Strange to see no gold in this sunset! But pearl gray and
silver sheen and shell pink filled the great gap of sky.
The curtains and shafts of colored light were wanting,
too. Yet withal there was exquisite beauty, rarer, more
delicate, quickly evanescent and soon gone.

Rock shaved and changed his clothes, thinking of
everything he could to keep away the tantalizing and
heart-depressing thought of the interview with Thiry so
soon to come. Yet behind every vague and swift idea
that he called up hovered the shadow of this girl and
the unfortunate circumstances in which she must be involved, and the fate that had lured him into her life.

He made sure, this evening, to be on hand before the
first supper bell rang. All the younger members of the
family, except Thiry, came at the call. The children
romped from one side and the boys raced from the other.
Alice, who had rung the bell and called, gayly, "Come
and get it," took her seat beside Rock.

89

"We're livelier when Ash and Pa are away," she said, smiling.

"So I notice. Sure hope they stay away long," he replied, remarking how singularly she spoke of Ash before her father. Rock kept roving eyes on the quest for Thiry. But he was looking the wrong way when her voice, almost at his elbow, gave him a pang that was both pain and joy in one. She and Mrs. Preston were bringing in the supper. The children were noisily merry; and the boy cracked jokes, some of which, vague riddles, Rock guessed might have reference to him. Mrs. Preston was the last to take a seat at the table, and she occupied her husband's place. Thiry, as before, sat opposite Rock, and when he could summon courage to look straight at her he suffered another twinge at the enhanced sadness of her face.

Nevertheless, Rock had such hold on himself that he amused and interested Mrs. Preston, brought smiles to Alice's face and shouts of glee from the children. But as soon as he had finished supper he excused himself and seeking the gloom of the pines, he gave himself up to turbulent anticipations.

The moon appeared long in rising, and Rock, patrolling a beat under the trees, both longingly and fearfully watched for the silver radiance over the rim. It came at last and found him unprepared. How could he bear to terrorize Thiry Preston by confessing his determination to stay?

At length he could not longer procrastinate. Skirting the edge of the pines, he circled the slope, and coming to the stream he followed that up to a level, and soon found the great pine under which he had talked with Thiry the night before. The far side of the Pass was blanched in moonlight; this side was dark in shadow. Rock was unable to see the rustic seat until he could almost touch the tree.

To his mingled relief and disappointment Thiry was not there. He sat down to watch and think. A light shone through the curtained window of her cabin.

Trueman could not rally any connected thoughts. He must wait until she came—until he could see and hear her. That moment would liberate him. He had waited at a rendezvous for many a girl—a situation always

90

attended with pleasurable and sometimes perplexing sensations—but his was not the same. How tremendous the issue of this meeting!

He heard the cabin door open. A broad light flared out into the gloom. Then Thiry appeared in the doorway, clearly defined. She wore white. She had changed her dress since supper. Trueman's heart gave a leap and then seemed to stand still while she stood peering out into the night. She closed the door behind her—vanished. But Rock heard quick light footfalls. She was coming.

Presently her pale form grew more distinct. She groped slowly toward the seat. Evidently her eyes were not yet accustomed to the darkness. Rock saw her put out her hands, feeling for the tree or the bench.

But before she touched either Rock reached up to take them.

"Oh!" she cried, evidently startled. "It's you—Mr. Rock."

"Yes." He did not let go of her hands.

"You're—late. I—I've been here twice," she said, with a nervous little laugh. No doubt she could not escape from the romance of this unusual situation.

"I'm sorry, but it took courage to come at all," returned Rock.

"Didn't it, though? . . . Mr. Rock, you—you are holding my hands. Please let go so I may sit down."

He released her and leaned back against the pine, conscious that her presence had ended his uncertainty. She sat down, quite close to him, and bent her head forward a little, as if trying to pierce the gloom.

"Miss Thiry, such eyes as yours ought to see through walls," said Trueman, sentimentally.

"Ought they? Well, they can't. . . . And, Mr. Rock, this is no occasion for holding hands or paying compliments."

There had been some slight change in her. Rock sensed less aloofness. The long hours, probably, had magnified; and constant thought had made him no longer a stranger. He would let her start the conversation. Then he would prolong it as far as fairness and consideration would permit. Suddenly the moon slipped up over the black rim, and magically the darkness lightened. A silver radiance touched the girl's hair and face. Rock, his own features in shadow, watched her and waited. The hour seemed to be the most momentous of his life. The night wind, sweet and balmy, was moving up from the Pass, roaring low in the tree-tops. How innumerable the nights he had listened to that music, always with a sense of its message! And the time of its fulfillment had come.

"Ash stole your horse?" she began, tentatively.

"Reckon I wouldn't say stole. But he sure borrowed Egypt," returned Rock, with a laugh.

"Egypt! . . . I knew you named him that."

"Yes. Much obliged to you."

"Who told you?"

"Lucy. I've sure a stand-in with her."

"So it appears. . . . I dare say you'll learn *all* our secrets," she said, a little irritated.

"Miss Thiry, things just gravitate my way."

"Don't call me Miss Thiry. If you must be formal make it Miss Preston."

Rock guessed that his apparent coolness and non-chalance had struck her a little provokingly.

"Thanks, Miss Preston."

"I should be pleased that you called Leslie's horse by the name I gave him. Most everybody knows. Ash certainly knows. And—that's why I can't be pleased or flattered."

"Lucy was, anyhow. . . . She said you loved the horse."

"Oh, I do. I've known him years, it seems. I used to ride him, too. How glorious it was! . . . But Ash caught me once—and then, well, I never got on him again."

"Your world revolves around your brother Ash," mused Rock. "Well, some day I'll put you up on Egypt, right here in your yard. . . . And some other day—maybe—I'll give him to you."

"Oh! . . . You couldn't—and I couldn't accept. . . . But that threat proves you—just—just what I've figured out you are."

"Good or bad?" queried Rock.

"Bad. You're a cowboy, many times over, dominated by a very devil. . . . Oh, your ears would burn if you knew all I thought."

"They're burnin' now. But I'd rather you thought bad

than not at all. If a man can't make a woman think about him, then his case is hopeless."

"Would *any* case ever be hopeless to you?" she asked, curiously.

"No. I've helped a good many friends whose cases seemed hopeless to everyone but me," he answered, significantly.

"With a gun, I suppose?" she flashed, perhaps both thrilled and repelled.

"Out here in the Southwest, sometimes you have to use a gun."

She was silent a moment, evidently not quite sure how to take him.

"I asked Al what you did when you found out Ash took your horse," went on Thiry, presently.

"What did Al say?"

"He said you were thunderstruck. You turned red as a beet, then white as a sheet. . . . And you swore something terrible."

"Al told the truth, Thiry," admitted Rock, with reluctance. "I never was so surprised—never so furious. New trick on me! My beautiful horse—that *you* had named—taken from me. . . . If you understand cowboys you may get some faint hunch of my feelin's."

"Mr. Rock, you see, then—how impossible Ash is!"

"Nobody or nothin' is impossible."

"Dad says the man doesn't live who can stand Ash's meanness."

"Well, I'm livin' and maybe I can. . . . You saw him this mornin'?"

"Yes. I was up early, helping Ma get breakfast. When the horses came up it wasn't light yet. I heard Dad jawing somebody. Then Range came in and told us. I never said a word, but I was sick. At the table Dad was sarcastic. He said things I'm sure Ash never heard before from anyone. But Ash never batted an eye. Then my mother had her turn. Finally I couldn't keep out of it, and I asked Ash why he'd stolen your horse. . . . 'Callin' me hoss thief, now?' he said, and I thought he'd strike me. I replied that it did look like stealing. This he didn't answer. Next I asked why he had taken him and—what he meant—to do with him."

Here emotion accompanied Thiry's speech, she grew husky, and faltered.

" 'Luce told me he'd called the hoss Egypt, which was your pet name,' said Ash. 'That's why I took him an' why I'm goin' to break a leg for him.' "

Only Rock's powerful hold upon himself, fortified by hours of preparation for anything, kept his anger within bounds.

"All because I gave him your pretty name! Tough on the horse. . . . And you were afraid to open your mouth! . . . Much you love Egypt!"

"Wait a minute, will you," she answered, not without anger. "I pitched into Ash Preston as never before in our lives. I—I don't know what all I called him. He took it—and, oh, he looked dreadful. But he never said a word. He got up, nearly overturning the table, jumped on the horse, and was gone like a white streak."

"I stand corrected," replied Rock, thickly. "I talk too quick. I'm sure glad you had the nerve to call him. If you hadn't—But what did your father say?"

"Dad took it all out in looking. He was flabbergasted. So were the boys. After they were gone Ma and Allie tried to console me, but I guess I was badly upset."

"Did you cry?"

"Didn't I? . . . It's a good thing you can't see my eyes."

"I can see them. . . . Well, Thiry, I suppose you want to know what I'm goin' to do about this horse deal?"

"Worry over that has made me sick all day. I don't want to hear, but I must."

"When Ash gets back, I'll go up to him nice and pleasant. I'll say, 'Look here, cowboy, if you want to borrow my horse, ask me for him.' "

"Mr. Rock, would you say that?"

"Sure. Or somethin' like it."

"Suppose he comes back without Egypt?"

"Then I think I'd better pass it off as if nothin' had happened. I'd ask your father. And if Egypt was crippled I'd go find him and end his misery."

"Oh, it's bad enough, without that wonderful horse being hurt. If you had to kill him—I—I think it'd be horrible."

"It sure would. But at least it'd be removin' one red flag from in front of this bull."

Then followed a long silence. During this interval Thiry looked down at her idle hands, and from them up at Rock, and back again. The horse incident had thrown them off the track of the purpose of this interview.

"Mr. Rock, you—you were to tell me something tonight?" she began, nervously.

"I have several things to tell you."

"You needn't tell me *one*. For I know that. I can feel it. . . . You're not going away."

"No," he replied, with a ring in his voice.

"Oh—Mr. Rock, I feared you wouldn't. All day long I've felt it. . . . But, oh, if you only knew! . . . It's not all for Ash's sake that I ask it. But for Dad and Mother, Alice and Lucy—for me!"

"Thiry," said Rock, with deep feeling, "last night I almost gave in to you. It was terribly hard not to. But tonight I have hold of myself. You can't persuade me. You can't drive me. I shall stay."

"Oh, you're selfish. You think only of your silly infatuation—"

"No, it's not selfishness or silly infatuation," he interrupted, with sudden passion that made her draw back. "I've thought all night and all day. Out of this torture has come two facts, which I believe as I do my own soul."

"What are they?" she asked.

"I believe I can serve you best by stayin' at Sunset Pass."

"And the other?"

"I love you."

She flung out her hands, protestingly, imploringly, and as if to ward off some incomprehensible peril.

"Mr.—Rock!" she gasped. "You dare make love to me—when we've never been together an hour—when I'm insisting you leave my home!"

"I'd dare that, yes, under any circumstances," he retorted, coolly. "But as it happens, I'm not makin' love to you."

"I declare, Mr. Rock, you are beyond me," she exclaimed. "What in the world are you doing, then?"

"Tellin' you a simple fact. I'm not likely to annoy

you with it soon again. But I sort of welcome this chance to prove somethin' to myself. You'll hear gossip about me and my love affairs, which you can believe if you like. But I know now I never had a real one before. It suits me to stake what I think I've become against the old True Rock. This needn't worry you one little bit."

"You speak in riddles," she replied, incredulously. "How can I help but worry—now, more than ever?"

"I shall leave you blissfully alone. I shall hardly be even polite if I see you at meal-time. Your brother Ash will soon see that there's one rider who's not mushy over you."

"To what end?" she went on, sharply. "Is that to deceive Ash, so you can stay here?"

"Partly. But I'm bound to confess that it's to spare you."

"Oh, you're not going to spare me," she cried. "You'll not leave me alone. And even if you did Ash would believe it only a blind—that you were with me during his absence."

"But sure Ash couldn't believe you a liar?" queried Rock.

"He'd make more of your avoiding me than if you were just friendly. It's a poor plan. Please give it up."

"No."

She began to twist her hands in her white gown. The agitation, which before he had marked, was possessing her again. The idea that he had decided to stay at Sunset Pass held some singular dread for her. Was it as much because of a possible fight between him and Ash as for some other reason? Rock concluded it was both. And while he weighed this in mind he watched her with penetrating gaze, steeling his heart against the tenderness that threatened to overwhelm him.

"If you really care for—for me—you will listen."

"Care for you!" he returned, scornfully. "You wait and see, Thiry Preston."

"Wait for what?" she demanded, almost piteously.

"Why, I reckon, for a little time."

With evident strong effort she controlled some almost irresistible fear or conflict. Her glance changed to one of deep and unfathomable mystery. She had discovered a latent strength. Rock divined she had been driven to

96

extremity. And he grew sickeningly sure that she was involved somehow with Ash and her father in something which would not bear the light of day.

"Trueman Rock, I want you to leave Sunset Pass," she said, leaning to him.

"So you've told me about a thousand times."

"Let's risk being discovered meeting at Wagontongue," she went on, and it seemed a certainty she was thrilled by her own deceit. "You can work anywhere. We'll take Mr. Winter into our confidence. We can meet in his store and spend an hour or two in his office. Then I'll arrange to stay with Mrs. Winter all night when I come to town. You can meet me there, too. I will go to Wagontongue every week."

"Why would you be willin' to do this unusual thing?" asked Rock, eager to lead her on and on. "I think I asked you that before."

"Didn't you say you—you wanted to be friends with me?"

"I sure did."

"It's your only chance. And I'm giving you that to get you—to persuade you to leave here."

"Thiry, I ask you again—*why* do you want me to leave?"

"To keep you and Ash apart."

"Is that the only reason?"

"It's the—the big one," she replied, with both voice and glance unsteady. She was not an adept at lying, even in an issue of tremendous importance.

"But that won't keep Ash and me apart. He will come to town when you do. He'll watch you."

"I'll choose the time when he is away with Dad. He won't know that I go to town."

"When he's away—where?"

"Why, on the range. Dad has large orders. The driving and—and the—the work will take up half his time from now on."

What a child she was, thought Rock! As transparent as crystal water! But she was withal a woman, with all a woman's power to surprise and waylay to attain her ends. He ruthlessly laid traps for her, but the sole reason was not only to lead her into betrayal.

"You would risk so much for me?"

"It's not for you, though I know I—I—*will* like you, if you let me. It's for Ash and Dad—all of us."

"It's very sweet of you, Thiry," he said, with just enough satire to belie the portent of his words, "but very little to risk my life for."

"No, Trueman, it may save your life."

"You call me Trueman?" he asked, amazed.

"Yes, Trueman. . . . We can deceive Ash. . . . The Winters will do anything for me. Ash will never catch us together."

"How long would you expect this sort of thing to go on? We couldn't keep it up forever, could we? And when it came to an end—and I worshiped you—what then?"

"I'd run the same risk as you."

"What of?—being killed?"

"No! No! No! You're tantalizing me. You know what I mean."

"Indeed I don't. Reckon some locoed cowboys would think you meant that you risked the danger of love."

"I meant just that, Mr. Trueman Rock," she blazed. "I'm human. Those nasty gossips in town, who call my love for Ash unnatural, can't understand. . . . I've a heart, though everybody doubts it. And surely it is not beyond the bounds of possibility for me to—to love some one. Especially if he sacrificed for me—proved himself a man."

"Thiry Preston, are you offerin' such a hope to me?" he asked, huskily.

"It's not a hope, but a chance—only a chance—and all I *can* offer."

"But a chance—that means a lot," he went on, without remorse. "I could be with you alone?"

"Yes, as long as you wished."

"Could I make love to you?"

"How could I keep you—from it?" she rejoined, her nerve visibly weakening. "But if you were kind—as I first thought you'd be—you wouldn't press—"

"Would you let me kiss you?"

If Trueman had expected her to gasp and droop, or flare up affronted at this bold query, he had reckoned without his host. Again some bolt had shot back within her, tapping a reserve spirit.

"Yes," she replied, white-faced and calm.

"Would you kiss *me*—now—to seal the compact?" he went on, as mad in the ecstasy of the moment, as stern to convict her.

"You drive a hard bargain," she murmured, bitterly. "I've never kissed any man save Ash and Dad . . . but I will kiss you."

"Very well," he replied, with a coolness that was the most magnificent deceit.

She stood up, took brave, but hesitating steps, until her knees pressed against his, and as she bent over, instinctively her hands went out. Rock saw them trembling. She was going through with it. A moonbeam caught her face. Rock, who had perpetrated this monstrous hoax, uttered a cry of poignant repentance. One second more would make it too late. Her face loomed close, strong in purpose, with veiled eyes, sadder than ever.

Rock seized her hands, and bending his head, he kissed one and then the other.

"Thiry," he whispered, "I would give almost my very life to have you kiss me. But not for this. . . . I led you on. I wanted to see how far you would go. . . . You poor, loving, blinded girl! What would you not sacrifice for this damned Ash Preston?—I tell you—you shall not. . . . I will stay here! You have no idea what a horrible temptation you gave me. To meet you often—to have you alone—to be able to kiss you! My God! . . . *Thiry!* I could make you love me. . . . But so help me God, I wouldn't have your love at such sacrifice. I'll win it square and fair—or never. . . . Now, I'll go, and I'll not speak to you soon again. Trust me, Thiry. Good night."

He kissed her hands again and rushed away into the moon-streaked shadows.

Chapter Seven

Four days passed, days full of hard labor for Rock and pondering thought, and slow absorbing adaptation to the most difficult and strangest situation he had ever encountered.

He conquered his sense of hurry, of having no time. Here he required a long hop, step and jump. Early at breakfast and late at supper he saw Thiry and then only to exchange a greeting. He did not look to see if she looked at him, though curiosity and longing consumed him.

By doing most of the fence work he made himself more than solid with the three brothers, particularly Al, who had taken a strong liking to him. He let them ride off up into the timber to cut pine saplings and snake them down to the pasture, while he dug the post holes and built the fence.

Opportunity would some day come for him to ride down to the old well on Slagle's ranch, and find out what was in it. He persuaded himself that he wanted to have plenty of time and be perfectly safe to pursue his investigations, but as a matter of fact he really was reluctant to find material proof of the Prestons' guilt.

Rock dreamed as well as thought while at work, and every day seemed to make more certain the thing that had transformed him. The hours alone were satisfying to him, but when he had to play his part with the boys, and the harder one before the other Prestons at home, then he found it most trying. How much better to have been riding the range!

It was now near the end of June and the summer rains were due. This season, next to autumn, was the most beautiful for a rider in the open. The range needed rain. The grass was bleached white, the waterholes were dry or stagnant pools, the streams, even in the Pass, were getting low. The boys who rode the range said it was burning up. The hottest weather, though, had passed. Each morning white clouds peeped up over the eastern gateway of the Pass, and then from all around they appeared to climb toward the zenith, gloriously white against the deep blue, swelling, darkening, mushrooming. But not yet had they brought the welcome rain. Each sunset added something of beauty and change to the one before. Rock gloated over them as a miser over his gold. Sunset Pass at sunset resembled his most poignant dreams; but it also gave him pause and forced him to watch and feel and realize. So that when he plodded in late to supper he was hard put to it to conceal his sadness.

On the fifth morning Al remarked, laconically, "We sure gotta hustle today, for Pa will be home."

"Why the particular hustle today, Al?" queried Rock.

"Pa has a way of slippin' up on us, an' it'd sure never do to be ketched loafin'. He wouldn't let us go to the rodeo and dance on the Fourth."

"I'd forgotten about that," rejoined Rock, with enthusiasm. "Are all the folks goin'?"

"Pa and Ma ain't goin', but sure the rest of us Prestons are."

"Includin' Ash?" asked Rock, casually.

"He never missed one yet that Thiry went to—leastways a dance. Allie and the kids will stop at Leslie's. Thiry said she was goin' to Winter's. Reckon you'll ride in with us? We aim to start on the first, so's to get in the day before the Fourth."

"I'll ask your dad," returned Rock, thoughtfully. It would be very much better, perhaps, for him to remain on the ranch. Yet the urge laid hold of him, persuasively at first, and then, augmented by a very contrary spirit, it grew compelling. He could look on at the rodeo, and take just a peep in at the dance, to see Thiry in a party dress. But then he would be certain to see her in the arms of some moonstruck cowboy. That sent a hot twinge through Rock—an unfamiliar sensation. It was his introduction to jealousy.

"Reckon, on second thought, I will go," he said to Al, and certain it was that this sudden, almost involuntary decision made him realize how far he was from knowing himself.

Late in the afternoon the brothers left off work and rode home. This time Rock went with them, listening to their cheerful talk about the prospect of the good time in town. The next day was Sunday, which Gage Preston made a day of rest when the riders were in off the range. And Tuesday was the 1st of July.

They reached the barns, to ascertain that Ash and the others had not yet come in. Rock, after caring for his horse, slowly sauntered up the slope to his cabin, finding himself subservient to an oppressive mood. Ash Preston would soon be back. What had he done with Egypt? And over against this cold speculation, with its incalculable possibilities, balanced the warmth of his assurances to Thiry. How could he fail her? Yet, equally impossible—how could he be otherwise than True Rock? While he was soberly debating the matter, and cleaning up for supper, he heard the clip-clop of trotting horses, then a rattle of wheels. With a start he went to the door. Scoot Preston was driving up on the seat of a big empty wagon. Two more wagons had topped the slope. Soon they halted before the cabins. Rock waited for riders to appear. And he was not disappointed. The burly form of the older Preston hove in sight, riding a roan and leading two saddle-horses. A little afterward, sight of Ash on Egypt shot a quick stab through Rock. The next instant he relaxed. The white horse appeared tired, but none the worse for the absence.

"Aw!" exclaimed Trueman, aloud, and his relief told him just how much he had cared—how he had resolutely put thought of Egypt from him. "Reckon I might as well go out and get it over."

But first he went inside. While pondering over how best to meet this situation and still be true to Thiry, he had buckled on his gun-belt. Suddenly the fact dawned on him, and he laid hard hands on the belt buckle. But he got no farther. There was more here to be true to than Thiry Preston; there was the code of the West. He had no right to face this vicious unknown problem, Ash Preston, without being armed.

Whereupon he strolled out leisurely. As he came in sight of the arriving Prestons, halfway between the cabins, Gage espied him, and with a start he wheeled about from the family, who were welcoming him, to dismount like

102

any cowboy, and hurried to intercept Rock. As he drew near, his deep gray eyes betrayed considerable anxiety.

"Wal, Rock, how are you?" was his greeting, accompanied by extended hand. "The boys say you-all got on fine. I'm sure glad."

"Howdy, boss!" returned Rock, cordially. "We got the fence job 'most done."

"Ha! You don't say? Wal, I'll be dog-goned. How'd you ever get thet out of them?"

Preston fell in step with Rock, though it was signficant that he kept a couple of yards distant. Rock replied with good humor, somewhat eulogizing the young Prestons. In this manner they approached the double cabin, where on the wide porch were collected the women and children. Ash was the only one of the returning brothers who got down on the ground. His movement was almost stealthy. Perhaps more significant than his father's action was his slow step forward and to one side.

"Cowboy, I shore hope you won't rile Ash—leastways hyar before the women," said Preston, hurriedly.

"Don't worry, boss," returned Rock, with a genial laugh. He had caught a glimpse of Thiry, who kept somewhat in the background.

Egypt was standing, bridle down, halfway between Ash and the porch. One glance told Rock that he was guant, dirty, and rough, but apparently as sound as ever. He whinnied at sight of Rock.

"Howdy, boys!" said Rock, nodding to the drivers on the wagons. Then halting beside Egypt, he turned to face Ash Preston. Despite his iron control a slight quiver strung his frame. How cool, intent, potential of evil menace this man! He stood at ease, hands on his hips, his black sombrero slouched back, his blue-flame eyes piercing Rock, as if to read his mind. Rock had met penetrating glances before, and this one shot little cold sparks along his marrow.

"Howdy, Ash! Did you like my horse?" he said, with perfect composure and entire absence of rancor.

Not improbably that was the last query Ash Preston would ever have anticipated.

"Best hoss I ever forked," he replied, without feeling of any kind.

"Thanks. Hope you were good to him."

"Wal, Rock, the fact is I begun bad," drawled Ash. "But he piled me in the brush. An' runnin' him over rough ground didn't phase him none. An' I reckon I ended treatin' him good."

"Did he pitch with you?" queried Rock, in genuine surprise.

"He's got any outlaw beat I ever rode."

"Dog-gone!—Leslie swore this horse never pitched in his life."

"Reckon thet was no lie, Rock. But I nagged him. He threw me, an' I couldn't get near him again thet day."

"Served you right," responded Rock, naturally. "It doesn't pay to be mean to horses. And see here, Ash, don't go borrowin' a horse from a rider without askin' him."

The tension relaxed, the charged atmosphere lost its fullness and suspense. Gage Preston laughed loud, as if explosion was relief. The women began to murmur. And Ash, though he betrayed little of what might have been his true state, eyed Rock with slow, cool smile, and slouched with clinking steps to the porch.

Thiry met him, reached for him in glad excitement: "Oh, Ash, I'm glad you're back—and you—and everything all right."

Ash wrapped his long arms around her, and hugging her closely, he bent his head over her. The action seemed eloquent, beautiful, and yet it carried a hint of bold raw nature. It pierced Rock like fire. Bending down to feel the legs of his horse, he kept that studious posture until he had recovered. Without a glance backward, then, he led Egypt down toward the barns. And he brooded in mind, muttering his thoughts.

"Cold, shiny rattlesnake ready to strike!—Sol Winter sure had him figured. . . . I just wonder. Reckon he thought I'd rave and curse. Sure he'd have come back at me. . . . And then a fist fight or gun-play!—Damn him, he wanted it. . . . Now what in h—can you do with a fellow like that?"

But Rock's heat and rancor lost itself in something worse—jealousy. It had seared him to see Thiry run to Ash, almost with arms outstretched, her face flushed, her eyes alight, her voice broken, to receive that strange caress. Yet was it a caress? What violence of emotion attacked Rock! He could not trust himself on the moment. He only knew he had fallen into sudden misery and must extricate himself.

Rock spent so much time caring for Egypt, cleaning and brushing him, and making him a comfortable bed of grass in a stall, that it was dark when he got back to his cabin. The supper bell rang. He had no appetite, and at this moment he strongly resented the need to keep on with the role he had assumed for Thiry Preston's sake. What use! He could not carry it on forever. Tomorrow, or next week, or month Ash Preston would go beyond the pale—beyond any man's endurance.

"Aw, I'm sore," growled Rock, and swore at himself. He had planned to overlook and overcome Ash's appropriating his horse so affrontingly. But that was nothing compared to seeing Thiry in her brother's arms. He had not calculated upon such a contingency. Still, Ash was only her brother; it was only a blood tie. Nevertheless, it rankled. He could not explain his reaction to this perfectly normal attachment between brother and sister. So he put it down to the account of his own defects.

It occurred to Rock, presently, that to live up to his apparently amenable attitude he must present himself at the supper table. To this end he hurried out, and fought himself all the way over, to present an agreeable front. Fortunately he did not arrive late, as the Prestons were just seating themselves at table, all of them more or less gay.

For the first time in five days Rock looked deliberately into Thiry's face. She gave him a grateful smile, wistful and wondering, as if she would make amends for doubt. It softened Rock, and though he did not glance at her again, he managed to get through the meal cheerfully. Afterward, to his relief, Preston called him into his cabin. It had two rooms, connected by a curtained alcove. The hands of women surely had given this interior its color and comfort.

"Have a drink with me, Rock," invited Preston. He was in high spirits.

"Sorry boss, but I've quit."

"Thet's so. I forget. Lord save me from influencin'

any man to break his word. Have a cigar, then. I shore recommend these."

"Thanks," replied Rock, accepting one. "Did you have a successful trip?"

"Best ever, but thet won't interest you," returned Preston, briefly. "I'll say, though, thet when the trip ended hyar I was some worried. An' when I seen you packin' a gun, I was scared stiff."

"Sorry, boss, but that oughtn't have bothered you. It's just habit."

"Ahuh!" returned Preston, giving Rock a dubious look. "But it was hard to figger you. Ash shore wasn't able to. An' you clean knocked the pins from under him. He didn't, an' neither did any of us, expect you to take thet dirty deal so nice an' friendly."

"What else could I do?" demanded Rock, spreading wide his hands. "I came out here to make friends, not enemies."

"Wal, I'm shore thankin' you. When we rode off last week I was shore mad at Ash. But I got over it, an' now I'm hopin' it won't be as bad as I feared. You've got Ash stumped. I heard him ask Lucy if you'd been runnin' after Thiry."

"Humph! What did Lucy say?"

"Lucy said you hadn't—thet you were seldom hyar, an' then never paid no attention to Thiry. Is thet so, Rock?"

"Reckon it is, since you left."

"You an' Thiry quarreled, I take it," went on Preston. "She didn't say so, but she has a way of makin' the boys leave her alone. I didn't think you'd be so easy, an' I'll gamble it won't last. Just before supper Thiry told me you'd acted wonderful with Ash—thet she'd misjudged you. Don't remember when I've seen the lass so strange. The truth is, Rock, I think she likes you an' hates the falseness of the situation. You've shore begun right, if you're in earnest about her."

Rock could scarcely believe his ears. Yet there was no mistaking Preston. He implied even more than he said.

"In earnest? Good Lord! I wish I knew how to tell you how earnest I am."

"Wal, I reckon now I savvy why you met Ash that

106

way. Guess I had the hunch. Rock, you're an upstandin' fine chap an' I like you. Thet bad habit you used to have don't hurt you in my estimation. So don't be backward tellin' me just how you feel about Thiry."

"Preston, the minute I laid eyes on Thiry I fell in love with her," replied Rock, with sincere depth and frankness. "It's changed my whole life. I used to be a free, careless hombre, runnin' after girls, ridin' here and there, drinkin', gamblin', fightin'.—But that's past."

"Thanks fer talkin' out," rejoined Preston, puffing at his cigar and bending deep inscrutable eyes upon Rock. "Course you mean marriage, cowboy?"

Rock jerked in his chair; his face reddened. "Preston—I never let myself have—such hope," he burst out, almost choking over his cigar.

"Faint heart never won fair lady," quoted the rancher. Then he frowned and added, tersely, "Declare yourself, like a man, if you want my interest."

"Boss—I—I don't quite savvy," replied Rock, uncertainly. "What more can I say? . . . Unless—I suppose, Preston, when a man falls honest in love he should have honorable intentions. If I had any they sure would be honorable. But, Lord, I never dared even dream of Thiry as my wife."

"But you'd like to marry her?" queried this astounding ranchman.

Rock stared a moment. "I'd be the happiest and luckiest fellow on earth."

"Wal, thet's talkin'," returned Preston, gruffly. "I was about changin' my mind thet you wasn't such a sudden fellar, after all. Do you want my advice?"

"Preston, I—I'd be most grateful for anythin'," replied Rock, bewildered.

"Thiry ought to be told."

"Aw, no! . . . So soon? Before I've proved what—It'd only distress her—do my cause harm."

"Cowboy, you don't know women," said Preston. "The very fact thet you came to me an' declared yourself, straight like your name, will go far with Thiry, an' all of us 'ceptin' Ash. An' even Ash couldn't help but see thet was right. He beat a cowboy once who dallied after Thiry without talkin' marriage."

"Like as not he'd try to beat me—if I did tell her,"

rejoined Rock, with a nervous laugh. The very idea threw him into a fever of panic.

"Wal, I'm appreciatin' your fine feelin's, Rock, so I'll tell her myself," replied the rancher, and turning to the open door he called, "Lucy."

"Preston!" gasped Rock, rising.

At this moment Lucy poked her disheveled head and bright face in at the door. "Daddy, did you call?"

"Where's your sister?"

"Which one? Thiry is here. But I don't see Alice."

"Wal, reckon Thiry will do. Send her in," said Preston, dryly.

Rock, standing as if paralyzed, heard the child call gayly, and then light, quick footfalls. Immediately the dark doorway framed a slender form in white, with wistful, expectant face and great, doubtful eyes.

"Come in, lass, an' shut the door," said her father, as he knocked the ashes from his cigar. There seemed nothing momentous in voice or manner.

She complied, and came forward hesitatingly, her glance going from her father to Rock.

"Thiry, come hyar," he went on, and when she drew close he put an arm around her. "Do you see thet big cowpuncher standin' over there?"

"Yes, Dad—I couldn't very well help it," she replied, and she just escaped being demure.

"Sort of pale round the gills, ain't he?" continued Preston, still in his dry, genial tone.

"Dad, I—I'm afraid he looks a—a little guilty," replied Thiry, constrainedly.

"Wal, it's not exactly guilt," laughed Preston, as he squeezed her slim waist. "Lass, Rock has asked your hand in marriage—an' I've given it."

"*Dad!*" she whispered, and leaned against him as if suddenly bereft of strength. Then she rallied, while the scarlet waved up from neck to cheek. "Are you crazy—or am I? You couldn't joke—"

Her blazing eyes flashed in doubt and fear from her father to Rock.

"Miss Thiry," replied Rock, finding himself under those wonderful eyes, "this is the most solemn—and terrible moment of my life."

Rock made her a gallant bow. Slowly she released

herself from her father's arm, with widening, darkening eyes, that seemed fascinated by Rock.

"Reckon it's sudden, lass," spoke up Preston. "But thet's this cowboy's way. An' fer one I kinda like it. Rock's some different from the others, Thiry. No ridin' round out hyar, makin' everlastin' excuses to get back to the ranch, pryin' you out at odd moments, worryin' your mother an' me—an' drivin' Ash to drink. No, ma'm, True Rock comes straight to *me*. I like thet. Your ma will, too, when I tell her."

"What do you think—*Ash* will say?" she broke out.

"Ash?—Wal, child, he's not your dad or your boss. You're no kid any more. You're a woman, free to do as you want. You shore don't have to ask anythin' of Ash."

"Father!" cried Thiry, incredulously, almost with horror.

In that exclamation of protest, of unbelief, of consternation, Rock delved further into this Preston mystery. It seemed to betray Preston's guilt along with that of his son, and Thiry's knowledge of it.

"Wal, lass, will you answer Rock now or do you want some time to think it over?" asked Preston, coolly, unabashed or unconcerned by her agitation. He was deep. He was playing a game that Rock sensed but could not fathom. His effect upon Thiry was also beyond Rock's ken.

"Mr. Rock, I thank you," said Thiry, through trembling pale lips, "for the honor you do me. . . . I'm sorry I cannot accept."

Rock bowed, with what little dignity he could assume.

"Thiry, wait a minute," said her father, as she made for the door. He caught her and held her, unmistakable affection in his grasp. "I'm sorry to upset you. But these things will happen. Don't think your dad wants to get rid of you. I'm powerful fond of you, Thiry. You always was my favorite. It's only thet lately—wal, I don't want to worry you about what might happen to me. I might not always be hyar to take care of you."

"Dad, what do you mean?" she asked, hurriedly.

"Nothin' much," he replied, enigmatically. "I'd like to have your future settled before—before long. An' Rock struck me about right. . . . Aw, there you're cryin'. Wal, run along. I shore can't stand a cryin' woman, not even you. An' it's no great compliment to Rock."

Thiry held her head high as she walked by Rock without giving him another word or glance, and he saw that she was weeping.

"Preston, I ought to knock the daylights out of you," declared Rock, wrathfully, when Thiry was gone. "What'n hell did you do that for?"

"Cowboy, you shore are an appreciatin' cuss," returned the rancher, with sarcasm. Signs were not lacking that he had hidden deep emotion from Thiry.

"If I ever had any hope to win Thiry, it's sure gone now," fumed Rock.

"Much you know about women," said Preston. "About girls, mebbe you did. But when it comes to women, love, an' marryin'—wal, my boy, you're a green hand. I had a hunch Thiry took a shine to you, an' now I know it."

"Man, you're drunk or crazy, as Thiry said."

"Wal, Rock, if she hasn't before she will now," replied Preston, imperturbably. "Thiry's whole-hearted an' fancy-free. I take it she just can't help herself. She knows now you want to *marry* her. Thet always fetches a woman, provided she ain't in love with some one else. Thiry is some like her mother, an' a lot like me. Slow to care for anybody. . . . Have another cigar, cowboy. I see you've mashed thet one."

Rock discovered that not only had he crushed the cigar, but he had burned his fingers.

"Preston, I can't be mad at you, but I sure want to be," returned Rock, resigning himself.

"Set down. I want to tell you about Ash," said the rancher. "Thet hombre shore put up one on himself. We all reckoned he meant bad by your white hoss, an' right off he started bein' mean. Did you know thet hoss? . . . Wal, I'm damned if he didn't throw Ash nine times. I only saw him get piled twice, but between me an' the boys it figgered up nine. You never seen the like of thet pitchin' hoss. He wouldn't stand fer Ash an' he wouldn't stand under him. The second day Ash couldn't even get a rope on him. An' he had to change his tactics. Reckon thet hoss is smart. Anyway, he knowed when Ash changed his mind, an' then he stopped buckin'. After thet Ash rode thet hoss as I never saw one rode before. He wanted

110

to break his leg. An' he put him to the rocks an' ditches an' logs—somethin' awful. I cussed Ash till I was out of breath. No good. But he couldn't hurt the hoss an' he shore did hurt himself. So he gave up. He showed respect fer a hoss the one an' only time in his life. So, Rock, it's ended far better than we ever dreamed it could."

"Yes. But will he take Egypt again?" asked Rock, anxiously.

"Ash will do anythin'. But you keep your hoss fer yourself. If you have to put him out on the range at night. You could hobble him out."

"I thought of that."

"Wal, try keepin' tabs on Egypt hyar at home. An' if thet doesn't work.—You'll shore be goin' in to town with the rest of the outfit. They're leavin' day after tomorrow. Thet reminds me. I run into thet pretty Mrs. Dabb, an' she said to tell you to be shore an' come to her dance."

"That's nice of her. Where's it to be held? At Dabb's house?"

"Nope. Not big enough. She's havin' the new town hall decorated."

"Well, in that case I might go," replied Trueman, thoughtfully.

"Say, cowboy, wasn't this Dabb woman an old flame of yours?" inquired Preston, with inquisitive good humor.

"Well, she wasn't exactly mine, but that wasn't my fault."

"Ho! Ho! I know the lady. Thet is to say I've seen her with the cowpunchers. An' she's shore a high-steppin' little filly. Reckon John Dabb was a damned old fool, marryin' thet young lady. . . . Wal, Rock, if she happened to be a little sweet on you yet it'd shore be lucky fer you."

"Preston, I fail to see how," exclaimed Rock, aghast. This rancher was certainly manifesting a complex and many-sided character.

"Wal, just you fool around Mrs. Dabb some an' make Thiry jealous," replied Preston, with a chuckle.

"By thunder!" exploded Rock, yet partly with a laugh. "Preston, you're a regular old devil, or else I don't savvy

111

you. Even if I could make Thiry jealous—which's preposterous, I'd never do it."

"Then you're a darn sight of a fool," returned Preston, complacently. "It won't hurt your cause none to let my lass see other women like you."

"Boss, you must have been a devil among the women, in your day," said Rock, slyly.

"Reckon I was, but my career ended sweet an' sudden."

"Well, how would you handle this particular case of mine, regardin' the dance?" inquired Rock, prompted by a spirit of mischief. He was getting a most unexpected, surprising, and pleasurable jolt out of this new contact with Preston.

"Are you a good dancer?"

"I used to be. Reckon I haven't forgot."

"Wal, then, as you're a handsome cuss, too, you want to make the most of your chance. It's to be a masquerade, you know."

"Masquerade? I sure didn't know."

"You get yourself up in some dandy outfit. Don't be a cowboy, or a greaser, or Indian. You might be a flash gambler, or a parson, fer their clothes look good on a fellar. Then first off be cold to Thiry an' sweeter'n pie to your old girl. But you want to be slick, cowboy. Don't carry it too far. Don't overdo it."

Rock laughed rather wildly. The absurdity of the thing so blandly suggested by Preston did not quite submerge a certain enticement. The nerve of it, the very audacity, the reckless assumption that he might make this wonderful girl jealous, took on him a hold hard to shake.

"Old-timer, I'm afraid I couldn't do it," replied Rock, with a grimace, as he flung his second cigar into the fireplace. "It'd be funny; it'd be great, if I dared. But it would be very unkind to Mrs. Dabb and—"

"Reckon it would be," interposed Preston. "But if you don't make up to her, some one else will. An' cowboy, smoke this in your pipe—thet feller might not be as clean-minded as you are."

"Thanks. I think I'll rustle now, before you get me locoed. Good night," replied Rock.

As he opened the door, abruptly, he almost bumped

112

into Ash Preston. Rock could not help wondering if Ash had been eavesdropping.

"Say, Rock, strikes me you've been in there pretty long," said Ash, with blue-flashing glance as direct as his speech.

"Hello, Ash!" retorted Rock, with instant laugh. "I shore was. It takes long to extract advance money from your dad."

"Haw! Haw! Mebbe I don't know that," returned Ash. "It's shore some job to get money due. An' dammit, you hit him first."

"Wal, Ash, I have some left. Come in," said Preston. "Good night, Rock."

Trueman strolled in the black shadows of the pines near his cabin. The night was pleasant, the wind at its old task in the tree-tops, the frogs along the creek were croaking drowsily of midsummer. The dark Pass, obscure and dreaming, seemed pregnant with life.

It took him an hour to throw off the spell incited by the rancher. To think he had been a party to a proposal of marriage to Thiry Preston! What if he had not been the genius of it?

The plot had thickened, and Rock saw no way of extricating himself, even had he so desired. He had shocked Thiry beyond measure. How impossible to confess that he had not made any offer of marriage! All things considered, now he was glad. He hoped all the Prestons would know it before they retired. In some unaccountable way he had won Gage Preston's regard and friendship. Nevertheless, he concluded that Preston had some deep motive besides a longing to see Thiry safely settled for life. What could that motive be? No matter how Rock looked at the problem, one fact stood out—whatever furthered his courting of Thiry Preston could only render Ash Preston more dangerous. Did Gage Preston's motive hide in that?

Rock tried to give it up and went to bed, where he listened to the sing-song of pines overhead and thrilled to the ridiculous yet enchanting suggestion of Preston's. To make Thiry jealous! The idea was just as tantalizingly sweet as it was dishearteningly silly. No girl could be made jealous unless she cared. And absolutely and insupportably he was sure she did not care for him.

113

One by one Rock's thoughts, ecstatic and dismaying by turns, brought him back to the conviction that Preston was deeply involved in crooked work and that Thiry knew it. If so, why did not the father aid and abet the daughter in getting rid of a new rider who was not exactly a dunce, at least in ways of the range? So the mystery augmented along with Rock's perplexity. Eventually his speculations wore him to slumber.

He awakened at dawn with an idea which must have generated in his subconscious mind while asleep. And it was that he should start toward Wagontongue ahead of the Prestons instead of waiting until they had gone. He wanted to stop long enough with Slagle to dig through the husk of that rancher's provocative reticence. Likewise, he wanted to ride over that part of the range which had been the scene of Preston's latest labors. With Preston at home, busy with manifold tasks left him, and his family on the road, there would be opportunity for Rock to confirm or disprove his suspicions.

At breakfast Rock asked permission to leave that day, instead of on the morrow, and it was readily given. He hurried down to the barns without having had a glimpse of either Ash or Thiry. The white horse had been watered and fed, doubtless by Al, whom Rock saw doing his early-morning chores.

Saddling Egypt, and leading the rested and mettlesome horse up to the cabin, Rock tied a couple of blankets behind the cantle, and rode away under the pines, without being noticed, so far as he could tell, by any of the family.

What he devoutly hoped was that Preston had not worked close to the Pass. The Flats, Rock had ascertained, were the wide gray cedar-dotted levels some miles this side of Slagle's ranch. Tom Preston had been given orders to drive the green wagon as far as the Flats. Trotting briskly along, his eyes ever and anon keen on the broad wheel tracks, Rock soon arrived at the bottom of the slope, where the ground spread wide and flat for miles.

He found where the wagon had left the road to halt in the first clump of cedars, and then it had gone on again, back to the road. Horse tracks and wheel tracks

114

were old stories to Rock. He could almost read through them the minds of riders and drivers.

A mile or more this side of Slagle's ranch, which was hidden in the rough hilly country west of the Flats, the wagon tracks and hoof tracks of saddle-horses turned off the road. Rock did not care to follow them until the Prestons had passed, and even then he would be extremely careful how he did follow. Ash Preston might have eyes as good as his own.

Rock, surveying the country ahead, concluded that unless Preston had made a cut-off to avoid passing Slagle's ranch, soon to meet the road again, he had surely been stopped shortly by rough going.

To Rock's disappointment, he found that Slagle was not at home. The rancher had probably taken his family to town, for there was ample evidence that he was absent only temporarily. Rock had nothing else to do but ride on, thinking that he might stop at Pringle's.

A couple of miles down the road Rock met the wagon tracks again, coming from across the Flats.

"By golly! looks like a short-cut, doesn't it? I guess not!" exclaimed Rock derisively. Then he discovered that these tracks were fresh, and made on the return home. The wagons had been empty. This was longer and harder going than round the road. Rock passed on a few hundred yards, to find where the Prestons had driven into the road on their outward trip. And still farther on he came to more tracks, older by some weeks.

Off to the west, on the gray rolling range, Rock espied straggling herds of cattle. Somewhere along here the Prestons had done their latest job of butchering beeves; and Rock was intensely eager to find the spot.

Chapter Eight

After pondering awhile, Rock decided he might safely risk some careful scouting around, provided he left no traces and kept keen survey of the several miles of road.

With this in mind he tied Egypt on hard ground, and taking to the thickest part of the cedars he mounted the hill. Emerging on top, to the right of the summit, he searched the rolling rangeland with the telescopic eyes of a range-rider. Rolling sea of bleached grass and gray sage, cedared ridges, green washes, clumps of cattle colorfully dotting levels and slopes, and endless monotony that waved away to the black rough horizon—these familiar objects were precisely what he had expected to see.

He concluded he would have to follow the wagon tracks, to find where the Prestons had last butchered, but the present was not the time to undertake that. Keeping within the cedars, he went on to the summit of the ridge.

The wind was strong in his face. It carried more than heat, and as he gained his objective point, he both smelled and saw dust in the air. Then something faint, but raw, an odor that was tainted!

Eagerly Rock came up behind a cedar, and from this cover he peered out and down. The slope on that side sheered steep and rough, down to an open draw, up which his keen sight roved. This draw appeared pale green, with a dry winding wash in the center. It led up to a wide pocket, where yellow water gleamed. Cows were bawling. White objects flashed in the sunlight, drawing Rock's gaze the quicker. Then he discerned a cabin and corral, covered with white spots, also men on horses, and some on foot.

Rock slipped to his knees, and crawling to a low thick cedar bush he half buried himself in it, and peered out. The good, or perhaps bad, luck that had always attended him on the range was operating now. Likewise were his sharp eyes and the keen brain behind them.

The white objects were cowhides, thrown over the corral fence, and nailed on the cabin, hair side down. There were seven riders, several still sitting their saddles, the others walking around. Voices floated up faintly to Rock as he crouched there, suddenly covered with cold and sweat. Bunch of cowboys snooping around! Many and many the time Rock had been a party to just this thing. Curiosity was a characteristic of any cowboy on a range where cattle mysteriously disappeared.

116

The cabin was very old, with roof caved in, and door and window vacant—like black eyes. The corral fence was down in places. Rock thought he remembered having once visited this deserted homesteader's ranch.

One of the cowboys, a tall fellow wearing a red scarf, turned some of the cowhides over to look at the under side. Presently he and the others on foot collected in a group round their mounted comrades, and talked. What would Rock not have given to have heard them! For there might have been nothing unusual about this, and on the other hand it might have been a serious colloquy. Watching like a hawk, Rock convinced himself that these riders were curious about Preston's butchering business. Nothing inimical to the Prestons manifested itself. A riding outfit might drop down anywhere. On that hundred square miles of open range there were many thousand head of cattle under different brands, and therefore a number of cowboys under different management. Judging by the past, these outfits were not likely to be particularly friendly toward one another. They all looked upon one another with suspicion. That was simply the life of the range.

Rock strained his eyes to take in all details of that red-scarfed rider's appearance, so he might recognize him some day. But the distance was pretty far, even for his sharp eyes, and he could not be sure. Presently the mounted riders galloped off, and those on foot took to their horses and followed. They rode up the ridge, westward from the cabin. The fellow with the red scarf, following last, halted on the brink of that pocket and took final survey of the scene. Was there something on his mind? Finally he rolled a cigarette. Rock saw a puff of bluish smoke. Then the rider followed after his comrades, who had disappeared over the ridge.

"Dog-gone!" muttered Rock, rolling out of his uncomfortable covert and wiping his perspiring face. "What to make of that? Maybe means nothin' an' then again—"

He counted the cowhides in sight. Thirteen! It was not a lucky number. But there might be several more hides on the far side of the log cabin. Even so, that was rather a small number, if the hides in sight represented all the beeves killed by Preston on this occasion. Preston had gone to town with three large wagons, one of which

117

Rock had helped load with hides. The other two, of course, had been loaded with beeves. How many? That was something Rock wanted to know—and meant to find out.

He resisted the impulse to go down into that draw. This could wait until a more favorable hour. Instead, he retraced his way to his horse, racking his brain the while.

"Aw, hell!" blurted out Rock, in disgust. "If it was anyone but Thiry's people I'd *know*. I do know, only I keep hopin' I'm wrong."

No doubt at all was there that the cowhides in plain sight over in the draw bore one of several of Preston's brands. If other stock besides Preston's had been butchered, which Rock did not doubt in the least, the hides with their telltale brands had of course been well hidden. Heads were easier to dispose of, and the risk of discovery through them was negligible. Three or four riders, taking as many heads, and riding out at night into rough places, could throw a good many into holes and brush, where not one in a hundred would ever come to light. And small matter if they did! What was the head of a steer on that vast cattle range? Hides, however, were branded to protect the owners. But if hides ripped from stolen beeves were carefully hidden, as Rock believed was true in the matter of Slagle's well, the chances were very few that the theft could ever be detected. Preston was safe for the time being if he relied on Slagle's well to conceal his thefts. For Rock could never betray him. The best that Rock felt he might do—in case he proved his suspicions—was to tell Preston and scare him from any further crooked work. The nucleus of that, indeed, was forming in Rock's mind.

Straddling Egypt once more, Rock rode down the hill toward Wagontongue. Should he go on into town or only so far as Pringle's? It struck him that he might be in a little too brooding a state of mind to stop over with his homesteader friend. He might ask too many questions.

Cedars and brush grew densely at the foot of this slope, where the road crossed a culvert over a deep wash. Rock's eyes, bent on the ground, suddenly espied the heel imprint of a rider's boot. It stopped Rock. If he ever had occasion

118

to study a track of any kind it became photographed on his mind. He had seen that heel track before. Slipping out of the saddle, Rock bent to scrutinize it. And he experienced a queer little cold chill.

The impression of the heel was well defined, but the toe part was dim. It pointed off the road. Rock found another, like it, though not so plain. But for his trained eyes the trail might as well have been made in snow. Whoever had made it, though, had stepped lightly. It led into the coarse white grass, down over the bank, to the edge of the culvert, where it vanished.

There was no doubt in Rock's mind that this imprint was identical with the one near Slagle's well. He had the little sticks with which he had measured that track. Taking them out, Rock was about to go back and measure, when his instinct prompted him to take a look at the culvert, now that he was down there. He walked on, stepping on stones.

The culvert was not the handiwork of masons. The aperture was large, to take care of a considerable flow of water during the wet season. Crude walls of heavy stone had been laid about ten feet high and the same distance apart. Logs and brush had been placed across the top. Above this a heavy layer of earth formed the road.

When Rock stepped into the mouth of the culvert he saw a lumpy floor, which at first glance he thought consisted of rocks lying on dried mud.

A foot track, the one he was trailing, brought a low exclamation from his lips. Bending quickly, with his little sticks he tried them. They fitted perfectly. Moreover, this one had been made recently.

When Rock rose from that track he knew what he was going to find. The tunnel appeared about a hundred feet long, with light shining in at both ends, and the middle dark. The numerous stones on the floor were of uniform size and shape, and he noted that the first of these lay back several yards from the opening of the culvert.

Rock kicked one. It was soft. Bending to feel of it and to look at it more closely, he ascertained that it was a burlap sack tied round something. He laughed sardonically.

"Cowhide," he said, and went on, kicking to right

and left. These stone-like objects were all hides tied up in burlap sacks. They were old. Some of them were rotting. Then toward the middle of the culvert, where the bags were thickest, he found that those in sight were lying on a bed of bags, flat, decomposed. Altogether, hundreds, perhaps thousands of hides had been destroyed there. He detected a dry, musty odor, but it was not strong.

Rock went back to the point where he had found the boot track. It was useless to attempt to conceal his own trail. He reflected that in a few days now the rains would come, and with water running through the culvert all traces of his having been there would be obliterated.

If fresh cowhides had lately been deposited in this hiding-place where were they? Rock searched the ground more carefully. Back from the opening it was difficult to see well. Nevertheless, he trailed the heel track a third of the length of the culvert, toward its center.

Naturally then he reached up to feel where he could not see. He had to put his toes in crevices between the stones to climb up and reach over the top of the wall. The thick logs placed across from wall to wall, and far apart, left considerable room along the top.

When Rock's groping hand came in contact with a sack he felt no surprise. This one was not soft. It appeared to hold heat. Grasping it firmly, Rock dropped to the ground and hurried with it to the light. He ripped it open. Quicklime, hot and moist! A fresh cowhide, wrapped with hair inside!

With hands that actually shook Rock unfolded the hide. No slight thing was this proof of somebody's guilt— about to be disclosed! The brand was clear—a half moon. Rock had never heard of it. He certainly knew all the old brands of that range.

He rolled up the hide, stuffed it in the sack, with the little quicklime he had spilled. And he put it back where he had found it. Then he struck a match. By the dim light he saw rows of burlap sacks, neatly stowed away.

Rock sneaked out of that culvert and into the cedars and round and up to his horse as if indeed he were the guilty one himself. Not until he was riding away down the road, positive that he had been unseen, did he recover his equanimity. To ferret out rustler tricks, trail stolen cattle and horses, and discover evidence of thieving practices on the range, had been part of Rock's long experience. It was all in the day's work. How vastly another thing here! That boot track had been made by Ash Preston. Rock knew it. Gage Preston was growing rich by butchering other ranchers' cattle. The very least implication Rock accorded to Thiry Preston was that she shared the secret, and therefore indirectly the guilt. And Rock loved her—loved her terribly now, in view of her extremity. When he got to that confession he seemed unable to escape from the tumult and terror it roused in his mind.

Egypt, left to choose his gait, had started off on his fast trot. He had many gaits, but this was his favorite, and it covered distance rapidly. He held to it steadily, except on the hills, when he slowed to a walk.

Rock scarcely saw the beautiful rangeland. He rode past Pringle's place before noon, scarcely aware of it. He was in no mood for friends. But in due time his emotion spent itself upon the resolve to save Thiry if he had to die to do it.

After that he gradually rounded to a coherent, if not a logically connected, sequence of thoughts. When cattle disappeared off the range, any range, in more than a negligible number, it always led, sooner or later, to speculation and private suspicion by every outfit, and usually investigation, also private, by the outfit that had suffered most. Rock recalled cases where quite extensive rustling had never been cleared up. Ranchers worked slowly in this regard. They might step on some one's toes. Generally when the perpetrators of crooked work were unearthed, it was accomplished by the cowboys rather than the ranchers.

Rock had no idea how far this extraordinary dealing of the Prestons had gone. It would take considerable time to find that out, if it were possible at all. But it had proceeded far enough to be extremely hazardous for them, and in fact for any riders connected with them. The situation would certainly become a delicate one for Rock, unless he betrayed Preston at once. This was unthinkable. Rock knew his own reputation had always been above reproach, as far as honesty was concerned. It would still hold good with the old cattlemen who knew him. But that could scarcely apply to new ranchers, new outfits,

121

who had come into the Wagontongue range of late years.

Rock believed that before another year was out, if the Prestons kept up this amazing and foolhardy stealing, they would be found out. Why could not Preston see this? He certainly did not lack intelligence. One remark he had made to Thiry had been thought-provoking. It might well be true that Ash Preston, having led or forced his father into criminal practice, dominated him wholly. Ash Preston struck Rock as a man without fear or conscience, and even without a heart, except where Thiry was concerned.

Rock's mind rejected solutions to this problem as fast as it created them. There was not any solution, at least at this hour of the game. Rock must know more, and if possible everything, before he could formulate any plan to stop Preston and save Thiry. If there were other suspecting riders, besides Rock, on the range, that fact could not be helped. Any moment one of them might stumble upon signs which would lead to discovery and exposure. Still, the possibility was remote. Slagle's well was known to none save old riders of the range, and they, no doubt, were gone. Then who would ever look under an innocent and open culvert along the road? No doubt in the world that there were other places as cunning! Rock did not want to find any more. Whenever he came to a bridged wash, he wondered if it, too, harbored sacks and hides, but he did not get off to investigate. The last and only proof he required was to see one of Ash Preston's boot tracks. That would prove what Rock was already sure of. Afterward he would wait until events shaped themselves to decide his future actions.

As the hours passed, Rock reviewed the whole knotty question again, without further enlightenment. He strove to bring reason and intelligence to bear, instead of a mounting antipathy for Ash Preston.

Late in the afternoon Rock encountered the first rain of the summer. It was only a shower, in the locality through which he rode, and while the glistening drops pattered down the sun continued to shine behind him. To the east, over the desert, a low far-spreading vivid rainbow stood out against a background of purple cloud. The odor of dust permeated the air, and the glistening sagebrush seemed conscious of refreshment. There appeared to be heavy rain off to the eastward. Rock felt the cool drops soak through the sleeves of his shirt. He took off his sombrero and let them wet his hair and splash his hot face. But soon the shower passed on.

It was long past dark when Rock arrived at Wagontongue. Upon inquiring of a Mexican, he found a stable where Egypt would be well looked after. Next he hunted up a restaurant to appease his own hunger, and then he went to the hotel and to bed. The long ride and the long hours of emotional and mental conflict had exhausted him. Not for years had he been so sunk in gloom. The urge to drink came upon him, and he laughed it away. He had need of stimulant, yes, but not that false kind. It was well that he fell asleep at once.

The sawmill whistle disrupted his deep slumber at six o'clock, but he enjoyed the luxury of the soft bed and linen sheets awhile before rising. Rested and fresh again, and with the bright gold sunrise shining in his window, Rock felt far removed from the brooding, fagged rider of the night before. He would find a way. He dared to pit himself against Ash Preston in anything. Least of all did he consider Ash particularly dangerous to face in fair gun-play. He was several years younger than Rock, and had been only five on the range. Calculating on that, and his own long experience, his instinct for divining an opponent's intent, and his swift hand, Rock felt a certainty of his power to beat Ash Preston to a gun and kill him. That question, not before deliberately thought out and faced, seemed settled. Indeed, it had arisen involuntarily, presupposing that Rock's subconscious mind had accepted the meeting as inevitable and had dealt with it. Rock resisted this strange thing, repudiated any certainty of conflict, and swore he would avoid that, but all the same the possible issue had been met in his consciousness, and without his consent had been decided upon.

"Cheerful way to begin the day," thought Rock, yawning and stretching. "Well, now I've got to do a lot of things. And sure I mustn't forget that masquerade rig. . . . But I'm not goin'. . . . I sure oughtn't to. . . . Would t be very risky—if I went for a little while—and kept disguised?"

123

After breakfast, which Rock partook of rather late, he went round to see Sol Winter. And meanwhile he had subdued himself to some semblance of the old order of cool insouciance, which state really had been natural before the fair face of Thiry Preston had disturbed his equilibrium forever.

Winter was sweeping out the store, his back to the door, and he did not see or hear Rock.

"Hands up!" said Rock, in harsh disguised voice, as he gave Winter a hard dig in the back with his forefinger, to imitate the prod of a gun. "Money or your life!"

"O Lord!" ejaculated Winter, swiftly dropping the broom and elevating his hands high. He had once been held up by a robber.

"Turn around," ordered Rock.

Stiff as a poker the storekeeper obeyed, white and tight of face. Suddenly he became transformed most ludicrously.

"Rock! . . . You—dod-blasted—son of a seacook!" he gasped out, dropping his hands, the right of which he extended shakily to meet Rock's. "Scared me—most to death!—Same old cowboy! My, you look good! All browned-up. . . . Dog-gone, I'm glad to see you!"

"Same here, old-timer," replied Rock, heartily "Reckon you look a little brighter, Sol."

"I've less worry, son, an' at my age worry tells. Fact is, I'm doin' fine again. Since payin' my debts, I've laid in more stock an' advertised it. We're goin' to make money, pardner."

"Fine. I'm sure tickled. Reckon I'll need a pile one of these days. . . . Any news, Sol?"

"Not much. Everybody comin' in for the Fourth. Amy Dabb's givin' the biggest dance ever held in these parts Masquerade. Won't that be a new one on the punchers? You ain't goin' to miss it, True?"

"I might drop in to look on a minute," returned Rock casually.

"Did you get an invite?"

"Sure. Amy sent me one by Preston."

"Thiry's comin'," said Winter, with anticipate pleasure. "Sent me word she an' Alice would stay tw nights with us."

"Wonder what she'll wear—and if I can recognize her?

nused Rock, with shining eyes. "I'll bet a hundred I'll know her pronto."

"Wal, True, you don't look much like a disconsolate lover."

"Don't I? By gosh! I am, all the same."

"No! Wal, that's new for you. How're things generally out Sunset Pass way?"

"Pretty bad, Sol. But there's too much of it to tell now."

"Bet you had a run-in with Ash!"

"Nope. Outside of stealin' my horse, Ash acted tolerable nice, for *him*."

"Stole your horse!—an' he's alive yet?" ejaculated Winter, his shrewd old eyes warm upon Rock.

"Sol, I took it as if I was complimented."

"True Rock, you 'pear rational enough, an 'you shore ain't drunk," returned Winter, reflectively.

"Honest, Sol. I'm tellin' you truth. Now what do you say?"

"Wal, all I can say is love works wonders."

"Does it? All right, old-timer. Let's hope it lasts. . . . But to leave off and talk seriously, Sol. I want to find out somethin'."

"What?" asked Winter, as Rock led him back into the store.

"Preston drove in here a couple of days ago," went on Rock, lowering his voice. "In the outfit were three wagons I know of. One was full of hides, which I helped pack. The other two were loaded with meat. Beeves! Now I want to find out how many beeves there were and where they went. But I don't want this information unless we can get it absolutely without rousin' the slightest curiosity or question. Savvy old pardner?"

"Wal, I'll be darned if that ain't funny," ejaculated Winter, his eyes narrowing to mere slits.

"Humph! Nothin' funny about it, as I can show you," said Rock, bluntly.

"Wal, mebbe I mean queer. For I shore can tell you right now what you're so damn keen about knowin'."

"Good Lord!" exclaimed Rock, with a quick breath, and he sat down heavily upon the counter. He had actually to nerve himself for the disclosure.

"Heard it quite by accident," went on Winter. "Jackson, who runs Dabb's butcher shop, once worked for me. An' if I do say it myself he liked workin' for me better than for Dabb. Wal, I went in last night to buy some beefsteak to take home. An' I seen a lot of fresh meat hangin' up. Shore I always was curious, but I never let on I was. All I said was: 'See you're stocked up plenty an' fresh. How're you ever goin' to sell all that meat before it spoils?"

" 'It won't last over the Fourth,' he said. 'Long as I got plenty an' can sell cheap to the Mexicans an' lumbermen, it shore goes fast. Wagontongue will soon stand another butcher shop, Sol, an' any time you want to talk business with me I'm ready.'

" 'I'll think it over, Jackson,' I said. 'I'm out of debt an' doin' well again. But where'll we get the meat? Reckon we couldn't cut in on Dabb's supply?'

" 'No, we can't,' he told me, 'but Preston is killin' now altogether instead of sellin' any more on the hoof. He's gettin' thirty dollars more by killin', on each head of stock. He'll sell to anybody. Today he shipped thirty-six beeves. Driscoll told me. Shipped them to Marigold.' "

Winter paused to see what effect this news might have upon Rock.

"Thirty-six!" muttered Rock, with unreadable face and voice.

"Yep. An' I counted ten beeves hangin' up on Jackson's hooks. All fresh. So that makes forty-six. Now let me see. Forty-six times thirty. . . . Thirteen hundred an' eighty dollars *more.* Hum! Not so poor, Rock.—What you want to know all this for?"

"Gee, Sol, you're a gabby old lady!" returned Rock. "I was just askin', because you and I might go into the meat business. . . . And say, who runs the Half Moon brand?"

"New cattleman named Hesbitt," replied Winter. "He's been on the range over two years. I've seen him but don't know him. They say he hails from Wyomin' has got lots of money, an' runs a hard outfit. Clink Peeples is foreman. You ought to know him, Rock."

"Clink Peeples. By gum! that sounds familiar. I've heard his name, anyway. What does he look like, Sol?"

"Onusual tall puncher. Sandy complected. Eyes sharp like a hawk's, but tawny. Light tawny. Somethin' of a

126

landy, leastways in town. Always wears a red scarf. An' ̶e's one of the gun-packin' fraternity. Clink will be in ̶own shore over the Fourth."

"Red scarf? Ahum!" said Rock, dropping his head. ̶"Clink? Where does he get that name?"

"Wal, somebody said he had a habit of clinkin' gold ̶coins at the bar."

"Sounds like the range," laughed Rock. "They sure ̶can call a puncher proper. . . . Well, Sol, I'll run along, ̶and drop in again."

He did run along, as if hurrying to get away from some ̶one; but it was only from himself and his coalescing ̶thoughts. Pretty soon some one was likely to come up ̶to him with one of Ash Preston's boots! Rock wondered ̶if he were lucky or unlucky. He concluded it was the ̶latter, for wherever he roamed, unfortunate persons and ̶untoward events centered around him.

Reaching Dabb's new store, where the windows were ̶full of merchandise of all sorts, Rock went in and hunted ̶up the suit department. It chanced that there was in stock ̶a black broadcloth suit, with frock coat, which might ̶have been made for him, so well did it fit. Rock ̶purchased it and an embroidered vest of fancy design, ̶a white shirt with ruffles in the bosom, a wide white collar ̶and a black flowing bow-tie to go with it. Lastly he ̶bought shiny leather shoes, rather light and soft, which ̶augured well for dancing. Not forgetting a mask, he asked ̶for a plain black one. None of any kind was available. ̶All false faces and masks of humorous design had been ̶sold.

Rock carried his possessions back to the hotel, certain ̶that some of his youthful cowboy sensations were not ̶wholly dead. While in his room he cut a pattern of a ̶mask out of paper, and taking this back to the store he ̶bought a piece of black cloth and fashioned it after the ̶pattern he had cut.

Then to kill time and to forget the burden on his mind, ̶Rock went about renewing old acquaintances, whom ̶he found in greater numbers than he had anticipated. ̶But he shied away from the saloons; not that he distrusted ̶his strength, but because he believed he had parted ̶company with that atmosphere for good and all. He met ̶cowboys on the street corners and stopped to chat; he met ranchers in the post-office and in the county clerk's hall, where he went to investigate cattle brands.

What with a late dinner and another visit at Sol Winter's store, a call at the stable to see Egypt, and then more leisurely random saunterings around town, the day passed by. After supper the hotel man, Clark, got hold of him and in a genial way whose intent was obvious to Rock, tried to pump him about the Prestons. Rock had met that same attitude before during the day, and though without apparent evasion, he did not commit himself. Then who but Jess Slagle stamped into the hotel lobby, in his rough range garb.

Slagle had been trifling with the bottle, but he was not by any means drunk. He was, however, under the influence of rum, and his happened to be a disposition aversely affected by it.

"Howdy, thar, Sunset Pass puncher!" he said, loud and leering.

"Hello, Jess! How are you? I called on the way in."

"Left home yesterday. Stayin' till after the fireworks. Are you goin' back to Preston?"

"Why, certainly! Like my new job fine," responded Rock. "I'm sort of a foreman over the younger Prestons."

"Rock, it was a hell of a good bet that Gage Preston would never put *you* to butcherin'."

"So you say. Well, I reckon 'most any rancher could figure I'd never go in for that kind of work."

"Ho! Ho!—Preston was figgerin' deeper'n that, Rock," returned Slagle, with evil eye. "Want a drink with me?"

"No, thanks. I've sworn off," replied Rock, shortly and he went out to walk in the darkness. Slagle's remarks did not set lightly upon Rock. They were trenchant with meaning. Slagle, of course, hated Preston, and naturally would be prone to cast slurs. But would he make two-sided remarks like that, just out of rancor? It would go severely with him if one of them ever came to Preston's ears. And rattlesnake Ash Preston would strike at less than that.

The night air bore the cool freshness of past rain, and the scents of a desert moistened and revivified.

Rock strolled to and fro, between the hotel lights and those on the corner. When would the Prestons arrive in

128

Wagontongue? The boys would ride it through in one
day, except perhaps one or two of them who would
accompany the womenfolk. They would require a day
and a half to make the journey, possibly a little less.
Rock, yielding to musings not wholly free from pain,
dared to dwell on a possible dance with Thiry. But that
was too wonderful to come true, at least now. He would
not be so weak and selfish as to jeopardize her evening's
pleasure, by asking. Still, he wanted to see her at that
dance, if only from some obscure corner behind the
crowd.

As he came again into the yellow flare of light, quick
pattering footsteps sounded behind him, and soon the
swish of skirts. A hand, small, eager, and strong, seized
his arm, and a feminine voice he knew rang under his
ear.

"True Rock, I've been on your trail all afternoon."

Chapter Nine

Rock stared down into the piquant flushed face of
his old sweetheart, Amy Wund.

"Now I've got you and I'm going to hang on to you,"
he said, with a roguishness that did not altogether conceal a firm determination.

"Why—how do—Mrs. Dabb? You sure—"

"Oh, Mrs. Dabb, he—!" she interrupted, flashing dark
passionate eyes up at him. "Call me Amy, can't you?
What's the sense of being so formal? You used to call
me 'darling Amy'."

There was no gainsaying that. And he did not admire
profanity from a woman's lips, no matter how pretty they
were. Amy's checked him up to reasonableness sooner
than could have any proper speech.

"Well, good-evenin', Amy," he drawled. "I've
forgotten what I used to call you. Reckon it's not just
good taste for you to remind me."

"Perhaps not, True. But you make me furious. I could do anything."

"Sure you could. But, for instance, do you think i' wise to hang on to me—this way—right in front of the hotel?"

"Let's get out of the light, then. I've got to talk to you," she replied, and pressing his arm tight she hurried him down the dark street.

"Amy, listen to sense. Oughtn't you be home?" asked Rock, gravely.

"Sense from True Rock? Ye Gods! When I was sixteen you *made* me meet you out, at night, because my father wouldn't let you come to our house," she retorted.

"That's so, Amy. I guess I was no good. But I've learned a little in all these years—at least enough to consider a woman's name."

"Thank you. I believe you have. And it's not true you were no good. . . . Now about my being at home. I suppose I ought to be there, since I took the responsibilit' of it. But it's an empty home, Trueman. I am alone most of the time. John has men come there to drink and play cards and talk business. He objects to my friends. He is as jealous as the devil. Just a selfish rich old man! I have money, horses. I think children would have made it a home, but there are none—and never will be."

"Aw, too bad, Amy," replied Rock, deeply touched "You never should have married Dabb."

"Father was in debt to John. . . . And I had to foo' that bill, True," she returned, bitterly. "But I didn' waylay you to talk about myself."

"How'd you know I was in town?" asked Rock, glad to have the subject changed.

"I heard it this morning. And I sure was thrilled. True did you get the invitation to my dance?"

"I did. Many thanks, Amy. It was good of you. I rather expected to be left out."

"Would you have been hurt if you had?" she asked curiously.

"Reckon I would. Men are such queer hombres."

"Are you coming, True?"

"Well, now, that's a horse of another color," he said "I'd sure like to. I might drop in for a little—to loo on."

"True Rock! You look on at a dance! Why, cowboy, are you growing old?"

"No, Amy, I feel far from being old. But there are reasons. You should know one of them, anyhow."

"You mean my husband?"

"Sure do. He never had any use for me after I quit him."

"All the same, Trueman. I could get him to hire you as foreman of the whole outfit. And that's a job. John is running thirty thousand head."

"You could not," returned Rock, incredulously.

"Do you want the job?" she retorted, with uplift of chin he remembered well.

"Why, Amy, no. I've got one job. Thank you all the same."

"True, that Preston job is a poor-paying one and a risky one."

"How do you know that, Amy?"

"I heard John say so. But let's get this dance question settled. Will you come?"

They halted at the end of the sidewalk, on the outskirts of town. The stars were shining brightly, and by their light Rock saw Amy's face, upturned to his.

"Amy, you make me angry," said Rock, though he was not so sure of that. "Here you are—an old sweetheart of mine, and now married to a man who hates me—coaxing me to come to a dance."

"That's why, Trueman."

"Then I sure better not come."

"Oh, that was partly a lie," she cried, in disgust at herself. "I can't even tell the truth any more. I'd like you to come for several reasons, Trueman."

"All right, fire away," he said, lightly.

"First for old times' sake. Then because certain of my friends say you won't come. Next because—well, True, I've been a darned fool. I've gone—a—a little too far with a certain cowboy. And I'm afraid of him. He's coming to my dance. And I thought—if you were there—I'd not be afraid, anyhow."

"A certain cowboy. Why certain, Amy?" he inquired, looking dubiously at her, aware she could not meet his eyes.

"Trueman, I might as well make a clean breast of it,"

she said, almost with defiance. "I'd met this fellow often. Oh, I liked him, I guess. But I wasn't crazy about him, and I never encouraged him until that day you snubbed me."

"Then what did you do?"

"I flirted—oh, worse than ever," she replied, and she had the courage to look shamefacedly up at Rock. "I've met him twice since. And the last time—I—well—"

"Amy, how far did you go?" broke in Rock, as she paused.

"Too far! . . . I let him kiss me—hug me."

"Amy Wund!" exclaimed Trueman. "It wouldn't have amounted to much before, but now I'm ashamed of you."

"But, Trueman, I came to my senses," she protested. "I don't want to see him again. But he'll come to the dance. . . . And they tell me he's a pretty wild cowboy. At that he's no boy, I'll tell you."

"Who is he, Amy?"

"I don't know his real first name. His last is Peeples. Clink, they call him."

"Clink Peeples. I've sure heard of him. Rides for this new rancher, Hesbitt."

"Yes. And Hesbitt——"

"One thing at a time, Amy. Is this the last reason you have for wanting me at that dance?"

"No, Trueman, there's another. A woman's reason, and therefore the most important."

"What is it?"

"I won't tell you."

"Very well, I reckon your third reason is enough to fetch me. I'll come."

"Oh, thank you, Trueman," she replied, in delight, squeezing his hand. "You always were the dearest, kindest fellow when anyone was in trouble. . . . Trueman, you could steady me. God knows I need it."

"Amy, I don't exactly trust you," said Rock, dubiously. "I never did. But that doesn't mean I haven't faith in you at all. You've got it in you to become a splendid woman. Could I help you—as a friend or brother? Be honest, Amy, I'd despise you if you lied."

"Yes, you could, and I'll be grateful for that—if I can't have more," she rejoined, won to sincerity by his force.

"All right. Shake hands on it," he said, earnestly, smiling down on her.

"But, True, I won't promise not to try to—to make you be more," she said, rebelliously.

"Don't talk nonsense," he returned, sharply. "Amy, will you consent to my callin' on your husband?"

"You want to see John?" she queried, astounded, her eyes opening wide. "What on earth for?"

"Well I think it might be a good idea," he rejoined, evasively.

"It might be at that," she agreed, her dark eyes full of thought. Then she tossed her head and laughed. "All right, go ahead. You have my consent."

"You're game, Amy. No one could say not. . . . Can I ask John anythin' I like and tell him what I want?"

"Trueman Rock, you son-of-a-gun!" she burst out, as if astonished into a corner. "Yes, darn you, anything except I was once in love with you—and that it's not utterly impossible for me to be so foolish again."

"I'll take good care you don't do that," he laughed, wondering why he had been so unkind. She was amenable, and perhaps not so dangerous as he had imagined.

"Trueman, I have something more to say," she said, hesitatingly, lacking her former confidence and spirit.

"Well then, say it. A woman always leaves the worst for the last."

"I think you'd better quit riding for the Prestons," she answered, her reluctance giving place to intense earnestness.

"Why?" he inquired, freezing a little.

"I'm afraid I can't explain what may be only my intuition. But I give you my word of honor, Trueman, that it's not because I—I might be jealous of Thiry Preston."

To do her justice, Rock had to admit to himself that the deceitful side of her seemed to be in abeyance at this moment. She was grave. Her eyes were big with perplexity.

"No? What is it, then?" he asked, tensely.

"I believe the Prestons are going to get more than the ill will of the range."

"That's a strong statement, Amy. On what do you base it?"

"True, I can't trace it down. But it must come from

133

many little bits of gossip I've heard. Some of it, by the way, from Peeples. Everyone knows, of course, that you took the job to be near Thiry Preston. It's a joke already. That's your side of it. Trueman, you have a reputation. Oh, I don't mean as a gun-slinger. That's old. Nor do I mean as a great rider, roper, and all such cowboy qualities. It's that you're true blue, honest, a man of your word. Why even my husband thinks that. For I asked him."

"I'm glad, Amy. I hope I deserve it. I certainly mean to. . . . But is there unusual interest in me, just now?"

"That's the point. There is, True. I could tell you a lot of things, if I could remember. One is—Clink Peeples said he reckoned Gage Preston would profit by your honest name. Isn't that a queer remark, Trueman?"

"It is—a little," Rock admitted.

"And here's another—more of a stumper," went on Amy. "Last night John had some men out to the house, as usual. They talked and smoked. When I heard your name I listened. Some one, I think it was Mr. Hesbitt, answered whoever had used your name first. 'I don't know this great cowboy Rock,' he said. 'But if he stays on ridin' for Preston, I'll not share the opinion you men have of him.'"

"Amy, that isn't a compliment to Preston," said Rock, ponderingly.

"It certainly isn't. And it means you'll lose your reputation. Trueman, there's something wrong about this Preston outfit. I can feel what I can't explain. You know I'm not a fool about everything. I was born here. My dad has been a cattleman all his life. He's away now, in Colorado. I wish he'd hurry back. I could get things out of him. John is close-mouthed, as most of these cattlemen are."

"They've all good reason to be," said Rock, laughingly. "They were cowboys once."

"Trueman, you don't need to tell me that. And don't beat around the bush or make light of it. I'm thinking of your good name. There's an undercurrent of feeling here and there—against the Prestons. It'll spread, if there's any reason for it. And then you'd be dragged in."

"Amy, I hope it's nothin' more than gossip," returned Rock, slowly.

"True, will you leave Preston? Please, you can get three times the money."

"No. I'll stick, Amy. I should think you'd know that. If there's anythin' in these hints I reckon the Prestons need me all the more."

"I always loved you for that very trait," she said, with passion. "But I wish here you didn't have it. . . . Oh, Trueman, I tell you I dread this job of yours. That wild, beautiful Sunset Pass! That lovely, strange Thiry Preston! She'll fall in love with you. How could she help it? And you'll be dragged in with them. You'll have to kill this Ash Preston. Oh, he's a snake! He insulted me vilely, right on the street. There's not room enough on this range for you and him. You'll fight. I feel it, Trueman. A woman knows. . . . Oh, it took years for me to get over your killing Hooker! . . . Don't hush me. I *will* tell you. . . . That poor cowboy, crazed by drink and jealousy! How he hounded you—and finally shot you—so you had to kill him to save your own life. . . . Trueman. I *don't want* you to kill another man!"

"Do you think I'm a bloodthirsty devil?" burst out Rock, repelled, yet sorry for her. "I don't want to kill another man. I won't, if I can help it."

She wiped her eyes. "Forgive me," she said, more composed. "I didn't mean to speak out like that. I know how you hate it. . . . Let us walk back now. You can drop me at my corner."

She did not speak again for several blocks. She held his arm closely. Rock did not have anything to say. The interview had surprised, annoyed, frightened and softened him.

"I don't suppose you'd care to see John tonight?" she inquired, releasing his arm and stopping.

"I reckon not. Tomorrow, if I cheer up."

"Cheer up!—Trueman, I'm sorry. I used to—Well, never mind. But you won't drink? Remember my dance is only a day away."

"No, Amy, I won't drink—before or after your dance."

"True, I like you better than I used to," she said, softly.

He bowed his thanks, not quite gallantly.

"Fact is, I never *liked* you," she retorted, quick to respond. "But let's not fight again. Still, making up used

135

to be such fun. . . . Trueman, what will you wear at my masquerade?"

"Look here, little lady, that's not fair. I won't tell you."

"You must. I'll never be able to recognize you. I remember how clever you used to be. . . . The unmasking will not take place until dinner. That'll be late, Trueman. And I'll want to know you, so in case I need you. . . . You may have to throw Clink Peebles out."

"So the honor of protectin' you falls to me," laughed Rock. "I've half a mind you're lyin'. But I'll stifle my suspicions. . . . Amy, I've bought a dandy broadcloth frock suit, black. Also a fancy vest, shirt with ruffles, flowin' black tie and black mask. The clerk in the store didn't know me from Adam, so he can't give me away. I'll come as a flash gambler."

"You'll look grand. Bet you make more than *one* heart ache," she returned, with a glance of mischief and regret. Then she extended her hand. "Good night, Trueman."

"Good night."

Next morning about eleven o'clock, Rock strolled out of the hotel on his way to see John Dabb.

He felt more like himself—his old self—than at any time since the cataclysm that had brought about his metamorphosis. How long, anyhow, had it been since he met Thiry Preston? Ages it seemed! Likewise his arrival at Wagontongue yesterday seemed far away. From the hour of his meeting Amy Dabb to the present moment, except for a half-night's sleep, events had multiplied. One after another of the persons whom he had conversed with, during that interval, had added with some obscure or casual remark, to the chain of calamity which was being forged around him.

Trouble, menace, always brought out in Rock the reckless, dauntless spirit which he shared in common with his type. Drink, in the past, had made him more reckless, but less dangerous. As there was to be no more drink for him there was no hope for the oblivion cowboys yearned for on occasions. Rock had to face the music. And by this hour he had waxed stern and calculating, sure of his vision, while outwardly he appeared the old cool cowboy of the range.

Rock asked to see John Dabb, and was shown into

136

that individual's private office. He walked into a richly furnished room, where two men sat smoking. One was John Dabb, not a great deal changed from the Westerner Rock had once worked for. He was a well-preserved man of fifty, scarcely gray, with the lean face, strong chin, thin lips, and yellow-flecked hazel eyes Rock remembered.

"Howdy, Mr. Dabb!" said Rock, easily. "Reckon you know me."

"Trueman Rock!" exclaimed Dabb, in great surprise. "I do. Amy told me you were here." Embarrassment succeeded his astonishment, which was perhaps what caused him to extend his hand.

"Hesbitt, this is True Rock, one of the real· riders we used to have," went on Dabb, recovering to introduce his comrade, who had also arisen. "Rock, shake hands with Hesbitt, one of our new ranchers.

Hesbitt bowed stiffly and spoke, without offering his hand. Rock looked squarely at him.

"Glad to meet you, Mr. Hesbitt."

His keen faculties, on edge now, gauged this man, unfavorably. Hesbitt was younger than Dabb, probably a man who had never been a cowboy, for he did not show the physical characteristics of the range. He was lean, sallow, hard, with sharp eyes close together and deep under bushy eyebrows.

"Well, Rock, to what am I indebted for this call?" queried Dabb, with curious coldness.

"Remains to be seen whether you'll be indebted to me or not. Reckon that's up to you," replied Rock.

"Don't want your old job back?" inquired the rancher, ironically.

"Not now, but if I lose out with the Prestons, I'd shore like my old place back."

Dabb was plainly puzzled and annoyed.

"Well, did you call to ask me that?"

"No, my business is a little more intimate."

"Indeed? Ahem—er, I hope it's brief," rejoined Dabb, stiffening.

"As brief as you want it," returned Rock, and then he took a slow step nearer to Dabb's companion. "Mr. Hesbitt, I heard this mornin' that your foreman, Peeples, was in town, wantin' to see me."

"Yes, he got in early, and I believe does want to look you up," said Hesbitt, deliberately, his deep-set eyes intent and unsatisfied upon Rock.

"Reckon he can't be particular eager," drawled Rock. "I've been up and down street, and in and out of the hotel all mornin'—lookin' for Mr. Peeples."

"Ah! I see. . . . I dare say he's very busy buyin' supplies," replied Hesbitt nervously. "May I inquire—er—what you want of my foreman?"

"Nothin' so important—that is, to *me*," said Rock, with emphasis on the pronoun. "I just wanted to give Peeples opportunity to meet me. And to tell him somethin'."

"What?" asked Hesbitt, whose sallow face slightly paled.

"Reckon I'd sure like you to know as well. I just want to give you a hunch. Not till two days ago did I ever hear of the Half Moon brand. And not till yesterday did I learn what outfit run it."

Manifestly Rock's cold biting speech impressed Hesbitt, but scarcely to the acceptance of its content. He knocked the ashes off his cigar, and picked up his hat from the desk, without deigning another glance at Rock.

"Dabb, your former cowboy's talk is queer, if true," he said, curtly. "I'll leave you to renew old acquaintance. Good day."

"Hesbitt, you're new to this range," rejoined Dabb, a little caustic. "I've told you before. And your Wyoming cowboy foreman needs to be told—or he'll get into trouble. This is not Wyoming. . . . I'm bound to tell you that Rock's talk is not queer. I'll gamble it's true. I never knew him to lie. And no old rider or cattleman on this range would *say* it, even if he thought it."

"Much obliged, Dabb," replied Hesbitt, heatedly. "I've told you something before—and it is that what this range needs is some new blood."

"Humph! Some of it is most d——liable to get spilled," said Dabb, harshly.

Hesbitt bowed and went out, jarring the door. Dabb bit viciously at his cigar.

"Some of these new cowmen make me sick. . . . Rock, help yourself to a smoke and sit down."

138

"Dabb, I sure appreciate what you said to him about me," replied Rock, losing his coolness. "Fact is I'm surprised, too. I'd been told you had no use for me."

"Rock, that's not the point," returned Dabb quickly. "When I knew you were honest, I was bound to say so. Your connection with Preston has started rumors. Hesbitt has been losing more stock than any of us. His outfit is a hard-nut bunch from Wyoming. They think they're—well, I don't want to repeat gossip. There's too much of it. . . . But whether or not I have any use for you I'd sure need to see proof of your dishonesty."

"That's straight talk. I like it and thank you. It makes what I wanted to say easier."

"Ah, I'd forgot. You had some intimate business. . . . Make it short, Rock."

"Dabb, did I ever do you any dirt?" queried Rock, by way of a start.

"You quit me, left me in the lurch," replied Dabb, testily. "I never overlook that in a foreman."

"But be fair, at least," responded Rock, earnestly. "I had to leave quick—or kill another man, and one very generally liked here, Cass Seward."

"You may have thought so. Cass was a friend of mine. He told me once you didn't need to run off. He could have fixed it up. Arrested you—and let you off. It was an even break, you knew. What was that fellow's name? Anyway, I know everybody was glad you bumped him off."

"Ahuh!—I'm sorry I didn't know that," said Rock, broodingly. Then he shook off dark thoughts. "Dabb, did you have anythin' else against me?"

The rancher thrummed on his desk, and puffed on his cigar, while revolving this query.

"Look me straight in the eye," went on Rock. "Man to man, Dabb. If you have cards on me lay them down. I'm comin' clean honest. . . . And a lot might depend on you doin' the same."

"What are you driving at?"

"Dabb, I'm askin' very little, at least for two Westerners like us. I've absolutely no ax to grind. I might want a job some day of you, but only on my merits. Now I'm askin' only a show-down. I want to know where I stand with you. I want you to believe in my sincerity."

"Rock, that's d—strong talk—coming from you. It's hard for me to think you might have some underhand motive."

"Don't think it. For there's none."

"All right, Rock, I'll meet you," replied Dabb, flushing darkly, evidently stirred. "Straight out then, I've sort of held against you—that old affair of yours and Amy's."

"Good!" exclaimed Rock, cracking a fist in his palm. "That's just what I wanted you to admit. Dabb, it never amounted to shucks. You know what gossip is in this town."

"You bet I know," said Dabb, grimly. "But even allowing for that—"

"Listen," interrupted Rock, leaning over to Dabb. "The old women here gave Amy the worst of that affair. She was pretty and vain—and had a way with the boys. But she was good, and if they ever said otherwise they lied. I was in love with Amy, perhaps a little more so than I was with two other girls. Amy knew this. She never let herself go. I'm sure she was fond of me, but there were other boys. And so we had it hot and heavy. But what I want to make clear to you, Dabb, is that Amy was never serious about me. I mean never in love as it was in her to be. And I'm satisfied that she never has been yet. Even with you—her husband! You'll excuse me, Dabb, but this is blunt straight talk."

"It is, by God!" Dabb said, strainedly. "And to what end, Rock?"

"Amy's happiness," flashed Rock. "I don't need to swear that, if you really know me, as you told Hesbitt. . . . I met Amy the day I arrived in Wagontongue and again yesterday. Dabb, she'd scalp me alive if she ever found out I told you this. . . . She's lonesome and unhappy. I don't believe Amy ever would have married you if she hadn't cared somethin' for you. But you've failed to win the best in her. Dabb, I don't suppose anyone ever dared to hit you this way. I don't care a d—how angry you get, if I can only make you see."

"You're making me see red, cowboy," replied Dabb, hoarsely, and the blood that he confessed colored his sight certainly showed in his face. "But go ahead. I've not the nerve to pull a gun on you."

140

"Dabb, I always had a hunch you weren't a bad fellow, under your skin. The range claimed you drove hard bargains, and the cowboys didn't exactly like you. Maybe that was justified. All the same, as ranchers go, you sure were white. . . . You're rich now. You don't have to eat, sleep, drink, whistle, and smoke business. Pay some attention to your young and pretty wife! Like you did before you married her!—Sol Winter told me you were as gay as any young buckaroo in town. Well, back-trail yourself. Take the girl away occasionally, to Kansas City or Denver. California in winter. . . . And before long, old-timer, you'll be glad. If you don't do this, sure as I'm sittin' here, Amy is goin' to the bad. . . . That's what I came to say and that's all."

Rock ended abruptly, forced by the older man's torture. Dabb writhed in his chair. Fury and shame contested with the sense of fairness that seemed dragged out of his depths. Suddenly he burst out into the wildest of range profanity.

"Fine, Dabb," returned Rock, with a laugh. "But do you mean it for me or yourself?"

The rancher wheeled in his chair, clawed at things on his desk, bent his head, and jerked it aloft, then with action growing slower and slower he lighted another cigar. When again he turned, his face was half enveloped in smoke.

"You are a—queer one—Rock," he stammered, with incoherence gradually clearing. "I don't know whether to order you out of my office—or to believe I'm the d—d old fool you make me out. . . . Anyway, it's too sudden. You've hit me where I live. And it hurts like sixty. . . . But you talk like a man. And I'm not yet so set in my mind that I can't learn from any man."

"It took nerve to brave John Dabb in his den, but I'm sure glad," replied Rock, frankly smiling, with all tension eased.

"I'm not convinced," returned Dabb, doggedly, "but I'm some staggered. If the truth turns out as straight as your talk—well, young man, you're on parole till I find out. . . . Now since you've presumed to advise me on a delicate matter, I'll retaliate."

"Throw your gun, John. I'm ready to duck."

"Quit Preston!" cut out Dabb.

141

"Why?" snapped Rock, just as sharply.

"I can't say."

"But *why* can't you say? If you feel a thing keen enough to show, why can't you give me a reason?"

"You know the range, Rock. Some things just can't be said."

"And why? Because they can't be prove."

"Exactly."

"Well, I'll stick to Preston until these damned underhand rumors are proved—or until somebody suffers for startin' them."

"That may work out too late for you."

"I've got to risk it."

"If you do any gun-throwing in defense of Preston, it'll ruin you."

"That depends. But it's far-fetched, Dabb. It's way out of probability."

"Not at all—if you're sweet on Thiry Preston," rejoined Dabb.

"Between you and me—I am."

"So!—That accounts. I'll respect your confidence, Rock. She's a charming girl. It's too bad that she. . . . There I go again. I'm as gabby as the old women. Suppose you run along and let me collect my wits."

Rock accepted his dismissal with good grace, feeling exultant over the unexpected response. However, as he was closing the door, Dabb called him back.

"I forgot something," he said. "I think I ought to tell you I've broken business relations with Preston."

"When?"

"Last Friday, when Preston was here."

"May I ask what were the business relations?"

"Preston had the small end of a cattle deal with me. I bought him out. And then I canceled all beef orders."

Dabb lowered his glance at this juncture and absentmindedly drew figures on his desk.

"How did Preston take that?" inquired Rock, after a moment.

"Kicked about the cattle deal. But I took it he was relieved to get out of selling me more beef."

"Relieved.—What you mean?"

"He just struck me that way. Didn't ask me why. I

142

vas glad. My reason was good, but I could scarcely divulge it to him."

"Mind tellin' me?" went on Rock, leisurely rolling a cigarette.

"Yes, I'd mind. It would necessitate violating someone's confidence. You'll have to find out for yourself, Rock."

"Reckon so. Well, I'm such a dumb hombre it may take me long.—By the way, Dabb, are you still head of the Territory Cattle Association?"

"No, I resigned. Hesbitt was recently elected."

"Gee! Sorry to hear it."

"Why so? Hesbitt is said to be a better executive than I was."

"He never was, a cowboy," returned Rock, significantly. "Good day, Dabb. Reckon I'll meet up with you at the rodeo and the dance."

"Likely. I can't very well take to bull-dogging steers again. But I'll drop in on Amy's dance for a couple if I break a leg."

"Now you're shoutin', John," replied Rock, gladly, and went out.

There were bustle and activity on the street. Wagon-tongue was filling up for the Fourth. Rock saw that the town hall had been gayly decorated in red, white and blue. Flags were showing. Youngsters were already setting off firecrackers. The hitching-rails were lined with saddle-horses. Down the long main street, wagons came toiling in from the desert. Cowboys, Mexicans, Indians were numerous, mostly in the vicinity of the saloon, Happy Days. Rock swore pleasantly to himself, in his assurance that he had walked in or out of this saloon, cowboy—happy and drunk, for the last time.

An hour of sauntering to and fro provided Rock with some amusement and interest, but his main object, which was to allow Clink Peeples the meeting he was reported to be seeking, did not materialize. Whereupon he went to get dinner, finding the restaurant crowded. After that he sat in the hotel lobby until he could not stand it any longer. Then in his room he killed some more time, dwelling again on his interview with Dabb.

It had been of both good and bad cheer—good in its intimation of possible contentment for Amy, if he could

only be instrumental in rousing the best in her instead
of inciting the worst; and bad for himself, inasmuch a
it added materially to the persistent, evil rumor hovering
like a gathering cloud over the Prestons.

In the afternoon, rather late, Rock walked round to
see Winter. He was received almost with open arms.

"Hey, you been drinking?" expostulated Rock, holding
his friend at arm's-length.

"Nope. That is, not red liquor. But I shore been
drinkin' in Thiry's sweet smiles an' words."

"No!"

"Yep. The Prestons got in early. Drove all day
yesterday an' half into the night."

"Dog-gone!—I didn't expect her till tomorrow."

"True, she has been in half a dozen times," went on
Winter, eager to reveal the momentous fact. "Asked for
you *every* time!"

"Sol, you lyin' old geezer! My heart might stand her
askin' once.—But six times! . . . I ought to choke you."

"Son, mebbe it's not all gospel truth. When she first
run in she was her old nice sweet cool self. Kissed me.
Said she an' Alice were all fixed up nice out at my house.
She asked if I'd seen you. An' I told her I hadn't yet
today, but thet you'd be in. Then she said Ash hadn't
come to town an' wasn't comin'. I was too surprised to
say more'n thet mebbe once she'd have a real good time.
She blushed at thet. An hour later she came in again,
somehow different. She bought buntin'. She was helpin'
Amy Dabb decorate the dance hall. Asked had I seen
you yet, an' I said no. She went out an' pretty soon came
back, a little more different. She had a red spot in each
cheek. An' so she came an' went, till the last time, a little
while ago, when she was with Amy. Then you bet she
didn't ask about you. He! He! He! . . . I'll bet you a
million Amy got in some good licks."

"Sol, you can laugh about that!" ejaculated Rock
with a groan.

"These here girls strike me funny. True, shore as you're
born, Amy had been fillin' poor Thiry full of guff about
how wild you was over her, an' mebbe was yet."

"Of course she had. It's terrible. Thiry will be disgusted
with me."

144

"Wal, she wasn't, not so you could notice it," said Sol, dryly.

"Reckon I've the rottenest luck of any cowpuncher who ever forked a horse," went on Rock, raving. "Here all day that fire-eatin' Dabb woman has been ruinin' me with my girl—when I've been tryin' to help her. If that isn't like her."

"What'd you do, Rock?" queried Winter, with quick interest.

"I went and made friends with John Dabb."

"You did? Holy mavericks! What was your idee, son?"

Rock heard Winter, but only vaguely, for he was rushing out to the door, where through the window he had espied Thiry Preston.

Fortunately Thiry did not see him until he emerged, to all appearances in a normal manner for a young man to step out on the sidewalk. The action, however, brought him right in front of Thiry.

"Why, hello!" he said, forcing a pleasant surprise to hide his rapture, as he doffed his sombrero. "Heard you were here. Really didn't expect you till tomorrow."

She greeted him shyly, with absence of that inhibited expression which marked her meetings with him at Sunset Pass. She wore a light-blue dress and a new bonnet, the rather wide brim of which shaded her face somewhat. Still, he saw that her cheeks were not pale and her eyes not tranquil.

"We started at daybreak yesterday morning," she was saying. "The boys were no good at all, and the youngsters simply mad to come—so Dad sent us off a day ahead."

"That's fine. The kids will have the time of their lives. Where are they?"

"Goodness only knows. In one of the stores somewhere. . . . Oh, Ash stayed home."

She spoke this as if it was an afterthought, scarcely important.

"That so?" replied Rock, with constraint, though he tingled. "Well. It's too bad, if you're disappointed."

"I'm so greatly relieved I—I don't know myself," she replied, with unexpected candor. "I don't remember a Fourth that Ash hasn't spoiled by getting drunk."

145

"May I walk with you a step?" asked Rock, changing the subject. "Where are you going?"

"You may. I'm on my last errand," she replied, and waved a gay hand at Winter, who was looking on with a broad smile.

Rock fell in with her short quick steps and made careful remarks about the weather, and the town being full of people, until they reached the baker's, where she said she was to order things for Mrs. Winter.

"I'll wait for you," said Rock.

"Are you afraid to walk into a bakeshop with a girl?" she asked, and the wide bonnet-brim tilted just far enough and long enough for him to catch a flash of gray eyes.

"Not—exactly afraid," confessed Rock, who, as a matter of truth, was scared into consternation because this could not really be actually happening out of a dream.

"From what I've heard—recently—you could march into a lion's den—for a—for certain people," she said, distantly.

"Ahuh, reckon I could—for—for a certain *person*," replied Rock, beginning lamely and ending valiantly. That brought the blue bonnet-brim down to hide most of her face. Rock, however, thought he caught a glimpse of a coloring cheek. He escorted her into the store, stood beside her while she gave her orders, and accompanied her out.

"I'm to wait here for Allie. She won't be long," said Thiry, stopping outside before the window.

"Hope she'll be late," returned Rock, trying vainly to find himself.

Presently she lifted her head so that the bonnet no longer could be anathematized. Rock devoured her lovely face before he realized it had never worn such an expression for him. Doubt, disdain, petulance!

"You're going to the dance," she said. It was not a question.

"Reckon I'll drop in for a peep," he replied, his heart giving symptoms of pyrotechnics.

"Are you going to mask?"

"Sure. It wouldn't be fun otherwise."

"Would you tell me what you'll wear?" she asked, sweetly—too sweetly not to be dangerous.

146

"Thiry, that'd spoil the fun. I sure want to fool you," he protested.

"Have you not already fooled me?" she went on, with bitterness tinged by pathos.

"I have not!" he shot at her, swift to speak his sudden passion. It startled her.

"Trueman Rock, you have a great deal to disprove and more to prove," she said, wide strange eyes on his.

"Thiry!" he gasped, suddenly beside himself.

"You would not tell *me* what you were going to wear—so I'd recognize you first."

"Of course I'll tell you," he burst out.

"I don't care to know now. . . . You would not see *me,* anyhow."

He could only stare mutely. His bosom seemed rent with a conflict—the objective belief in anything she might utter, and the bewildering undercurrent that betrayed her. Wild recollection of her father's sly predictions further added to his state.

"Mr. Rock," she went on, without the scorn, "I had better explain my rather bold words. This dance was to be the first gay happy time for me—since I grew up. Dad somehow prevented Ash from coming to town. He filled me with—with beliefs about how *you* would make it wonderful for me. I have no one but my brothers, and they all have their girls. I—I dreamed myself into . . . no matter what. . . . Then I come to town to have my ears filled to burning—all day long. The dance was to be given for you! You wouldn't even dance with any other woman but *her!* You were an old lover renewing his vows! You——"

"Thiry, hush!" interposed Trueman, in rage, despair, and exaltation, all bewilderingly mingled. "I told you I didn't care what anyone said to you about my old affairs. But if *you* care, then I hate the very thought of them."

"Trueman, I don't know how much, or why, or if I care. But I trusted you and that woman has killed it."

"Oh no, Thiry, don't say that," he implored.

"But there's a secret understanding between you and her—for this dance."

"Yes, there is. But it's sure not sentiment on my part," he replied, humbly. "Thiry, if you won't trust me, I shall

147

have to give her away. And I never did that to a girl in my life."

"How could I trust a man who would betray any woman—much less her?"

"You couldn't. And I deserve that rebuke. But, Thiry, I'm dumfounded. Dear child, be reasonable. Why, I was going to get *my* happy time just spying upon you from some corner. I never dared hope to get to dance with you. Good Heavens!"

"Trueman, I meant to dance only with my brothers, and perhaps one or two of the boys I know—and all the rest with you."

"Thiry Preston, you tell me this—this—" he cried, and failed to find adequate conclusion.

"Yes, I tell you," she retorted. "I couldn't do it at home, because I didn't know. But that's no difference."

"Of course it isn't. I should have made some wild dream come true. But, Thiry, it's not too late."

"Oh, it is," she said, disconsolately, yet she seemed to hunger to be persuaded. "She has spoiled—"

"Listen," he broke in. "I meant to befriend Amy Dabb. She needs it, Heaven knows, as you will see for yourself tomorrow night. But if you let her jealous tongue spoil *anythin'* for you, I'm through."

"Trueman, I could forgive a great deal, I think, but no bold lie," she murmured, her grave eyes piercing him.

"I would not lie to you, to save my life," he returned, in weary cold finality.

"I apologize. It is I who am a little suspicious," she returned, softly. "Trueman, I make this excuse. I'm not used to intrigue, to deceit. . . . Oh yes, I'm a woman and I haven't told you my real feelings. And I cannot. But I could never cope with Mrs. Dabb. She read my soul and tortured it. She thought I might l—like you and meant to destroy."

"Thiry, did she destroy what little there might have been?" asked Rock.

She averted her face. "I don't know. I'm all excited. When I get back home I'll be appalled. But, oh, I—I want to have this dance! You'll understand me, Trueman, won't you? That's one thing I do trust."

148

"I'll do my best. But you are strange. Sure there never was a girl like you."

"In what way?" she asked, giving him again the gray sweet wonder of her eyes.

"Thiry, I could not find words here," he replied, striving for calm. Indeed, where or when could he ever do justice to her strangeness, her inconsistency, her innocence and simplicity? "Perhaps at the dance—"

"Perhaps at the dance—then—if you disprove much and prove more I will—"

The arrival of Alice Preston, breathless and pink and merry, checked Rock's impassioned reply that otherwise he could not have resisted, even if Thiry had never completed her thought-compelling sentence. The girls, laughing and talking, started for home, and Rock accompanied them toward the corner.

Just before they arrived there, a man and a woman hove in sight. Evidently she was trying to hurry away from him.

"I tell you no—no!" she cried, in a rage. Then Rock recognized the voice and the blazing black eyes. Amy Dabb! The man was a tall rider. He wore a red scarf, and his face was almost as red.

"See heah, sweetheart, you cain't come thet with me," he drawled, blocking her way.

"Shut up, you d—fool! Some one might hear you," she cried, passionately and low.

Rock with a stride and a leap was upon them.

"Somebody did hear you, Amy. Rustle now, with the girls," said Rock, sharply, as he gave the rider a hard thrust backward and then confronted him.

"Howdy, Mister Red Scarf!"

Chapter Ten

The red-scarfed rider had evidently had a drink or two, but he appeared level-headed, and slowly the evilish geniality with which he had accosted Amy Dabb faded into cold, watchful speculation. His tawny gaze swept Rock from head to foot, and back again.

"Howdy, Mister Big Hat!" he replied, with capital imitation of Rock's greeting to him.

"My name is Rock."

"Aboot had thet reckoned," returned the rider, guardedly.

"You're Hesbitt's foreman, Peeples," went on Rock, "He told me you were lookin' for me."

"I shore was."

"Ahuh. Reckon you didn't look very hard," rejoined Rock, in slight derision.

"Wal, I cain't say there was any particular call to rustle."

Thus these two range-riders measured each other. Rock's reaction was vastly diverse from that following his encounter with Ash Preston. The foreman of Hesbitt's outfit appeared to belong to that type of cowboy whom Rock was wont to believe the salt of the earth.

"You're not drunk," replied Rock. "How's it you insult a married woman on the street?"

"Is thet any of your bizness?"

"It shore is. I'm an old friend of Amy Dabb's. Rode for her husband. Reckon it's not exaggeratin' to claim I'm his friend, too."

"All right, Rock, I apologize," returned the foreman, readily, though resentfully. "But honest to God, it shore ain't because I think I ought to."

"I heard what she said, and your answer. Peeples, you ought to be horsewhipped for that. Then you wouldn't let her pass."

"Aw, hell! She shore wasn't thet way when we was

150

alone indoors, last time I seen her," said Peeples. "She plump surprised me—made me sore."

"No wonder, if you thought bad of her," rejoined Rock, feeling his way. This man could be talked to. "Reckon you don't know Amy well. She's a lonesome and unhappy girl. She met you, liked you, because you're a good-lookin' and interestin' cowboy. And I reckon she let you hold her hand—maybe kiss her, though that's pretty reckless even for Amy. You scared her, most likely. And afterward she got to thinkin', remembered she was married, and made up her mind next time to cut you. It's the way of some women, Peeples. Tough on a fellow, but he's to blame. Now, tell me square, don't you think it was kind of low-down to brace her, right on the street?"

"Rock, I reckon it was, if she's what you seem to think," responded Peeples, staring hard. "I shore didn't. . . . An' how aboot my takin' you as a slick hombre—a liar—sweet on her yourself, an' wantin' the inside track?"

"Peeples, you can take me any way you like," responded Rock, speaking hard. "But if you do it that particular way you've got trouble on your hands right now."

"So I aboot reckoned," nodded the rider. "Strikes me I've got to take a lot for granted aboot you. Shore you know more aboot me than I do aboot you. It ain't a very square deal all around."

"I would take your word, if you shook on it," replied Rock.

"Wal, I guess I'd take yours."

"All right, Peeples. We're gettin' somewhere," said Rock, more heartily. It always warmed him to be taken seriously when he was in earnest. "I'll give you my word, confidentially. I'm not sweet on Amy Dabb. Only want to help her, before it's too late. . . . And more, I am darn good and awful sweet on some other girl."

"Rock, when occasion comes I can be as high-falutin' as you or any other man," responded Peeples, even more heartily. "Much obliged for your confidence. I'll ask Amy's pardon—tell her plumb straight she overdid it a little, an' advise her to cut thet game with cowboys in future."

151

"Fine. We can shake on that, anyway."

"Let's drink on it, too," responded the other, as they gripped hands.

"Peeples, I'm off liquor for good."

"You don't say. What's the matter? Is it religion or the girl?"

"Maybe both," laughed Rock. "Now, Peeples, tell me why you were lookin' for me?"

"Easier'n your other cracks," replied Peeples, laconically. "I kept hearin' aboot you out on the range. Then lately you come back an' went to ride for Preston. Thet made me curious, an' I reckon I jest wanted to meet up with you an' see for myself."

"See what?"

"Wal, you know how one cowboy sizes up another."

"Ahuh. Very often wrong, Peeples," returned Rock, with gravity.

"Shore. But we're old hands at this range game. You might be a deep an' clever cuss, an' so might I. But I reckon it'd be a poor idee to gamble on."

"It'd be a losin' bet."

"Rock, do you know one of them queer range shadows is creepin' over the Prestons?"

"I've heard so," replied Rock, gloomily.

"How many of them shadows did you ever heah aboot that didn't grow wuss?"

"Not many," admitted Rock. "But I'm hopin' this one will blow over."

"Natural. But if it doesn't—if it clouds up black—you're shore goin' to get rained on, cowboy," said Peeples, with dark significance.

"Peeples, I like Gage Preston," went on Rock. "Do you know him?"

"Shore. Like him fine, too."

"I didn't take to Hesbitt," mused Rock, as if making comparisons.

"Shore I never did, either," admitted Peeples. "None of the outfit never did. But—wal, I'm responsible for his stock. An' you can bet your bottom dollar I'd never be responsible for Preston's."

"Neither would I. My job is bossin' the younger boys, the twins and Al. Do you know them?"

"By sight. . . . See heah, Rock, does Preston split his outfit?"

"Yes. And I'm sort of handlin' the small end of it. These boys are pretty young. We don't have nothin' to do with Preston's butcherin'. Of course I've only been with them a little while. But I know for a fact that it's two years and more since Preston made his younger sons do any of the bloody work."

"The hell you say!" ejaculated Peeples, with a dancing of the brown flecks in his tawny eyes. "Hesbitt doesn't know thet. It's shore news. Mebbe it explains why all the cowpunchers who ever rode for Preston left quick an' spoke well of all but Ash."

"Peeples, I don't see that," complained Rock.

"You don't? Wal, these punchers went heah an' there, all over the range, speakin' good of Gage. If they had knowed any bad they shore would have told it. But if—I say *if*, mind you—there was anythin' off color, they had no chance to see it, an' didn't stay long enough to suspect. All the same, Preston had the benefit of honest cowboys in his outfit. D—deep an' slick, *if* thet's the secret."

"Aren't you imaginin' a lot, Peeples?" queried Rock, made testy by the rider's keen deductions.

"Shore. But how'd you figger if you was me—on the outside?" demanded Peeples.

Rock found that an embarrassing and confounding query.

Peeples spread his hands. "You know d—well you'd figger same as me," he said, succinctly. "An' now aboot your connection with Preston. Speaks high for him to have you in his outfit. True Rock, clean an' square range-rider! Old hand at the game! Rode for the best ranchers in the Territory! . . . Sounds awful good when some new cattleman like Hesbitt or some wonderin' puncher gets to talkin'. . . . Rock, if Preston keeps you out there it's a safe bet he *is* rustlin' an' will ring you in with him, by hook or crook."

"So that's your angle?" muttered Rock, in deep thought. "Suppose I were to tell it to Ash Preston?"

"Wal, you'd drive me into a gun deal. An' you'd be breakin' confidence. I took it you aboot asked my opinion. After all, Rock, I cain't prove nothin'."

153

"I'll keep my mouth shut," rejoined Rock, and indeed his lips were tight as he spoke.

"All right, thet's what I'd expect. An' I'll say a little more. It always struck me thet this bizness of Ash Preston's chasin' the punchers away from Sunset Pass, on account of his sister, was aboot half fraud. I'll bet thet's a put-up job between Ash an' his father."

"I don't know. Sure he tried to chase me away," acknowledged Rock.

"An' played hell doin' it! Ash would have a sweet time chasin' me, too, you can lay to thet," retorted Peeples, as he spat emphatically. "An' last, Rock, take my hunch for what it's worth. As I'd take yours. . . . Grab the girl an' raise the dust away from Sunset Pass. For if anythin' ever comes of this deal—as I suspect—an' you're still with Preston in any capacity, I swear I cain't see how you'd ever square yourself on the range."

The new town hall was the finest structure in Wagontongue, and the civic authorities, who happened to be mostly members of the Cattle Association, were proud of it and its expression of a progressive and prosperous community.

It was of Spanish design, low, rambling, many arched and aisled, painted white, with red tiled roof. Whoever designed it must have had in mind a place for public functions as well as business. The outside had been draped with flags and bunting in celebration of the national holiday. Two aisles with arched walls formed the outside of a large patio. Here and everywhere gay many-colored Chinese lanterns hung, singly from the tops of the arches, and in strings across from wall to wall. Flowers and desert shrubbery lined the walks and circled the fountain, where water tinkled musically. Many chairs had that day been added to the few benches up and down the aisles, in the vine-bowered corners, and along the walls. The large hall, which was to answer many purposes for the townspeople, had been cleared and cleaned, its floor polished, and its ceiling rendered bewilderingly colored with endless streams of bunting. It was empty except for straight chairs set against the wall, on all sides, except at one end, where the platform had obviously been arranged for an orchestra. Flags and sage and evergreen furnished the interior decoration, very simply and attractively.

Trueman Rock strolled from the town hall, which he had inspected along with a multitude of visitors, back to his hotel. The street was full of people. Lobby and saloon were noisy, smoky. He went to his room to avoid the crowd. Events had multiplied already this day. What would the dance and the Fourth bring about? Rock was inclined to the idea that it might be just as well for him to spend the rest of the day in his room. When he left it next he would be in masquerade.

Rock made himself comfortable in a big chair before his open window, and prepared to rest, smoke, and think the tedious hours away.

He ran over in mind a few of the many singular events of the last two days. Thiry Preston's astounding, bewildering, unbelievable attitude! That had not come first, but it always stood first in reflection. His talk with Sol Winter about the beeves, with Amy Dabb about her affairs and the masquerade, with John Dabb about his wife, with Clink Peeples about Amy and the Prestons. That morning Rock had met Hesbitt face to face, to be coldly snubbed. This from the new president of the Cattlemen's Association was not reassuring. Ash Preston was in town, hiding. Al had confided this bit of dismaying news. He had discovered it quite by accident, through a Mexican, and believed that Ash had ridden in under cover of night. The Mexican has said Ash was not drinking. This was even more disturbing than the fact of his presence. Rock had cautioned Al not to tell Thiry. It was possible Ash would not recognize Thiry in her masquerade, and she would have some hours of pleasure, at least till she unmasked. But what was Ash up to? Last night the Cattlemen's Association had met, and though the conference was not supposedly secret, they had most certainly locked the doors on many ranchers and cowboys. This news went the rounds of the hotels and saloons.

After Rock had ruminated over these matters he relegated them to oblivion and returned to the puzzle about Thiry. He could not attend to it soberly; be could not reason it out calmly. Nor could he trust his ecstatic

155

convictions. Gage Preston was a calculating, lying father, trying, for some occult reason, to urge Rock on. Sol Winter was a loving, dreaming old fool. And Rock called himself something similar, minus the old.

Yet how incontestable. Thiry's strange looks and words! They were facts. He knew he was now madly in love, but he could still hear and see. What in the world had gone on in her mind? Preston had incited something. She had committed herself to something before she left Sunset Pass. It did not matter in what degree she had committed herself—for he was involved. How that thrilled through Rock! Then Amy Dabb had shown the cloven hoof. That stirred heat in Rock's veins. He could fancy her pouring confidences into Thiry's innocent ears. False confidences that Rock thought would have hurt and poisoned and destroyed—killed what little interest he might have won from Thiry.

Nevertheless, Thiry had seemed to have admitted him, most probably with all unconsciousness, into a strange intimacy that was not compatible with her desire to have him leave Sunset Pass. This softening, whatever it portended, created a tumult in Rock. No matter if she did not know! Some day, when it was too late, he could tell her. What an exalting prospect!

Thiry had been upset by Amy Dabb, had been rendered angry, doubtful, full of scorn—and, yes, jealous! That was the most amazing thing of all. Thiry was a girl—like other girls—except, of course, lovelier by far, sweeter by far. If she were jealous—if it were actually true—then he owned Amy Dabb a great debt. Amy was certainly the kind to make a high-spirited, complex girl like Thiry very uncomfortable indeed—strike fire from her, put her on her mettle! If Thiry had secretly or even unconsciously been tenderly stirred by her father's avowal of Rock's love, that would account for her reaction to Amy and to him. And Rock sat out the afternoon, thinking, dreaming, with music in his heart.

Darkness had long set in when he left the hotel. He had waited till late, and then the task of donning his masquerade had not been inconsiderable. His appearance, at least of late years, had not occasioned him any bother. But now he was hard to please. Half the time he believed he had never looked so well, and the other half he imagined he looked huge, awkward, silly. At least, however, he managed to satisfy himself sufficiently to venture forth, amused at himself, keen as any cowboy for his first dance. It was well, he thought, that he had purchased a black hat. Its shape troubled him, but would be all the better for his disguise.

In the lobby of the hotel there had been a number of people, several in masquerade, and most ridiculously garbed. Rock tried his disguise, voice as well as suit and mask, upon the clerk, Clark the proprietor, and the porter. They had not recognized him; wherefore he headed toward the town hall, treading on air.

The public square, in the center of which stood the hall, appeared crowded with noisy youngsters, scattered groups of men and women, many Mexicans of both sexes, lounging Indians, whose colored raiment vied with the others, and a host of cowboys in their range clothes.

Rock ran the gauntlet of merry jests, admiring glances from dusky eyes, laughter and query, to the entrance at the main corridor of the hall. Inside the door was a gate, guarded by men, one of whom was the town sheriff, very important and pompous, with his silver badge conspicuous. Two placards struck Rock's eye. One read: NO ADMITTANCE TO ANYONE NOT IN MASQUERADE. And the other sign, larger, read: CHECK YOUR HARDWARE AND BOTTLE.

"Howdy, gambler!" greeted the sheriff. "Scuse me while I search you. Mrs. Dabb's orders."

His second slap at Rock located the gun under the long frock coat.

"Ha! Not on the hip! Hangin' low, eh? Wal, cowboy, unbuckle an' pass."

The heavy gun belt went into the hands of an attendant, who deposited it on a shelf where already a row of weapons glittered. Rock received a ticket.

Rock passed on down the corridor to where it opened into the patio. There was music somewhere and sound of voices and laughter. Then he saw masqueraders in goodly numbers, and he strolled down the right aisle, where under every arch gay young people, safe in their disguises, ogled the strollers and made remarks. The lights from the lanterns were just strong enough to lend glamour and softness to the Spanish aisles, the beautiful patio and the brightly clad maskers.

Cowboys were present in numbers, all masked, some of them with ludicrous false faces, and some in chaps and boots and spurs, in gaudy vests and blazing scarves. Among the girls, three out of five were dressed in Mexican garb, no doubt owing to its color and charm. Rock noticed one girl, striking in Indian costume of exceeding richness, who he stared at as she passed by alone. He strolled around the patio, peeped in at the dance-hall, the floor of which shone like a shield. A few masqueraders in a group were just inside, gayly guessing at one another's identity. The musicians had not arrived.

Arriving at the main corridor again, Rock halted against the wall to watch the fast arriving guests come in. It would indeed be a gala night for Wagontongue. From outside came the faint reports of firecrackers. Merry laughter everywhere! All seemed most curious, friendly, yet aloof in their own safe disguises. So far there did not appear to be any comic costumes, although there were many huge-nosed false faces.

A girl, slight of stature, passed Rock to peer at him with challenging eyes, disguised if not hidden by a red mask. Her costume was Spanish, gold and black, very graceful and pretty. It could not be Amy, for surely she would wear something magnificent. A masker in cowboy attire accosted her, to be gayly repulsed. She passed on, and Rock forgot her in his growing, searching gaze for some one he would know the instant she appeared. What would Thiry wear? Guests were arriving more thickly now. Rock heard the tuning of orchestra instruments. There were bustle and excitement, confusion owing to the evident fact that all were strangers. A clever masquerader, impersonating a negro preacher, passed; Rock noted a woman, typical of the pioneer West; then came an Irish laborer, covered with dust, red-headed, with a stubby pipe stuck in his false face; next a Spanish matador, admirably gotten up in what must have been a real bullfighter's costume. A shepherd boy came arm in arm with a dairy maid. These two knew each other, surely. A cowboy—Rock knew he was one from his bowed legs—presented a capital counterfeit of a cavalry officer, though his costume had seen better days. Then entered a bandit, an outlaw, a miner, and a clown. Rock decided that the masculine contingent was to afford the humor of the occasion; the feminine departed rarely from the eternal vanity. But that pleased Rock. Let the men play ugly, funny parts; let the woman typify beauty.

Some one took his arm lightly.

"Buenas tardes, señor," said a low voice at his elbow.

Rock bowed gallantly to the slim creature on his arm. He did not recognize her, but saw that she was the Spanish girl in gold and black.

"Buenas tardes, señorita," replied Rock, peering into the black holes in the red mask.

She averted her face and walked with him, surely aware of the attention they roused. Rock grudgingly accorded her the admiration she deserved. He had wanted to save all for Thiry. Surely this could not be Thiry, although a Spanish costume like this was deceiving. Her little head, half hidden by the mantilla, did not come up quite to his shoulder. Thiry was taller, and not so slim.

Rock grasped suddenly that there appeared to be a little pressure on his arm, a gradual but sure guidance of his steps. Being intent upon this unknown lady who had taken possession of him, Rock had not observed where they were heading. He was to find that they were entering the dance-hall, where many masqueraders had assembled, plainly awaiting the mysterious first partner that chance might bestow upon them. This Spanish girl was enterprising, not to say bold. Rock felt himself further drawn into the subtle charm of the atmosphere. Then the orchestra burst into music, a languorous Spanish waltz, once Rock's great favorite. The girl who had led him there swayed to the rhythm, toward him, slowly lifting her hand to his shoulder.

"You handsome gambler! You don't know me!" she cried, in arch reproach.

"Amy!" exclaimed Rock, incredulously.

"Sure. Do you like me in this costume?"

"Great! You sure are a Spanish girl. Fooled me plumb good."

"Not a soul recognized me," she said, in delight. "I'll tell no one but you. . . . Come, this is your old favorite waltz."

Before Rock new what was happening she was in his arms, light as thistle-down, and they were whirling, gliding to dreamy strains that found the old chord deep in his memory.

"Trueman, hold me tighter," she whispered, and leaned back against his arm, to look up at him. The dark eyes seemed inscrutable wells under the red mask.

"Behave yourself, Mrs. Dabb," he returned, warningly, with a laugh. "Reckon I don't know quite all due my hostess, but sure not that."

"Hold me tighter, True. This may be the last wicked, happy time of my life."

"Hope you don't expect to die?" queried Rock, in mock alarm.

"Well, if you won't, I'll have to hug you," she went on, and she did, to Rock's confusion. "Oh, I could hug you and kiss you before everybody! . . . Trueman, *what* did you do to my husband?"

"Did I do anythin'?" asked Rock, helpless in the unexpectedness of this attack. His old knowledge of Amy's resourcefulness tried in vain to fortify him.

"Did you? . . . Trueman, he came home the other day, at noon—something unheard of," she went on, swiftly. "He told me you'd been in to see him. That you had raked him over the coals. That you had cleared up something about you and me! . . . Then he told me he had been sore and jealous for a long time. He admitted being mean, selfish, suspicious. He'd neglected me shamefully. He would turn over a new leaf. He would try to be young again. . . . Oh, he knocked me cold! . . . Since then he has been like he was when he courted me. . . . And most amazing of all, he's to drop in here tonight—in masquerade. He wouldn't even tell what he'd wear."

"Good Lord!" said Rock, under his breath.

"You should say thank the good Lord."

"Sure I meant that."

"How'd you do it, old boy? It's a miracle.—And maybe it's not too late. I was—I guess, on the ragged edge."

"All past, Amy," he said, cheerfully.

"I don't know, Trueman. You can't kill the devil so quickly. But I'm happy tonight—as I haven't been in years. . . . But I forgot to tell you something else. I

160

oughtn't tell you. But I can't act a lie tonight. You know I was scared of Clink Peeples. I wondered what you'd do to him. I didn't dare turn round after you pushed him away from me. I ran. Well, today I met Peeples. Really, Trueman, I don't believe it was flattering. Anyway, he apologized for insulting me. He owned up to a shameful opinion of me—for which he said I was part to blame. All the same he said he'd ask me to marry him if I was single, or ever were. Then he advised me to 'lay off the cowpunchers'! Fancy that! . . . Now, Trueman, what did you do or say to Clink?"

"Amy, it was nothin' but talkin' square," he replied, frankly.

"Square," she murmured, wonderingly, as if she had an unexpected glimmering. Then leaning her head forward to his shoulder she grew silent. Rock was reminded that the better side of Amy had always come uppermost when she was dreamily, happily excited. When whe was jealously excited she was about as tractable as a wildcat. Round and round they swung amid the colorful murmuring throng. The scrape and thud of cowboy boots drowned the patter and slide of lighter-footed dancers. Then suddenly the music ceased.

"Trueman, you always were such a wonderful dancer," murmured Amy, still under a spell.

"Dog-gone! I clean forgot I was awful worried about my dancin'," replied Trueman. "Why, Amy, I haven't danced in years!"

"I wish I had every dance with you."

"You flatter me, Amy. But it sure tickles me."

"Of course you'll dance often with Thiry Preston?" she asked, the old jealousy flaring up.

"Reckon I haven't the nerve yet to ask even one. Besides, I probably won't recognize her."

"Bah! That girl couldn't disguise herself in a burlap sack," returned Amy, flippantly.

Amy's last words added to Rock's sudden realization of what thin ice he was skating on.

"Trueman, I'll have to stand for you paying some attention to Thiry," went on Amy, passionately. "But be careful. You don't want me to go to the devil. . . . If you dance more with her than with me—Lord help *her!*"

161

"Amy! What nonsense!" returned Rock, sharply. "I don't like your hint. . . . But don't let anythin' spoil this dance for you. There's very little chance of my dancin' with Thiry."

"*Quien sabe?*" she replied, mockingly. "Come, I'll have to go out. Many of my guests are not here yet. I want to watch."

Amy must have had certain duties as a hostess, for outside she slipped away from Rock and mingled with the laughing, curious assemblage. He made no effort to follow. She had at first roused all his kindlier feelings, then she had alienated him. He feared Amy Dabb could not be influenced or led except through submission to her imperious will.

Rock haunted the long corridor, studying the new arrivals, that were still coming in numbers. When the music started up again, most of the masqueraders went into the hall, if not with partners, then hoping to find them. Rock remained at the entrance to the patio, and was standing close to the wall, when a small party entered the corridor and came quickly down. There appeared to be half a dozen youths in nondescript masquerade, and several girls, two of whom, attired in white, stood out prominently.

"Look!" spoke up a woman to her neighbor on a bench near Rock. "That girl in white. Colonial wedding-gown! Isn't she just lovely? Who can it be?"

On the other side of Rock a cowboy, standing at ease, punched his comrade.

"Pard, see what's comin'," he said, pointing. "How'n hell would a fellar ever get close enough to thet dame to dance?"

"Wal, he shore couldn't hug her in thet outfit. More'n likely he'd tangle his feet," replied the other, with a chuckle. "So I ain't a-goin' to try."

These remarks caused Rock to take a second glance at the entering party. The girl in simple white was too small of stature to be Thiry; and her companion was too gorgeously arrayed. Nor did the third young lady inspire Rock with any thrilling interest.

It struck him that the girl in the wedding-gown was certainly worth looking at. At first she did not appear to be masked at all, but as she drew closer he saw that

162

he wore a close-fitting mask, scarcely any whiter than her powdered face. Her hair was done up in some amazing style and as colorless as snow. Arms and neck, of exquisite contour, likewise were of a dazzling whiteness. The gown, one of those hoop-skirted, many-ruffled affairs Rock had seen in pictures, took up the space of three ordinarily dressed women. Indeed, there appeared scarcely space enough for the girl to pass him.

Trueman flattened himself against the wall, as he had observed the two cowboys do. Nevertheless, the young lady so marvelously gowned was forced to sweep her skirts aside to avoid contact. She came on. Rock could not determine whether or not her face was beautiful, but he certainly imagined it was. The momentary halting of the party, evidently to choose a direction, brought his Colonial masquerader so close to Rock that he meant to step forward and allow her more room. But she seemed to be looking at him, though her eyes were hardly discernable. He felt suddenly rooted to the spot.

"Gurls, you shore passed the dressin'-room," remarked one of the youths.

They turned, some of them laughing, and the wonderful girl in white pressed close to Rock in passing, still apparently gazing at him. As the soft, fluffy, perfumed gown swept him, Rock felt a hand touch his—slip a folded paper into his palm with quick pressure. Then she passed and he leaned there staring. She vanished with the others.

Rock's trembling fingers tightened on the paper. It was a note. That girl had been Thiry. In one glance she had pierced his disguise. And he had been far indeed from returning the compliment. What a joke on him! His vaunted perspicacity, his vain sense of a lover's assurance, went into eclipse. And in its place shot a thrill at her cleverness, her superb masquerade. Swift on that followed a shock at the significance of her action. Coming down to earth with a jerk, Rock peered into his palm at the note, then rushed off to find a light by which he could read it. All the swinging lights were Chinese lanterns and those stationary on the walls were dimmed by colored paper. Finally he found one under which he thought he could discern the writing, and here, after a keen glance around, he opened the note.

163

I will know you the instant I lay eyes on you. Will you me? I am in terrible fear, but I will come to the dance, cost what it may.

Ash is in town, hiding. I do not know what he means. It may be there is some other reason for his action. Allie and I will go to the Farrells' to dress, and come with their crowd.

Ash never saw my great-grandmother's wedding-dress. He won't recognize me, when he comes. *For he will come!* You must keep close watch over me, else I would not dare take the risk. He is capable of stripping me before the crowd. I will dance with the Farrell boys a little—the rest with you. I shall not stay till they unmask. I want to go before he knows me. You must take me away before that.

It may be madness. But I let my heart become set on this one dance. I grow furious at the thought of giving it up. I don't know myself of late. I *will* come—if only to—

Thiry.

Rock did not draw a breath during his swift perusal of this note. Then he gasped—and devoured it again. Though he could not believe he was awake the words were there, on white paper, in ink, clear and firm, in even, beautiful script.

What did they betray? He could not subdue his pounding heart, but he strangled the leaping, whirling, rapturous thoughts. Her letter betrayed terror, yet a woman's willful longing for a little freedom, a little joy of youth. She asked his protection. Thiry Preston—who not long before had begged him to leave her! When Rock read again the sentence in which she confessed that Ash was capable of stripping her before the crowd, in his sudden realization of its content he froze in deadly fury. But it shook him and passed with the realization that she had promised to dance mostly with him. Lastly she did not know herself. She would come, if only to—To what! Rock stormed at his insane hopes. This girl was admitting him into sweet and heart-lifting intimacy, but he must not be wild in his judgments. Why was she going to come? If only to—outwit Ash Preston once in her life! If only to—have a little of the pleasure she had been weak enough to dream of—that all girls yearned for! If only to—see how true had been Amy Dabb's confidences! If only to—confound her awakening heart with the shamelessness of a man! If only to—yield to irresistible temptation to see if Trueman Rock was the lover of Amy Dabb! Any one and all of these intentions might have been in Thiry's mind while she penned that impulsive, poignant letter.

Rock placed the note inside his vest and strode back toward the corridor, his breast throbbing, his head high, his step buoyant, his nerves vibrant.

As he entered the corridor, Thiry came out of a door halfway down and seemed to float toward him. They met, both aware of others present. Rock, removing his hat, made her an elaborate bow.

"Lady from Virginia, I salute you," he said gallantly.

"Sir Knight of the Card Table," she replied, and offered her hand.

Rock clasped it and kissed it with the old-fashioned courtesy due the character she personified. But they acted no more. She seemed silently confused as he led her to the patio. There in the subdued glow of the lanterns they were comparatively alone.

"Thiry! You paralyzed me," he said, at length. "I didn't know you. I didn't *know* you. . . . And, oh, how lovely you look!"

She murmured her thanks. They stood under an archway beside the fountain. The falling water tinkled in harmony with the soft strains of music. For them it was neither the place nor the time for calmness.

"How ever did you know me?" he asked.

"I just did," she replied.

"But how?"

"It was the way you stood."

"Reckon that makes me awful happy—an' fearful, too, Thiry."

"You!—You have little to be fearful about. But I—"

"Never mind. If I ever had eyes I'll use them tonight. I'll let no insult, no humiliation touch you. . . . Thiry, where'd you get that gorgeous gown?"

"It was my great-grandmother's wedding-dress. We are from Virginia."

"Virginia? Your father told me Missouri."

"Yes, after the war. I was little then. The war ruined us and we moved to Missouri."

"Ahuh! . . . Thiry, I always wondered about you. Was Preston a rebel?"

"All Prestons were rebels."

"You too?"

"Yes, as far as a child could understand. But those days and influences are past forever, thank God. . . . Ash is the only one of us who is still a rebel."

"Fine feathers make fine birds," rejoined Rock. "You were always pretty to look at, in anythin'. But now you're—oh!—beyond the poor compliments—and hopes, too, I reckon, of a range-rider."

"I'm glad you like me, Trueman, but don't rub it in," she said, naïvely. "In a few days I'll bake bread and milk the cows again."

"You'll be all the better for that."

The music ceased and the gay dancers poured out of the hall to promenade in couples and quartettes and crowds, all intent, it appeared, to peep under masks and find one another out.

"My brothers—the twins and Al—and the Farrell boys know me, of course," said Thiry, as if remembering where she was. "We must find them. Then after a few dances I'll be free—if—if you—"

"Thiry, there's no if—now or ever," he replied, unsteadily.

"Will you dance while I dance?"

"No. I'll watch you—and see if anyone else is watchin' you."

"Oh, but surely you must *want* to dance some?" she queried.

"Only with you."

"Not Amy Dabb?" she flashed, with odd inflection of voice.

"Not Amy Dabb," he said, turning to find her face averted.

"But, Trueman, she is your hostess. If I remember correctly, she meant to embody the duty of all her masculine guests in *your* attendance."

166

"Did she?" replied Rock, a little nettled at her satire. "You mean she gave you a hunch I'd dance all *my* dances with her?"

"Something or other like that," murmured Thiry.

"Reckon she was just talkin'. She was wrong."

"Then *I* was wrong to believe her. Forgive me. . . . But I didn't see how you could be so—so—such a liar."

"Thiry, I couldn't lie to you," he returned, with low voice ringing. "Save me agony by believin' that now. For some day you'll know."

"But you must dance with your hostess—at least once," said Thiry, hastily.

"Once.—Would you stand for it once?"

"*I!* . . . Stand for it? I fear you—"

"No," he interrupted. "Now don't get proud. I might stand it out at the Pass. But not here, with you in that dress. . . . I mean, straight out—do you *want* me to dance with you instead of Amy Dabb?"

"Yes, I do," she returned, hotly. "She hurt me. She said catty things all in a nice way. She offered to lend me a dress. She made me feel a—a country bumpkin. . . . I told you before what she hinted about you. It's selfish, little, miserable of me to want to show her.—But she made me almost hate her."

"Thiry, my obligation is paid," replied Rock, trying to contain himself. "I have had that one dance with Mrs. Dabb. She met me. I didn't recognize her until she made herself known. It's over. So there."

"I'd like you to dance with Allie," returned Thiry, shyly. "She won't tell on you. For that matter, it'd be fun, if we can fool her."

"Fine. Let's find her and your friends."

Chapter Eleven

Thiry had introduced Rock to her sister Alice as Señor Del Toro of Las Vegas. And Rock felt that so far as dancing was concerned he had acquitted himself creditably. But his stock of Spanish words was much

167

more limited than Alice's, which, now that the dance had ended, began to be embarrassingly manifest.

He had enjoyed this dance with Alice more even than the one with Amy Dabb. Alice was like a fairy on her feet and Rock could not have forced her out of step if he had tried. And as for dancing, this time he put his mind on it, endeavoring to do it well. He was thinking, perhaps, of the dances with Thiry so perilously close.

"Señor, hadn't we better talk English?" inquired Alice, mischievously.

They were sitting in one of the corner bowers of the patio, a place Rock had spied out and which he thought would not be known to many. His idea was to get Thiry there.

"Certainly, señorita. I thought you were Spanish, too. I speak English," replied Rock, disguising his voice.

"I think I've heard you."

"Indeed? Where, may I inquire?"

"At my home—Sunset Pass."

"Then I have had the honor of being at your home? Sunset Pass? I don't recall it. But I've been asked to so many *haciendas*."

Alice laughed merrily. "You look very grand as a Spanish gambler, but you're really one of my Dad's cowpunchers."

"Alice Preston! You smart little rascal!" ejaculated Rock, greatly amused. "Then we didn't fool you at all?"

"Oh yes, you did! I was taken in, all right, and I was thrilled to death. But I grew suspicious before the dance was over."

"Well, sure it was fun. I'm glad you discovered me, for now I can talk. . . . Allie, doesn't Thiry look just gorgeous?"

"Yes, she's lovely. You'd hardly know her. Thiry carries this sort of thing off beautifully. Her masquerade is the finest here, don't you think?"

"Reckon I know, Allie. She's got them beaten a mile. But you look pretty sweet yourself. I'd choose you about next, if I was a judge."

"Thanks. You're a cowboy, all right. . . . But about Thiry—I almost wish she had not come."

"Why?" asked Rock, anxiously.

168

"She's worried half to death. She's game, and only I who know her would even guess it. She's afraid Ash will come here and discover her."

"But, Allie, doesn't Thiry sort of overdo it? Isn't she oversensitive? Sure Ash can't do very much mischief."

"You don't know Ash," returned Alice, concisely. "If he catches her in that dress he'll ruin it. Ash hates to see Thiry make herself so beautiful. I remember when I was a kid, how Ash used to rave if Thiry fixed herself up for a party. If he recognizes her here—good-by to great-grandmother's wedding-gown. It took two hours for Thiry to coax mother to lend her that gown."

"By George! I can't understand it, Allie!" exclaimed Rock, in low anger, clinching his hands. "Why, Allie, to spoil that gown would be vile!"

"He'd do it. But Thiry hopes to fool him. You must help, somehow, Mr. Rock. . . . My sister doesn't say a word, but I guess you had more than a little to do with her wanting to come so bad."

"I wish I could believe that," replied Rock, slowly. "You know she refused to marry me?"

"Yes, Dad told us. But, goodness, Mr. Rock—think how sudden you were! What could you expect?"

"Sure I deserve that. I didn't expect more than I got," went on Rock, eloquently, and then he bent his head close to the girl's. "Allie, can I trust you?"

"Why, of course you can!" she rejoined, manifestly thrilled.

"I'd like you to know what meetin' Thiry has done for me. I used to be a pretty tough cowboy, they tell me. But I can never be again what I was. I will never care for any other girl—no matter what Thiry does to me. I just worship her. To say I love her isn't enough. Please don't think this just the ravin' of a wild cowboy. I'm no boy any more, Allie. I'm thirty-two, old enough to know my mind, don't you think? . . . Well, I'm beggin' you to trust me, to believe in me, and to be my friend. I'll give my word you'll never, never be sorry. . . . When we get back to Sunset Pass I'll not distress Thiry, I'll content myself findin' some way to serve her, and all of you. I'll keep away from her, if that is possible for me, while Ash is there. . . . Will you stand by me, Allie?"

"You bet I will," she replied, with surprising vehemence.

"That makes me your friend for life," said Rock, feelingly.

"Thiry is unhappy, not like her old self. It's the way Ash nags her. Why, she can't call her soul her own. I get so furious. I wouldn't stand it. But Thiry loves Ash as much as I hate him."

"Allie, don't say that. He's your brother."

"I don't care if he is. I ought to be ashamed. But I'm not. I never *felt* like his sister. And you can bet he never treated me as if I were."

"There goes the music," replied Rock, and he arose. "I'll take you back to the hall. . . . Allie, our dance was fine. And I just couldn't say how much our talk means to me."

"Trueman Rock, I can't help but like you," she said, with a serious abruptness that reminded him of Thiry. Rock divined from her words and look that he had been on trial. Then at the door of the hall she squeezed his arm and left him.

Rock became all eyes then. He was no longer a masquerader, nor a lovelorn shadow of his lady. He shifted in one moment to the cool, searching cowboy on a trial. His searching gaze was concerned with the masculine element of that gay crowd. If Ash Preston was there, Rock determined to locate him. It seemed extremely unlikely that Ash would mask and dance in order to spy upon Thiry, but Rock, believing the fellow was capable of anything, had to satisfy himself. He lounged around the door of the hall during two dances before he convinced himself that Ash was not among the cowboys dancing. Then he strolled down one long aisle and up the other, peering at every man and into every shadow. Likewise he searched the patio. Then he went into the corridor and toward the entrance, where the deputy and his sheriffs still held forth, faithful to the duty imposed upon them. When Ash Preston came in he would have to be masked and he could not hide a gun from those laconic Westerners. This afforded Rock relief. Returning to his post just inside the dance-hall door, he took up his vigil there.

Another dance had just started. The big hall was a

wonderful spectacle of movement, color, youth, beauty, and humor, for some of the cowboys were enough to make anyone laugh. They were growing noisy, too, but it was only hilarious fun. Rock did not see an objectionable thing. Certainly there had never been such a dance before in that country. They were making the most of it, and Rock, in his mind's eye, could see them telling around the camp fires of the future the story of that wonderful affair.

Then he espied Thiry, conspicuous in white and notable for her grace. She was dancing with one of the lanky youths with whom she and Alice had come. Either he was a capital dancer or inspired by his partner. As they came around in the gliding circle she espied Rock over her partner's arm. What a smile she gave Rock! It made his heart beat faster. She appeared flushed under the white mask and powder. No doubt of her enjoyment! Probably for the hour she had forgotten the menace of Ash Preston. Soon that dance ended, and as the laughing throng pressed in a stream out the door, some one—a woman—thrust her face close under Rock's.

"Traitor!" she whispered, and went on. The wine-dark hot eyes, through the red mask, the gold-and-black Spanish gown, so striking on the slender figure, belonged to Amy Dabb.

Trueman whistled to keep from swearing. He had actually forgotten Amy. Dance after dance had gone by, and he had never even seen her. But suppose he had! His dismay was short-lived, in that he looked around from the disappearing Amy to see Thiry close at hand, coming alone.

"Señor del Toro, you look lonesome," she said, gayly. "Are there no charming señoritas here?"

"I can see only one."

"You have not danced?"

"Once, with Allie. Sure she is a bird."

"Then you enjoyed it?"

"Wonderful! And the little minx soon saw through my disguise."

"Come. The rest is yours," she said, and took his arm.

"Have you enjoyed yourself?" he asked, as they mingled with the merry masqueraders in the patio.

"Oh, so much! It has been such fun. And I remembered I loved to dance. Then the music, the costumes, the excitement—oh, I can't tell you."

"Has anyone discovered you?"

"Only one I know of, Amy Dabb. She was quick to see through it."

"Well. Did she say anythin'?"

"I rather think so."

"What?" asked Rock, intensely.

"She said: 'Hello, Thiry! You look great. But wedding-gowns don't always mean wedding-bells.' "

"Humph! That was sweet of Amy, now. She has a nasty tongue, as I well know. . . . Thiry, I reckon there's not a young man at this dance who wouldn't ring weddin'-bells for you."

"Rash flattery, Trueman," she retorted. "There must be many. I know five boys who are madly in love with their prospective partners."

"Five? . . . You mean six!" rejoined Rock.

"No. There are Al and Tom and Hal, my brothers. Then the two Farrell boys. I don't know anyone else here."

"Thiry, I make number six," said Rock, and quickly looked away, too guilty to dare to see how she took his remark. She made no reply at all. In silence they went the rounds of the patio, then up one arched aisle and down another, back to the dancing-floor. The music blared out. From behind, the eager masqueraders pressed, and Rock found himself in the hall.

Thiry looked up with inscrutable eyes.

"You broke your word. You make me remember," she said, reproachfully, as she gave way to his encircling arm.

A pang shot through Rock, but he did not think it was remorse. The miracle that tore him was his possession of this lovely girl. She was in his arms. She yielded to, rather than resisted, the close embrace he could not have forsworn to save his life. Rock was vaguely aware of the swaying, gliding, circling dancers, the grotesque masks, the low roar of voices mingled with sliding feet, and the unavoidable contacts. But the enchantment was Thiry, whose grace equaled Alice's, whose clasping hands and slender form unconsciously belied her reproachful words.

172

That dance was brief as a fleeting moment, but endless in its intangible mystery and joy.

Again they strolled under the magic rose and purple of the dimming lanterns, and on to the secluded bower in the patio. Here the stars shone white and watchful through the foliage. Somewhere a guitar twanged low melody and a girl's sweet voice in Spanish accompanied it. The water tinkled off in the darkness.

"It's very—warm," murmured Thiry, as Rock leaned over her in the shadow.

"Take off your mask," he suggested.

"No, señor."

Trueman took her hand in his. It was an almost instinctive action on his part. She made no attempt to withdraw it, greatly to his surprise and joy.

"Trueman, you must take me home soon," she said, as if coming out of a spell. The time and the place, the languorous atmosphere of this Spanish edifice, which, though new, seemed old in beauty and romance, the music, the dancers, the youth had indeed called to Thiry Preston.

"Oh no, not now. Just one more dance," pleaded Rock. "You said the rest were mine."

"But I'd forgotten."

"What?"

"Ash will come any moment. I feel it—here," she whispered, her hand on her breast.

"Thiry, he is not here now. I've looked clear through every man in the outfit. Please risk it."

"Well, then—one more."

But at the end of this dance she forgot again or could not resist the joy of the hour. Once more Rock led her to their shadowed corner, once more he held an unresisting hand.

"Take off your mask," he begged again.

"Can you put it back on—right?" she replied, a little tremulously.

"Sure I can."

Then she was unmasked under his worshiping eyes, under the dim rose light of the lantern above and the far, white, and knowing stars. Once she lifted her eyes to him—eyes that betrayed the spell of the moment—then no more.

173

"You do not talk, señor," she said, trying for conversation.

"How can I? . . . I'm holdin' your hand."

"Oh, so you are!—Well, let go."

"Pull it away," he whispered, daringly.

But she did not.

Rock won her to stay one more dance, reveled in his power to persuade her, though his conscience flayed him. What risk he might incur for her! But he gambled with his happiness.

"Trueman, we must go now," she said, nervously.

"Yes. But don't you hate to?" he returned, jealously.

"No. I'm too thankful for—for all it's been."

"Thiry, you are warm. We must get somethin' to throw over your shoulders when we go out."

"I have a shawl."

They reached the patio. Something had happened, as Rock guessed from excited voices. A girl cried out in dismay.

"Hey, look out there!" called some one, unmistakably a cowboy.

"He snatched at my mask," replied a girl, angrily.

"He got mine," added another woman, shrilly. "The mean thing. That's no fun."

Rock drew Thiry to the right, out of the press.

"Some cowboy snatchin' masks," he said, hurriedly.

Suddenly into the open space before him leaped a lithe figure of a cowboy, wearing a red handkerchief as a mask. He was as quick as light—so quick that Rock scarcely guessed his purpose in time to thwart it. But Rock was on the wrong side of Thiry. One sweep of hand tore Thiry's mask from her white face! She cried out and spasmodically clutched Rock's arm.

The cowboy appeared to leap up. He snatched off the red handkerchief that masked him, to disclose the livid face of Ash Preston. His evil eyes, like coals of blue fire, flashed over her face, her bare neck and arms, her spreading ruffled gown.

"Ash," gasped Thiry, clutching Rock's arm tighter, "meet Señor del Toro—my masquerade partner!"

"Señor 'ell!" he bit out, incredibly cold and fierce.

174

Like a snake's head his hand shot out, to fasten in Thiry's bodice and tear with fiendish swiftness.

In one single action Rock freed himself from Thiry and struck Preston on the side of the face. He went down with a thud. Women screamed; men shouted excitedly; and all spread back hurriedly. Up bounded Preston, with catlike quickness, his hand flashing back for his gun. But it was not there. He had passed the sheriff and had forgotten. If it were possible his wolfish face gleamed fiercer. His tawny hair stood up.

"Greasér, I'll kill you for thet!" he ground out.

"*Carramba!*" replied Rock, and made at Preston with terrific fury. His onslaught was like a battering-ram. He cared nothing for Preston's sudden blows. He broke through them, beat him back, and knocked him against the wall. Ash fell, but got up cursing, to come back wilder than ever, his face the redder for blood. There was a swift interchange of blows, then one from Rock staggered Preston. Another swift and hard, hitting solid like an ax on beef, sent Preston in a long fall. Before he could rise Rock plunged upon him, beat him with right, left, right, left—tremendous blows that made Ash sink limp. Rock seized him by the neck, choked and shook him as a terrier with a rat, and rising, dragged him to the fountain and threw him bodily into the shallow water. Ash lay on his back, his head just above the surface, and though still conscious he did not have strength to get up.

Rock, remembering his mask, felt for it and found it intact. That helped release him from the grip of an awful anger. Thiry's white mask lay where Preston had dropped it. Snatching it up, Rock whirled to see some woman in the act of covering Thiry's naked shoulders and bosom with a shawl.

"Come—we'll—get out—of here," he panted, hoarsely, and placing a firm hand under her arm he led her away from the gaping crowd, down the corridor toward the outlet. The voices of excited people grew fainter. Rock halted long enough to produce his check and get his gun-belt, which he threw over his left arm.

"What's up in thar?" queried the sheriff, sharply eying Rock.

"Some fool cowboy snatchin' masks off the ladies,"

replied Rock, and hurried Thiry out, through the crowd of Mexicans, to the street and darkness.

Thiry was weak. She leaned on his arm. Still she kept up with his rapid steps. Not for three blocks did Rock speak, nor did she.

"He—didn't know you," she burst out, then. "Called you greaser!"

"Yes, that's the only good thing about it," returned Rock, stirring to recover under such pressure as he had never experienced. He was wringing wet with cold sweat and quivering in all his muscles. A knot of fire within seemed to be loosening. His mouth was dry, his tongue thick.

"My God! What shame—what disgrace—distress I've brought on you!" he muttered when he could speak.

She was sobbing a little and clinging to the arm with which Rock upheld her.

"He tore my waist—almost off. Oh, I don't mind the shame of that—so much. But the gown mother treasured. She loved it so. . . . She'll be heartbroken."

"What's a dress?—That can be—mended," he panted. "But I kept you there. Too long! It was my—fault—my fault."

"I was to blame, too," she said, loyally.

"If I had only left when you wanted to go!" he returned, fiercely. "After my promise to you! God! what luck I have."

"Trueman, I shouldn't have gone. I knew something dreadful would happen. I *told* you. . . . Only he was worse than I ever saw him."

"Worse!—He was a hydrophobia skunk!"

"Oh, Ash! . . . My brother!" she cried, brokenly.

Her grief tortured Rock, but he did not have it in him to retract his words. What language could do justice to Ash Preston! They hurried on, to the edge of town, down the pine-skirted road. The night was starry, almost cool, and the wind moved through the tree-tops. Presently they reached Winter's house, which sat back among the trees. Rock saw a light. He wanted to say good night to Thiry at the gate, but could not. She still clung to him. At the porch he halted, and helped her up. It was shaded there by trees, but he could still see her pale face and the great eyes, strange and dark in the night. Before he

176

knew what he was doing he clasped his arms round her, as she stood a little above him. She did not repulse him, but she pressed her hands against his shoulders. Thus they looked at each other in the shadow.

"Forgive me, Thiry," he implored.

"There's nothing to forgive," she faltered.

"I'll go to my room before anyone sees me. Ash didn't know me. He never will."

"*She* will tell," said Thiry, hopelessly.

"Who? Allie? Oh no. She'll be as true as steel," he declared.

"Not Allie. I mean that jealous woman."

"Amy Dabb!" exclaimed Rock, with a start. "She did know. But she'll have no chance tonight. Reckon your noble brother couldn't hear if she tried to tell him. But they'll pack him out of there pronto. Tomorrow I'll find some way to shut her mouth."

"Yes, you will," said Thiry, with sad derision. "Don't waste your breath, Trueman. Don't ask her. Perhaps it will not occur to her that Ash didn't know you."

"Then let's hope for the best . . . that I won't have to run away to avoid a real fight with Ash."

"Real! I'd like to know what you'd call what you had. But it was one-sided. Scared as I was, I saw that. . . . Trueman, you were wonderful. Oh, if it had not been my brother!"

"He deserved it, Thiry," returned Rock, passionately. "Admit that."

"You beat him terribly. It—hurt me—so. . . . But, oh, he did deserve it."

Rock tightened his arms a little, drew her closer.

"Thiry, kiss me good night," he whispered, suddenly.

"Trueman!" she exclaimed, and tried to draw away. But he held her, and as she turned her face he managed to kiss her cheek.

"Now you've done it!" she cried.

What he had done she did not say, but she ceased to pull away. That emboldened him. Still he drew back the better to see her averted face.

"What's one more offense?" he queried. "I've ruined my hopes tonight—or I have found them glorified. . . . Oh, Thiry—how I love you! . . . Kiss me good night."

"No!" Yet she seemed weakening. He felt her quiver in his arms.

"Then let me kiss you? . . . It might be the first and last time. For if Ash finds me out I'll have to leave this country. Else I'd have to kill him!"

"You'd go away for me?" she flashed, suddenly quickened and revivified, and her hands went to his shoulders.

"I promise you."

"You love me so much?"

"Thiry girl, I love you more than I can prove."

Blindly, with unreckoning impulse, she bent and met his upturned lips with her own. Quickly, with a gasp, she broke away to stare a moment, as if some realization had stricken her, then she fled across the porch and into the house.

Ash Preston did not return to Sunset Pass for a week after the Fourth. Rumor drifted down by a rider that Preston was hunting for the Mexican who had beaten him at the dance.

It was an anxious and brooding time for Trueman Rock, more, perhaps, because of Thiry's unconcealed dread than for his own sake. Nevertheless, he never drew an easy breath, despite the rumor, until Ash returned, sober yet showing the effects of a prolonged debauch. One moment Rock stood on the porch, his hand quivering, while Ash strove over from his cabin. Sullen, his face black and blue, still swollen, he presented no encouraging aspect. But manifestly that moment proved he did not know or suspect Rock had been his assailant. Then the suspense of this meeting for Rock ended when Thiry almost fainted in Ash's arms. Not improbably her relief was so great that she succumbed under it. Certainly, however, no one save Rock took it that way.

"Aw, Thiry, I'm sorry," rasped out Ash, while he held her on the bench. Tears were streaming down his bruised cheeks. "I was drunk thet night. . . . I'll never go to town no more."

How utterly incongruous his repentance seemed to Rock! Pity could not abide in Rock's heart—not for this man.

This had happened in the middle of the afternoon,

upon Ash's arrival home. Gage Preston was absent. It was Rock's opinion that Gage did not care to be present when Ash met Thiry and Rock. A maddening flash of thought came to Rock, following the collapse of his reinforced nerve. This issue had only been postponed! All the anxious speculation, the worry wearing into dread, the sickening realization that Thiry was growing strained, pale, the waiting suspense, and then this sudden release—all these in vain!

Yet, even a respite, considering Thiry, was something blessed, and for which he gave profound thanks. Supper that night no longer seemed something like a funeral feast. Gage Preston came in late, and his gruff heartiness, his steely glance, embracing Ash and Thiry and Rock, were strangely at variance. Rock felt that after a short absence, in which incalculable changes had taken place, he was about to see a new phase in Preston's complex character.

Rock did not tarry with the family. He carried away with him a look from Thiry's eyes—the first in which she had met his since that unforgettable last moment on Winter's porch—and it drove him to pace under the pines, to throw back his head, to fill his lungs with the sage-laden air of the Pass, to cast exultant defiance up at the silent, passionless white stars.

He paced a beat from the open back to the gloom of the thick-spreading trees. On the soft mats of pine needles his feet made no sound; against the black shadow of the slope his figure could not be seen. But his own sharp eye caught a dark form crossing in front of a cabin light. He heard a voice low but clear—Gage Preston's: "Ash, come hyar."

Then two dark forms made black upright bars, to obliterate the light, then passed on. Rock watched, crouching to peer through the gloom. Suddenly he made them out, perilously close upon him. Silently he sank behind the log by which he had crouched, immensely glad that it lay between him and the approaching men.

"What you want?" growled Ash.

"Not so loud, you — — — —!" replied Preston, in low harsh tones. "I want to talk."

"Wal, I ain't in no humor."

"Sit down there," ordered Preston, with heavy contact of hand upon his son's person.

179

Rock felt the jar of the log where evidently Preston had pushed Ash. Noiselessly craning his neck, Rock saw the dim figure of the father, bending over. Then Rock espied Ash sitting not ten feet from where he lay. It seemed to Rock that cold blood oozed from his very marrow. If caught there he would have to fight for his life. Almost he ceased to breathe. The pounding of his heart sounded like a muffled drum.

"What the hell's got into you?" demanded Ash.

"What the hell's got into *you*—thet you hang on in town, lookin' for trouble, makin' more fer me?" countered the father, sternly.

"Some greaser punched me, an' I stayed to find him."

"Punched you! Aw, why don't you be game? He beat you till you were senseless."

"Ahuh. Wal, if you knowed it why'n hell bother me? It don't make me cheerful."

"But I needed you hyar," replied Preston, trying to stifle rage that would not down. "There's work no one else can do."

"But, Pa, I wanted to kill thet Señor del Toro," protested Ash, almost plaintively.

"Bah! Señor del Toro? Why, you lunkhead, thet make-believe Spaniard was Trueman Rock!"

"Hell, no!" snapped Ash, hotly. "I had thet hunch. But I was wrong. Next mornin' I went to Thiry. I told her thet black-masked pardner of hers was Rock an' I was a-goin' to kill him. She fell on her knees. An' she wrapped her arms around me. An' she swore to God it wasn't Rock. . . . Pa, I had to believe her. Thiry never lied in her lfe."

"Mebbe I'm wrong," choked Preston, as if a will not his own wrenched that admission from him. "But whoever he was he gave you plumb what I'd have given you. Everybody says so. Wade Simpson told me. An' Slagle said it only today."

"Ahuh? Wal, two more fer bullet holes," drawled the son, in deadly menace.

"Talk sense," fumed Preston. "I'm shore gettin' leary about you. Man alive, you can't shoot everybody on the range. An' haven't you any decency? To rip Thiry's dress half off before a crowd. Why, you — — — —!"

180

"Aw, Pa, I was drunk. When I see Thiry with her shoulders an' bosom all bare—before them men—I said by God she'd stand naked before them an' me."

"Drunk?—Man, you were crazy," retorted the father, hoarsely. "You'll never live thet down. But thet's nothin' for you to care about. The thing is you disgraced Thiry. You shamed her. You hurt her so she's been ill. She—who's loved you all her life!"

"Shet up, Pa," wailed Ash, writhing. "I can stand anythin' but thet."

"Wal, you shore have a queer streak in you. Yellow clear through when it comes to Thiry. But fer her you'd be a man. An' we could go on with our work thet's callin' fer all a man's brains."

"I'll make it up to Thiry," returned Ash, hurriedly. "She'll forgive me. I'll never do thet no more."

"You can't be relied upon, as you used to be," returned the rancher, bitterly. "Now listen, somethin's up out there on the range. I've done some scoutin' around lately. I've talked with the Mexican sheepherders. Too many riders snoopin' around Sunset Pass! Today I seen some of Hesbitt's outfit. An' Slagle asked me sarcastic like why Clink Peeples was over hyar so much. . . . Ash, there's a nigger in the woodpile. I shore don't like the smell."

"Clink Peeples had better keep away from the Pass."

"There you go again. What good will it do to throw a gun on Peeples? If they're suspicious, thet'd only make them worse. . . . What'd you do with them last Half Moon hides?"

"I hid them."

"Where?"

"In a good place, all right."

"D—you! Didn't you take them to Limestone Cave, as I ordered you?"

"I packed some there. It was too far, an' I was tuckered out. I hid the rest under the culvert."

"But I told you not to hide any more there. I always was scared of thet culvert. Once a big rain washed some out. It could happen again."

"Wal, it ain't too late. I'll take Boots tomorrow night, an' we'll pack the fresh ones over to Limestone."

"No. The ground's soft since it rained. You'd leave

181

tracks. An' thet's too risky with these new riders searchin' around. Better leave them. An' we'll lay off butcherin' fer a spell."

"Lay off nothin'. With all them orders fer beef? I guess not. Pa, there's room fer a thousand hides down in the old well."

"Ash, I tell you we'll lay off killin' till this suspicion dies down," said Preston, in hoarse earnestness, fighting for patience.

'Wal, I won't lay off, an' I reckon I can boss the boys," replied Ash, implacably.

Then Preston cursed him, cursed him with every hard word known to the range, and some besides, cursed until he was spent from passion, when he fell heavily to a seat on the log.

"This hyar rider, Rock," spoke up Ash, as if he had never heard the storm of profanity, "when you goin' to fire him?"

"Rock? Not at all," replied Preston, wearily. He was beaten.

"Wal, then, I will. He's been around too long, watchin' Thiry, an' mebbe us, too."

"Ash, haven't you sense enough to see thet Rock's bein' hyar is good fer us?" asked Preston, girding himself afresh. "Never was a rider hyar so trusted as Rock. Thet diverts suspicion from us. It was lucky he came."

"But he might find us out."

"It ain't likely. Shore he doesn't want to."

"He might stumble on to it by accident. Or get around Thiry an' scare it out of her."

"Wal, if he *did*, thet wouldn't be so bad. She could keep his mouth shut. He loves her well enough to come in with us. Only I'd hate like hell to ask her to do it."

"An' if she did win him over, what would *he* want?" hissed Ash.

"Huh! Reckon thet's easy to answer. An' I'm tellin' you, Ash, Thiry would like Rock if she had half a chance."

A knife plunged into Ash's vitals could scarcely have made him bend double and rock to and fro, like that thrust of Preston's.

"She'd like him, huh? So thet's why she made me promise not to pick a fight with him. . . . Hell's fire!"

"Wal, Ash, if circumstances come up we can't help or beat, what'n hell can we do? I told you ages ago thet Thiry is bound some day to love some lucky rider. It can't be helped. An' it might be Rock. Which'd be most infernal lucky fer us."

"Lucky fer him! Haw! Haw!—I'd shoot his heart out."

Preston rose to loom darkly, menacingly over his son.

"You can't murder him in his sleep, or shoot him in the back. Thet'd look bad in Wagontongue. It'd just about ruin us. An' if you call him out to an even break—why, Ash, he'll kill you! Savvy? You shore ought to be keen enough to see it. Rock is cold as ice, as quick as lightnin'. He has a hawk eye. I'm warnin' you, Ash."

The son leaped up as if sprung. "So help me Gawd! You're tryin' awful hard to keep us apart. Haw! Haw! ... No, Pa, I don't savvy you!"

Chapter Twelve

Long after the Prestons stalked away Rock lay behind the log, thinking over the peril he had been in and the revelation that had accompanied it.

Late he stole like an Indian to his cabin, made his bed inside, and barring the door, lay down just as he was. Sleep was neither desirable nor possible. The certainty of the Prestons' guilt was not the staggering detail of that disclosure. Rock pinned down some grim facts.

Thiry had lied to deceive Ash as to her escort at the dance. Ash did not know then, but sooner or later he would find out. There was more suspicion directed toward the Prestons than Rock had known. The case was growing critical. Gage Preston knew it. He wanted to avert catastrophe; but for this vicious son he not improbably could have done so. But Ash Preston dominated father and brothers. He would ride to his doom. Rock had met many of that Western type, and every single one of them had died with his boots on.

Preston had told his son that Señor del Toro was Rock. Here Rock had an icy, sickening portent—one which he had been on the verge of before—Preston wanted to force a fight between him and Ash. He knew that Rock would kill his son. There seemed no other possible interpretation. He had deliberately suggested they persuade Thiry to make Rock one of them. By fair means or foul! This betrayed Preston's extremity. Lastly the cunning Ash was growing suspicious of his father.

Out of all this only calamity could come to Thiry, unless Rock by some means was able to avert it. He was at his wits' end. He had never heard of such an overwhelming predicament as the one that now struck him to desperation. If he could only call Ash out and shoot him! But this would break Thiry's heart and make him an object of horror in her eyes. He simply could not do that—not to save Gage Preston from jail and Thiry from disgrace. At length, worn out by contending tides, he rolled over and went to sleep.

In the morning he watched from his window until Ash left, then went out to breakfast. The children were there, gay and chattering as usual. Thiry did not appear. Preston came out while Rock was eating and said:

"Rock, I've a job for you that'll take you away some time."

"Fine. I need some real work," replied Rock.

"Reckon you'll find it that. The boys are gettin' a pack outfit ready. They know where to go. I want five hundred head of two-year-old steers in the flat down there by Slagle's ranch. By August."

"Boss, it can't be done," protested Rock.

"It's got to be."

"With three half-grown cowpunchers?"

"Wal, you've been hollerin' fer some real work. Pack an' rustle."

"You're the boss, Preston. But are you sure you won't need me more right here?"

Preston bent toward Rock and lowered his voice. "It ain't what I'd like or need. I had no idee last night thet I'd send you off this mornin'. But it popped into my head."

"Ahuh! Who popped it?"

"Thiry. She asked me to. Ash is wuss than ever before. An' fer once Thiry seemed to be thinkin' of somebody else but him."

"How is she feelin', Preston?" asked Rock, anxiously.

"Wal, she perked up when I told her I'd send you."

"Suits me fine. Don't mind tellin' you, boss, that Ash is almost gettin' on my nerves."

"Haw! Haw! Almost gettin', hey? Wal, if you ain't made out of stone I'll eat my hat. My nerves *are* shot to pieces."

Rock got up and stepped over the bench, without looking at Preston.

"Small wonder, boss. Reckon you'd do well to hawg-tie Ash an' hang round the Pass for a month."

This speech had been the outcome of impressions Rock had received from Preston's manner and words. He spoke it curtly, with never a glance, then walked away toward his cabin. It did not suit Rock just then to leave the Pass without a hint to Preston. He believed it would be interpreted that Wagontongue gossip had reached his ears and might be worth heeding. Let Preston ponder over that advice and see how far he got. This might pave the way to something deeper.

Rock repaired to his cabin and rolled his bed and packed the things he would need. Several times during the process he went to the window to peer out. The clip-clop of hoofs drew him again. Ash and Boots Preston were riding by, headed east. Rock's quick eye noted saddle-bags, blankets, ropes. And he guessed that the contrary Ash meant to disobey his father and remove the fresh hides from the culvert to a better hiding-place.

"Ride on, you lean-jawed wolf!" muttered Rock.

When they were out of sight, Rock wavered between two strong desires—to see Thiry before he left and write to her. The better course would be to write, because he could put on paper what there would be no chance to speak. No sooner did he decide than he realized it was an opportunity not to be lost. Therefore, with lead pencil and paper he sat down to his little table and began, with hand that he could not keep steady and heart which accelerated a beat for every word.

Thiry Darling,

Your Dad has ordered me away for several weeks, maybe more. I am glad to go, though not to see your sweet face for so long will be terrible. But I shall work like a beaver, and content myself with thinking of you by day and dreaming of you by night—with praying for your happiness and welfare.

I want you to know this, so that while I'm gone you may remember me often. My conscience flays me still for what I brought upon you at the dance. But I don't ask forgiveness for that so much as for what happened on Winter's porch. Still, if I had no more to sustain me, Thiry, through what seems to be the hardest trial of my life, that kiss you gave me would be enough. I know you meant only unheeding gratitude. But nevertheless you kissed me, and I can never be a rational being again.

Don't worry, Thiry dear, about Ash, or me, or whatever it is that is wrong. You can't help it. And it will not turn out so bad as you think. Nothing ever does. I believe that if you were to fall into some really dreadful trouble I could save you. Now what do you think of that for a fellow's faith in himself? Of course, by trouble, I mean something concerning Ash. I must not deceive you, dearest, your brother is the kind of range man that comes to a bad end. You must face this with courage. You must realize that he might involve your father, you, and all of your people in something through which you could suffer.

It is no use to try to change Ash. You waste your strength. The more you do for him the less he will appreciate. I think you can only pray and hope for the best. You will have a good long rest from my disturbing presence, during which time you must think earnesly and fight for that endurance women of the West must have.

My mother and sister tried the pioneer life for a while. It was too much for them. But you are of stronger stuff. Remember that Allie and Lucy must find their spirit in you.

186

I shall think of you every sunset, and see you come out to watch the Pass.

Ever

Trueman.

Returning to the Preston cabin, Rock looked for Alice to deliver his note to Thiry, but as she was not there he ventured of his own accord. Slipping it under the door of Thiry's cabin, he beat a rather precipitate retreat. Nevertheless, he heard the door open, and turning saw Thiry pick up the missive, and then stand to look at him. It was too far away to see her expression. Rock waved his hand. Would she return his salute? She did not, to his dismay. Still he turned again and again to look over his shoulder as he hurried away. Finally she waved, then quickly shut the door. Rock's dismay was transformed to delight. She had his letter and she had waved good-by. He could not have asked or hoped for more. That would serve him well during his sojourn in the woods.

In half an hour he sat astride Egypt, bound down the Pass. This trip would be a welcome respite, and from every angle favorable for him. Two hours later he was climbing the benches into the black timber, and late that afternoon he halted with the boys in a wild and sylvan spot to make a permanent camp.

He had ridden along that babbling brown stream, but he could not recall the exact location. The huge pines shaded boulders covered with green moss; open forest stretched away on each side; the brook came rushing down from the higher country above; deer grazed with the cattle wild horses trooped up to whistle and look, and then race away with manes flying. This was the edge of the mountain range where thirty thousand head of mixed brands roamed, wilder than the deer.

"Boys, your dad has stuck us with a job he thinks we can't do," observed Rock, at the camp fire. "Five hundred head of two-year-olds by August."

"Can't be did," replied Tom, throwing up his hands.

"By thunder! What's eatin' Dad these days?" exclaimed Harry.

"Let's fool him once," added Al, with spirit. "For some reason or other he wants us holed up out here like

a lot of gophers. There's another dance in town along
early in August. An' if you-all want a hunch—there's
somebody who says I gotta be on hand."

"That's the talk, Al," said Rock. "If we can find a
canyon or draw somewhere close we'll drive what we
round up each day, and fence them in."

"Good big draw over here. Water an' grass. Once been
fenced in, but the poles are down. Reckon we could fix
it up pronto."

Before they went to bed Rock had imbued the brothers
with something of his own will to do or die. Next morning
they were up in the dark, had the horses in at dawn,
breakfast before sunrise, and on the drive when the first
tinges of rose colored the rims of the Pass.

It was another old story for Rock, though he had never
herded cattle with such a horse as Egypt. This fact and
the forest with its multiple aspects of wild beauty and
lonesome solitude, and the oft-recurring memory of Thiry,
so poignant and sweet, made the hours seem days and
the days weeks.

It rained every day, mostly summer showers, with
rainbows bent from cloud to forest. The dry dusty brush
grew green with renewed life; the pines and oaks were
washed clean; the streams sang bank-full of amber water;
the aspens began to take on a tinge of gold.

One night Al got in latest of all, weary and sullen.
Rock new something untoward had happened, but he
waited until the lad had eaten and rested.

"What did you run up on today, cowboy?" queried
Rock, at length.

"I was up under the Notch," replied Al, "an' first
thing I seen a couple of riders high up, watchin' me. I
didn't let on, an' went on drivin' same as if I hadn't seen
them. Reckon they never lost sight of me all day."

"Dog-gone!" ejaculated Rock.

The twins were silent, which fact did not argue for
a favorable reception of this news.

"See any brands except ours?" asked Rock, pertinently.

"Shore did. Lot of Half Moon stock scattered all
over."

"The devil you say. I thought Hesbitt ran the Half
Moon outfit low down on the range."

"We heard in town he was goin' to change," replied Al.

"Any two-year-olds in that bunch?" asked Rock.

"Reckon most of them."

"Ahuh! And how many of our brand?

"Pretty scarce. I won't bother to drive there tomorrow."

Three days later, miles east of the Notch, Rock's alert eye caught sight of riders above him on a slope, keeping behind the trees, and no doubt spying upon him with a glass. Though boiling with rage, he went right on driving as if he were none the wiser. On the return to camp he came to the conclusion that one of Hesbitt's outfits was deliberately on the trail. This roused more than anger in Rock. The situation around Gage Preston was narrowing down critically. Rock thought it best not to acquaint the brothers with his discovery. They were doing wonderful driving, and soon the five hundred head would be all rounded up, ready to be moved down into the Pass.

But a couple of days before this longed-for number had been herded into the canyon-corral, the thing Rock expected came to pass. Early in the morning, at breakfast hour, a group of riders, five in number, rode down upon the camp.

"Boys, reckon I don't like this," said Rock, gruffly. "But you take it natural-like, and I'll do the talkin'."

As the riders entered camp Rock rose from his seat beside the camp fire to greet the visitors. They were seasoned range-riders, a hard-looking quintet, not one of whom Rock had ever seen. They probably belonged to the Wyoming outfit which had come from the north with Hesbitt. It took no second glance for Rock to decide they did not know him by sight or reputation.

"Howdy! Just in time for grub," he said, heartily.

"Much obliged, but we had ourn," replied the leader, a bronzed, rugged cowman, with bright bold eyes that roved everywhere.

"Say, you must crawl out early mornin's," drawled Rock, going back to his seat and lifting plate and cup. "Get down and stay awhile."

His invitation was not accepted or acknowledged.

"Gage Preston outfit?" inquired the leader.

189

"Part of it," replied Rock, not so cordially. He meant presently to show that he was thinking hard.

"Round-up or drivin' a herd?" went on the interlocutor, visibly cooler.

Rock set down his plate, his cup, and slowly turned on his seat.

"We're drivin' five hundred head of two-year-olds down the Pass. Reckon another day or so will make the full count," rejoined Rock.

"Big job for so few punchers. Anybody else with you?"

"No."

"Where you got the herd bunched?"

"We fenced a canyon across the creek," returned Rock, pointing eastward.

The leader was evidently finding Rock a man about whom he had begun to have uneasy conceptions.

"Don't know the lay of the land," went on the leader. "Haven't rid long on this range."

"Shore you didn't have to tell me that," replied Rock, bluntly. "You're from Wyomin', an ridin' for Hesbitt."

"How'd you know thet?"

"Reckon nobody else would brace *me* this way."

"You? Which one of the Prestons might you be? I've seen Ash Preston out on the range, an' you're shore not him."

"I might be any one of the other six Prestons," rejoined Rock, with dry sarcasm. "Hadn't you better hand over your callin'-card before askin' me to introduce myself?"

"I'm Jim Dunne, foreman for Hesbitt," replied the rider.

"All right. How do, Mr. Dunne? A blind cowboy could see your call isn't friendly. Now what do you want?"

"Wal, we've come over to have a look at your herd," answered Dunne.

"Ahuh!" Rock, with suddenness, stood erect. He strode halfway across the camp space to confront Dunne. "Just to see if by accident we didn't round up a couple of Half Moon steers?"

"Wal, I ain't sayin' nothin' about accidents," returned the other, no doubt stirred by Rock's caustic query.

"Dunne, you bet your life you're goin' to look over

190

our herd," snapped Rock. "Then I'll call you plumb straight."

One of Dunne's men whispered to him, with visible effect.

"Say, are you this fellar Rock?" he asked, suddenly.

"Yes, I'm Rock. Reckon that doesn't mean anythin' to you. But maybe it will later."

"Wal, I can't see as there's any reason to be riled," returned Dunne, shifting in his saddle, evidently now wanting to conciliate Rock.

"That's because you don't know this range," said Rock, curtly, and then turned to the Preston brothers. "Boys, we'll drive the steers out of the canyon for inspection. We'll head them down into the Pass. Then we'll pack and go on in."

Rock relentlessly held the Half Moon outfit on both sides of the corral gate while the cowboys drove the steers out in single file and in twos and threes. It was Rock's task to head them down toward the Pass, which was easy after the leaders got started.

Dunne made several weak attempts to call off the inspection, but Rock rigorously held him and his men to a count of every steer that passed the gateway. It was a long, tedious job.

"Dunne, between you all you've seen every head of stock we've driven," said Rock, when he had dismounted to face the men.

"Reckon we have," rejoined Dunne, and made as if to mount his horse.

"Stay on the ground," ordered Rock. "You didn't see one Half Moon brand, did you?"

"Who said we was lookin' for Half Moon brands?" blustered Dunne.

"Bah!—Out with the truth! You didn't see one Half Moon brand?" demanded Rock.

"Can't say I did."

"And you punchers? Neither did you?"

"No, Rock, we didn't," replied the one who had whispered to Dunne. "An' if we'd had our way this deal wouldn't hev come off."

"All right. . . . Dunne, go for your gun!" commanded Rock.

"What!" ejaculated Dunne, hoarsely, his face turning yellow.

"Can't you hear? . . . Any man who thinks me a rustler has got to back it with his gun."

"Rock, I—I—we—Throwin' guns wasn't in my orders."

"Dunne, you don't fit on this range," replied Rock, in bitter scorn. "Keep out of my way hereafter." Then he turned to the other riders. "Reckon you're not willin' parties to this raw deal Dunne gave me. Any self-respectin' cowboy, if he calls another a rustler, knows it's true and is ready to fight. . . . Tell Hesbitt exactly what happened here. If you don't I'll hold it against you. Tell him rotten gossip on the range isn't proof of an outfit's guilt."

"All right, Rock, we'll shore give Hesbitt the straight of this," replied the rider.

The four mounted men rode away, and Dunne made haste to get astride and follow. Rock called after him:

"Dunne, I reckon all the Prestons—Ash in particular—will take your insult to me home to themselves."

The three young Prestons with Rock certainly took it so. Through the whole affair they had been pale, set-faced, silent. After Dunne and his men left they broke out, Al worst of all.

"But, True, look ahere," he protested, when Rock tried to quiet him, "it means we Prestons are suspected of rustlin'."

"I reckon so. By that particular Hesbitt outfit. But, Al, that isn't much to rile you. This Wyomin' outfit is sort of new. They want to boss the range. I met Clink Peeples, another Hesbitt foreman. He's not a bad fellow."

"What's Dad goin' to say?" queried Al, wide-eyed.

"What's *Ash* goin' to *do*—that's the thing?" returned Tom, tragically.

"Looks bad to me, boys," added Harry, gloomily. "Clears up some queer remarks I heard in town."

"Let's rustle home."

Rock agreed to that last, whereupon they bent united efforts to breaking camp.

On the third day following, early in the afternoon, Rock and his cowboys left the herd of steers in the meadowland below Slagle's ranch, and rode on home, a weary and silent four, scattered wide along the lane.

The labor of the past few weeks had been so strenuous and the application to it so zealous that Rock scarcely realized the lapse of time. What had happened at Sunset Pass during the interim? He hoped but little. What pleasure he might have had in driving the herd down to the Pass, ahead of schedule, had been spoiled by the advent of the Half Moon outfit and the necessity of revealing it to Preston.

Rock asked the brothers to keep their mouths shut, but strict observance of their promises was not likely. Indeed, by the time he had shaved and changed his clothes, there came rapid footfalls, followed by a thump on his cabin door.

"Who is it?" he called, for he had taken the precaution to lock the door.

"Preston. Open up," came the peremptory reply.

Rock slid back the bar, whereupon Preston stamped in, with Ash close behind him.

"Howdy, boss!" said Rock, cheerfully, and nodded to Ash. But his geniality did not inhibit a lightning scrutiny of both men, especially the latter.

"Al busted in with a wild story," broke out Preston, waiving a greeting. "Said Hesbitt's outfit spied on you while you was drivin'? Then they rode into your camp. Five of them. Feller named Dunne in charge. He was mean as a skunk an' said he'd look your herd over. But when you called him an' he found out who you was he tried to hedge. . . . Al says you made him inspect every steer you had—an' after that dared him to throw a gun. . . . Al was terrible excited. Darn fool blurted thet all out in front of the folks. . . . Rock, was he just loco, or is he exaggeratin' a little run-in you had with one of Hesbitt's outfit's?"

"Boss, Al told the truth, and put it mild at that," replied Rock, and turned to tie his scarf before the mirror. In the glass he saw Preston's eyes roll and fix with terrible accusation upon his son. "Sit down, both of you," went on Rock, and presently faced them again. Ash was coolly rolling a cigarette, his face a mask. Preston had been drinking of late, but appeared sober, and now, though grim and angry, met Rock's glance steadily.

193

"Wal, thet's short an' sweet," he said, with a gruff laugh. "So you come in only a little short of five hundred head?"

"Four eight, if we counted correct."

"Wonderful job!" exclaimed Preston, as if the eulogy had to be paid. "Never expected you till mid-August. What you think, Ash?"

"Rock, how'd you get such work out of Al an' the twins?" queried Ash, from a cloud of cigarette smoke.

"They were plumb fine," replied Rock, with enthusiasm. "I couldn't ask any better boys."

"Wal, thet pleases me. Too bad such a fine job had to end bad," said Preston. "How'd they take this suspicious deal?"

"Mad as hornets."

"Wouldn't be Prestons if they wasn't. . . . Rock, suppose you tell us everythin' thet come off."

Thus adjured, Rock began a minute narrative of the situation from the day Al caught the two riders spying upon him from the slope. When he reached a point where he too had observed watchers, Preston interrupted with a curse, then:

"Al didn't tell me thet."

"He never knew it. I thought I'd better keep it to myself until I saw you," returned Rock, and then went on with the story, which the rancher allowed him to complete.

"So you invited Dunne to draw?" he queried, rising with his eyes like lights behind transparent veils.

"Boss, I did. Reckon I was good and sore," admitted Rock. "But what could you expect of me? He made me out a rustler, though he crawfished yellow on it. Besides, that insult extended to my boss, didn't it?"

"It shore did," rejoined Preston, thick-voiced. "Rock, suppose Dunne couldn't have been bluffed? What then?"

"Say, you call yourself a Westerner?" queried Rock, derisively. "Gage, you haven't been long out here, or you'd never ask a fool question like that."

"All the same, I'm askin' it an' I want to know."

"I'd have bored him," answered Rock, provoked to something he seldom yielded to. "And I told Dunne to keep out of my way. If I meet him—"

194

"Wal, Rock," interposed Ash, in a voice that made Rock's flesh creep, "I'll see to it I'll meet him first."

"Cowboy, I never expected you'd stand up fer me thet way," burst out Preston, genuinely moved. "Course I never knew you. It means more'n I can tell you, havin' my youngsters be with you then. I just can't thank you."

"Don't try," returned Rock, turning it off with an easy laugh.

"Wal, would you mind givin' me your angle on this deal?" went on Preston, relaxing to earnest anxiety.

"'Most as short an' sweet as the other. Hesbitt is a new rancher here. He doesn't know our range. He's never been a cowboy. There's been some rustlin', as you know. Like in my day here years ago. Reckon Hesbitt has been losin' most of any of you ranchers. He's sore, and his outfits are tryin' to be Wyomin' smart. They've picked on you. That's my angle."

"Wal, by——! it's as clean an' sharp as everythin' else about you," returned Preston, perturbed. "Ash, did you savvy thet?"

"Shore, but I ain't awful impressed," replied the son, puffing smoke. Rock could not see his face, but he had further reason to respect Ash's cunning.

"Rock, do you figger thet other old-timers hyar have the same angle?"

"I'd say so, unless some one like Slagle. But naturally he'd be quick to think ill of you."

Preston paced the room, gazing down at the bare rough-hewn floor.

"Reckon this hyar deal wouldn't be particular bad fer me if it wasn't fer our butcherin' bizness," he remarked, as if thoughtfully to himself. Rock, however, divined that was a calculating speech.

"You hit it, Gage. There's the rub. My hunch is you must quit the butcherin'," said Rock, deliberately, his eye on Ash. He anticipated that individual's reaction.

"I will, by thunder!" replied the rancher, wheeling instinctively to face his son.

Ash rose out of the cloud of smoke. At that moment, for Trueman Rock, nothing in the world could have been so desirable as to smash that face. Ash took no notice of his father's decision. He flipped his cigarette butt almost at Rock.

"I'm butcherin' tomorrow, Mister Rock," he asserted.

"Butcher and be darned!" retorted Rock, absolutely mimicking the other's tone.

"You're gettin' too thick out here," said Ash, backing to the door, which he opened. "I told you once to clear out. This's the second time. There won't never be no third."

"See here, Ash, I'm not tryin' to run your affairs. I was just givin' my angle. Take it for what it's worth. As for clearin' out—well, I'll consider that. Reckon I don't want to make trouble between you and your folks."

Ash backed out the door, his wonderful blue eyes like fire under ice, then he stalked off the porch toward his cabin.

"Gage, that bull-headed son of yours will be the ruin of you," said Rock, turning to the rancher.

"Lord! don't I know it!" groaned Preston from under his huge hands. His massive frame wrestled. Up he sprang, to lift clenched fists, and broke into an ungovernable rage that both astonished and mystified Rock. The rancher's face turned a purple hue; his thick neck bulged almost to bursting. He stamped and cursed and swung his arms, as a man of strength and will baffled and defeated. The paroxysm subsided, and he grew composed, but if there was not actual hate in the set glare of his deep gray eyes, then Rock erred in his belief.

"Boss, some way or other you must persuade Ash to give up the butcherin', at least for a while. Make him think so. Anythin' to gain time."

"Rock, why don't you persuade him?" queried Preston, significantly.

"Me!" ejaculated Rock, shot through and through with an impression he hoped was false. He did not betray that he had grasped Preston's dark hint.

"Thiry an' I have kept him layin' off since you left. I reckon we'd better try the same again."

"Yes, try whatever worked. But don't oppose him, Preston."

"Wal, I guess not. I'll let him cool off a bit, an' tackle him after supper."

Rock remained away from the supper table, though

196

the second bell rang. He found in his pack enough to satisfy him. He did not feel hunger. It was a trying hour as he watched from his window. There was little sunset color, owing to heavy clouds. Thunder rumbled off in the hills, and as dusk fell quickly, sheets of pale lightning flared along the horizon.

Presently Rock saw Preston, accompanied by Thiry, come out of his cabin and cross over to enter Ash's. A light flashed from the window. Rock's first thought was to creep under that window and listen. But for risk to Thiry he would have done so; however, he decided to go down through the grove and come up between Ash's cabin and Thiry's, and wait for her.

It was quite dark when he slipped out. The air was sultry, and smelled of brimstone and rain. Lightning had struck somewhere near the ranch that day. He stole among the trees, and making a half-circle he came up to the bench under Thiry's pine, and sat down there to wait, thrilling with aniticipation of soon seeing her white form emerge from the blackness.

But an hour passed. She did not come. Another went by! The light burned in Ash's window, and now and then a dark form cast a shadow. The conference was still going on. Rock knew surely that Thiry had not left Ash's cabin; he had watched for that, all the time he had circled it.

The night threatened to be stormy. The stillness gave place to a moaning of the wind, and thunder rumbled nearer. Drops of rain pattered on Rock's bare head. The lightning flared brighter, showing the black mountains and the Pass leading to them.

All the lights except that one in Ash's cabin were now out. The hours passed, strangely full for Rock. The longer he waited, the less impatience he felt. He had been drawn into the whirlpool of this Preston catastrophe, and he would stick it out, come what might. How the wind moaned overhead! It was like a knell. And the weird flashes of lightning along the battlements of the horizon fitted the melancholy sound.

It must have been long after midnight when Rock heard a door close. He waited, straining eyes and ears, beginning to wonder if he had been mistaken about not missing Thiry. He reassured himself. Another door closed, and that he was sure had come from Preston's cabin. How pitch black it was at a little distance! Then a pale sheet of lightning illumined the heavens. By its aid Rock discerned a white form, gliding swiftly. Thiry! He must not frighten her, and decided to call out when she came near enough. The pale sheet lightning favored him once more. She was so close that the lightning shone live silver fire on her bare head. He moved to intercept her, peering to pierce the gloom. He did not want to speak loud, so he waited.

Out of the blackness a slender vague shape glided, like a specter. The darkness was deceptive. Rock let her get right upon him, so close he could have touched her, and his heart suddenly contracted violently.

"Thiry! Thiry!" he whispered, unable to make his voice clear or steady. He heard her gasp. Like a statue she stood. He had a poignant instant of remorse for succumbing to his selfish longing to see her. This would alienate her further.

"Thiry! Don't be frightened. I waited. . . . It's Trueman," he whispered.

"You!" she cried, and seemed to loom on him out of the shadows. Her arms swept wide and that extraordinary action paralyzed Rock. The next instant they closed round his neck.

Chapter Thirteen

Rock stood stiff and immovable as the pine tree by his side, but his mind, his heart received the fact of that embrace with tumultuous violence. Scarcely had Thiry clasped him when she uttered a cry and released the convulsive hold, her hands unlocking and sliding down from each shoulder as if bereft of strength.

"Oh—I'm—beside myself!" she whispered.

Taking her hand, Rock led her to a seat on the bench under the pine, where she sank almost in collapse, her head bowed. Rock resisted his natural impulses—crushed down the exultation of the moment.

"Thiry, why did you—do that?" he asked, in a low whisper, holding her hand tight.

"I—I don't know."

"But dare I take it—as 'most any man would such action from a girl?"

"It's done . . . I'm amazed—shamed again at myself. What must you think of me?"

"Reckon I think all that's wonderful and beautiful. But I think also I'm entitled to an explanation."

"Trueman, how can I explain what I scarcely realize?" she said, with pathos. "I'd been hours with Dad and Ash. Oh, it was sickening. We begged—we prayed Ash to give up—plans he has. He was a fiend. So was Dad. But I kept trying till I was exhausted. . . . It must be two o'clock. . . . As I came across to my cabin I was thinking of how you met that Half Moon outfit. How you resented suspicion against Dad! My poor sick heart must have warmed to you with something—surely with gratitude. You seemed my only friend. I was wondering how I should thank you—tomorrow. . . . Then you rose right out of the black ground. What fright you gave me! And when you spoke I—I just—"

She faltered and broke off leaving him to guess the rest. Rock's compassion overcame his more powerful emotions.

"Thiry, you've explained how upset you were—and why. But that would not make you fling your arms round my neck."

"I'm guilty," she replied, distantly. "If you can't be understanding—generous—then take it how you will. . . . After all, I belong to the Preston outfit."

These words, tinged with bitterness, accompanied by the withdrawal of her hand from his, gave Rock the cue. This was his hour. His intelligence recognized it, but his conscience would not let him rush madly to take advantage of her weakness at this critical time. So watching her dim pale face against the black pine, he pondered. He seemed scarcely prepared for the opportunity which now knocked at the gates. Yet always with this Preston problem he had vacillated, procrastinated. He hoped to put off the inevitable.

"Trueman, it's late. I must go in," she said.

"Reckon you can spare me an hour," he returned, his voice gruff with the strain of his emotions.

"Indeed no! I must go. Good night," she replied, nervously rising.

He grasped her arm, not gently, and pulled her down on the seat, this time closer to him, and he held her.

"You stay here. Reckon I might remind you that Ash is not the only bad hombre on the range."

To judge from her shrinking, and the trembling of her arm, his speech both frightened and angered her. Rock thought it just as well. The tremendousness of this Preston situation, and its threatened catastrophe, had kept him at top pitch of mental strain for weeks. It could not last. But he divined it must grow worse before it could become better. And he seemed gradually forcing the issue.

"Very well, if you detain me by force," Thiry said, coldly. "Why were you waiting for me at this unheard-of hour?"

"I saw you go into Ash's cabin, and I thought I'd wait till you came out. Reckon it never occurred to me you'd be so long. But I kept waitin'. At that the time flew by."

"Then you were spying on me—on us?" she queried, a quicker note in her voice.

"Reckon so, if you want to use hard words. But sure my strongest motive was just to see you, talk to you a minute."

"Well, since you've done that, please let me go."

"Thiry, you upset everythin' when you put your arms round my neck," he said.

"Don't harp on that," she flashed, hotly. "I never did such a thing before. I—I couldn't to any other man. It just happened. If you want to spare me let me forget it."

"Could you ever?"

"I might make myself."

"Reckon I'll never let you," rejoined Rock, stubbornly. "You've froze up the last few minutes. That hurts. I have my own battle to fight, and you're not helpin' me."

"Your battle! . . . Trueman Rock, if you had a hundreth part of my battle to fight—you—you'd flood the range in blood."

"I love you. My life is wrapped up in you. . . . And don't we read that self-preservation is the first law of nature?"

200

"The most selfish, yes."

"Thiry, let me make your battle mine," he pleaded. "Tell me what weighs so upon you. Tell me your secret."

"I—I have no secret," she replied, shakily.

"Don't you trust my love?"

"Oh, I would if I dared," she whispered, in poignant pain.

Rock had wrenched that truth from her. Therein lay her weakness, the vulnerable spot upon which he must remorselessly make his attack. If she did not already love him, certain it seemed that he could make her. This horrible secret was clamping her heart; and Ash's baneful influence was like a poisonous lichen.

Rock felt assailed by insurmountable temptations. He would not stifle his conscience, but every moment he became more convinced that in order to save her he must play upon her weakness, force her to confession, betray his knowledge of her guilty sharing of Preston's secret. He strove for self-control. In vain!

"Thiry, you might dare anythin' on my love," he began.

"Oh no—no! If it were only myself."

Rock realized that Thiry was governed by her emotions. She was too honest for base secrets, and certainly too honest to hide her love, once she realized it. Rock became more convinced that she did feel tenderness for him, perhaps unconsciously, and he could not stem the torrent of his hopes and fears.

"Thiry, there are only two people in all the world—you and me."

"How silly, Trueman. You *are* selfish."

"Well, if it's selfish to love you—worship you—to want your burdens on my shoulders—to save you from trouble, disgrace—to make you happy—then indeed I am sure selfish."

What a delicate instrument she was for sensibility! Through her wrist, which he held, he felt the intermittent slight quiverings, then at the word disgrace a distinct shock. Hurriedly she rose, and all but released herself.

"Do you speak of love and—and disgrace in one breath?" she queried.

"Yes. And you understand," he replied, sharply.

"I—I do not."

201

"Thiry darling, I can forgive your falsehood to all except me."

"What!" she cried, pride and fear in one gasp. She shook in his grasp.

It did not take much of a pull to get her into his arms, and in another moment he had her helpless, lifting her from the ground, her face close under his.

"Thiry, don't you love me a very little?" he asked, deep tenderness thrilling in his voice.

"No! . . . Oh, let me go!" she implored.

"Be honest."

"I can't be . . . I'm such a liar."

"Thiry, I love you so wonderfully. Ever since that minute you stepped in Winter's store. . . . Didn't you like me then—or afterward?"

"I suppose I did. But what's the use to talk of it. . . . You're holding me in a—a—most shameless manner. . . . Let me go."

"Reckon I'll hold you this way a long time. . . . Till you say you love me a little."

She essayed to free herself, but her strength fell far short of her spirit.

"Then you'll hold me until daylight—when Ash will see you."

"Well, say a little short of daylight. Reckon I can get along with that for a while."

"Oh—please—please! . . . Trueman, this is outrageous!"

"It sure is. 'Most as outrageous as your deceivin' me."

"How have I deceived you?" she demanded, vibrating to that.

"For one thing—carin' about me a little. You do, don't you, Thiry?"

"Care about you? I suppose I—I did, else I couldn't have been such a fool as to go to that dance. But what's caring? . . . It certainly doesn't give you license to hold me against my will."

"Well, I reckon that depends on what you mean by care. I'm arguin' you love me a little bit. Sure I've prayed enough for it."

"You pray! You're a fine Christian," she retorted, scornfully.

"Christian or not I've sure prayed you'd love me."

"Then your prayers have been unanswered—as mine have been," she said, in mockery.

"Thiry, I must make sure."

"How?"

"Reckon first off I'll kiss you a couple of thousand times and see if I can tell by that."

"You wouldn't dare!"

"Wouldn't I, though. Sure I'm a reckless cowboy. Now watch me."

And with action at strange variance with his bantering words he bent to kiss her hair again and again and again, and then her ear, and last her cheek, that changed its coolness under his lips.

"There!" he whispered, and drew her head back on his shoulder so her face would be upturned. To his piercing eyes the darkness was as if it were not. "Sure *they* were only worshipful kisses. . . . Do you hate me for them?"

"I couldn't hate you. . . . Please let that do. Let me go—before it's too . . . Trueman, I beg of you."

"It *is* too late, Thiry, for both of us," he whispered, passionately, and he kissed her lips—and then again, with all the longing that consumed him.

"Now will you confess you love me—a little?" he asked, huskily.

"O God help me—I do—I do!" she cried, and her eyes seemed deep accusing gulfs.

"More than a little? Thiry, I didn't expect much. Sure I don't deserve it. . . . But tell me."

"Yes, more." And she twisted to hide her face, while her left arm slowly crept up his shoulder, and went half round his neck. "That's what was the matter with me."

"When did you know?" he asked, amazed in his incredulity.

"Just now. . . . But I knew there was something wrong before."

"Thiry, bless you!—if this's not a one-sided affair, kiss me."

"No—no. . . . If I give up—we're ruined," she whispered, tragically.

"Sure we're ruined if you don't. So let's have the kisses anyhow."

"Trueman, since I never can—marry you—I—I mustn't kiss you."

"Darling, one thing at a time. By and by we'll tackle the marryin' problem. I'd go loco if I thought you'd be my wife some day. . . . But just now make this dream come true. I want your kisses, Thiry."

"I daren't. . . . It's not fair."

"To whom?"

"You."

"I'll risk it. . . . Thiry, I'll compromise. I'll be generous. Just one—but not like that fairy kiss you gave me on Winter's porch."

"Trueman, if I give *one*—it means all . . . ten million will follow," she said, tremulously.

"Dear, I'll save the nine hundred and ninety nine thousand, and so forth. . . . Come."

And lifting her head he turned her face to his.

"You are wrong to—to master me this way," she rejoined, mournfully. "If you knew—you might not want it."

"Master nothin'? I am *your* slave. But kiss me. Settle it forever!"

How slowly she lifted her pale face, with eyes like black stars! In the sweet fire of her lips Rock gained his heart's desire.

Then she lay in his arms, her face hidden, while he gazed out into the stormy night, across the black Pass to the dim flares along the battlements of the range. His victory brought happiness and sorrow commingled. In the tree-tops the mournful wind did not presage a future without strife. But the precious form in his arms, the mortal flesh that embodied and treasured an infinitely more precious gift—her love—lifted his spirit and bade him go on.

"Now," Trueman, explain what you meant by my—falsehood to all?" she asked, presently.

"Are you quite prepared?" he returned, gravely. "Sure it's not easy to rush from joy to trouble."

She sat up, startled, with hands nervously releasing their hold. All about her expressed doubts, misgivings, but she had no inkling of what he had to reveal.

"Thiry, you are keepin' Ash's and your father's secret from all."

204

"Trueman!" she cried, as if her own mind had deceived her ears.

"They are cattle thieves. Beef thieves. So are your brothers Range, Scoot and Boots, along with them."

"O my God!—You know!" she almost screamed, and slipped to her knees before him.

"Hush! Not so loud! You'll wake some one," he said, sternly, placing a firm hand over her mouth. "Get up off your knees."

But she only leaned forward, clutching him, peering up into his face.

"Trueman, how do—you know?" she gasped, convulsively.

"I suspected it when I first came. I found signs. Quicklime! That made me suspicious. Slagle's well is half full of hides. Sure those hides have not the Preston brand. . . . Then over near where they butchered last I came on the same boot track that I'd seen down near the slaughterhouse. I trailed that track. It led under a culvert. There I found hundreds of hides, tied up in burlap sacks. Most were old, but some were new. I opened one. That hide had a Half Moon brand! Down here at your barn, one day, after the dance, I measured Ash's boot track. It was the same as that one I'd trailed. . . . But for real proof, I heard your Dad and Ash talkin' together. One night I happened to be out, thinkin' of you, watchin' like tonight. Your father and Ash came out, right to the log where I sat. I lay down. . . . And I heard them talk about this. They gave it all away."

"Oh, you were a spy!" she burst out, in hot agonized words.

"I'm afraid I was."

"I knew—it would come. . . . It will—kill me," she wailed, brokenly. "Oh, to make love to me—while you were spying on my brother—my father!"

"Little girl, I told you to speak low. . . . Reckon it does look pretty bad to you. But it's not so bad as it looks—so far as I'm concerned. But, Thiry, you're in this secret and you would be held guilty in some degree in court, if your part in it was found out. And let me tell you Ash would hold no secret. He would drag even you into it!"

"Oh, no! No! No!"

205

"He would. And there's the danger for you."

"Court!—Danger? . . . My God! you mean they'll be arrested—and I will be dragged in with them?"

"Reckon that is liable to happen," he replied, wanting, stern as the task was, to impose upon her once and for all the peril of the situation.

"You'd betray us!" Swift as a striking snake her hand darted out and snatched his gun as it rested against his thigh. Leaning back, she extended it with both hands. "I'll kill you!"

"Thiry, if you believe I could betray you or them—shoot!" he replied, swiftly.

"You will not tell?" she flashed.

"Never. You sure got me wrong."

She gave vent to a shuddering sound. The gun fell from her hands. She swayed. He could see her eyes were tight shut. Then she sank forward, her face on his knees, and clinging to him she broke into low sobs, every one of which was like a knife-thrust to Rock.

He let her have it out, and stroked her hair, and her tight fists, one of which clenched his scarf, the other his coat sleeve. She did not recover soon, though presently the sobs gave way to soft weeping. Then he held her closer, scarcely seeing her or the black pine-streaked gloom, or the stretching flares of yellow light along the horizon. He was seeing something blacker than the night, more sinister than the shadows. As a last resource, to save her and her father, he could kill Ash Preston. That would kill Thiry's love, but protect her name and insure a chance for her future happiness. But for Ash, this blundering, thieving work could be halted in time to prevent discovery. The range was lenient. Preston already saw the error of his ways. He could be amenable to any plan. Ash was the stumbling-block.

At this brooding juncture of Rock's meditations he became aware that Thiry was stirring. She rose from her knees, while still clinging to him, and she sank beside him on the bench, to lean against him, face uplifted.

"Can you forgive me?" she whispered.

"Thiry, you talk nonsense sometimes."

"But I might have shot you."

"Sure I thought you were goin' to."

"I was out of my head. I should have known you

would never betray us. . . . My wits were gone. Everything went but a hot terrible fury. Oh, Trueman, I am a Preston."

"Well, I reckon I don't want you anybody else."

"Can *anything* be done to save us?" she queried, appealingly.

"It must be done, Thiry. Sure I don't know what. My mind's not workin' any better than yours."

"I dare not breathe a word of this. They would kill you."

"Never give Ash a hunch that I know. He'd come pilin' after me with a gun. Don't tell your father anythin'. . . . There's no great hurry. We've got time. I'll find some way."

"You promise me?"

"I swear it," he replied, solemnly.

"Oh, Trueman, you are my one hope. To think I've tried to drive you away! . . . That I nearly shot you! . . . How little I know myself. But I do know this: if you stop this selling of stolen beef—if you prevent it before they're arrested—I'll—I'll love you with all my heart and soul."

"Darling, I will do it somehow," promised Rock.

"I'll go now," she said, rising, and swaying unsteadily.

He lifted her in his arms and walked toward her cabin.

"Am I an empty sack, that you pack me so easily?" she whispered, with a little intimate laugh that thrilled him.

"Not so I'd notice it," he whispered.

At the door of the cabin he set her gently upon her feet. She still held him with one clinging hand, and that unconscious act was balm to Rock's distracted heart.

"I am glad now you came to Sunset Pass," she whispered. "But you've added to my fears. It's now you, too, who might fall under the Preston shadow."

"Did you read my letter—that I slipped under your door, before I left?"

"It is here," she said, touching her breast.

"Read it again. Be brave, Thiry. Don't give up. . . . Never lose faith in me. . . . Good night," he concluded, and loosing her hand he kissed it, and fled silently into the darkness.

Forty-eight hours later Rock rode into Wagontongue.

Gage Preston had been more than glad to give him leave of absence, sensing no doubt in Rock something not inimical to his precarious fortunes. In a note to Thiry, Rock explained the reason for his going, importuning her to wait patiently, and not to be victim to imagined evils—that somehow he would find a solution.

He rode into Wagontongue the old True Rock of earlier and wilder range days. Yet though that was a fact, in defiance, in cool exterior, no day of his life had ever seen the passion, the will to invent and achieve, that one single moment now embodied.

Though plan after plan had formulated on the long ride in, only one seemed a solution—to call Ash Preston out and kill him. Against this idea he fought, knowing that it had for him a drawing power not solely based on consideration for Thiry and the Prestons. This spirit dominated him in times past. He wanted to surrender to it now, and argued with himself that the most this trip might accomplish was to relieve the tension at Sunset Pass. However, that was no inconsiderable accomplishment, for his presence acted upon Ash Preston like a red flag flipped in the face of a bull. With him gone, perhaps Thiry and Gage could restrain Ash for some weeks. And even days of grace now were precious.

When Rock dropped in to see Winter it was not with any definite purpose; but that night he and his old friend locked themselves in a room at the hotel. There were range channels open to Winter to which Rock had no access. The Preston situation was graver—actual accusations had been made, it seemed. But by whom was not manifest. Winter talked while Rock listened. It did not take long to impart information that was endless in its possibilities.

"Sol, old-timer, I'm in deep," said Rock, at the conclusion of Winter's confidence, and he opened his palms expressively. "Thiry loves me!"

"Shore," replied Winter, sagely wagging his head. "But you wouldn't take her an' leave the country?"

"Reckon I couldn't think of that yet."

208

"Do you know anythin' thet makes Preston's guilt shore?"

"Yes, but I promised Thiry not to tell it."

"But you can go to Preston an' tell *him* you know. Scare him to sense."

"Yes, I can. More—I know I can stop him."

"Good. That seems a solution. It's not too late. Go back pronto."

"Sol, Gage Preston can't call his soul his own. I reckon Ash led him into this and now has got him buffaloed. Nothin' on earth or in heaven can stop Ash Preston."

"Nothin'?" echoed Winter, but the incredulity of the West rang in his sarcasm.

"Nothin' but lead!"

"Ahuh! . . . Wal, I never yet seen thet kind of a hombre miss meetin' it. . . . Leave him out. Now, Rock, I've an idee. If Dabb an' Lincoln know what I know—an' it's a good bet they know more—they will *tell* you. Thet obviates any broken promise on your part. Dabb is human. Lincoln is the whitest man in these parts. They're both rich, an' they rule the Cattle Association. Hesbitt is only president. What Dabb an' Lincoln say is law. . . . Now you go to them."

"But, Sol, good Heavens! What for?" queried Rock, impatiently.

"Son, you are so deep in love thet you ain't practical. If you can get Dabb an' Lincoln to sympathize with you an' Thiry, thet'll be sympathizin' with Preston. Ten years ago there was a case somethin' like this, only instead of a rancher bein' a butcher he was a rustler. Rich, too an' in respectable standin', till some slick cowpuncher tracked his outfit down. Wal, his friends got him to make good what he'd stole, an' saved him from jail, if no worse. Preston's case ain't so bad, thet is, yet. . . . Trueman, I've grown gray here. I've been raised with these ranchers. I know them. . . . If you've got the nerve an' the wit you can keep Preston from ruin an' Thiry from a broken heart."

Rock leaped up, inspired, suddenly on fire with the vision Winter's sagacity had conjured up. He pushed aside table and chair, and hugged his startled friend.

"Old-timer, I've sure got the nerve and you've supplied the wit."

Rock did not have a restful night, and loss of sleep added somewhat to his haggard looks. Next morning Clark, the hotel proprietor, jocosely twitted Rock, saying he had heard that Rock had sworn off drinking.

"Sure I have," replied Rock.

"You don't look like it. . . . Wal, no doubt you've got your worries—hangin' with that Preston outfit."

Other acquaintances of Rock's remarked about his visit to Wagontongue, and did not hide their curiosity.

When Rock presented himself at Dabb's office he encountered more that was significant.

"Hello, Rock! You sure look rocky," replied Dabb, in answer to his greeting. "Hope you haven't been drunk."

"No. Only worried."

"Too bad. Have a chair and a cigar. I've been hopin' you'd run into town."

Dabb appeared cordial. He had a cleaner, brighter look, and had evidently paid attention to his appearance.

"How's Amy?" queried Rock.

"She was fit as a filly when I saw her last. She went to Denver to visit. Expect her home next week. Reckon she's goin' to give another dance this fall."

"Gosh! Wasn't that Fourth of July dance enough?" ejaculated Rock.

"It was a great success. Biggest affair we ever had out here. . . . Too bad you couldn't stay for the unmaskin'. You sure made up fine as Señor del Toro."

"Humph! Then Amy told you."

"Yes. But not till next day. I saw you lick that Ash Preston. Can't say I didn't enjoy it," rejoined Dabb, with a laugh.

"Well, I can say I didn't," said Rock.

"Accordin' to Amy you had your hands full before that fight. She was inclined to be sore, Rock. Told me you paid no attention to her. I was there, masked as a padre. Had heaps of fun."

"I'm sorry if I hurt Amy's feelin's," replied Rock, dejectedly. "God knows I can't afford to lose my few friends."

"What's the trouble, Rock? Things goin' bad out there?"

"They've gone from bad to worse. . . . John, I told you I was in love with Thiry. Well, *that* wasn't so bad. But now she's in love with me. And the situation is hell."

"Man, you've only yourself to blame. You were advised not to go. I myself told you not to stay."

"I loved the girl," replied Rock, simply.

"Humph!" said Dabb, chewing at his cigar. "You fell in love with Thiry before you went out there?"

"Of course. Otherwise do you suppose I'd have gone?"

"Probably not. . . . Well, that puts another light on it. . . . Why don't you run off with her?"

"Run off? John, you know I've many faults, but runnin' off was never one of them."

"You run off from me, you son-of-a-gun," retorted Dabb, good-naturedly. "But after you told me, I respected your motive. . . . Rock, gettin' serious, are you goin' to stick out there?"

"What else can I do?"

"And go under with Preston?"

"Reckon I must—*if* he goes under."

"Naturally you have your hopes. . . . Rock, some of us cattlemen know you haven't looked for anythin' shady about Preston."

"How do you know?" asked Rock, curiously.

"Well, that question came up the other night at our Association meeting. Hesbitt gave you a hard rub. Over this Preston scandal. Tom Lincoln an' I an' one or two others took exception to Hesbitt. We claimed you not only weren't in with Preston on anythin' crooked, but you hadn't trailed around lookin' for it. The reason, of course, was you were sweet on Thiry Preston."

"John, that was most damned good of you," returned Rock, warmly. "If I could be cheered up that might do it. But I'm sure down. . . . You an' Lincoln figured that if I had looked for shady work I'd have found it?"

"Sure. We knew that. No outfit could fool you."

"Well, what then?"

"Not so easy. But personally I believe you'd have come to me for advice an' help."

"I don't know that I'd have presumed so far," went on Rock. "But I'll tell you what I came to town for. I was goin' to see Amy and persuade her to help me out of this terrible mess. More for Thiry's sake than mine."

"Good gracious, Rock! You pay Amy a high compliment, if you think she'd help you."

"I'll gamble she would. Amy has a heart of gold. Sure, she has to be persuaded. But the good side of Amy is the stronger."

"You're right, Rock. Amy takes a lot of handlin', an' I'm findin' out—I don't mind tellin' you, to my happiness. . . . Of course, the only way Amy could help you would be through me."

"I have to admit that. But much as I'm buffaloed, I didn't have the nerve to come direct to you."

"I see. What's worryin' you now, Rock?"

"Hesbitt's outfits are after Preston," replied Rock, and he gave Dabb a detailed account of Dunne's maneuver at the Notch camp, and what had come of it.

"You dared that foreman Dunne to throw his gun?" exclaimed Dabb, gravely, removing his cigar.

"I sure did."

"Rock, that was a bold move an' a wise one. Reckon it was the only way any honest range-rider could meet such a raw deal. But suppose you meet this Dunne again, in more favorable circumstances for him, an' he shows fight?"

"I'd hate it, but I'll sure go through with my call. No cowman can insult me like that. He'll either crawl again, as he did then, or shoot."

"Rock, I'm darn glad you told me this. Reckon it didn't seem important to you—that I knew—for you'd have told it quick. But it is important."

"How so?" asked Rock, curiously.

"Well, in the first place it vindicates Lincoln an' me, in our stand for you. An' it will stump Hesbitt."

"Ahuh!—Then this new rancher is dead set against Preston?"

"Is he? Well, I guess. An' he has his outfits r'arin'. . . . Now, Rock, the strange thing is, Hesbitt has been losin' a good deal of stock—most Half Moon brand—an' his men can't locate them. Hide nor hair! . . . But other men have!"

212

"Dabb, what're you tellin' me?" shouted Rock, fiercely. He did not need to dissimulate.

"Don't yell, cowboy. Walls have ears," admonished Dabb. "Rock, now listen. You once rode for Jess Slagle. You know him. Preston ruined Slagle. An' Slagle has hung around out there to get even. Reckon he's in a fair way to do it. For he has tracked the Prestons down. But he wants to get his money back, or some of it. Sure he knows if he threatens Preston with exposure he'll only get shot for his pains. So he came first to me."

"Aw, this's awful!" groaned Rock. "Jess Slagle. . . . An' he has tracked Preston down?—What to, John?"

"Fresh Half Moon hides hidden close to where Preston last butchered. He can show these any time. I called Tom Lincoln in to talk it over. We advised Slagle to keep mum an' wait."

"What was the idea in that?" demanded Rock.

"Well, we're all ranchers, you know," replied Dabb, meditatively, as if the query had before presented itself to him. "In a little way, more or less, we've all appropriated cattle not our own. Reckon we hate to make a move. The stolen cattle were not ours, you see. It'll mean a fight. An' we've passed the buck to Hesbitt."

"No, John, by Heaven! you've passed it to me," returned Rock, with passion.

"Now, Rock, you don't want to take this deal on your shoulders," protested Dabb.

"Would you? I put it up to you straight," demanded Rock, eloquently. "Suppose you loved Thiry. Suppose she loved you, and you'd found out what a sweet girl she is. . . . That if her father went to jail it'd break her heart—or kill her. . . . Now what would you do?"

"Rock, I'm damned if I know," replied Dabb, red in the face, and he slammed his unsmoked cigar to the floor. "It's a cropper. An' I hate to be beaten by anythin' in the cattle line."

"Dabb, here's what I'll do, and I'm sure thankin' you for the hunch," returned Rock, passionately. "I'll buy Slagle's silence. I've five thousand dollars in the bank. I'll stop Gage Preston's stealin' before it's too late. . . . And if I have to, I'll call Ash Preston out!"

"No! No!" exclaimed Dabb, violently. "Not that last, anyway. . . . Rock, will you never settle down to peaceful

213

ranchin'? You might be a credit to this range. And you'd lose the girl and ruin her happiness, sure."

"Well, it might be the only way out," returned Rock. "Suppose you come to my house for dinner tonight. I'll have Tom Lincoln. We'll talk it over."

It was an interminably long day for Rock. His reasoning told him if there was an escape out of this range tangle Dabb and Lincoln would help him to find it. Nevertheless, the suspense, on the heels of all the other emotion, was almost insupportable.

The days were growing shorter and it was dusk when he walked out to the mansion that was John Dabb's home. What a place for little Amy Wund to preside over! His remembrance of her then was kindly and grateful. Surely she must have had much to do with John Dabb's transformation.

Rock was admitted to a cheerful library, and the presence of Dabb and Lincoln.

"Howdy, Rock! Get down an' come in," was Dabb's greeting. "Glad you came early. . . . Tom, you remember True Rock, don't you?"

Lincoln was a little gray withered cattleman, bright of eye, lean of face, not apparently a day older than when Rock had last seen him. He looked like a Texas Ranger, and had been one in his day.

"I shore do," replied Lincoln, extending a lean hand. "Howdy, Rock! Do you remember when you first come to Wagontongue an' got sweet on my girl? An' I chased you out of the yard one night?"

"No, Mr. Lincoln, I don't remember, but you're probably right," replied Rock, joining in the laugh on him.

"Well, Tom, his girl-chasin' days are over. Sit down, friends, an' smoke while I talk," said Dabb. "I've got two more fellows comin' after dinner, an' we'll have a little game of draw after. . . . Now, Rock, I've talked your trouble over with Tom, an' here's his angle. I'm bound to say I think it a solution to a nasty problem. At that it hinges most on you. . . . Go back to Preston an' tell him the truth. That he's found out by some cattlemen, an' he must quit his butcherin' stolen cattle before Hesbitt gets on to him. Tell him he's to come before the Cattle Association. That means Tom an' me, an' Hesbitt, sure, but we can handle him. We'll keep the deal out of court an' Preston out of jail, provided he comes to us, pays Slagle off, an' squares Hesbitt for the stock he has lost. Then Preston, an' his four sons, especially this Ash Preston, who's the ringleader, no doubt, must leave the country."

"Wonderful fair and fine of you gentlemen," returned Rock, instantly, his set face breaking. "Reckon I couldn't find words to thank you. I won't try. Preston doesn't deserve this. Sure it is generous."

"Wal, Rock, it's aboot this heah way," put in Lincoln, with his slow Southern accent. "We shore can afford to be generous because Preston hasn't stole from us. Then we don't want the range slandered by such a raw case. Who'd ever think the Prestons would stoop to that? Mrs. Preston is a nice woman and the girls are ladies. Shore they cain't be in the secret. We'd like to keep Preston out of jail for their sake."

"All right, Rock. What do you say?" queried Dabb, as if in a hurry to get it over. "Will you settle it?"

"Yes, with one reservation," replied Rock, grimly.

"An' what's that?"

"I can manage Preston. But when Ash finds out, he'll fight. He can't be persuaded or frightened."

"Shore. An' your reservation is you'll have to kill him," interposed the imperturbable Texan as he flicked the ashes off his cigar, his bright eyes on Rock.

Rock did not make any reply.

"Darn tough on the girl. My wife says she loves this particular brother," added Dabb, regretfully.

"Reckon it's tougher on Rock, but *quien sabe?* You shore cain't ever tell aboot a woman," rejoined Lincoln.

"We'll go in to dinner," said Dabb, opening the door. "Rock, how'd you like a little poker afterward?"

"I'd like it fine," replied Rock, shaking off a cold black spell, and fetching a laugh, as they went out. "That is, if the limit is worth while."

"See heah, cowboy, the limit in Dabb's house is the roof," drawled Lincoln.

"I'll hate to take your money, gentlemen," responded Rock, "but a chance like this seldom comes along for me."

215

Chapter Fourteen

Before sundown of another day Rock reined his sweating horse in front of Slagle's cabin, and dismounted to approach that individual, who, probably having heard him, had come to the door.

"Slagle, I want to talk Dutch to you," said Rock, without any greeting.

"Thought you looked kinda serious. Any trouble brewin'—er happened?" returned Slagle, permitting Rock to lead him aside.

"Dabb told me you'd come to him with proof of Preston's guilt."

"The devil he did!" ejaculated Slagle.

"Yes, and my business with you is to buy your silence."

Slagle showed further amazement and interest. He listened intensely to Rock's story.

"Say, cowboy, air you makin' this offer on your own hook?" he queried.

"Sure. I told only Sol Winter, who had my money banked."

"What on earth fer? Rock, excuse me, fer appearin' to insinuate. But it looks darn queer."

"Jess, I'm honest. I'm not in on the Preston steal, and you sure know that. I'm tryin' to stall the thing off. Now I figure you as pretty sore, and I don't blame you."

"You ain't makin' no mistake there," growled Slagle.

"Well, what'll you take to keep mum?"

"Rock, this hyar don't set right on me. Lord knows I need money, but I ain't so low down I'd take a cowboy's savin's. What's your idee? You shore can't care thet much about Preston."

"Jess, you're wastin' my time," replied Rock, impatiently. "I love Thiry Preston and I'm goin' to save her dad because of that."

"I savvy. Shore call it decent of you. Makes me want

216

to act square with you. An' the fact is, Rock, I couldn't prove anythin' on Preston now."

"Why not?"

"The Half Moon hides have been moved from where I found them."

"You don't say? Where was that?"

"Over the next hill hyar, under thet big culvert."

"Well, no matter. You did find them, and your word would convince ranchers, if not a court. My offer stands. What'll you take?"

"Rock, hev you got backin'?"

"No. I've my own money. Cash!"

"How much you got?"

"Five thousand."

"Whar'd you ever get thet much?—Rock, I'm afeared you must 'a' been a road-agent somewhere," he said, jocularly, and he paced up and down thoughtfully. "Wal, I hate to take you up, Rock, an' I wouldn't if I didn't feel shore you'll get it back, or some, anyhow. Say I take half of what you got—twenty-five hundred. Preston will have to pay you. An', Rock, I'll pack an' rustle out of hyar pronto."

"You'll leave the range?"

"You bet. An' darn glad to."

"That's fine, and better. It may be a long time till somebody else gets proof on Preston. And it's time I'm gamblin' on. . . . Here's your money, Jess. I'm askin' two promises."

"Ahuh! What are they?" queried the homesteader, his eyes popping at the roll of greenbacks.

"Keep Preston's secret and don't get drunk before you leave."

"Reckon thet's easy. Rock, I'm much obliged to you. I've got another chance in life."

"I hope you'll be successful," returned Rock, stepping over to his horse and mounting. Slagle followed him, and laid a red-haired hand on Rock's chaps. His eyes held a scintillating prophetic light.

"Rock, I'd be willin' to bet all this hyar money, five to one, thet if you save Gage Preston, you'll hev to kill Ash."

Spurring Egypt sharply, Rock swore lustily at the vindictive homesteader and galloped away.

Though Rock put the white horse to a finish that concluded a wonderful day's travel, it was well after dark when they reached the Pass. Lights were burning in all the Preston cabins. At the barn Rock encountered one of the Mexican lads, and turned Egypt over to him. With that he stalked back through the grove. Peering into the kitchen door, he espied Mrs. Preston and Alice and Lucy at their evening chores.

"Howdy, folks! Is it too late for a bite and a cup of coffee? I've had nothin' since yesterday. Starved isn't the word!"

"Why, Mr. Rock, you sure look it," replied Alice, gayly.

"Cowboy, it's never too late in this chuck-house," returned Mrs. Preston. "Come in and sit down."

Heavy boot thuds out on the porch attested to the approach of men. Rock certainly did not keep his back to the door.

"Who come in, Ma?" queried Preston, outside.

"A poor starved cowpuncher," replied his wife.

"Dad, it's only Mr. Rock," added Alice, quickly, with a knowing glance at Trueman.

Outside some one violently slapped what sounded like a pair of gloves on the table.

"Pa, didn't I tell ye?" growled Ash Preston's unmistakable voice. "Thet hombre can't keep away from Thiry— — — —!"

Footfalls, sharp and quick, rang off the porch to thud on the ground. Silence ensued. Rock turned to the women. Mrs. Preston had her head bent over her stove, but Alice's eyes met Rock's, flashing, intelligent, resentful. Then Preston's dragging steps approached. The doorway framed his burly form.

"Howdy, boss!" greeted Rock.

"Back so soon? Reckoned you'd stay out your leave," replied the rancher, with gloomy penetrating gaze on Rock.

"I rustled back," said Rock, meaningly.

"Bad news?"

"Reckon all I got is good."

"Ahuh. . . . Wal, come in, soon as you want to," concluded Preston.

Alice and her mother set before Rock a bounteous

218

meal and while he gave ample evidence of appreciating it, they asked questions about the town. Rock imparted all the information he could muster.

"Oh yes, I near forgot," he added, presently, with a wink at Alice. "Yesterday I run into your beau, Charlie. He shore pumped me about you."

"My beau! Trueman Rock, I—I— He's not that," exclaimed Alice, blushing furiously. The mother's quick look was not lost on Rock.

"Excuse me, Allie. I just naturally thought he was, from the way he talked. Sure does need two to make a beau, doesn't it?"

"Certainly it does," returned Alice, and behind her mother's back she gave Rock an eloquent glance, accompanied by the motion from a threatening little fist. Rock opened both mouth and eyes, in remorseful enlightenment, then went on with his meal. Mrs. Preston had occasion to go out the back door.

"You wretch!" whispered Alice. "Mother thinks I'm too young. . . . And I'm crazy to go to that next dance."

"I'm sure stupid, Allie. . . . Lucky boy! . . . Heigho! I wish I could go."

"Can't we all, Trueman?—Thiry spoke of it today," Alice bent close to Rock's ear. "She's crazy about you."

"Allie—you wretch! It can't be true."

"It is so."

"Aw! How can you think that way?"

"I accused her of being."

Rock leaned closer to the tempting lips, as if they were dispensing music.

"Well?"

"Thiry denied it. But she got red as fire—then mad."

The entrance of Mrs. Preston put an end to this whispered exchange. Soon afterward Rock strode out to seek Preston. On the porch he halted, and gazing out at the spectral pines and up at the blinking stars, and across the thick void toward Thiry's bright window, he called on all the passion and wisdom that might come through hope and prayer. The moment he confronted Preston the climax of this situation would have been set in motion.

"Rock, you didn't break any laigs gettin' hyar with thet good news," growled Preston, as Rock entered.

"Reckon you won't be r'arin' for me to hurry, after I start," replied Rock, closing the door and facing the rancher with intent unmasked gaze. "Preston, not a whisper of what I say must be heard by anyone but you."

"Come close then, an' talk low."

Whereupon Rock drew a chair up to Preston's, and eying him squarely, whispered:

"Preston, the jig's up!"

"What you mean?" hoarsely rejoined the rancher, as if shot through with something that froze his vitals. He knew! It was only an outburst.

"You're found out."

"What's found out?"

"Your butcherin' stolen cattle."

"Who knows?"

"Slagle found Half Moon hides under that culvert above his place. He told John Dabb. Dabb told Tom Lincoln. Then me."

Preston's eyes set with greenish glare; his face, too, took on a greenish-white cast and otherwise changed grotesquely.

"My Gawd!" And as if to shut out the revealing light he covered his face with nerveless hands.

Rock's first thrill came with the rancher's reception of this news. It augured well. But he let the revelation sink deep. He waited.

At length Preston lifted his haggard countenance.

"How can Slagle prove thet—on me?"

"He can't. The hides were there, and now they've been moved."

"Ahuh. Wal, then, I'll deny everythin' an fight them."

"Gage, _I_ can prove you guilty," whispered Rock.

"You can? . . . How?" returned Preston, with solemn glaring eyes.

"Ash's tracks. I trailed them. I measured them. I got his boot track here in the corral. I saw that same track leadin' down to the culvert and under it. I compared them. I ripped open one of those burlap sacks. The Half Moon brand!"

220

"Ash!" And the hissed word was a curse.

"Yes. You've split on Ash Preston."

The big hands clenched, and opened wide, and plucked at the grizzled locks.

"Rock, you wouldn't ruin me?"

"No."

"An' you shore couldn't break Thiry's heart?"

"Do you need to ask?"

"Does anyone else have the proofs on me—like you?"

"No, not yet. But I'm not the only trailer on this range. Somebody will trail your sons, as I did Ash. *If you don't stop them!*"

"Ha! Then it ain't too late?" he queried, huskily, and the corded veins in his neck bulged, his temples throbbed and reddened.

"No."

What a rasping breath escaped the broad chest!

"Does anybody else suspect—beside the four you named?"

"Hesbitt's outfits are scourin' the range. They suspect. But they don't know. Reckon sooner or later they'll hit on somethin'. Old sign. It might not convict, but it'd ruin you just the same. And any fresh sign—Preston, you'll all go to jail!"

"Rock, are you comin' in with me—an' Ash—an' Thiry?" asked Preston.

"I'm in with you and Thiry now. Not Ash. . . . But clean and honest, Preston. I've laid my cards before Dabb and Lincoln. They know me. I couldn't be crooked now—not to save your life and Thiry's happiness."

"Ahuh!—What's the deal?"

"If you'll agree to what I lay before you we can stall off the worst."

"What you mean by worst?"

"Ruin for your family. Jail for your sons. Perhaps bloodshed."

"Ha! thet last is shore as hell with Ash in it. . . . Rock, I get a hunch you've been workin' to ward off this ruin. Fer Thiry's sake?"

"Naturally I think of Thiry first," went on Rock, with deep emotion, warming to the impending argument. "But also I'm thinkin' of her mother and sisters—and the boys who're as innocent as they are. In fact for all of you."

221

"Can you save us? Not countin' Ash. He's outside of any deal. An' on him we'll stumble. Through Ash will come this worst you harp on."

"Listen," whispered Rock, bursting with his message. "I've shut Slagle's mouth. I've bought his silence. He's leavin' the range."

"Lord Almighty! . . . How'd you do it? What'd you give him?"

"Twenty-five hundred dollars."

Preston whistled low. "Of all the fellars I ever seen, you— Rock, I'm goin' to square thet with you."

"Sure you are. You're goin' to square it *all*. . . . Listen. Come to town with me. I've got it all fixed. Dabb will call a meetin' of the Cattle Association council. That means him, Lincoln and Hesbitt. To keep this out of court you will agree to pay Hesbitt for his Half Moon stock. Dabb and Lincoln have promised me they'll handle Hesbitt. It will all be done in secret. Then you and your sons who were in this deal must leave the country."

"Fair enough, but I reckon I'd rather fight."

"Preston, don't let pride and anger blind you. By fightin' you will lose your golden chance. We all believe Ash roped you into this butcherin' stolen cattle."

"He shore did. He was killin' stolen steers long before I ever knew. Then it was too late to stop him. An' I drifted in myself. All so easy! Only a few head of stock at a time! Nobody could ever guess! An' now. . . . Rock, I'd almost as lief croak as face thet council. They might let me off, but they'd tell. It'd leak out."

"Preston, you're not thinkin' clear. You don't see this right. Straight out you've fallen to worse than rustlin'. If you don't take this chance—for the sake of your womenfolk—you'll ruin them. And you'll be as bad as Ash. You're no fool. I'd say, if it weren't for your wife and daughters, you should *quit* this crooked work and fight the whole range. If you met up with a bullet, well and good. . . . But you're not alone. You've got wife to think of—daughters, innocent boys. . . . By Heaven! Preston, I can't let you ruin Thiry. She's guilty now, to some extent, for she shares your guilty secret. Ash would drag her with him."

"He shore will—unless you kill him!" muttered this implacable father.

"But if I do—Thiry will hate me," replied Rock.

"Mebbe she would. We Prestons shore can hate, but we don't change from love to hate."

"D—you, Preston," fumed Rock. "I've had a feelin' more than once that you'd not stop me from drawin' on Ash."

"Hell, no! An' you would have long ago if you'd had the guts you once was noted fer. . . . But Thiry has got you locoed. . . . Come in with us, Rock. We'll fight this deal, sell out, an' go to Arizona or Utah."

"No!" replied Rock, fiercely.

"Wal, then, I'll think your idee over good an' hard. Rock, my not acceptin' it pronto doesn't mean I don't appreciate your wonderful offer an' all thet prompts you. I shore do. It may be the best way to save them. But the wife—Thiry, Allie, Lucy—they'd have to know, an' I'd almost shore rather die in my boots than tell them."

"Man, we don't have to tell. No one but Thiry will ever know."

"All right. Thet's much in its favor. I'll think it over. . . . Meanwhile, I'll stop Ash if I have to hawg-tie him. An' you better take the boys an' go off in the woods somewhere. They deserve a vacation. But no goin' in to town. Take them huntin'. It's 'most turkey season. An' let me know where you go."

Well as Trueman Rock knew that country, it was his fortune to be taken by the Preston boys to high hunting-grounds which he had never visited or heard spoken of on the range.

It was up in the mountains back of the Pass, about a day's climb on horseback, eight thousand feet above the low country. Up there early fall had set in and the foliage was one gorgeous array of color. The camp, which was where they threw their bed-rolls and built their fire, lay in a mountain meadow, at the edge of a magnificent grove of quaking asps. Behind on a gentler slope stood scattered silver spruces and yellow pines, growing larger as they climbed, until on the ridge above they massed in the deep timber line, which like a green-black belt circled the mountain under the gray grisly weathered and splintered peaks.

A golden glamour seemed to float over that grove and to enrich all objects under the aspens, the fallen poles, the rocks and grass, the camp equipment, and the men themselves. It was cast by the golden sunlight falling through the dense aspen foliage, not a quivering leaf of which did not burn pure gold. Even when there was no wind the leaves fluttered, as if endowed with life that was trembling, dying.

Rock fell in love with this place more than any in which he had ever dropped a saddle. How poignantly he needed the beauty, the color, the solitude! He had come up there on the ragged edge of utter desperation. But scarcely were the boys out of sight and the horses grazing along the green-bordered brown stream, still and deep, when Rock began to feel something at work on his restless, seeking, undefeated mind.

The hour was along toward sunset, and the brothers had gone off to hunt a little before the day ended. Rock felt grateful to Preston for this respite up under the peaks. Like scales he cast off the outer and worn vestments of his mental strife.

Across the meadow, scarcely half a mile wide at this its upper end, rose a slow undulating mountain slope, in hue so varied and brilliant that it did not seem actual landscape. Scarlet vines covered the boulders and outcropping of rock at the edge of the wood. A grove of oaks, sturdy, spreading wide their branches clad in green-bronze leaves, had thrived to the elimination of spruces, except a few giants that could not be choked out. Back of these oaks, aspen, maple, and pine thickets vied in gold, purple, and green to excel one another. Soon the vast panoply of black timber belt submerged the lower thickets, except in open spots here and there that shone like gold and cerise and scarlet eyes out of the forest. Above the timber line gulches with threads of white snow wound toward the peaks. And lastly the bold steel teeth of rock bit at the blue sky.

A very faint moan of wind floated down from the pines. From some lofty height an eagle whistled piercingly, and as if in reply, on the wooded ridge an elk bugled. Snowbirds were cheeping back in the grove, and on the wing somewhere wild canaries were twittering, both series of notes totally different, yet pregnant with the same portent—autumn was at hand. The wood behind the aspen grove gave forth familiar sounds of nature, the screech of jay, the chatter of squirrel, the crack of antler on dead wood, the rustle and tread and brush of denizens of the wilderness.

Rock dreamily heard all, so restless, so soothing; and yet within them he seemed to hear a step upon his trail. It was the haunting future.

Then a rifle-shot rang out, to crack in echo, to peal along the slopes, and roll away suddenly. Nothing like a gunshot to transform Trueman Rock. He left off his meditations, his watching, listening, waiting absorption, to take up camp tasks. Action was better than rest.

Then the brothers returned to camp, Al with a wild turkey, the twins with nothing. And the atmosphere of loneliness, of solemn solitude, of presageful nature, seemed less in evidence. How quickly Sunset Pass, with its work and problems, fell off the shoulders of the Preston boys! They were young. Rock envied them, though he rejoiced that the trials of the range had not yet settled on them.

"Gee! I seen a big buck," said Harry, excitedly. "Couldn't get a bead on him."

"Hope Dad doesn't send for us soon," replied Tom.

"Aw, it's great, but I hate to miss that dance. Somebody will jilt me," sighed Al.

In the morning Rock was awakened by the gobbling of turkeys. The boys slept on, blissfully unaware that their favorite game had almost invaded their camp. Rock crawled out, revolver in hand, and soon espied the big birds at the edge of the grove. A gobbler stood up straight, head high, his purple-and-black breast puffed, his beard hanging low. Rock's hand moved and stiffened, his gun boomed, the turkey fell. A roar of wings attested to the flight of his flock. Shouts behind Rock indicated the alarm, consternation, and delight of the brothers. Securing his gobbler, Rock walked into camp and laid it before the roused Prestons.

"By golly! right in camp!" ejaculated Tom.

"How far was he off?" queried Harry.

"Pretty far. Most fifty yards, I'd say," replied Rock.

"You nailed him with a six-gun?" queried Al, in wonder and disgust. "Say, you can't shoot a-tall! Reckon I'd just as lief not be Dunne when you meet up with him."

Thus the hunting began for Rock, and he entered into it heartily. A white frost glistened on the grass, ice had formed in the pans; the meat the boys had hung up was frozen stiff. Therefore Rock sanctioned the boy's plan of killing wild game to pack down to the ranch. Hung in the shade, it would not spoil.

"Boys, you try for turkeys and deer," suggested Rock. "And don't miss an elk, if you see one. I'll climb for a sheep."

For a rider used to horses it was no child's play to mount to the heights. Rock tortured his lungs and his long legs. He sighted a few rams, but they passed out of range. And he was not a good enough sheep-hunter to stalk his game properly. Nevertheless, every day he climbed the slopes, watched for hours from the crags, and returned to camp late, tired physically, yet rested and strengthened in his mind. It was good to get away from the Pass and think with clarifying vision. It was well, too, to be alone, for in the past weeks he had fallen back upon an old habit—the drawing of a gun to bring back and insure the swiftness that had once been his. This action alone was grim indication of his extremity. He dared not slight it, though he fought against admitting the reason for it to his consciousness.

The days passed until Rock had no idea how long he had been absent from the Pass. Nearly a fortnight, he guessed. Then came Indian summer, that enchanting brief period of smoky warm, still days, and floating amber and purple haze in the air.

Al Preston left to go down home for supplies. This threw Rock into a fever of uncertainty. What news would he fetch back? What message from Preston? Would Thiry write? The day was long, the night interminable, the second day unbearable. Rock wandered in the open forest across from camp, wanting always to be in sight of the trail that came up from below. Mid-afternoon ought to see Al ride in. That would allow ample time for the slow pack-horse. He sat on a pine log in the open forest above the oak grove. The smoky haze, the purple veils, the warm, swimming air, so full of fragrance and dreamy languor, the riotous mosaic of autumn colors, the melancholy birds, the dim sun still high and red above the slope of the mountain—these held Rock in strong grip, making it possible for him to wait.

Then a gray-laden pack-horse emerged from the green wall across the meadow. Rock suffered both thrill and pang. Next came a dark horse holding a slight rider that could not be Al Preston. Who could it be? Not the youngest Preston lad. Perhaps it was some boy Al had brought or sent. For Al was not in sight. Another pack-horse cleft the dark green gap where the trail emerged. And after it Al on his big bay. The foremost rider waved to the boys in camp. How they yelled! Rock watched with eyes starting and expanding. What was there strangely familiar about that rider? Yet he knew he had never seen him before. Rock never forgot a mounted rider. Suddenly he leaped up madly. Thiry!

He ran. He leaped the brook. He made the camp in bounds.

"Thiry! Of all people! . . . Aw, I'm so—glad to see you," he panted.

"Howdy, Trueman!" Her smile was strained and she scarcely met his eager gaze. He had never seen her in rider's garb. Could that make such difference? She wore a tan blouse, with blue scarf, fringed gauntlets, overalls, and high boots. She looked like a boy until she dismounted. Rock had a wild desire to snatch her in his arms.

"Boys, throw my pack and unroll my bed," she said. And while the boys obeyed with unified alacrity she led the stunned Rock away from camp, under the golden aspens, into the forest.

"Glad to see me?" she asked, looking ahead at the windfalls and the splashes of brilliant hues.

"Glad!" he echoed, as if words were inadequate.

"You don't show it."

"Thiry! . . . I'm loco."

She still held his hand, that she had taken openly before her brothers. Rock could not shake off his trance. Still, it did not seem the Thiry he knew. Her cheek was warm with a golden tint, partly from the exposure of the long ride, partly from the reflection of the leaves above. The blood did not come and go, like a life current under a peal shell. She halted beside a great fallen spruce with rugged seamed bark. "Lift me up," she said. And when he had complied she held him with strange hands, and looked into his eyes as she had never before. A black squirrel squalled from a silver spruce that towered over them. All around the forest inclosed them, standing and fallen timber, sapling pines and sturdy junipers, patches of aspen, white-stemmed with dead gold foliage, quaking as with a tremor of their roots. The thick tang of pine filled the air.

"Kiss me," this unknown Thiry said, not shyly, nor yet boldly, yet somehow unnaturally for her. When Rock obeyed, restraining himself, in his bewilderment, she put her arms around him and her face against his neck.

"Bad news, Trueman dear," she said, as if forced.

"Sure I could have guessed it. But it's welcome, since it fetched you."

"Ash made a killing of Half Moon steers and shipped the beef from Wagontongue," went on Thiry, talking by rote.

Rock's frame jerked with the hot gush of blood through his veins, but he did not voice his anger and dismay. And he remained mute. Her monotone, the absence of any feeling, the abnormal something about her, fortified him to hear catastrophe which would dwarf what she had already told.

"Dad wants you to come in with us—share our fortunes, our troubles—our sins . . . help us fight these enemy outfits. . . . If we——"

"We?" he interrupted, in bitter heat.

"Yes, we. Ash and Dad and I—and my three brothers . . . and *you.*"

"I! . . . And what do *I* get for spillin' blood for thieves? Ah, that is Preston's game. He wants me to kill—to spread terror among those Wyomin' outfits. . . . And my reward will be——"

"Me," she said, without emotion.

"With Ash Preston's consent?" demanded Rock, angered to probe to the depths of this proposition.

"Dad claims when you become one of us—Ash will have to consent."

"Thiry Preston!—You ask me to do this thing?"

"Yes," she droned. But he could feel a changing in the stiff form against him.

"You ask me to be a thief—a killer—to save your rotten

228

brother, your weak and crooked father?" he flung at her, in a stern and terrible voice.

"I—ask—you."

In violence, almost with brutal force, Rock shook her, as if to awaken her out of a torpor.

"No! No, you poor driven girl!" he cried. "I would die for *you,* but I'll never let you ruin your soul by such dishonor. They have blinded you—preyed on your love. Your brother is mad. Your father desperate. They would sacrifice you. Ash would agree to this, meanin' to shoot me in the back. . . . No, Thiry. . . ."

"You—will not?" she sobbed.

"Never. Not even to have you."

Suddenly, then, he had a wild weeping creature in his arms, whose cries were incoherent, whose beating hands and shaking body wrought havoc to the iron of his mood. "Oh, thank God—you won't!" she wept, lifting streaming eyes and working face. "I prayed you'd—refuse. I told Dad you'd never, never do it. . . . I told Ash he lied . . . he'd never let you have me.—But they made me—they drove me—all night they nagged me—until I gave in. . . . Trueman darling, say you forgive. I was weak. I loved him so—and I'm almost broken. . . . But you lift me from the depths. I love you more—a thousand times. Let come what will. I can face it now."

Hours later Rock kept vigil over a sleeping camp, where near him lay Thiry, in deep slumber, her fair sweet face, sad in repose, upturned to the watching stars. Beyond, her brothers were stretched in a row, likewise with dark faces still and calm in the starlight.

Rock's heart was full to aching. The night was exquisite, clear and cold, with blue velvet sky lighted by trains of stars, white sparks of fire across the zenith. The night wind sighed through the aspens, soughed in the pines, and roared low up on the mountain slope. Coyotes barked and wolves mourned. Whatever might betide on the morrow, or thereafter, this night was his in all the fullness of requited love, of protective possession. He had forgotten the prayers of his youth, yet it was certain that he prayed. There seemed infinite strength in the grand dark mountain above, and a mystery all about him, in the ceaseless voice of dying insects, in the murmur of wild nature.

In the rose light of dawn, while the Preston boys whistled and shouted at the camp tasks, Rock and Thiry again wandered under the silver spruces, the golden aspens, the scarlet maples, back to that bit of primal forestland.

"Don't go back to the Pass," Thiry was pleading.

"I must. I'll go alone."

"But I'm afraid. If you meet him—Oh—you will! . . . Trueman, I couldn't hate you. Once I thought I might. . . . Oh, don't go!"

She wound her arms around his neck and clung to him with all her might.

"Take me away—far away across the mountains," she begged, her lips parting from his to implore mercy, and then seeking them again. "It's the only way. I am yours, body and soul. I ask nothing more of life but that you spare him—and take me. . . . The boys will let us have a pack. We can cross the mountains. It is not yet winter. . . . Then somewhere we two will live for each other. I will forget him and all this horror. And you—will never—kill another man."

"Thiry girl, hush; you are breakin' me," he cried, spent with the might of agonized will that denied her kisses, her lissom pressing form, her clinging arms. "That would be the worst for us both. It would brand me with their guilt and drag you down. . . . No. I shall go alone—make one last stand to save your father."

Rock rode the zigzag descending trail down to the Pass in four hours—another splendid performance of the sure-footed, tireless horse.

There did not appear to be any untoward condition at the ranch that obviously affected the womenfolk. Preston had ridden off early that morning to a general roundup on the range, at a place called Clay Hill. Ash Preston and his three brothers were off somewhere, probably also at the roundup, on their return from Wagontongue. No, they had not driven the beef wagons to town this time.

"Reckon I'll ride over to Clay Hill," muttered Rock, as if to himself.

"Stay for dinner. It's ready," said Mrs. Preston.

"When will Thiry and the boys be in?" asked Alice, thoughtful eyes on Rock.

230

"Before sundown, sure. They were packin' when I left."

"Was Thiry mean to you?" whispered Alice, in an aside. "She had one of her cold, queer spells."

"No, Allie, she was wonderful good," replied Rock. "Why did you ask?"

"You look so—so queer," returned the girl hesitatingly. "You're neither Señor del Toro nor Trueman Rock this day."

"Now, Allie girl, how do I look?" queried Rock, essaying a smile that would not break, which made him aware of the cold tightness of his face.

"Sort of dark, and far away. Older, Trueman, not like yourself. I'm afraid all's not well between you and Thiry," she said, plaintively.

When he ventured no denial, evidently she convinced herself that her intuition had foundation. The children, whom nothing affected adversely, drew Rock out of his brooding calm during the meal. Soon afterward he was riding down the Pass to take the trail up on the range.

The old ranch, where Preston had installed the slaughter-house, had lately been the scene of extensive butchering. It made a hideous blot on the beautiful autumn landscape. And the stench outdid the appearance in hideousness. Clouds of buzzards sailed over the grewsome spot, and hordes of the grisly birds hopped around.

As Rock rode by Slagle's old well he satisfied himself, even from the saddle, that the dim, unused trail was not so dim. Rock cursed the bull-headed fool who was recklessly marching to his downfall, dragging father and family with him.

Rock climbed out of the Pass, up to the rolling rangeland. It unfolded from this height before and below him, in magnificent stretches, its vast monotony of gray now broken by dots of red and patches of gold. The melancholy season hung over the rangeland like a mantle. But it was invisible; it might have hidden in the smoky blue haze. Slopes and swales, leagues of level land, ridges fringed by cedars, round gray mounds and limitless stretches of green—all were bare of cattle. That added to the desert atmosphere. A brooding silence, that seemed emphasized by the incessant hum of insects, lay over all.

231

How barren of life! Not a hawk or a gopher or a jack-rabbit! Far in the distance the range faded in pure obscurity. And through the autumn haze a magenta sun burned, but dully, so that Rock could look into it with his naked eye. And as he rode on, at a swinging lope, while the sun imperceptibly lowered, so the faint magenta hue gained on the gray and green.

Clay Hill was a famous old roundup ground. The gray bare knob of clay rising over a grassy level had given it a name. There were several cabins near the springs that gushed from the base of the hill.

Rock's keen eye snapped at the old-time scene. Dust and color and action! Herds of cattle, fields of horses! So he rode on down through the cedars, now unable to see the bright variegated plain, and again catching an ever-growing glimpse. Not until he rounded the southern corner of Clay Hill, where the trail ran, and came abruptly upon the first cabin, horses, wagons, men, did he grasp that something was amiss. What could check a general roundup in the middle of the afternoon? No cowboys on guard! No cutting or branding! No movement, except a gradual straggling of the herds! The men he saw were in groups, and their postures were not expressive of the lazy, lounging, careless leisure attendant upon meal hours or cessation of work.

Rock had permitted himself no anticipations. But now he divined the hour he had long dreaded; and instead of halting, as if momentarily checked by an invisible blow in the sinister air, he spurred his horse and rode down upon the men, scattering dust and gravel all over them.

He was off, throwing bridle, gloves, and in two swift jerks he got out of his chaps.

"What's up?" he demanded of the six or eight cowmen who backed away. In the first sweeping glance he did not recognize one of them.

"Fight busted the roundup," replied a lean-jawed rider, whose face showed drops of sweat and pale freckles.

"Jimmy Dunne shot," replied an older man, warily, his narrow slits of eyes shifting all over Rock.

"Dunne! . . . Is he dead?"

"No."

"Who did it?"

"Ash Preston."

"Where is Dunne?"

"Layin' in the cabin thar."

Rock brushed the men aside, to encounter more, all of whom he saw with lightning gaze.

"Get out of my way," he ordered, sharply, and forcing entrance to the cabin, he surveyed the interior. A line of dusty, sweaty cowboys fell back, to disclose a man lying on the floor, with another kneeling in attendance. A pan full of bloody water, the odor of rum! Rock saw a face of deathly pallor, clammy and leaden, and eyes black with pain. Yet he recognized the man. The kneeling one was ministering clumsily to him. Rock stepped in and knelt, to take up Dunne's inert wrist and feel for his pulse.

"Dunne, I hope you're not bad hurt," said Rock.

At that the other man looked up quickly. It was Clink Peeples.

"Howdy, Rock! . . . I don't know, but I'm afeared Jim is. . . . Still I'm no good hand at judgin' bullet holes."

"Let me see."

The angry wound was situated high up on the left side, and it was bleeding freely, though not dangerously. Rock, calculating grimly, saw that Preston had missed the heart by several inches. The bullet had no doubt nicked the lung. But there was no sign of internal hemorrhage.

"Has he been spittin' blood?" asked Rock.

"No, I reckon he hasn't. I shore looked for thet," answered Peeples.

"Did the bullet come out?"

"It went clean through, clean as a whistle."

"Good!" exclaimed Rock, with satisfaction. "Dunne, can you hear me?"

"Why, sure," replied Dunne, faintly. A bloody froth showed on his lips. "Rock, reckon Preston—beat you—to this job."

"Reckon I'd never have done it. . . . Listen, Dunne. This is a bad gunshot, but not necessarily fatal. If you do what you're told you'll live."

"You—think so, Rock? . . . I've got—a wife—an' kid."

"I know it," returned Rock, forcefully. "Understand? . . . I know."

"Rock, thet's shore—good news," panted Peeples,

233

wiping his face. "I was plumb scared. Tell us what to do."

"Make a bed for him here," replied Rock, rising. "But don't move him till he's bandaged tight. Then awful careful. Make him lie quiet. . . . Heat water boilin' hot. Put salt in it. Wash your hands clean. Get clean bandages. A clean shirt if there's nothin' else. Fold a pad and wet it. Bind it tight. Then send to town for a doctor.

"Thet's tellin' us," returned Peeples, gratefully. "Frank, you heard. Rustle some boys now."

"Peeples, was it an even break?" inquired Rock, coolly.

"Wal, I'm bound to admit it was. So we've nothin' on Preston thet way."

"What was it about?"

Dunne spoke up for himself, in stronger voice: "Rock, I had the—proofs on him—much as I didn't—have on you."

"Ahuh! . . . Don't talk any more, Dunne," replied Rock, and turned to Peeples. "Do you know what proof he had?"

"Rock, I don't know a damn thing. Jimmy's not a man to talk," replied Peeples, in such a guarded way that Rock construed his words to mean the opposite.

"Did he accuse Ash?"

"He shore did. Braced him soon as he got here with his outfit. I didn't see the fight. But thar's a dozen fellers who did. You talk to them."

Rock did not need, except out of curiosity, to question anyone further. Besides, he knew Dunne had spoken the truth. If there had been any doubt, Dunne would have kept his peace.

"Where are the Prestons?" asked Rock, stalking out.

"Over at the third cabin," replied some one.

"Are they inside, holed-up, lookin' for trouble?"

"Shore lookin' for trouble, but not holed-up, by any means. Ash is stalkin' to an' fro over thar, like a hyena behind bars."

Rock elbowed his way out of the crowd. Soon his glance fell upon those he sought, and in him surged the instinct of the lion that hated the hyena. Ash Preston stalked to and fro, away from the cabin, and when he faced back toward the watching men he appeared to do it sidewise. Two of his tall brothers sat together, back to the cabin wall. A third, probably Range Preston, stood in the doorway, smoking a cigarette. Apart from them sat Gage Preston, his burly form sagging, his bare head bowed. His sombrero lay on the ground. Rock's impression was that Gage awaited only the sheriff.

Long ago Rock's mind had been made up and set. He grasped at inevitability—strode forth to meet it, aware of the low excited murmur that ran through the crowd behind him.

Ash, espying Rock, halted in his tracks. The two brothers rose in single action, as if actuated by the same spring. Range Preston stepped outside to join his brothers. Gage Preston did not see, nor look up, until Rock hailed him. Then, with spasmodic start, he staggered erect.

Ash Preston, seeing that Rock had sheered a little off a direct line, to approach his father, hurled an imprecation, and fell to his swift, striding, sidelong stalk.

"Rock, I'm done," rasped Preston when Rock got to him. "So double-crossin' you like I did means nothin' to me."

"Preston, have you been in any of these last butcherin' deals?" queried Rock, sternly.

"No. An' so help me Heaven, I couldn't stop Ash."

"Why did you send Thiry—persuadin' me to come in with you?"

"Thet was why. I wasn't beat then. I figgered I could fight it out an' I wanted you. So I drove Thiry to it. . . . But now! . . . You had it figgered, Rock. I'm sorry—sorry most fer Thiry, an' Ma, an' the girls. If I had it to do over again, I'd——"

"Do it now," interrupted Rock, ringingly. "Come with me to Wagontongue."

"Too late! Too late!" returned Preston, hopelessly.

"No! The situation is no worse—for you. For him it *is* too late!—Come, Preston, be quick. There'll be hell poppin' here in a minute. Will you give up—go with me?"

"Rock, by Heaven! I will—if you——"

"Yell that to Ash!" hissed Rock, strung like a whip-cord.

Preston, with face purpling, shouted to his son, "Hey, Ash!"

"What you want?" came the snarling answer.

"I'm goin' to town with Rock."

"What fer?" yelled Ash, as if stung.

"Wal, just off, I'm gettin' a marriage license for Thiry!—Haw! Haw! Haw!"

What was that raw note in Preston's thick voice—in the laugh which rang loud, clear? Did it connote revenge or hate or menace of the moment, or all combined?

"I say what fer?" yelled Ash, dancing up and down.

"To pay your thievin' debts, you—!"

"Preston, get to one side. Quick!" warned Rock, risking one long stride forward, when he froze in his tracks, his right side toward Ash, his quivering hand low.

Ash Preston spat one curse at his father—then saw him no more. Again he began that strange sidelong stalk, only now he sheered a little, out toward Rock, forward a few strides, then backward the same, never turning that slim left side away from Rock. Rock learned something then he never had known—Ash Preston was left-handed. He approached no closer than thirty paces. Then he did not or could not keep still.

"Howdy, spy!" he called.

"Glad to meet you, beef rustler," returned Rock.

"Am givin' you my card pronto," called Ash, louder, more derisively.

"Gave you mine at the dance. But I got six left! *Carramba!"*

That stopped the restless crouching steps, but not the singular activity of body. Ash's muscles seemed to ripple. He crouched yet a little more. Rock could catch gleams of blue fire under the wide black brim of Ash's hat.

"Señor del Toro!" He had recognized the Spanish word.

"Yes. And here's Thiry's mask—where she put it herself," flashed Rock, striking his breast. "See if you can hit it!"

At the last he had the wit to throw Ash off a cool and deadly balance—so precious to men who would live by the gun. When Ash jerked to his fatal move Rock was the quicker. His shot cracked a fraction of a second before his adversary's. Both took effect. It was as if Ash had

236

been hit in the head by a club. Almost he turned a somersault.

Rock felt a shock, but no pain. He did not know where he was hit until his right leg gave way under him, letting him down. He fell, but caught himself with his left hand, and went no farther than his knees, the right of which buckled under him.

Ash bounded up as he had gone down, with convulsive tremendous power, the left side of his head shot away. Blood poured down. As he swept up his gun Rock shot him through the middle. The bullet struck up dust beyond and whined away. But Ash, sustaining the shock, fired again, and knocked Rock flat. Like the first bullet this one struck as if it were wind, high on his left shoulder. He heard two more heavy booms of Ash's gun, felt the sting of gravel on his face. Half rising, braced on his left hand, Rock fired again. He heard the bullet strike. Terrible fleshy sodden sound! Ash's fifth shot spanged off Rock's extended gun, knocked it flying, beyond reach.

Preston was sagging. Bloody, magnificent, mortally stricken, he had no will except to kill. He saw his enemy prostrate, weaponless. He got his gun up, but could not align it, and his last bullet struck far beyond Rock, to whine away. Ash's physical strength had not matched his unquenchable spirit. He actually tried to fling the empty gun. It flipped at random. To and fro he swayed, all instinctive action ceasing, and with his ruthless eyes on his fallen foe, changing, glazing over, setting blank, he fell.

Gage Preston hurried to Rock's side. Men came running with hoarse shouts.

"Help me—up," said Rock, faintly.

They raised him, speaking in awed voices. Then he dragged them, half-hopping, careless of his dangling leg, over to the writhing Ash, in time to see his last shudder.

"Ah—uh!" gasped Rock, in emotionless finality, with strength and sense slowly failing into oblivion.

Chapter Fifteen

When Rock came to his senses again he was lying on the floor of the cabin where seemingly only a few moments before he had given advice as to the proper care of the wounded Dunne.

He gazed around up at the grave faces of cowboys and cattlemen, at Gage Preston, who, grim and white, was binding his leg, at Peeples, still working over the prostrate Dunne.

"Preston, how is it—with Rock?" asked Dunne, huskily.

"Wal, the top bullet glanced off the bone," replied the rancher. "Ugly hole, but nothin' fer this fellar. The leg shot, though, is bleedin' bad."

"Bind it tight," whispered Rock.

Dunne moved his head in slow action, until his cavernous eyes, supernaturally bright, rested upon Rock.

"Say, Rock, it didn't take you long to get—heah on the floor with me."

"Seems long," said Rock, weakly.

"Matter of ten minutes, mebbe," explained Preston, as he wrapped and pulled with swift powerful hands. "Hyar, somebody help me . . . hold thet end tight."

Rock became conscious of awakening pain, of a burning in his breast and a dull spreading fire in his right leg. Presently Preston rose from his task, wiping his bloody hands, and the voices of watchers ceased.

"Somebody get Rock to town pronto," he said, gruffly. "Ain't safe to let him wait fer the doctor."

"Lon Bailey has his four-seat buckboard," replied a cowboy. "We can take out the hind seat, an' fix a place for Rock to lay."

"Rustle now," replied Preston, and then bent his gloomy gaze down. "Rock, if the artery ain't cut you've nothin' bad. No bones broke."

"Gage, I'm—sorry," whispered Rock, faintly. "No—other way."

"Ha! You needn't be. Shore, I'm not," rejoined the rancher.

"Will you—come to town?"

"Tomorrow. Me an' the boys will see Dabb. Mebbe it ain't too late."

"It—never—is, Preston."

"I'm thankin' you. Good-bye an' good luck," he returned, and stamped out.

Rock closed his eyes.

"Say, fellars, nobody hain't told me what happened to thet Ash Preston," spoke up Dunne. "He's done fer me, an' most the same fer Rock. If you-all let him—"

"Daid," interrupted a blunt cowboy, without solemnity.

"Preston had the side of his haid half shot off," replied another range rider. "Shot clean through the middle an' then plumb center. He died orful hard."

"Rock, you heah me?" said Dunne. "I had you wrong—an' I'm askin' pardon. . . . An' fellars, if I have—to die—I'll go happy."

Merciful unconsciousness did not return to Rock. When strong and gentle hands lifted him into the buckboard he knew agony. When the swift wheels ran over a bump or a rut in the road it was like a rending of flesh and bone. He set his teeth and endured, his brain in the vise of sensorial perceptions. The miles covered, the black night, the white stars, the cold—of these he was aware, but they meant nothing. Gray dawn and Wagontongue found him spent and in a daze of agony.

Rock was lying in the pleasant sitting-room of the Winters' home where a couch had been improvised for him. It was late in the day, according to the slant of the sun rays, coming through the low window above his bed. He had awakened to less torture, but he could move only his one arm and head. A fire crackled cheerfully in the small grate. Outside the window waved the branches of a pine tree and a soft sough of wind came strangely, like an accompaniment of something sad in the past.

Another day Rock awoke to rest, if not ease, and slowly the stream of consciousness resumed its flow.

The little doctor was cheerful that day. "You're like

239

an Indian," he said, rubbing his hands in satisfaction. "Another week will see you up. Then pretty soon you can fork a hoss."

"How is your other patient?" asked Rock.

"Dunne is out of danger, I'm glad to say. But he will be a good while in bed."

Sol Winter came bustling in with an armful of firewood.

"Mornin', son! You shore look fitter to me. How about him, Doc? Can we throw off the restrictions on grub an' talk?"

"I reckon," replied the physician, taking up his hat and satchel. "Now, Rock, brighten up. You've been so thick and gloomy. Good day."

"Wal, son, I almost feel young against this mornin'," said Sol, cheerfully, as he kindled the fire. "Shore is some fine mornin'. First frost."

"Sol, do you reckon you could shave off this brush on my chin? It's sure irritatin'."

"Wal, I'll guarantee to get it off," replied Winter, with a warming laugh. "There, we'll have a fire pronto."

Then Mrs. Winter entered with breakfast for Rock. She was a slim, plain, busy little body, with gray hair, kindly eyes, and a motherly manner.

"Mawnin', Trueman!" she greeted him, smiling. "Sol says the bars are down an' heah I've rustled you fruit, rice, egg, toast, and coffee."

"Mother Winter, you're no less than an angel," returned Rock, gratefully. "Sol, help me sit up in bed. . . . Oh, I can if you'll lift me."

"Hurt much?" inquired Winter, when the desired position had been attained.

"Reckon—a little. Now, fetch it to me, Mother Winter."

"Do you hear the church bell?" she asked, as she deposited the tray on his lap.

"Sure. Then it's Sunday?"

"Yes, and another Sunday you might go to church, with a crutch."

"Me go to church? . . . Lord, can't you see the congregation scatter?"

"Trueman, there's news," said Winter, after his wife left the room. "Might as well get it over, huh?"

"I reckon so," rejoined Rock, slowly.

"Gage Preston paid me the money you gave Slagle. Yesterday, before he left."

"Left?" echoed Rock, putting down his cup.

"Yep, he left on Number Ten for Colorado," replied Winter, evidently gratified over the news he had to impart. "Go on with your breakfast, son. I'll talk. I've been wantin' to for days. . . . Rock, it all turned out better'n we dared hope. They tell me Hesbitt was stubborn as a mule, but Dabb an' Lincoln together flattened him out soft. I got it all from Amy, who has been most darn keen to help. Rock, thet little lady has a bad conscience over somethin'. . . . Wal, with the steer market jumpin' to seventy-five, even Hesbitt couldn't stay sore long. They fixed it up out of court. Dabb an' Lincoln made it easy for Preston. They bought him out, ranch, stock, an' all. Savvy those foxy ranchers! They shore had a chance an' they fell on it like a turkey on a grasshopper. Cost Preston somethin' big to square up, but at thet he went away heeled. I seen him at the station."

"Did he go—alone?" asked Rock, gazing away out of the window at the distant pine slopes.

"No. His three grown sons were with him. All slicked up. Shore is an adventure for them. Looked to me they didn't care much. At thet, there's darned little gossip. The rest of the Prestons are in town, but I haven't seen them. Funny Thiry doesn't run in to see me. I met Sam Whipple's wife. She saw Thiry an' Alice, who are stayin' at Farrell's. She said she couldn't see much sign of Thiry's takin' Ash's death very hard. Thet shore stumped me. But Thiry is game."

"Reckon she—they'll all be leavin' soon," returned Rock.

"Don't know, but I'll find out pronto. If they *did* leave, like the old man, without seein' you, or at least one word of thanks—wal, I'll change my idee of them."

"Sol, you can't expect them to thank me for—depletin' their family somewhat."

"I didn't mean thet. . . . Wal, I'll go out an' do some work around the barn. First off, though, I'd better shave your whiskers. There's likely to be callers, an' shore Amy, 'cause she said so."

241

"Sol, I don't want to see anybody," replied Rock, hastily.

"Wal, I'm shore sorry, but I'll be darned if you won't have to. Suppose, for instance, Thiry would call!"

"You're loco—Sol," choked Rock. "She couldn't stand sight of me. . . . Please—don't—"

"Son, I may be loco, at thet," replied Winter, with remorse, and evidently he controlled desires to argue the point.

He went out, leaving Rock prey to rediscovered emotions, stronger, darker for the sad resignation. He had sacrificed his love to save Thiry's father, and therefore her, from ignominy. The thing could not have been helped. It had from the very first, that day in the corral here at Wagontongue, been fixed, and as fateful as the beautiful passion Thiry had roused in him. He had no regret. He would not have changed it, at cost to her. But with the accepted catastrophe faced now, there came pangs that dwarfed those of gunshot wounds. His heart would not break, because he had wonderful assurance of her love, of the sacrifice she had tried to make for him. How that memory stung and vibrated over him! His sluggish blood stirred to swift heat. She would go away with her family, and in some other state recover from this disaster, forget, and touch happiness, perhaps with some fortunate man who might win her regard. But she owed that to him. And he realized that when the poignancy of first grief had softened, he would find melancholy consolation in the memory of the service he had rendered her.

Who was Trueman Rock, to aspire to the possession of Thiry Preston? Who was he but a lonely man, a rider that had always been and ever would be a rolling stone, good only to use his fatal gift in summary justice on some worthless scoundrel of the range?

"Son, lady to see you," announced Winter, not long after he had made Rock presentable.

"Who?" asked Rock, with a start that seemed to rend his healing wounds.

"No one but Amy."

"Tell her I'm sleepin' or—or somethin'," implored Rock.

"Like hob he will," replied a gay voice from behind

the door. And Amy entered, pretty and stylish, just a little fearful and pale, despite her nerve.

"Well, how do, Amy?" said Rock, and then he laughed. Amy's presence was always difficult to deny gladly.

"Trueman, are you all right?" she asked, timidly, staring at his long shape under the coverlet.

"Pretty good, Amy, thanks. But it was a close shave, the doctor says. . . . One inch one way for one bullet—and my artery would have been severed. And two inches lower for the other bullet—well, Amy, my heart would never have broken again."

"Don't—don't talk so," she cried, shuddering, as she sat down near him, and took his hand. Her face appeared singularly white, almost pearly. "Oh, Trueman, I've been in a horrible state ever since I came home."

"Well! I'm sorry, Amy. How so?"

"I hate to tell you, but I've got to," she replied. "For it was my last, miserable, horrible trick! . . . Trueman, the day I got back I met Ash Preston on the street. I told him you—you were Señor del Toro. He laughed in my face—called me a jealous liar. Wanted to kill Thiry's partner! . . . But afterward I began to fear he'd believe me and I fell to worrying. It grew worse as I realized— until I finally suffered the tortures of the damned. You cannot imagine what I felt when they fetched you here— all shot up. . . . Trueman, I don't want to abase myself utterly in your sight, but—well, I am a chastened woman."

"You wildcat!" stormed Rock, stern eyes on her.

"Forgive me, Trueman. After all, be didn't kill you—as I hoped in my madness. And out of evil, good has come."

"It was wicked, Amy."

"Don't I know? . . . It made me merciless to myself. It opened my eyes. I told my husband, and since then we've grown closer than we ever were."

"Then, Amy, I forgive you."

Quick as a bird she pecked at his cheek, to lift a flushing, radiant face. "There! The first sisterly one I ever gave you. . . . Trueman, I am the bearer of good news. You are a big man now. Yes, sir, in spite of—or perhaps because of—that awful gun of yours. But your honesty has gone farther with John and Tom Lincoln.

I have the pleasure of telling you that you've been chosen to run the Sunset Pass Ranch for them. On shares."

"Never, Amy, never!" cried Rock, shivering. "I shall leave Wagontongue again—soon as I can walk."

"Not if *we* all know it," she retorted, as she rose, with inscrutable eyes on him. "You've got more friends than you think. . . . Now I'll go. I've excited you enough today. But I'll come again soon. Good-bye."

Winter came in, upon Mrs. Dabb's departure, with humorous remarks that in no wise deceived Rock. His friends were all very good and kind, but they left him indifferent.

"May I come in?" asked a girl's high voice, with an accompanying tap on the open door.

"Wal, he looks powerful ferocious, but I reckon you can risk comin'," said Winter.

Whereupon Alice Preston entered, gayly gowned, and far brighter of eye than Rock would have expected to see her that day.

"Señor, may one pay one's respects?" she asked, coming to his side.

"Allie, you—well, I almost said, darlin'," replied Rock, suddenly warmed by surprise and gratitude.

"Trueman, you're just a day late," she said, roguishly. "I became engaged yesterday."

"Allie—Preston!" ejaculated Rock. "You—only sixteen years old!"

"Mother said the same thing. But Dad didn't know anything about it."

"Who's the lucky boy?"

"Charlie Farrell."

"Allie dear, I don't know that I ought to allow this," said Rock, gravely, "but seein' I'm crippled an' can't very well stop it, I'll say bless you, my child."

She sat down on the bed and took his hand in both hers.

"Trueman, I think you'd make a good dad at that. . . . Does my news cheer you up?"

"Sure does, Allie—for you. . . . I can never cheer up again for myself."

"Pooh!" she exclaimed, in sweet derision. Indeed, she was wholly amazing and inexplicable to Rock. He wondered if she had any other news. He wondered at

244

a hint of suppressed excitement behind her smiling, talkative manner.

"Are you leavin' Wagontongue soon?" he queried.

"Me? I guess not. Do you think—"

But a squeak of the door and a deep expulsion of breath from some one entering checked her. Rock gave such a start that his stiff injured leg actually reminded him of its condition. Thiry had entered. She leaned against the wall. She was bareheaded, and her soft hat dropped from nerveless hands.

Alice gave Rock's hand a thrilling squeeze and jumped up. "Reckon this is no place for sister Allie!" and she beat a precipitous retreat, closing the door behind her.

"Thiry!—how good—of you!"

Haltingly she approached, as if the impelling force that drew her was only slightly stronger than something which held her back.

"Trueman, are you—all right?" she asked, apparently awed at the helpless length of him there on the bed. She, too, sat down beside him, and her eyes, black with thought and pain, followed her reaching hand, to rest on the coverlet over his knee.

"Reckon I'm 'most all right—now," he replied, sensitive to her touch.

"Mr. Winter told me everything," she went on, "but *seeing* you is so strange. . . . Can you move?"

"Sure. All but my left leg."

"Was that broken?"

"No, I'm glad to tell you."

"Then you can ride again?"

"Some day."

"And the other hurt—was that here?" she asked, pale, almost reverent, as she laid a soft hand high upon his left shoulder.

"Lower down—Thiry."

Fascinated, she gently slipped her hand down over the bandage.

"Here?"

"Still lower."

Then she felt the throbbing of his heart. "But, Trueman—it couldn't be there."

"You bet it is."

"What?"

"The hurt you asked about."

"I was speaking of your latest wounds," she replied. Then she looked him squarely in the face, which she had failed to do before. How tragic, deep with sorrow, yet soul-searching that gaze! It changed. "I had to fight myself to come," she said. "There was a cold, dead, horrible something inside me. . . . But it's leaving! . . . Trueman, you're so white and thin. So helpless lying there! I—I want to nurse you. I should have come. . . . Have you suffered?"

"A little—I reckon," he replied, unsteadily. "But it's —gone now."

"Has Amy Dabb been here?" she asked, jealously.

"Yes. Today. She was very nice."

"Nice! . . . Because she wheedled John Dabb to offer you the running of Sunset Pass Ranch?"

"Oh no—I mean, just kind," returned Rock, uncertainly. He was of half a mind to believe this delirium.

"Trueman, you will accept that offer?" she queried, earnestly. "I don't care what Amy says. I know it was my father's advice to Dabb."

"Me ever go to—Sunset Pass—again? Never in this world."

"Trueman, you would not leave this country?" she asked, in quick alarm.

"Soon as I can walk."

"But *I* do not want to leave Sunset Pass," she returned, with spirit.

"I'm glad you don't. Reckon that's a surprise, Thiry. . . . It's very beautiful—out there. Perhaps, somehow, it can be arranged for you. Allie is engaged to young Farrell. Isn't that fine? . . . Some one, of course, will take the place. . . . Is your mother leavin' soon?"

"She is terribly angry with Dad," replied Thiry, seriously. "You see, mother was not in the secret. . . . But I think some day she'll get over it—when Dad makes a new home—and go back to him."

"She ought to."

She edged a little closer, grave and sweet, and suddenly bent over to kiss his knee where the bandage made a lump, and then she moved up to lay her cheek over his heart, with a long low sigh.

246

"Trueman, did you think I'd—hate you for killing Ash?" she whispered.

He could not speak.

"I thought I would. And it was a sickening, terrible blow. . . . But before that same night was over I knew I couldn't hate you. . . . And I believe, even if I hadn't learned what changed it all, I would have forgiven you—some day."

"What—changed—all?" burst out Rock, in insupportable suspense.

"What Dad told me."

"Thiry—have mercy!"

"Ash was not my brother," she said, in smothered voice, and her hand sought his cheek.

That dear bright head on his breast seemed to be lifting his heart rather than pressing against it. A thousand thoughts tried to pierce to clarity.

Rising, Thiry slipped to the floor on her knees, and leaned upon her elbows, clasping his hands, regarding him with remorseful tenderness.

"My brother Range beat the others home that night, with the news of the fight. I stole to my room. Allie stayed with me. Afterward she told me I raged I was going out to kill you. But that was only madness. . . . I had my terrible black hours. Thank God they are past. . . . I knew we were ruined—that Ash in some way had brought it about. Perhaps my love for him turned then. Allie begged and pleaded and prayed with me. How she hated Ash! And what a friend she was to you! . . . But I want you to know that even then believing Ash my brother I'd have forgiven you in time. I know it. After the agony was spent I was learning how deathlessly I loved you. . . . Sometime in the night late Dad came to me. Never had I seen him gentle, sad, defeated, yet something better for that. . . . He told me not to take it too hard—not to visit the sins of others upon your head. You had been driven to kill Ash. Some one *had* to do it, for the good of all, and no one but you *could*. He told me how he had inflamed Ash. Then the fight! . . . Ah, God, he did—not—spare me. . . . Then came the story, torn from his most secret heart. Ash was not his son, but the illegitimate son of a girl who he had loved long ago, who, abandoned and dying, gave him her child.

247

That child was Ash. And Dad said he was what his father has been. . . . I was not yet born. But when I came, Ash was my playmate. I remember when we were children. He was always vicious to everyone except me. And so I grew up loving him, perhaps for that. . . . Next day I went to mother, and she corroborated Dad's story. It seemed I was delivered from hellish bonds."

"Thiry darlin'—there must be somethin' in prayer," cried Rock, fervently.

"I was to learn how you had bought Slagle's silence—how you persuaded Dabb and Lincoln to force Hesbitt to settle out of court—oh, how from the very beginning you had meant good by all of us! Yet I could not drag myself to you. It took time. I had such dreadful fear of seeing you lying in danger of death, bloody, pale, with awful eyes that would have accused me. . . . Oh, I suffered! . . . But now I'm here—on my knees."

"Please get up?" asked Rock, lifting her to a seat beside him.

"Now will you accept Dabb's offer and take me back to Sunset Pass?" she asked, bending to him.

"Yes, Thiry, if you will have it so," he replied. "If you love me that well."

She gave him awakening passionate proof of that. "Dear, I understand better. Dad told me you were one of the marked men of the ranges. Our West is in the making. Such men as Ash—and those others you—"

Sol Winter came in upon them.

"Wal, I knocked twice an' then I says I'd better go in." He beamed down upon them. "Son an' lass, I'm glad to see you holdin' each other thet way—as if now you'd never let go. For I've grown old on the frontier, an' I've seen but little of the love you have for each other. We Westerners are a hard pioneerin' outfit. I see in you, an' Allie, an' some more of our young friends, a leanin' more to finer, better things."

DEAL YOURSELF IN...
ON A FULL HOUSE OF HITS FROM
THE KING OF ADULT
WESTERN ENTERTAINMENT,

ZEKE MASTERS

Follow Faro Blake, the Wild West's wiliest gamblin' man into the arms of dozens of beautiful women—into the hot center of twofisted trouble—in these sensational adventures you might have missed.

THE BIG GAMBLE 44083/$1.95
LUCK OF THE DRAW 44084/$1.95
THREES ARE WILD 43907/$1.95
DIAMOND FLUSH 43997/$1.95
RIVERBOAT SHOWDOWN 45412/$1.95
FOUR OF A KIND 45413/$1.95

POCKET BOOKS Department ZMW
1230 Avenue of the Americas
New York, N.Y. 10020

Please send me the books I have checked above. I am enclosing $_____ (please
add 50¢ to cover postage and handling for each order, N.Y.S. and N.Y.C. residents
please add appropriate sales tax). Send check or money order—no cash or C.O.D.'s
please. Allow up to six weeks for delivery.

NAME_____

ADDRESS_____

CITY_____STATE/ZIP_____

270

MATT BRAUN'S
WEST
IS THE REAL WEST!

And a Matt Braun novel
is your guarantee of
authentic western
adventure!
Follow the adventures of
Matt's great western hero
Luke Starbuck—in these
novels you may have missed!

JURY OF SIX 43804/$1.95____
TOMBSTONE 82033/$1.95____
HANGMAN'S CREEK 82031/$1.75____
THE SPOILERS 82034/$1.95____

POCKET BOOKS
Department WMB
1230 Avenue of the Americas
New York, N.Y. 10020

POCKET BOOKS

Please send me the books I have checked above I am enclosing $____
(please add 50¢ to cover postage and handling N Y S and N Y C residents please
add appropriate sales tax) Send check or money order—no cash or C O D s
please Allow six weeks for delivery

NAME_____

ADDRESS_____

CITY_____ STATE/ZIP_____

164